Praise

"L. Timmel Duchamp
publisher, and critic."

The Jane Austen Book Club, and
We Are All Completely Beside Ourselves

"Duchamp writes some of the most rewarding science fiction stories you can read today; she is simply and unarguably among the best."

—Samuel R. Delany, author of *Dhalgren* and *Nova*

"…a unique, essential voice."

—Jeff VanderMeer, author of
the The Southern Reach Trilogy

,

Special Honor for the Marq'ssan Cycle

The 2010 James Tiptree Award jury awarded a special honor to L. Timmel Duchamp's Marq'ssan Cycle, noting the importance of this stunning series, which envisions radical social and political change.

Praise for Never at Home

2011 Tiptree Award Honor List for
"The Nones of Quintilis" (from the collection)

"L. Timmel Duchamp's stories are intense, tricky, heartfelt, and most of all, interesting; they take on big themes in a clear way, but also at the same time swirl with complications, moments of poetry, life itself."
> —Kim Stanley Robinson, author of the
> Mars Trilogy and *Galileo's Dream*

"*Never at Home* is an intelligent, sensitive, important collection of short stories..."
> —*The New York Review of Science Fiction,*

"L. Timmel Duchamp sees the world from an angle inclined at about 25 degrees to the rest of us. Her stories make you feel odd, as if the ground shifted in mid-step and your foot has come down somewhere you weren't expecting. In this collection she explores in many ways the theme of belonging. They are some of her best stories: unfailingly original, emotionally intense, and suffused with intelligence. I am in awe of this book."
> —Carolyn Ives Gilman, author of
> *Isles of the Forsaken* and *Halfway Human*

Books by L. Timmel Duchamp

Novels

The Marq'ssan Cycle

Alanya to Alanya

Renegade

Tsunami

Blood in the Fruit

Stretto

Novellas

The Red Rose Rages (Bleeding)

De Secretis Mulierum

Fiction Collections

Love's Body, Dancing in Time

Never at Home

Edited Fiction and Nonfiction

Missing Links and Secret Histories: A Selection of Wikipedia Entries from Across the Known Multiverse

Narrative Power: Encounters, Celebrations, Struggles

Talking Back: Epistolary Fantasies

The WisCon Chronicles, Volume 1

The WisCon Chronicles, Vol. 2: Provocative Essays on Feminism, Race, Revolution, and the Future, with Eileen Gunn

The Waterdancer's World

L. Timmel Duchamp

Aqueduct Press

Seattle

Aqueduct Press, PO Box 95787
Seattle, WA 98145-2787
www.aqueductpress.com

Copyright © 2016 by L. Timmel Duchamp
First edition, first printing, October 2016

ISBN: 978-1-61976-109-4
Library of Congress Control Number: 2016914683
10 9 8 7 6 5 4 3 2 1

Cover and Book Design by Kathryn Wilham

Cover Illustrations: Swimmer 357500279 Copyright: Kluva/
Shutterstock;
Ice flowers background 13034917 Copyright: ArTDi101/Shutterstock

Printed in the USA by Thomson Shore, Inc.

For Joshua B. Lukin,
Treasured Friend, Intrepid Thinker, Outspoken Comrade

I'm interested in a poethics that recognizes the degree to which the chaos of world history, of all complex systems, makes it imperative that we move away from models of cultural and political agency lodged in isolated heroic acts and simplistic notions of cause and effect. Similarly, the monolithic worldview that leads to assessments of success or failure in the arts based on short-term counts of numbers persuaded—for example, the size of the audience—is particularly misguided. Although news media operate on the premise of a single worldwide field of events, from which the most important are daily chosen for review, human culture has always consisted of myriad communities with very different interests, values, and objectives. There are disparate "audiences" to define the character of culturally significant events and no way to know which will have the greatest effect on our multiple futures.

—Joan Retallack, *The Poethical Wager*

Preface

Humans have been living on Frogmore for nearly a millennium (in standard years). Since the history of the planet's human habitation is inextricable from the human inhabitants' struggle for independence from the Combine's Council for Developmental Strategy, accounts of Frogmore's history written by off-planet historians who have never set foot on Frogmore usually adopt a simplistic framework casting it as the story of failed civilization and descent into barbarous parochialism. My account, which relates only a portion of that history, refuses that framework and insists on seeing our planet's history as a hard-won achievement of autonomy that must often have seemed at best unlikely, at worst impossible, to those waging the struggle.

In constructing the account that follows, I've selected certain documents for inclusion as well as narrativizations of well-documented events and supplemented these with excerpts from published texts of the day in order to provide context about life on Frogmore five centuries ago. This is, of course, a standard methodology used by professional historians everywhere, most of whom just happen to live on Pleth, where all but two universities in the galaxy are located. Most historians agree that the events I choose to focus on constitute the turning point in Frogmore's history, but they will likely consider my narrativizations and selection of extracts biased and presumptuous, simply because my focus supports a radically different understanding of the planet itself as well as of the nature of the conflict. Unlike Pleth's most eminent historians, Frogmorians need more sophisticated accounts of their history, accounts that ring true for them and celebrate the achievement that one Combine-centered history calls "a sad day for galactic civilization, a defeat for everyone involved."[1]

I've chosen to relate this history primarily through the perspectives of five individuals, none of whom appear in the standard histories discussing Frogmore: Claire Gaspel, Ariel Dolma, Nathalie Stillness, Madeleine Tao, and Inez Gauthier. In addition to these, I begin my account with a brief narrative from a fifth point of view intended to provide additional context. Claire Gaspel's journals have been preserved because she was a "First Daughter" of the inhabitants descended from a group of reproductive surrogates who were among the planet's first human settlers; I've included extensive verbatim extracts from Gaspel's journals and Ariel Dolma's personal correspondence. I've also included extracts from anthropologist Nathalie Stillness's Frogmore journal, composed when she was on-planet doing fieldwork here. Decades after the events described herein, Jurist Madeleine Tao wrote a memoir of her professional life, a memoir rich in mature reflections on juridical process. And finally, the fifth perspective, the best-documented of the five, is that of Inez Gauthier, a financier and the daughter of General Paul Gauthier, who oversaw the Combine's occupation of the planet. I've chosen to make the Gauthiers the dominant focus of the narrative not only because the source material documenting their activities and influence on the planet is so plentiful, but also, and more importantly, because they played such a critical role in the eventful years leading up to Frogmore's break from the Combine.

The supplemental material I've included comes from the following sources (publication dates, Frogmore dating, given in parentheses):

1   This is the phrase used by Hortense Park in her magisterial *Backworld Issues: The Combine's Long Struggle for Civilization on Five Underdeveloped Worlds*.

Frogmore's Destiny: A Manifesto for Independence (5.III.501; written 8 years after the events in the book).

Frogmore: The CDS Fact Book (475).

A Traveler's Handbook to the Galaxy, 49ᵗʰ Edition (492).

Enoch Fulmer, *A Star-Hopper's View of the Galaxy* (490).

Madam X, *Frogmore's First Circle: Life in Amanda Kundjan's Circle* (495).

Imogen Alençon, *The Trouble with Frogmore* (497).

Alexandra Jador of Pleth, *The Art of Holodrama* (489).

Daniel Sayles, Confidential Memo to the Standing Working Committee for Frogmore [to which no one who appears in this book had access] (492).

I'd like to thank the Frogmore Historical Society for the grant that funded my travel to Janniset, which made this account possible, and the Narrative Sciences Department of Frogmore Central University for providing a sabbatical as well as leave-time for writing this account. Thanks go, too, to Gervais Tao, who generously shared family holos and other documentation with me; to the Daughters of Paula Boren for permission to publish selections from Claire Gaspel's journals; to the Frogmore Historical Society (again!) for allowing me access to its archive of epistolary documents and to quote from Ariel Dolma's letters to Livvy Kracauer; to numerous colleagues in my department who helped me work through the epistemological issues entailed by my departure from the standard narratives of galactic history; and, finally, to my partner, Gisela Kimura, who spent many hours reading drafts of this narrative and commenting on them freely and at length.

Exact citations and sources for my account are, as always, available on request.

Louise Ducange
Frogmore Central University

Zero

SADORA LUMNI

Sadora stood at the room's singular, small window, gazing down into the marsh below at the iridescent purple shells of the creepers foraging in the slow-bubbling sludge; though ponderous, their movements were oddly graceful. They might have an ugly name, but they were her favorite amphibious species. The day's mistflowers' lavender cast especially flattered the beauty of their shells.

Behind her, Solstice said, "The grant's been renewed."

Sadora turned. Solstice's eyes were shining. She held out the screen she'd been using, and Sadora went to her, took the screen, and sat down with her at the table. "So you'll be able to keep waterdancing?" Sadora said. Not a real question. But Solstice had been worried that this might be the year she'd be cut off and have to go to teaching full time. That, or take a job in the Capitol District at Frogmore Central University. Solstice always said it was a mystery how she got any funding at all, given how few public appearances she made, and those rarely attended by people with full connections. But Solstice had always refused to see how extraordinary her resume must look to the outsiders handing out the grants—and how smug they probably felt when telling their friends they were funding "an art form native to Frogmore."

"The renewal comes with an invitation," Solstice said. Her rough, throaty voice grew husky. "Or should I say a 'command performance'?" Though the traces of triumph glazed Solstice's eyes, her tone sounded wry to Sadora's ear.

"From the Executive Regional Manager?" Sadora wondered aloud. That would certainly account for the wryness. "Or a member of parliament?"

A grin spread over Solstice's face. "The Governor herself, Sadie. I'm to give an evening performance at the Governor's Installation and teach three workshops at Frogmore Central."

"Wow. Congratulations, sweetie." Sadora looked down at the screen, but the officialese of the text made it attention-repellant. "Sounds like a lot of work—and expense. All told, three breakdowns, set-ups, and moves of the tank. Are they paying for that?" If they weren't, the expense would seriously eat into the grant. Of course any amount of hardship would probably be worth it, but since Solstice had to teach part-time in the dome to supplement the grant, it wouldn't be easy. And of course that wasn't even taking into account the need to rent a room in the Capitol District for at least six days, maybe even as many as ten.

Solstice laughed. "Yes, silly. Do you think anyone would perform for them if they didn't? The letter specifies expenses plus an honorarium of 500 credits."

Sadora stared at her. The grant paid 1000 credits—to cover an entire year. Five hundred for a few days' work seemed extravagant beyond measure.

"We'll need to get time off from our jobs, of course. But since we both work for the dome, that shouldn't be a problem. And if we have to, we can always trade shifts with co-workers rather than get them to substitute for us."

"We?" Sadora said. "*Us?* The invitation is to you, Solstice."

Solstice looked inquiringly at her. "This is a joint project, isn't it? There'd be no waterdance without the tank and fluid. Remember that pathetic tank I was using when we first met? And you also collaborate with me on thematic conceptualization and design the special effects. How can it not be to *us?*"

Sadora set the screen down on the table. That all might be true, but as far as the people funding the grant were concerned, she provided technical assistance, not creative input. The thought flattened her. "Yeah," she said, somehow all that she could manage. What was the matter with her? Making Solstice the face (and name) for their work had been her own idea, after all. (As had been applying for the grant in the first place.) When the outsiders looked at Solstice (at least when she was wearing a cap concealing her head hair), what they saw was someone who looked like themselves. Someone who was eligible to vote and was thus a full citizen. Someone they could believe capable of being an artist—which they would never believe about anyone retaining the skin and exoskeleton all natives of the planet were born with.

Solstice took her hand. "What is it, Sadie? Do you have reservations about this? It seems to me that this might be our big break." She lifted her hand to stroke Sadie's cheek. "But you are so much more perceptive than I am, I know I'm probably missing something."

Conscious that Solstice would likely take any sign of withdrawal the wrong way, Sadora restrained herself from drawing back. Solstice's lack of sensitivity had been something they'd had to work through—and something Sadora considered a result of Solstice's years on Pleth, not a basic trait of her character (as Solstice had decided to believe). "Well," she said slowly, trying to think her way through the vague thoughts she felt needed formulation, "I think that right from the start you're going to have to be clear about what you want to achieve and how much you'll be willing to compromise to get there."

Solstice drew her hand away and sat back in her chair. "You mean, whether I'm hoping to achieve important things with my work, rather than mere professional success and public recognition?"

"Something like that." Sadora brushed her fingers over the grainy surface of the cheap printed table. "The reason you need to think about it is because if you do something that makes Them really uncomfortable, they'll likely drop you back into oblivion." Or worse. Though "worse" was an unlikely consequence for someone of no consequence anywhere, not among the Families, not even in their own dome.

"I don't want anyone to just think this is a pretty display of a body acceptable to the outsiders," Solstice said. Sadora noted that the expression settling on Solstice's face was bringing out the squareness of her jaw and couldn't stop herself from smiling. "If we can finish working out the logistics of the time-tripper piece," Solstice added, "I'd like to perform that one."

"How much time do we have?"

"Almost three months."

Sadora realized that she had just said *we*. We'll be all right, she thought. Just as long as Solstice doesn't start thinking of herself as one of Them...

They managed to get some of the shifts during their projected absence covered, but had to do some trading—and work some of the traded shifts before they left rather than after their return. The extra work was harder on Solstice than on herself; nurturing and stimulating small children was tiring in a way that maintenance work was not. But most of the remaining work preparing the new waterdance was Sadora's, so that was all right.

Most of the worry and all of the uneasiness was Sadora's too, though. Following Solstice's advice, she compelled herself to learn the habit of keeping her hair trimmed close to her scalp. Even people from the Families living in the Capitol District did that, Solstice warned her. Anyone without head hair was liable to freak out seeing one of the "unaltered" (the politest words of the plethora used to name people like Sadora) wearing their hair long (or wearing non-opaque cling-ons that made their exoskeletons clearly visible). Basi-

cally, the hardest part of their preparations involved anticipating such "nonsense."

Sadora threw a small party a few days before she and Solstice left for the Capitol District. Sadora wanted the people
closest to them to know why they would be spending time
away. And maybe, if she was honest, she hoped that outside
validation might make people take their waterdancing col-
laboration more seriously, though she knew that outsiders'
tastes and preferences tended to be a source of derision in
Family culture. The party had been solely her idea, of course.
Solstice always claimed she was antisocial and had no social
skills. But Sadora suspected that was a story Solstice told herself to shield herself from the power of her family's ostracism of her and repeated experiences of rejection that had
followed her return from Pleth.

"I understand her wanting to adapt her body for dance,"
Sadora's sister Lee said shortly after Sadora had introduced
them to one another. "But why couldn't she at least leave
some spalls in her skin? It's as if she's rejecting who she is—
trying to be one of *Them*."

"She still has her head hair," Sadora had pointed out.
"And she hasn't acquired neural hardware. *They* don't see
her as like themselves, and they never will, unless she takes
that last step. Which I don't see her doing."

Both her mother and Lee, though a little repulsed by Solstice at first, had gradually warmed to her. And their pity
for her ostracism had eventually morphed into indignation.
Like the few friends Solstice had made in the dome, they'd
even come to take pride that *their* dome had welcomed her in
and trusted her with their children. The Daughters of Violet
Cho prided themselves on their humaneness, and they had
a history of seeing things differently from Solstice's family,
the Daughters of Bessy Darracott, who had a reputation for
being ornery.

Sadora's mother brought a platter of cheese to the party, Lee brought fruit, her cousins brought pastries and breads, and Solstice's and Sadora's respective workmates brought beer and a selection of sparkling water. Sadora's workmates also brought their drums and tambourines, and though only the fittest could dance, everyone sang themselves breathless.

Later, after they'd collapsed into hammocks and shifted from sparkling water to beer, they reminisced about other times, told amusing anecdotes, gossiped, and finally spoke of the projected trip to the Capitol District and acquaintances in common known to be living there. When they were all well lubricated, Ari asked, "You're going to do the dance about the time-tripper, right?" He had been among those who'd been the audience for their final trial run.

Solstice said yes, she and Sadie were pretty happy with the shape it was in.

"What do you s'pose They'll make of it?" he wondered. "Will They even recognize it when they see it? Do any of them even know about time-trippers?"

Solstice and Sadora looked at one another. That was a question they'd never thought to ask. Solstice said, slowly, "I think some of them know about it—as a kind of myth or legend. I mean, I found mention of it in a travel book when I was on Pleth."

"They know about mistflowers," Sadora said. "They can't help but know mistflowers exist."

"But probably not about the relationship between mist-flowers and time-trippers," Solstice said softly.

"That dance, I think, is really for *us*," Ari said.

"Though They'll probably think it's about Them," Lee said.

Sadora grinned. "Isn't everything?"

Everyone laughed, and the moment passed, and they talked about the birds nesting in Shona's Grove dive-bombing a juvenile green raptor who'd foolishly taken them for prey.

When the first probes the Council for Developmental Strategy sent to the Bellarius System yielded the intelligence that one of its planets was loaded with riches just begging to be mined, most of the sitting councilors paid scant attention to aspects of the planet likely to pose obstacles to development. Toxic atmosphere? Nothing domes and environmental suits couldn't cope with. Punishing gravity? Magnetic slabs beneath the domes and exoskeletal prosthetics or genetic modifications everywhere else would solve *that* problem.

The councilors knew that they themselves would never have to set foot on the planet. What mattered was the potential wealth, just waiting to be exploited. And in fact, since the atmosphere was already toxic and only workers would actually be living on the surface, they'd have no pressing concern to worry about ecological impacts the way they had to do with most of the worlds they administered. For capital investors, it never got better than this.

The Council named the world Frogmore, in deference to the Frogmore Investment Group, one of the primary sources of venture capital for the first wave of development projects. Candide Gael constructed the first dome on the site of the area that soon came to be known as the Center, which over the centuries has grown into a thriving metropolis with a population of twelve million. By the second century, the Center had grown too large to be accommodated by a dome of any size. Smaller domes were constructed in other areas to service the planet's many mining projects. Because the impenetrability of the atmosphere makes above-ground lower-atmosphere navigation risky, most transport is via either high-speed train on the surface or high-atmosphere rocket.

— *Frogmore's Destiny: A Manifesto for Independence*

One
INEZ GAUTHIER

Hovering in the air above her dressing table, the holo-images of the four designs exhibited their features as Inez Gauthier subvocalized, in sequence, "charming smile," "sardonic smile," "sneer," and "frost." The images floated in the air like heads detached from their bodies, but the designs they wore flowed with such controlled precision that no one would have taken them for anything but models. The design-dresser stood by, silent and attentive, listening to his employer's comments, waiting to be cued for his opinion.

"*Aurora* is too subtle," she said, dismissing it from the display. She subvocalized "mild surprise," "astonishment," and "shit-eating grin." "Scratch *The Diva*," she said. She needed something to complement the pelt, not upstage it. So which should she choose? *The Gala*, or *The Deliberate*? For several minutes she strode about the room, clad only in cling-ons, caught up in furious thought. It was a question, she repeated several times to herself, of the total effect she wished to achieve. It must be dramatic, but not overbearing. Just as her choice of powder—

The general chose that moment to barge in. "Inez!" His peremptory tone wobbled perilously close to querulous. "Where are my star sapphire earrings?"

The design-dresser lowered his eyes and assumed the demeanor of a piece of noninteractive furniture. The general's daughter drew breath and stared at the image in the holomirror, at her nipples peeping through her nearly sheer cling-ons. Though the silver sparkles in the lavender powder served the total effect, she decided she should have stuck with the usual gold sparkles, since the silver made her skin an ugly gray.

"Inez! Did you hear me? I can't find my star sapphire earrings!"

The general often barged into his daughter's dressing room, and even into her bath. When, fresh from University, she had first settled into his household, she found this mortifying. But consciousness of her own embarrassment had taught her to accept these intrusions as a simple fact of life, without significance. Only the unsophisticated suffered the agony of embarrassment. One who had grown up at the hub of the universe, one who had been educated in the finest institution on Pleth, must never be so gauche as to experience even the slightest twinge of it. To fuss about her father seeing her naked ∼ on more than one occasion he had even had the bad taste to walk in on her while she was engaged with a sexual partner ∼ would be to expose herself to the general's contempt. After all, the general himself was almost never alone. He boasted to one and all that he issued orders and received briefings at every hour of the day and night, while eating, jogging, playing eye-hand coordination games. And while to his intimates he copped to being something of a hedonist, he took a curious pride in his ability to, when occasion demanded it, take care of business while executing a dump.

Requests that she retrieve some item or other for him annoyed her considerably more. Evergood, his personal attendant, carried in his supplemental memory the codes identifying every personal item the general owned. The first time he had said "Inez, where is the mate to this Arcturian camelhair wristband?" she had dished him a haughty stare and wondered aloud why he hadn't asked his personal attendant that very question. She had repeated this treatment every succeeding time he had asked her where he had put a personal possession, until finally he all but desisted from doing so.

While she would never claim to be the brightest star in the galaxy, when it came to her father's moods, she had no difficulty doing the math. He took care, naturally, not to let his irritation get out of hand with her, just as he always took care not to punch out his closest aides or his second-in-command. He might yield to an urge to assault the governor (though only in private, of course) but never someone he depended on for attending to details of which he himself had little grasp. That first year she had joined him on Frogmore—shocked at the remoteness, crudity, and naked barbarism of the planet—she had been forced to lay down a few ground rules. And so dramatic had been her methods of dealing with him that though the general often danced close to the line of transgression, he nevertheless refrained from testing (much less crossing) it.

Taken by itself, her father's testiness could have pointed to any number of developments and been explained in terms of several causal factors. But given the other symptoms he'd been recently displaying, her diagnosis was weariness with one- and three-night stands. A never-ending stream of partners satisfied his sexual needs and stroked his ego. But whenever he was forced to rely solely on his daughter for emotional security, a huge chasm of anxiety opened below the complacent emotional surface he usually displayed. Lately the general had taken to indulging in self-pitying drunks, extreme interest in his appearance, reminiscences about past liaisons, yearning speeches about escaping "this dunghill of a backworld," and long sessions in the therapy-cube, as well as settling into a prolonged period of sexual abstinence. His daughter, therefore, considered it only a matter of time before he'd be thrusting a new lover on the household.

The prospect of his forming a new sexual liaison left her ambivalent. At the beginning of his liaisons, the general would be interested in pleasing his new lover and revel in a certain freedom from the small tyrannies his daughter had

gradually (out of the irritation of weeks of enforced attention to him) taken to exercising over him. And Inez would finally have some peace. If the new lover proved to be grasping
or even simply obnoxious, though, the arrangement would
create a major headache for everyone in the household. In
any case, Inez would always and ever be there, a permanent
fixture in the household and ultimately the only person the
general believed understood him, and so after he had become
satiated with partnership, the new lover would leave, and the
whole cycle would begin again.

The general's daughter flicked a look at her father, subvocalized *boredom*, and pointedly studied the remaining designs. Suppressing the retort that sprang to her lips ~ let us
by all means get this over with, it doesn't matter who she is,
only that she'll be willing to spend half her waking hours
keeping track of your star sapphire earrings, your Borragian
onyx death's head ring, and the myriad other items you are
determined to thrust upon your other's consciousness ~ and
said in a voice as smooth and cool as the design base covering
the skin on her face, "Have you asked Evergood, General?"

The general glared at her; his design's eye-globes magnified the effect so splendidly that if anyone but her had been
on the receiving end of it, they would have been quaking in
their boots. "The fool is powdering my cape with Aurelian
Dust, something he should have done earlier."

"Consider: You've already put your face on while I haven't
even chosen my design yet," she said. "I thought you didn't
like waiting for me?"

"What you need is a schedule and the discipline for keeping to it. I never cease to be amazed at the results of a civilian
education. You're slack, woman!"

She aimed her right index finger at the holo-image of
The Deliberate and raised her eyebrows at the design-dresser. "If Evermore's busy, you might try looking in your jewel
boxes," she said.

The design-dresser inquired whether he should begin. Inez turned her long, bony back to her father and seated herself at the dressing table, gave the design-dresser the go-ahead, and messaged her attendant to let her know that she'd need to replace the silver powder with gold.

The general stomped off, unsatisfied. Had he really expected her to run over to his quarters and rummage through his jewel boxes for him?

Ninety standard minutes later, Inez shared a vial of one of the milder Barejo inhalants with her father. All five star sapphire earrings dangled from his ear. "I'm not *feeling* it," the general complained after they'd emptied the vial. "You should have chosen something stronger. You know I hate going to these affairs without getting up a decent level of intensity."

Inez stared past her father's head at the shifting tapestry glittering in the air behind him. "It's obvious, Daddy." She enunciated *Daddy* with special clarity to produce the aura of mockery she needed to evoke whenever using this form of address to him. "You've been living on this planet too long. Your senses have dulled, have become like theirs. It's their inability to respond to any but the most dramatic—no, *melo*dramatic—cues fed them. They've a coarse taste for extremes. Which is all the more obvious for their persistently mis-taking the word *subtlety* to signify *preciosity*."

She gazed at the tapestry: her perceptions had been heightened by the inhalant, even if his hadn't, for the ordinarily indiscernible shifting of patterns and colors in the tapestry now tantalized her, whetting her appetite for more solidly corporeal pleasure. She glanced sidelong at him. "Consider, Daddy, their absurd fashion for dueling." She had introduced the fashion when she'd first arrived, to test the natives' gullibility as to how the societies of the more advanced worlds in the galaxy behaved. Though the elites had eventually discovered the prank, their dueling had grown ever more elaborate, theatrical, and challenging, even penetrating the culture of Frogmore's professional class. Inez chuckled at the thought of her design-dresser dueling with, say, Amanda Kundjan's design-dresser: an absurdity she was tempted to share with her father. Intricate, she judged the elites' dueling, but never *subtle*. The last she had heard, more than two hundred books had been written on the subject.

"I wonder," the general said, his eyes glinting behind his amber-tinted eye globes, "that you still find their dueling a matter for amusement. That joke lost its savor years ago." The general's design spurted into an attractive pattern of pulsating oscillations that after a few seconds subsided into gentle swirls of the design's paler colors. Inez studied the pattern as she tried to guess what particular facial response had triggered it. Perhaps the most intriguing aspect of a new facial design lay in the need it forced on interlocutors to decipher a fresh set of patterns, shapes, and colors. For social occasions the challenge of deciphering as yet unlearned designs could be exhilarating, stimulating, and provocative (thus holding their interlocutors' boredom at bay). For business situations transpiring in evening hours, however, such designs could prove frustrating, even disastrous. Low-level staff, of course, tended to conform to a limited number of designs, and sometimes workplace rules dictated which—if any—would be permitted. Needless to say, everyone they encountered that evening would be devoting their utmost attention and powers of memory to grasping the essence of the general's new design.

The general continued dissing her. "I'll be astonished if anyone consents to sit beside you at dinner. You know how the natives feel about time-trippers. It's been bred into them like an instinct. Surely you must have noticed how they use the time-tripper to symbolize death, anxiety, and impotence?"

Inez laughed.

The deepest, thickest shade of chartreuse spread over his design—including the eyepieces, which she had previously thought to be stable tints. "If you weren't my daughter, the minute you showed yourself in public wearing that thing you'd be thrown straight into detention—unless you were first torn limb from limb. As I recall, they have laws against transporting any part of time-trippers—even those safely dead—outside the coastal zones."

"My pelt has been neutralized," Inez said. Careful not to look at them, she stroked the scales she had been assured had been treated with a chemical to seal in the poison and dull the scales' deadly sharp edges. But a strange frisson of anxiety and revulsion rippled over her, and she removed her hand—with feigned indifference—from the scales. At once the sensations that had been revolting her ceased. She tried not to think about the manifest correlation between the touching and the feelings the touching had apparently evoked and concentrated instead on the beauty of the scales. Some had been silvered, others had been left in their natural phosphorescent state. The whole pelt shimmered, deadly and sharp, coldly beautiful against the rich russet tones of her skin. Besides the effect of the whole, the individual scales, taken singly, offered their own subtle patterns and colors and textures that drew the eye and had the tendency to fascinate the beholder to the point of mesmerism.

She smiled at the general, aware that that movement of muscles in her face would set warm earth-toned streams rippling and flowing through her design. "Besides," she said, "those laws are mainly for the protection of natives who might be foolish enough to attempt to capture time-trippers—or to sell them."

"I only hope," the general said, "that the ill-feelings you stir up tonight won't get in the way of this new Brainnard mining project."

"What nonsense. That deal's in the bag. Anyway, I doubt anyone in the governor's circle is so fuckwitted as to let an unrelated cultural hang-up interfere with their getting their hands on such a windfall." She knew well that the general's entire staff considered that the major difficulty lay in the bitter infighting being waged by the governor's circle, the local managers of the Brainnard Region, and the unofficial coalition composed of local managers from all over the planet, who never stopped trying to disempower the governor. No one but the governor's circle, the Brainnard managers, and the Combine seriously mattered in the affair.

"While we're on the subject," the general said, his voice suddenly grating, "I think it would be wise to avoid even mentioning the Brainnard project tonight. We can't afford slip-ups with this one."

Inez gritted her teeth. So she had once fucked up a deal with a careless slip. *Once!* Eight local years should have been long enough to have proven herself reliable. But no. The general *never* forgot that old error—and never let her forget it. "You've such confidence in me," she said, "that I wonder you tell me anything." In fact he couldn't keep from babbling to her about every matter, large and small, that claimed his attention. She, after all, understood him. And that wouldn't change, even when the general had finally immersed himself in a new personal liaison. No matter how well the new lover "understood" him, he couldn't afford to risk gabbing indiscreetly to just anybody.

"Yes, Captain?" the general called out, staring past her.

Inez looked over her shoulder and saw Handler and Glance standing just inside the threshold.

"Are you ready for the scores, sir?" asked Handler.

"Yes, yes, Captain, let's have them."

For the next fifteen standard minutes, the general and his daughter pored over the scores of the blood chemistry, reflexes, and coordination tests (as of the last standard hour) of available craft operators and the staff security detail, and discussed who should be assigned to crew the general's craft and constitute his security detail for the evening. Most of the outcomes were obvious—some so obvious that they all knew (without speaking of it) that Glance would be docking and suspending two of the officers in the pool for failing to meet the minimal chemical standards applying at all times to officers.

As usual, though, the choice of pilot entailed considerable discussion. The general and Handler, his chief ADC, predictably favored the cleanest blood chemistry over the best reflexes and coordination score (which for unknown reasons seldom seemed to coincide). Lieutenant Glance, the officer charged with overseeing the evaluation and assessment of all craft and security operatives, however, as usual insisted that superb coordination and reflexes rendered a slightly muddied blood chemistry irrelevant on the grounds that the impurities in the top scorer's blood manifestly had not diminished their abilities and concentration to any appreciable effect. Inez agreed with Glance, but the general and his chief ADC together outranked her and the second, rather lowly ADC. Since Inez knew how to play on her father's most deep-seated fears about above-ground navigation on such a fog-shrouded world, she and the lieutenant prevailed. The general's attitude could be characterized as terror—wild, unreasoning terror that had been planted in him on his very first day on the world, when two craft in his escort had collided at high speeds with an errant civilian craft, resulting in the permanent deaths of five individuals in his escort and injuries for many more. His first official act on the planet had accordingly been to tighten its licensing laws. The rate of deaths and injuries in above-ground traffic had declined dramatically, allowing the general to instruct his critics that that achievement alone sufficed to justify the extent of his role in the planet's affairs.

After Handler and Glance left the room, Inez broke out another inhalant. The general complained that he wanted something stronger, but she ignored him. She felt certain that tonight was the night, and she didn't want him making a mess of a decision that would affect their lives for the next several months.

Half a standard hour later, the general and his daughter entered the antechamber on the roof. She was so bored with the general's boredom that she was close to stamping her feet and screaming. She needed to get off the planet, needed a break from the general, needed above all the refreshment of a civilized world.

The thought of getting away to one of the better sort of worlds, though, only exacerbated her mood. In the past she had tried doing that a few months at a time, since the general would not allow her more time than that away from him. But during such trips she always re-discovered the horrifying fact that Frogmore had left an indelible mark on her. The beautiful soul that had once illumined her existence had been scuffed and tarnished, making it invisible to the other beautiful souls she knew to be her equals. Only the constantly re-evoked memory of life before her arrival on Frogmore— years spent growing up on cultured, sophisticated worlds— made it possible for her to live with the humiliations and pique that trips off Frogmore now brought her.

Zagorin, that pillar of sour and stuffy stiffness, awaited her in the departure lounge. She held Inez's tissue-thin cape and the set of eating utensils they had decided would work with *The Deliberate*. She hesitated, patently wishing to avoid contact with the pelt she had earlier refused to handle when dressing the general's daughter. "Don't be an idiot," the latter said to her attendant. Naked face scrunched with distress, Zagorin took back the cape and, arms fully extended to protect her body from accidental contact with the pelt, draped it around her employer's proud shoulders.

Handler opened the hatch, said that visibility was currently seven meters, and announced that all preparations for departure had been completed. His Aurelian-dusted raw silk cape swirling, the general stalked out into the hot, muggy fog, and his daughter followed. Neither bothered to activate their respirators since the walk to the craft would expose them to at most four breaths of the mist-heavy air.

Colonel Farquhar (recently returned from the Brainnard Region) stood at attention before the hatch of the craft he would be riding in, and the general addressed some pleasantry to him as he and his daughter passed him. Though second-in-command and of a first-rank family based on Janniset, he, like all the general's other officers, had to attend social functions in uniform. Inez took note of his formal, unsmiling bearing and admired his sleek, full-shouldered figure, which the tight, black, ruby-accented uniforms that all the general's officers wore rendered a pleasure to her eyes. His stern, bare face, seemingly impervious to the wisps of fog drifting about him, admirably symbolized the peacekeepers' brave and stalwart mission. But how, she wondered, did he endure having to show a bare face to the world for as long as he was posted to this hellhole?

All those naked mouths, ever on display, made sexual voyeurs of everyone who looked on them. Inez felt certain that most of the officers must be uncomfortably aware of that fact. Did Colonel Farquhar resent the general for the latter's standing order that all officers on Frogmore (excepting the general himself) must always appear in public barefaced and in uniform? Did it gall the ADCs who attended far more functions than the general's daughter (who simply would not put up with an event or three every spacing local day) always to be obliged to wear the gold-braided emblems of their rank visibly upon their clothing and to put up with that absurd "Peacekeepers of the Galaxy" holographic insignia declaring TO UPHOLD PEACE AT ANY PRICE always in the same place on their breast pockets, pulsing like a logo on corporate livery? She imagined it did, but she'd never gotten intimate enough with any of her father's officers to ask.

One of *his* rules for *her* banned her from sexual partnering with any of his officers. "Surely with the native population of the entire planet to choose from you won't be lacking partners," he had put it to her. But the officers' naked faces piqued her erotic interest as the naked faces of many of the natives never could; when the natives went barefaced, it was usually because they knew no better, while the officers, all from advanced worlds, did so as a point of discipline. She abided by her father's rule, however—though only because he himself followed the same rule. If he hadn't, she would have done as she pleased in the matter.

The general and his daughter entered his personal craft; the officers and crew had of course assembled themselves on each side of its hatch into the sort of tight, clean formation the general liked to see. "Stavros," the general said, pausing to address the pilot. "You barely squeaked by, your blood chemistry was muddied again. This is not acceptable, Lieutenant. There's a reason we set standards."

Inez glanced at the other officers' faces and fumed silently at her father's insistence on making a point of the pilot's blood chemistry. Stavros's eye, memory, and experience far outweighed the trifling impurity of her blood. Thinking now of the towers that lay between the Commander's Residence and Lake Kundjan, of the Lake itself (not to mention the traffic), and of the tendency of the mistflowers to confuse the system's sensors, she broke out in gooseflesh. She could not remember ever having felt safe on Frogmore when flying with any other pilot. Whenever anyone else piloted her, she spent the entire trip with teeth clenched, toes curled, and fingernails dug into her palms. With Stavros at the helm, though, she had at times actually forgotten the danger.

As the general continued to harangue the pilot, his daughter grew so irritated that she spread the palm of her hand flat against his back ~ yes, she did like the feel of the Aurelian dust so rich and gritty on the raw silk ~ and, barely restraining herself from shoving him, interjected when he paused to let Stavros answer, "Are we boarding or aren't we? Or do you propose that we spend the night inhaling fog?"

Head reared back, he only snorted loudly in reply and said, "See to it, Stavros." As he stepped through the hatch, his daughter smiled at Stavros—and realized that the pilot would have no idea of how to interpret the flow patterns of *The Deliberate.* She imagined saying to her, "Let's space him when we get over the lake, shall we?"

Inez followed her father through the hatch, seated herself, and fastened her safety straps. Wanting to avoid seeing her father's nervousness, she closed her eyes. But closing her eyes opened her to the image of her own seat ejecting out into the lake, settling onto its floater, and rocking erratically, just above the surface, as she breathed in microscopic particles of mist-flowers that would soon be doing terrible things to her central nervous system. By the time she opened her eyes, the quiet, high-pitched whine of liftoff had been succeeded by the low throb of cruise. The general—likely fearful that she might level the charge of cowardice at him—had left the shutters open, thus exposing both of them to the constant realization that one could see nothing out there, not the ground, not a light, not a tower, just *nothing*, though many tall, thrusting towers and bustling air traffic lay all around them.

They had Stavros at the helm, the general's daughter reminded herself. She had heard people say—Handler among them—that Stavros had a sort of sixth sense when it came to spatial perception. Lightning-quick access to supplemental memory, attention to charts, the craft's instruments, and the constant readouts provided by the auto-navigation system constituted Stavros's tools, just as they did any other pilot's. But those who enjoyed the privilege of crewing in her cockpit told tales of Stavros's announcing this or that lying out there in advance of navigational readouts. Stavros, unlike every other pilot on her father's staff, never had near-misses.

The general's eyes were closed. Things had been dull, quiet, and predictable lately, so it was unlikely that he was in communication with headquarters. Smiling, his daughter relaxed her left hand and placed it over the general's right, which, gripping the end of his armrest, now resembled a claw. "Poor Daddy. Are you having a bad time?" she cooed at him.

Behind his globular eye-pieces, the general's eyes snapped open; his head whipped sideways, and he glared at her. "You're so obvious, Inez. Admit it: my lack of appreciative wonder and admiration for your time-tripper pelt galls you."

Inez sighed. "Your nerves are all shot to hell, aren't they." She patted his hand. "You should try relaxing. I know you don't like tranqs, but surely you must have one of those biofeedback apps in your personal package. You could access it now and by the time we land would feel as good as if you'd just had an hour in the therapy-cube. Really, Daddy. I don't know how you've managed to live on this planet for nineteen local years without cracking. And considering that Stavros—"

The general snarled. "Shut up, Inez!" He threw off her hand, and his design shuddered with convulsions of purple, yellow, and puce.

Disgusted, Inez turned her head away and deliberately stared out at the fog. But her eyes kept straying to the reflection of the three dim cabin lights on the surface of the window, beacons tempting her with their tangible, visible reality. From time to time she wondered if they were above the lake yet, but not once did she consider asking their location of the crew. Neither she nor the general really wanted to know. If they had, they'd be running the holo of their progress now playing in the cockpit. Instead, she labored to recapture her excitement over her pelt. She reminded herself that word would spread around the entire planet, that the notability of her audacity would not be contained within the governor's circle. From the natives she expected shocked condemnation and respectful admiration corresponding respectively to their backworld traditionalism and consciousness of and interest in the more advanced worlds. In a way, she mused, it would be a test, especially for the ambivalent types, for instance the governor herself. This insight so gratified her that she turned to her father to share it with him. But the little twitches flickering over his (still) purple, puce, and yellow visage made her queasy, and she returned her gaze to the window. Had there been a recent crash she hadn't heard about?

They might well be over the lake now.

To his daughter (but to no one else) the general often inveighed against the governor for insisting on maintaining her principal residence and military HQ on the artificial island in the middle of Lake Kundjan and threatened never to set foot again in the Governor's Installation. But since it could be approached only by air, the Installation lay physically out of the reach of the malcontents and insurgents that plagued the governor and local managers. Time-trippers and Frogmore's other comparably deadly creatures did not live in fresh water, which was fortunate, given how many accidents occurred over the lake.

At least they did not have to worry about sabotage. The fact that sabotage of government and military craft had never been a problem, as the general liked to point out, proved the insurgents had no way of getting hold of the weaponry the general imported in vast quantities from off-world. "If they had it, they'd use it," he said again and again to the few vocal persons in the governor's circle who argued for curtailing arms imports on the grounds that they would eventually fall into the hands of the insurgents.

Politics? You go into the military, and they make you a general, and what happens? In fact I'm nothing more than a policeman, here to ensure that the people of the planet abide by the laws their democratically chosen government promulgates. This isn't my idea of engaging in politics. The military apparatus provided by the Combine is neutral vis-à-vis this planet's politics... We're simply here to keep the peace, which a handful of malcontents seem determined to destroy. The general had used those very words so many times that his daughter had come to realize he must keep them handy in an autovocalization block. Which suggested that they were some sort of formula or definition for him...though serving what purpose? Rote explanation had its uses but could also get in the way. One could so easily reach for it and then find, mid-flow, that that wasn't what one wanted after all, that one had somehow gotten pushed into a corner because of the very fluidity and ease rote explanation presented as it slipped casually off one's tongue—and be unable to stop the recitation or alter it in progress.

Consciousness of the low hum and rising whine of landing-mode jerked Inez out of her stream of thought. She glanced at the general and observed the tendons in his forearms visibly bulging under his cling-ons as his hands clawed and clutched at the armrests. *Stavros,* she repeated to herself. *Stavros, Stavros, Stavros.* As though in response to this invocation, the sound of the engine abruptly cut off, and Stavros messaged them. <<We've landed on the Governor's Installation and are prepared to deboard at any time, General and Madam Gauthier.>>

Her heart lifting, her excitement resurging, the general's daughter clasped her father's hand and smiled at him. "Stavros is good," she said. "You can always count on her, General."

They unstrapped and rose to their feet, but then had to wait for the general to regain the firmness of his knees. "Tonight something good will happen to you," his daughter told him. "I can feel it in my bones."

The general gave her a look she had not yet seen pass over his design and half-laughed. He hadn't the faintest idea of what she referred to.

The most singular of Frogmore's many striking physical aspects is the ecology of its lower atmosphere, which is inhabited by numerous organisms collectively referred to as the "Scourge." Most of these organisms, of course, are microscopic; all are eukaryotic. The Scourge renders the air on the surface oxygen-thin to variable degrees and appears to the naked eye as a dense fog that impedes visibility, which ranges from 1.5 meters at its densest concentrations to 40 meters at its lightest. At times this fog is marked by the presence of phosphorescent particles that suggestible individuals take for signs of supernatural presence.

The five largest of these organisms are colloquially referred to as "mistflowers," which many people mistakenly assume to be identical with the Scourge rather than a subset of it. Mistflowers exude a pungent sometimes sweet scent that varies in fragrance and strength, depending on the concatenation of the cycles of each of the five species as well as on other factors such as stage of life-cycle, barometric pressure, velocity and direction of the wind, temperature, levels of oxygen and carbon dioxide, etc. Three species produce spores, and two species produce seeds that, when ingested through inhalation or dermal contact, impact the human central nervous system with effects ranging from euphoria in mild cases to violent hallucinations in moderate cases to, in the most extreme cases, temporary unconsciousness or death.

It is rumored that several local religious cults harvest mistflowers when the Scourge manifests in very light, glowing shades of lavender, and that they then ingest these during collective rituals. Our fact-checkers, however, have not been able to verify this.

—*A Traveler's Handbook to the Galaxy,* 49th edition

Two
INEZ GAUTHIER

In line with the family tradition, Inez had been raised to assume all responsibility for managing the family's finances. The "tradition" had been invented by the general's great-grandmother, who had begun life as a lowly assistant clerk in the carbon-filament industry that dominated the economy of the planet too optimistically named Evergreen. No one knew the details of how the first Inez Gauthier had founded the family fortune, simply that she had. And when her son Hugo had devoted himself entirely to politics, the family tradition had been hatched. In time he had produced a daughter— the general's mother—whom the first Inez Gauthier had trained and prepared to assume responsibility for managing the family fortune once she herself no longer chose (or was able) to do so. The general's mother never did succeed her grandmother, however, for Inez Gauthier had outlived her granddaughter, who had been killed in a freak mining disaster while inspecting the site of one of the family's mining interests. She had then helped her son raise the next—male, of course—generation (namely the general), who had naturally gone into politics and eventually been made a general and put in charge of the Combine's peacekeeping force on Frogmore. Because of his mother's early death, the general had had the second Inez Gauthier made while he was still on Pleth. The first Inez Gauthier had raised the second Inez Gauthier, trained her—and then retired. Her great-granddaughter had at first hoped that after suitable time off she would want to get back into the game;

later she'd realized that given how swiftly and constantly
"the game" changed, getting back into it would be nontrivi-
al—and thus was unlikely. But that was something she didn't
like to think about.

Stuck on Frogmore for the duration, she felt compelled
to import at least some cultural life and do what she could
to assist local efforts in developing an indigenous arts scene.
To this end, she had founded the Inez Gauthier Institute for
the Arts. And once the general's daughter had taken the lead,
it hadn't been long before members of the governor's circle
began promoting and funding local talent. Careful to conceal her skepticism, Inez lavished praise on all such efforts
and went to great lengths to incorporate them into the work
of the Institute. She sponsored master classes given by imported talent for local talent; she arranged tours for the imported talent to various regional centers; she even supported
and promoted the most promising of the local talent brought
to her notice. The governor, from time to time, smiled and
praised her for having "created a Renaissance on Frogmore,"
but Inez knew exactly what the governor thought of her.
Four local years past, she had partnered regularly with one
of the governor's closest aides. She doubted the governor's
sentiments had changed much since then.

So when the governor received the general and his daughter and at once launched into an enthusiastic riff on the dance
troupe from Janniset—among the Institute's current artists-
in-residence—now touring Frogmore's regional centers,
Inez gently remarked that the Institute's artists-in-residence
always found Frogmore and its permanent fog simply *fascinating*. The governor responded with an affable barrage of
clichés about how fortunate Frogmore was to be exposed to
off-world culture in a voice that conveyed nothing more than
polite flatness. Like most Frogmorians, the governor restricted her facial designs to variations on the natural form of her
face, especially in the fashioning of ocular- and oral-orifices,

and in this particular design (which Inez knew cold, since she had seen it on the governor dozens of times before), the governor's eyes were not only visible but magnified in order to make them the dominating feature of the design. Inez noted the darting of the governor's eyes as she tried to avoid seeing the time-tripper pelt; and observing the fidgeting of the governor's hands, she realized that rather than being routinely irritated by the customary ironic comments about the planet's supposed fascination for off-worlders, the governor was acutely uneasy.

This elated Inez. But then the governor's chief protocol officer, Bath, stepped forward, offered his arm, and led Inez at a stately pace to Danilla, the governor's number-three offspring. Glancing around, she saw that the governor's top military aide was glued to her father's right flank. No one appeared to be staring at her, but she detected a flurry of whispers in the native deviation breaking out behind her. Very well, she thought. If they wanted to pretend she hadn't struck a spectacular coup, she would allow them—for a while.

Inez was taken aback to discover that Bath had not only surrounded her with Danilla's entourage during the pre-banquet reception, but had also relegated her to Danilla's table for the duration of the meal. Ordinarily at such affairs she occupied a seat at either the governor's or her number-one offspring's table, while her father, of course, always sat at the governor's right hand (excepting rare occasions on which a member of the Council for Developmental Strategy had come to Frogmore on a fact-finding trip). Such a dramatic departure from the customary protocol needed parsing.

"Sunrises, sunsets, mountains, even lakes and oceans—which on Pleth are not poisonous—and the vivid green sky!" Danilla's design glowed, and the radiance of her voice veritably pulsated in her gracefully moving, subtly shaded visage.

Inez envied the design—so stunning, so masterly, that she knew Danilla must have had it specially created for herself while at university on Pleth; it had that personal flavor and dynamic that only design geniuses could tap.

"When I see such things in holos," Zak Dennison said, "I can't help but think they're products of the imagination, dummied up by clever holomakers."

Danilla's design softened into gently whirling dreaminess. "Before I went to Pleth, my idea about mountains and lakes or any object of physical geography and its external appearance—experienced by eye rather than simply by perception of its *insides*—were as abstract as my notions of equators, poles, and lines of latitude and longitude." Danilla turned to the general's daughter. "Imagine, Inez, I had no conception of things one could experience spatially within as having an *outside*—except in small ways, as with sleep cocoons." Her design leaped into reds and oranges spiked with streaks of indigo. "Imagine what it would be like never to see one's sleep cocoon from the outside, to carry only the experience of its interior space around with one. That's what it's like growing up on Frogmore!"

"Brilliantly put," Inez said. "I get an almost physical sensation from what you're describing." *Almost?* A sudden urge seized her to desert her father, to say *to the void with the new Brainnard Project* (by which the Gauthier fortune stood to reap billions of SCUs). For a few dizzy moments her breath seemed trapped in her body, her throat too tight for respiration.

Estine Gael protested. "That's going too far. We have gardens, we can see what *they* look like, we aren't entirely interior on this planet."

Danilla laughed. "Gardens! A few patches carefully protected by fog-burners and bombarded with artificially produced ultraviolet light. That's pathetic, Estine! One might as well claim the agricultural production units as gardens, too!"

Gardens. The gardens at the Commander's Residence, the most extensive and creative of any on the planet, hardly merited the name. Danilla had gotten that right. But when the Brainnard Project paid off, perhaps then it would be possible to do something truly *grand*... She said to Danilla. "Your description reminds me of sensing one's genitals purely by feeling—until that first time one sees one's own vulva in the mirror, during orgasm."

Conversation at Danilla's table ceased.

Inez hadn't intended to offend or embarrass them; she'd just assumed, the way the conversation was going, that they'd be like any standard knot of young people and have a good time playing with the image she offered them. It hadn't occurred to her that they were as prudish as the older members of the governor's circle, even if they did behave like quiet little juniors when in the presence of their elders. She laughed into the silence. "Obviously this analogy only works for women." Every one of them seemed to be at a loss for either how to respond or find some way of changing the subject. Remarkable! Though this group seemed to have tacitly forgiven her for breaking the time-tripper taboo, they apparently could not cope with the mention of something so personal.

Inez had been keeping an eye on Zak Dennison. It had been a couple of years since they'd partnered, but she'd sensed a flare of sexual tension between them when he'd politely offered her his wrist earlier. Like everyone else at the table, he appeared now to be preoccupied solely with managing his food. *What a cunning little instrument!* she imagined complimenting him to break the moment's stone silence. It was cunning, though, in the way it did much of the work of eating for him without either straining his patience at delicately dissecting the food morsel by morsel or massacring the arrangement of the dishes for his own convenience. The advanced worlds didn't have such instruments, since people never ate in formal herds the way they liked to do on the backworlds. She'd thought that perhaps he might be interested in reviving their partnering, but in light of his withdrawal into silence, it now struck her that it was more likely that Bath had instructed Zak to distract her and he had just been following orders.

Altina, seated facing Inez, put down the long curved spoon she'd been struggling (and failing) to manipulate with grace and said, "Rumor has it that after dinner we're to be treated to a performance of waterdancing. Are you familiar with that form of the art, Madam Gauthier?"

Virtually everyone at the table laid down their instruments and abandoned their arduous attempt to get food past their designs, assured now that the conversation was back on safe ground. Hypocrites, Inez thought scornfully. As though they didn't all detest eating in public as much as any civilized person! Still, she made the kind of polite interrogative response that encouraged everyone within comfortable range to chime in with replies.

As the meal progressed, she grew certain that Bath had assigned Danilla and Zak to handle her. Though rated only the "number-three offspring" of the governor ~ Frogmorians employed the most wretched expressions for ranking everyone and everything in sight ~ Danilla often represented the governor in ceremonial and diplomatic roles. Inez's respect for Bath soared as she considered the intricacies of such last-minute alterations in table arrangements and the ad hoc deployment of eight individuals who had likely been briefed for an entirely different situation. She appreciated his tactic of surrounding her with individuals relatively attuned to her interests and oriented toward the more advanced societies to the end of keeping her from causing a disruption at the governor's table. And yet she had to wonder: what social threat or political repercussions did they fear that could possibly outweigh the priority of the Brainnard Project? Could this all, really, be due to her wearing her time-tripper pelt? Or was something else going on?

Alone among her siblings, Danilla had taken to Pleth without homesickness or repulsion to off-planet differences and had even developed an enthusiasm for the ways of the advanced societies. Probably the governor had encouraged Danilla to become comfortable with the ways of the advanced worlds in the hope that she would in time develop the connections and savvy that Frogmore now depended on Inez to provide. Inez doubted Danilla would ever succeed to the degree the governor thought possible, but she admired and respected her for trying.

One human server removed their food-messy plates while another meticulously placed a new load of dishes in appropriate hot and cold spots in the table. When the servers withdrew, the inner round of the table rotated about a quarter-turn. Danilla leaned sideways; her shoulder all but touched Inez's. "For you, Inez," she stage-whispered, gesturing at the platter of pastries now directly before the latter's section of the table rim. "My mother ordered Lanike flour pastries to be served just for you."

Inez rolled her eyes, secure in the certainty that no one knew her design well enough to perceive it, and helped herself to the two smallest pastries on the platter. The governor's ostentatious presentation to the general's daughter of some item made from Lanike flour had become an enshrined ritual over the last few local years. The ritual might bore her, but once Nathalie Stillness had explained it to her, she had taken great care not to betray the slightest indication of impatience at being offered her favorite food at each function sponsored by the governor. According to the anthropologist, the humoring of an eccentricity (especially when that eccentricity belonged to a difficult person whom one felt some compulsion to please) allowed those who did the humoring a sense of indulging an irrational quirk and—depending on the way in

which the eccentric behaved when having her whim gratified—thus imparted a feeling of superiority and patronizing
graciousness to people who would otherwise feel frustrated
or even powerless in the circumstances. If the eccentric *demanded* such gratification, then naturally the whim would
be resented. But if, on the other hand, the whim presented
its gratifier with an opportunity to concede a favor, then the
gratifier would tend to experience positive feelings from the
performance of the act.

Aware of the governor's number-three offspring watching her manage the difficult task of conveying a bit of pastry
into her biological mouth ~ her carved jade utensil with its
long hook made it *possible*, but the point was to eat as gracefully as one would *sans* facial design ~ Inez grew irritated.
She sensed the entire table watching her. Yes, she did have a
sort of mania for Lanike flour, but what did that matter, since
she detested eating *any*thing in public? Even the most practiced banqueter must find it nerve-wracking to be watched
so closely.

When she had swallowed the bit of pastry she had managed to get inside her mouth, Inez said, "My compliments,
Danilla. The compote filling superbly complements that
wonderful fatty nuttiness that so characterizes Lanike flour.
And the brilliance of using it in pastry! It's perfect for showing off that superb texture unique to Lanike flour."

Satisfied, Danilla allowed her to return to the general conversation, which had wandered onto the subject of a resort
situated on the Fidalgo Peninsula. The general's daughter
leaned back against the cushions and slid down onto her spine
into a more relaxed position. Her lightly shod foot encountered something human. Slewing her gaze to the right, she
saw she had aimed correctly, for Zak's design had taken to
spinning in a luscious red and brown swirl. This she interpreted as interest, though given her unfamiliarity with his design

it would take some doing to confirm…which observation explained to her why new designs tended to sharpen her interest.

The general's daughter bided her time. Although she would have liked to have gotten a rise out of one of the more staid ministers seated at the governor's table, she had to admit that sitting with Danilla and her entourage, though bland, did not make her want to scream and throw things. Once the meal had been concluded, the protocol officer would be powerless to keep her under wraps, short, that is, of canceling the entertainment and sending everyone home early. He could, she supposed, direct her table companions to keep her tightly encircled in an attempt to keep her visibility to a minimum, but she doubted their power to contain her once she and they had left the table.

When the guests were herded into one of the Installation's medium-sized theaters, she mingled freely. She was disappointed, though. If there were any comments about her pelt, they were made in the native deviation. And since she could not read most of the designs around her (much less know who specifically wore them), she reaped no reward whatsoever.

Her father had already taken a seat on the inner platform, and she examined him for signs of infatuation; she detected none. She had only once interfered with the natural course of events and steered her father toward someone she thought would be easy to have around, but though it had been simple getting him together with the person she had chosen, she found that she had miscalculated in her assessment of the woman's personality, for she didn't have what it took to sexually satisfy the general.

The innermost platform was reserved for the nine Most Important Persons present. The governor's mania for ranking far outstripped the military's penchant for precisely spelled-out hierarchy and at times embarrassed even the chain-of-command-loving general. So of course she was placed beside her father. Seating the general's daughter anywhere but on that platform would have been scandalous—and likely have led to a serious diplomatic breach (besides call the future of the new Brainnard Project into question). She recalled Zak and her game of footsie with him as she made a beeline for the seat beside her father, and looked over her shoulder. And then she realized he would never have followed her onto the MIP platform without an explicit invitation. Her gaze ranged over the company, skittering about in search of the green-streaked silver cap he wore fitted tightly over his apparently shapely skull—and caught several people gaping at her. Her pulse quickened. *So they do see it! And know exactly what it is. Even as they pretend they don't.*

She did not spot Zak. Thwarted, her desire for him grew from a thread to a trickle to a stream rushing through her limbs, belly, and groin, fed apparently by his frustrating absence. Long-forgotten images and evocative fragments and her slight (but intense) knowledge of his body—as it had been then, anyway—impressed itself on her consciousness: the firm, round curves of his (admittedly knotty) legs and thighs and buttocks, for some reason exceptionally prominent ~ and she smiled as she grasped the reason: their contact under the table and, of course, the skintight pants clinging to his lower body tonight ~ their warmth and furriness and—

The general radiated grumpy gloom. "So there you are," he said as she sat down beside him. "Where'd you disappear to? One minute you were there, the next you were gone. Didn't even *see* you in the banquet hall."

"You have the governor's clever protocol officer to thank for that." She patted her father's shoulder. "Imagining he was keeping me out of trouble, I expect," she said, noting the minister seated on her father's other side, eavesdropping.

The general turned his head to stare at people occupying the next platform out. Constantly his gaze moved from

person to person, always seeking—though he himself probably did not realize it. Imagine not knowing what oneself
were so relentlessly up to!

"I asked Legs what he thought of your wearing that
pelt," he remarked in a bored tone of voice, as though his
statement weren't extraordinary.

His daughter tried picturing the look that would have
crept over the military aide's naked face. Serving as commanding officer for so long had in certain respects warped
the general's diplomatic demeanor. Set loose with a senior
officer like Legs, he tended to slip into that more familiar
mode, as though some other mechanism overrode his ordinary caution simply because his interlocutor happened to be
military, regardless of *which* military he or she happened to
belong to.

"I hope," the general said, "this performance isn't going
to bore me to tears the way the last one she foisted on us did."

"Offspring number-three assured me we were to see
something quite special," his daughter murmured, aware
of vibrations on the platform suggesting that the rest of the
"Most Important People" had arrived. "I gather it's a local
art form the governor's circle has recently discovered." *Local
art form* could mean anything, though surely given the governor's sensitivity to the influence and superiority of the Inez
Gauthier Institute for the Arts, she (or her staff) would take
care not to throw just anything at them.

The lights in the theater began dimming before all the
occupants of the innermost platform had finished settling
themselves. The governor, the general's daughter surmised,
was taking no chances. This annoyed her as Bath's other tactics had not. She leaned into the general and asked him if he
thought they might want to get up and wander about during
the performance.

"We don't even know what it is yet," he said.

In the near-dark that had descended over the theater, the translucent barrier shielding the performance area from the audience shimmered. The general pulled a fresh vial out of his pocket and broke it open. He inhaled deeply from it, then held it out to her just as a musical sound (of the gradual sort that at its inception had too few decibels for human ears to perceive) became audible. Suppressing the urge to slap his hand, she pushed it away.

The shimmering barrier winked out, revealing an enormous tank flooded in spots by golden light. In the lighted areas a few plant-like objects—suspiciously resembling those that were the scourge of the planet—drifted so sluggishly that the general's daughter thought that the fluid in the tank must be thicker than water. The thin stream of sound bifurcated, and a new texture overlaid it. Up into the lowest patch of light, up out of the inky fluid—entering from a door at the bottom of the tank, Inez conjectured—a long sleek figure moved slowly in corkscrew rotation, arrow straight. A construction or a person? The long smooth cylinder of body thrust out its limbs—four in all—looking for a moment like a stick-figure until ~ the rotation now slowed ~ the arms lifted up and up and up, nearly reconstituting the first straight, smooth image—and revealed the narrow shoulders and flaring hips of a woman.

The general made a noise in his throat. His daughter peered through the dark at him, but forgot his reaction when she heard gasps and mutters and hisses from the audience above and behind her. Looking quickly back at the tank, she saw that the dancer had thrust herself into a horizontal position, body extended in the fluid as though she were lying on her side, her back to the MIPs. For a few seconds she puzzled over the reason for the audience's reaction. A flash of recognition altered her perspective from one split-second to the next, and Inez understood they were reacting to the dancer's costume. The image she presented was unmistakable—the phosphorescent scales, the way she held her feet together in imitation of the tapered tail-end, the way her wings, which appeared to be growing out of her shoulder blades, floated easily in the reddish viscous fluid, the bony crown of a crest blossoming out from the back of her head...

What an embarrassment for the governor, Inez thought, fascinated. If only she could understand the relation between the outrageousness of her own appearance and the governor's deliberately introducing this new dance form to public notice...

For the next few minutes she focused sharply on the artist's precise execution of this strange form of dance. She remained emotionally untouched—cold even—as she tried analyzing ~ on going into shock she *always* analyzed ~ what was happening. And then, in an eruption of extraneous thought, she wondered if the governor had, on seeing the time-tripper pelt that clothed the body of the general's daughter, considered canceling the performance.

All her laborious thinking broke apart and disintegrated, its fragments dispersing into oblivion as something eerie happened inside the tank. The music, now a drone punctuated by barely audible spurts of wailing, cued her to prepare for something weird-to-frightening. The light in the tank altered, changing the reddish tint of the viscous fluid to a purplish-green that shaded subtly into the inky depths, transforming the dancer into a mottled mass of phosphorescence whose neck and face, excepting her eyes, became indistinguishable from the fluid. Tempted to go right up to the glass of the tank, Inez almost rose to her feet. But a tightening in her belly, a shivering of her limbs, the chill evaporation of sweat from the back of her neck, held her fast.

Her eyes. Not that they could be seen clearly. Simply that one noticed they were there. What a clever design, thought Inez. But the thought shattered as the dancer's body streamed out behind her and her forehead pressed flat against the glass ~

she's addressing *us*, she's oriented herself to *us*, to *me* ~ and suddenly the tank filled with the plants, or rather new parts of the tank became visible, and the flowers—yellow, purple, brown, some of them barely distinguishable—swarmed in a profusion that filled the tank and clustered about the dancer.

Bile flavored with a faint taste of the pastry she'd nibbled at dinner surged into Inez's throat. Those plants, touching a *human.* Those poisonous noxious plants that rendered this world all but uninhabitable...

Predictably the filthy Scourge exploded, and the tank became a mass of dirty yellow-brown fog. Illumination played over the entire tank, making the fuzzy outlines of the dancer and the plants less distinct than they would have been had they been cast in silhouette. Inez grew aware of her father shifting, fidgeting, clearing his throat—and reaching for a fresh vial. He muttered something under his breath that she could not make out. All around her spectators were murmuring and shifting as the yellowish-brown fog in the tank grayed.

When the audience's tension had almost reached the point of revolt, the figure of the dancer exploded into movement too blurred and fuzzed by the fog to be distinguishable. Wondering what the dancer might be doing in the midst of the filthy murk, Inez bent her entire attention on it. Her concentration broke only when an electric thrill—a shock, even—ran through her fingers past her wrist, up her arm to the shoulder. Gasping, she barely caught the cry of surprise before it leaped from her throat: she suspected from the way her fingers tingled that she had been stroking the pelt without having been aware of it.

"What is it?" the general—leaning into her, his cheek touching her ear—demanded in a whisper.

"Nothing!" his daughter fiercely whispered back.

The dancer whirled like a fiery top, shooting off sparks in all directions, sparks that buried themselves in the murk. A margin of the murk began receding from the edges of the tank, and a heavy bombardment of light revealed expanding patches of reddish viscous fluid that seemed far more transparent than the original fluid had been (though that, Inez thought, might simply be a matter of perception, given its contrast with the murk filling most of the tank). The murk continued to obscure the dancer—visible only as a whirling column of spark-shooting fire. But it continued, too, with increasing rapidity, to retreat from the periphery and concentrate itself in the center, until finally the sparks flying at tangents to the whirling column shot into visibility and, no longer swallowed by the murk, stuck to the walls of the tank, tiny specks glowing phosphorescent.

At last the dancer became clearly visible, and the final traces of fog were drawn *into* the fiery column, *into* the dancer's body. The image had not been one of the fog being burned away by the sparks, she realized, but of the fiery column—the dancer, or the dancer as time-tripper—consuming the fog, consuming the filthy spawn of the plants, consuming ~ no plants whatsoever now floated in the reddish, nearly transparent viscous fluid ~ the plants themselves. When the last of the fog had been drawn into the whirling column, the dancer's whirling did not cease or even slow ~ Inez expected now to be shown the human lineaments of the dancer ~ but instead she vanished abruptly.

The tank, brilliantly lit, appeared to be empty. And then the lighting changed swiftly, at a blink, and inky patches again drifted sluggishly, plants wafted leisurely, almost innocently, in the now purplish-green viscous fluid. After a few long seconds—Inez's fingers tugged one another in impatience at this absurd anticlimactic absence ~ surely that wasn't the end of it? It was badly designed if it were ~ the dancer popped into visibility—not rising from the depths, but simply appearing in the midst of an illuminated patch, a figure golden and phosphorescent, near-motionless, relaxed.

And blinked out. Only to pop into visibility five long seconds later in another patch of light...

Then came a repeat of the first graceful series of movements, except that this time the dancer twined the stems and leaves of the plants around her arms and legs.

The piece ended with the tank's plunge into total, inky blackness.

The house lights came up. For a time—it seemed a long, long time to Inez, who sat in near paralysis—a hush hung over the theater. Finally the governor hauled herself to her feet, officially breaking the silence. All at once people were chattering, the crowd set into noisy motion as though the silence had never been, as though paralysis had never gripped them.

"Governor." Inez, confronting her, forced the words through a tight throat. "I must meet that dancer."

The governor fixed her cold, magnified eyes on the general's daughter. "It was to your taste, the waterdancing?"

"That's what it's called?"

"It's apparently from the Spieden Region."

The Spieden Region, Inez recalled, was an area of islands and coastal lands of little proven use. The Fidalgo Peninsula, home to the resort so favored by Danilla and her cronies, lay in that region. She pressed the governor. "Will you arrange an introduction?"

The governor shrugged. "Of course. Bath can do it now, if you like."

The general touched her shoulder. "Must you do it now? Can't this wait—"

"I'll invite her back with us," Inez whispered, deducing from the blank abstracted look in the governor's eyes that she was communicating with her protocol officer.

The governor's eyes snapped back to attention and settled on the general's design (which his daughter had decided she loathed). "Perhaps you will join a few of us upstairs while Inez is meeting the waterdancer?"

The general held up his hand. "I'll decline on that this evening," he said. At this degeneration into military syntax, his daughter rolled her eyes. The inhalants were taking their toll. "I'll escort Inez. Frankly, that dancer impressed the hell out of me." His elbow jostled his daughter's arm. "As far as I'm concerned, she makes that last group you spent a fortune on look like klutzes."

"They're having problems with the gravity," Inez said, her tone defensive, for she had heard this criticism from him before. Even with all the usual ameliorations used in daily life on Frogmore, dancers from less mass-cursed worlds had generally found coming to terms with the planet's gravity beyond them.

"But that must be why she dances in that fluid. I imagine it's some sort of ultra-buoyant concoction," Minister of Culture and Education Maslin suggested. "Dance cannot of course *flourish* on a planet like ours. But the will to dance, apparently, will out." Maslin's design coalesced into obvious pink. "And creativity devises its own innovations for coping with physical limitations."

Maslin had long since made it clear that he considered himself to be Inez's hot rival. He wished his own name to be stamped on the so-called "Frogmore Renaissance," and he wished to be considered the architect of The New Frogmore, a planet to which (perhaps a few dozen years down the line, true, but what are a few decades in the larger scheme of the galaxy?) the most culture-craving of the advanced worlds would flock. On first hearing the term "Frogmore Renaissance," which Minister Maslin himself had coined, Inez had laughed in disbelief. But it did explain why, despite his perception of rivalry, the Minister of Culture and Education so often went out of his way to be friendly to her.

Bath's arrival spared Inez the obligation of conversing with the minister. With his characteristic blend of no-nonsense speed and ceremony, the governor's chief protocol officer swept her and the general out of the theater and through a door in the corridor that concealed an elevator. They descended one level; Bath led them through a maze of rooms of every size and dimension, resembling those at the Institute and at the Commander's Residence. The governor, Inez surmised, must have made off-planet consultations before building her theater complex, just as Inez, in her desire to meet the most stringent standards for such facilities, had done.

Bath led them into a dressing room. A small dark woman, her naked face marked by chitinous spalls, lay in a hammock, swinging. "Who are you?" Bath demanded.

The casual look on her face, her relaxed swinging in the hammock, held as she stared at Bath with frank curiosity. She said something in a soft, lilting voice, something Inez did not understand, for she had never bothered to learn the Frogmore deviation from Standard. It had come as a surprise to her that the deviation could be so different as to be incomprehensible on first hearing. Frogmore, after all, had only been around for about 500 standard years.

"Hmmmph." Bath turned to Inez. "This is the dancer's attendant."

The woman made a choking sound in her throat. Inez stared. The attendant, for some reason, was laughing. At *them?* The woman sported a naked face, cheap, loose clothing, and an ugly set of exoskeletal adaptations common among the directed classes on Frogmore. Inez wondered irrelevantly whether the adaptations Frogmore's elites were born with and had removed during their university years on Pleth were quite this ugly. Perhaps this woman's casual scorn for the sophisticated lay in her newness to civilized life?

"Where is Madam Balalzalar?" Bath asked her, his dry voice chillier than usual. "And answer in Standard. We are civilized people here."

"She's in the bath," the woman said in oddly accented Standard. "She needed to relieve the strain on her muscles and remove the traces of tank fluid from her skin as soon as possible. Clogs the pores, that gunk does."

Bath's toes tapped a faster and faster tattoo on the bare algolynite floor. "Then you had better tell her we're here, hadn't you."

The woman moved slowly, not rolling out of the hammock but sitting up first and then sliding out. As her feet touched the floor, a threshold behind her deopaqued, and a woman dressed only in cling-ons came into the room. She stopped short and looked at Bath, the general, and his daughter, then swung her gaze to where her attendant stood with one hand still on the hammock. The attendant said something in the Frogmore deviation. The dancer nodded and looked quickly back at the protocol officer, the general, and the general's daughter. The dancer's face had smooth brown skin, unmarked by chitinous spalls. Her eyes—bright, clear, almost black—studied the protocol officer's face. "Yes?" she said, breaking the silence. Even in that one syllable Inez heard the rasp furring the deep, quiet voice.

The protocol officer's body stiffened, then shifted, presumably to assure unambiguously the orientation of his address. "Allow me, General and Madam, to introduce to you Solstice Balalzalar." He turned slightly in the dancer's direction. "You are honored to meet General Paul Gauthier and Madam Inez Gauthier." He looked at the general. "And now, unless there is some other way I can serve you, I will leave you in privacy."

"Yes, yes," the general said, never taking his eyes off the dancer.

The protocol officer held out his wrist in a pro forma manner, indicating that he did not expect them to go through with the wrist-ritual, bowed, and left the room.

The dancer's eyes moved back and forth between the general and his daughter—and came to rest on the time-tripper pelt. Inez noted the long expressionless stare that finally moved from the pelt back to Inez's design-mediated face.

Inez suffered a pang of regret that the dancer could not see into her eyes. Something in that face—frighteningly naked yet as unperturbed as the attendant's had been while under Bath's fish-cold eye—compelled her, made her long for direct contact.

"You were magnificent, Madam," the general said, breaking the silence.

Inez had forgotten her father's presence. Both she and the dancer looked at him, and she saw with shock that he had found his next liaison.

"Thank you," the dancer said. "Then you weren't horrified. Many people are, you know. The topos runs close to the taboo." She glanced at the pelt, as though its fascination were irresistible to her gaze. "Though I suppose it couldn't horrify *you*." She looked again at Inez's design. "But of course. You are from off-planet. Which makes all the difference. The dance meant nothing to you."

"We will want to see more," the general said, all eagerness.

The dancer's gaze strayed to the general's design. Only now did his daughter notice that the dancer, like her attendant, had *head hair*, clipped short but clearly visible. She also saw the hard muscular body under the diaphanous cling-ons, saw the lack of the exoskeletal adaptations so evident on the attendant's body. And yet, the dancer showed her face without the least self-consciousness. "Thank you," the dancer said, "for your appreciation. Whether I will dance again in the Capitol District isn't certain, though it's likely, since the Minister of—"

"But it *is* certain," Inez interrupted. "I speak on behalf of the Inez Gauthier Institute. And I'm anxious on the Institute's behalf to pursue your future association with the Institute."

The dancer's eyes watched her without expression. What was wrong with the woman? She should be leaping for joy at having made it, at having secured the future of her art! Was it possible she didn't understand what the Institute—or who she, Inez Gauthier—was?

The dancer smiled faintly. "Perhaps something can be arranged," she said. She glanced over her shoulder at the attendant, standing, still, with one hand on the hammock. Then she looked back at Inez. "I don't want to be rude, but I'm exhausted almost to the point of collapse. We could, as you say, pursue this another time…"

Exhaustion! Of course. That must be the reason for her lack of responsiveness.

"How utterly disappointing," the general said. "We were hoping we could induce you to relax with us in more comfortable circumstances."

The dancer looked again at the general. After two or three seconds, her eyes hardened into coldness—not the glazed fishy cold of the protocol officer's eyes, but a remote cold that reminded Inez of holographs of tundra worlds without atmosphere or carbon-based life. "I'm exhausted," she repeated, inching a few steps backwards, as though to announce her imminent withdrawal.

"Understandable," the general murmured, never taking his eyes off her. "Perhaps dinner tomorrow evening?"

"Sir?"

Inez struggled to understand the dancer's lack of response to the general. Even if the dancer took the Institute lightly, she surely knew who the general was!

The dancer folded her arms over her breasts. "If we could work out the details tomorrow…"

Inez linked arms with her father. She could sense him about to push and knew instinctively that it would be a mistake. She had no doubt that the dancer, were he to press her now, would refuse in a way that would scorch them both. She mustn't let that happen, or the general would end up opposing, out of pique, any sponsorship of the dancer the Institute might undertake. "Yes," Inez said. "I think that's an excellent idea." She bowed and pinched the general's elbow. "Good-night."

"Good-night, Madam." The general bowed. "Until to-morrow evening," he said.

The dancer also bowed. "Good-night."

Inez whisked her father out of the room and, following the directional signals at the top of each archway, back to the main level. The dancer must be coming down off too many stimulants, she thought.

"She's magnificent," the general said as they stepped into the elevator.

"Even with head hair?"

The general sighed. "Provincialism. It won't last."

His daughter wished she could share his confidence. Something about the dancer's nonchalance bothered her, although, given what she knew of her father's sexual pro-clivities, she could easily imagine that the dancer's hint of hauteur would only inflame his desire, leading him to imag-ine all the (to him) delicious ways she might exert a strict, contemptuous domination over him in private. The thresh-old winked open, and they stepped out of the elevator. "At least she doesn't have the exoskeletal adaptations," she said.

"Hmmm?"

"Never mind. It probably wouldn't have mattered if she did." Well at least she had been right about the timing, even if it had never occurred to her that its object could be some-one so thoroughly unlike themselves.

For years I've heard rumors that natives in the Goncourt Region (and, sometimes, the Spieden Region) have, after placing microphones in strategically determined positions along the coast and floating on the surface of the ocean, recorded the sounds made by mistflowers, which they then select and mix to create what is called the Music of Mistflowers. According to the rumors, the natives who do this claim that the Music of Mistflowers is the true voice of the planet, singing their stories for those to hear who would. It is said that they listen to this "music" as an accompaniment to collectively ingesting the flowers, in order to "attune" themselves with the planet their ancestors chose to occupy.

I once asked a botanist about this, and whether she had any idea of what sort of sound these plants might actually produce. *Music* must be meant metaphorically, she said. "For no plant that I've heard of has the ability to deliberately produce sounds."

Perhaps not. But the more I thought about it, the more I wanted to believe these coastal people collect the sounds and combine them into something that could be called music, resembling the songs of various avian and mammalian species we all recognize as music designed for their own, rather than human, ears.

　　—Enoch Fulmer, *A Star-Hopper's View of the Galaxy*

Three
CLAIRE GASPEL

26.V.493

Here begins the journal of Claire Gaspel, First Daughter of Joan Kincaid, who is First Daughter of Dana Ahmed, who was First Daughter of Ariel Decautur, who was First Daughter of Clare Chavez...all of whom trace their line of first daughters back to our First Mother, Paula Boren, who came to Frogmore in Year 6 & bore her first daughter, Ariel Nisa, in Year 9.

Oh it's hard starting like this. Not knowing what I should be saying. There's something so intimidating about keeping an official family journal & knowing it will be given a place in a long line of other (better!) journals. How much easier for the aunts to keep their unofficial journals. For one thing, they only need to make entries when they have something special they want to say or have a point they particularly want to make. On the other hand, thinking about those nearly five hundred years' worth of journals, I can take comfort in knowing how relatively insignificant mine will be. Both Mother & Grand Mother Dana are keeping journals, so I'll have time to get the hang of it before mine will become anything more than a minor account supplementing theirs.

Today at my coming-of-age party I was talking about this with Daisy, & she suggested I go back & read all the other journals to get a sense of flow & of what I find interesting—so I'll have an idea what our descendants might find interesting in my journal. I'd already planned to do some reading (though maybe not *all* of the past entries of the daughters of Paula). For years now, Grand Mother, Mother, & the aunts have been so careful in selecting bits for me to read that I'm dying to see what kinds of things were in the parts they wouldn't let me read. & I have to admit I'm keen to find out what's in certain more recent journals (including the unofficial ones) since there were things that happened in my childhood that I *know* they were holding out on. But entries in others' journals become available only ten years after they're written. That's the rule. Obviously a good one: because who would write the truth if they always had to worry about everyone reading everything practically over their shoulder?

Maybe I should start by listing Grand Mother Dana's precepts, as a set of guidelines, to remind myself of them & also to help me relax about the scariness of the obligation.

> #1: Always write the truth. No white lies, no fudging, no sweetening of the facts. Just the truth. The truth as fully as you can tell it. (The fuller the better.)

> #2: Don't consider anything too trivial to write about. Be as inclusive or scattered as you have the time & energy for.

> #3: If you're grinding an ax, writing out of malice, or to justify yourself, it will show through no matter how clever a writer you are.

> #4: Always remember you are a First Daughter. Everyone in the line of First Daughters has obligations, one of which is to maintain the continuity of our history. Therefore, don't fail to make at least two entries a week, no matter how busy, tired, or dispirited you are. Make it a rule for yourself, a rule you won't allow yourself to break for any reason whatsoever. Preferably you should make daily entries, but I—who have been writing an official journal for forty-five years now—

know that that's not always possible. Be diligent & disciplined; demand a minimum of yourself. If you do, you'll *make* the time, for First Daughters always make time for carrying out their special obligations as First Daughters, even if other obligations must be stinted in the process.

#5: Don't ever go back & add things to previous entries, or edit or alter the entries in any way. That way lies falsehood. I would be very disappointed in you if I should ever discover you doing such a thing.

(These were Grand Mother's verbatim words.)

Well, though I haven't said anything of substance, at least I've made a start. I realize that judging by this first entry I may turn out to be a really lousy journal-keeper (& I know there have been some too dull or badly written to read, Grand Mother's told me about them). But I hope not. So whoever's reading this, try to be patient. I may improve; practice often helps. At least I know it does in other things. & Grand Mother says it usually happens in journal-keeping, too.

27.V.493

I don't dare complain to any of the other adults in the household. After all, they've been putting up with this all their adult lives. & they warned me not to say anything to the youngsters lest I make them dread adulthood.

But what a shock! I'm a wreck, actually. How do the adults manage? Now I understand why they're all so pleased at my achieving adulthood—it gives them (for a while, at least, until Chandra outgrows her infant-cocoon) an extra sleep cocoon to share in rotation among the adults, & even though I make an extra adult, everyone will get a little bit more time in sleep-cocoons. Actually, I found the experience of sleeping in the open so horrendous that I asked Grand Mother if I could sleep in a cocoon in the daytime (taking a long nap, sort of) because I felt so horrid. (I've never gone without sleep before, I had no idea how your body aches without it! My eyes burn, & my head is throbbing, my stomach is a twisted mass of knots, my hands are trembling.) She gave me a stern look & said that I must face up to the responsibilities of adulthood.

Apparently we can't afford one sleep-cocoon per person. She showed me the household budget, & it seems almost everything is taken up by necessities like oxygen, water, & food—& sleep-cocoons are especially expensive because you have to pay SCUs for them since they come from off-world. Why, I asked her, aren't they made on Frogmore? Why can't they be cheap-printed? She snorted & said that was a question I should be able to figure out the answer to for myself, that I knew enough about economics & politics to understand a thing like that.

She was irritated with me, I suppose, for suggesting that some of us could sleep in the daytime, and for asking why we can't sleep in shifts.

Today Mother left for Birth-Home to undertake her final pregnancy. All of the adults are pleased at the effect of her absence on the sleep-cocoon rotation—though as I just realized, the more babies we produce, the more the rotation gets stretched among a growing population of adults, eventually. Still, as more of us earn SCUs our income will presumably increase enough to purchase more sleep-cocoons—or so I have to hope!

Since this is Mother's last pregnancy, I am supposed to start thinking about how it will soon be my turn. (That's Grand Mother's word, not mine. Four years seems like a long time to me.) Will I find a mate by then, or will I conceive through a casual partnering? Mother, I know, is looking forward to taking up her work full-time. It hasn't yet been decided whether I'll pair with Marcy or Erin or Lydia. They're all in the same generational cycle with me, so the question turns on which of the four of us have the closest work-interests for forming pairs. All that, Grand Mother says, will be decided in the next three years. It's a little frightening to consider how many important decisions (decisions that will shape much of the rest of my life) will come to be made in the next four years.

Last night when I was sharing a bath with Marcy she hinted a sympathy for all the "shocks" I have coming to me. Of course Marcy doesn't have the whole fix on my situation, since she isn't a First Daughter. Still, I think I probably have more in common with her than with anyone else in the household. Let's hope that my work interest won't be closely related to hers, since we'd then pair up and one or the other of us would be away a good part of the time, separated as we share the same work, taking turns with the babies, with never any time for one another.

I'm so exhausted from not sleeping that I can't get my brain to work anymore. So I'll end this & see if I can find someone to share a bath with. Hopefully I'll feel better tomorrow. (Though, truthfully, I doubt it—my turn in a sleep-cocoon doesn't come until the night after next.)

Excerpt from the journal of Paula Boren
4.X.6

We all knew it would be hard. They told us so. And they put each of us through rigorous physical and psychological screening before finalizing our contracts. But *this* hard? A part of me is always screaming (silently, of course) for escape, back to the ease of Delphi. How will I make it? I keep asking myself. But then in the evenings, before collapsing for the night (and somehow we've all learned to sleep without cocoons, and of all things that may have been the hardest, for if ever we needed the kind of sleep the cocoons gave us it's now), we come together as a group, and our sense of purpose, our contentment at the chance to pursue our arduous but exhilarating ambition of freedom, fills us—oh so visibly, we can see it in one another's eyes, we hear it in our voices as we recite together the litanies we've composed for our mutual strengthening, and when we break up to go to our beds, we can feel it in the hugs we share. Our now knobby, rather bizarre arms still are arms that have the power of imparting the warmth of love. At least, this is true for me—how sad if others can't feel the same now that our bodies are different. I admit that I find something disgusting about the modifications, but we understand the price we must pay for wanting to live on this planet and eventually procreate—what good would carbon filament rein-forcements in our bodies do our children? Any child born in a normal condition wouldn't last long in this gravity, and that's the simple fact we must always bear in mind when we feel that loathing creep over us. But I keep reminding myself that though now and then we suffer moments of embarrassment and sometimes of hesitation when we see a burst of revulsion or the onset of alienation in another's face, we are learning to live with these changes, we are finding a way to think of them as instruments of our liberation and as the base of our future history.

We do have one relief to look forward to, and that is an end (someday) to having to wear the protective clothing and masks at all times we are out-of-doors. It's a mat-ter of the biologists making a final determination that nothing else in the atmosphere other than the Scourge can harm us. And then only for prolonged periods out-of-doors will it be necessary to wear the spacing bulky gear. We will have to carry respirators, true, and continue to go through decontamination every time we re-enter our enclosed areas.

We are, in fact, considering the idea of building a dome once we're on our feet. But that's years away, since although we started free and clear, we're already in debt because of the outlays we've had to make in getting ourselves established on the surface.

To think that during our period on Pittikin, when we were adjusting in light gravity to our clumsy new bodies, we were all so impatient to get to the surface we could think and talk of nothing but what it would be like here, of all we would do. The reality has been something else. But no, I'm *not* discouraged. Just consider (apart from the ease, of course) what we'd be doing were we still on Delphi. The very thought is enough to make me thankful to be here, hard as it is.

30.V.493

Imagine, after sleeping all her life in a sleep-cocoon, when Paula Boren & the other First Mothers came to Frogmore, they had to give up their sleep-cocoons entirely. It makes me ashamed for minding so about having to share a limited number of cocoons. & yet, at the same time it makes me feel I have something in common with her—in spite of her being so remote in history, in spite of her strangeness. (Her feelings about exoskeletal adaptations, for instance. When it's the off-world people who look so strange to *us*. & of course though they wear caps over their heads, we all know what those caps are hiding, which makes them—& those Frogmore people who slavishly copy their ways—grotesque & sinister.)

Grand Mother Dana announced at table this evening that Ariel Dolma, a cousin of my generation (but at the third level), would be coming to stay for several weeks. Later I asked Daisy if she knew anything about it, & Daisy told me that Ariel comes from a distant branch of the Family, a materially well-off one. Her parents have a life partnership & are both weavers. Daisy hinted at trouble, some sort of conflict between Ariel's father (who is an outsider) & the Family. Not surprising, of course: there often is conflict when paternity is a part of the Family organization, at least that's what Daisy says. Daisy also told me that Ariel was in training for being a midwife, that she'd already served an apprenticeship at Birth-Home & had just finished two years at University in the Capitol District. & now, before assuming a full-fledged position at Birth-Home, she has to undergo special instruction from Grand Mother. Daisy says she has no idea what it is, only that there are several positions that require special instruction from the current Grand Mother. (Which means I'll eventually know.) It will be interesting to see what it is that Grand Mother will do when Mother takes over from her. Since Grand Mother's mother died so young, we haven't had a Matriarch in my memory. I could find out about this by looking through the Matriarchs' journals, I suppose. But I barely have time to read Paula's.

Speaking of time, there's not much left before I have to leave the dome for work. & then, after work, I have to study. Grand Mother keeps harping on the need for First Daughters to educate themselves. Maybe she'd like me to qualify as a teacher, so that I can stay closer to home than most of us are able to do? Who knows? Not me. I'm almost as in the dark now as I was before my coming-of-age.

Excerpt from the journal of Paula Boren
12.XV.7

The argument seems interminable. Will we ever manage to write a charter we can all agree on? And will we ever get to the point of actually having our own children? What a strange sound that has: our *own* children. Sometimes the strangeness comes over me, and the very idea seems inconceivable. Yet we *did* think of it, and we know that at one time humans did bear and raise their own children. The word *mother* once meant something different than it does now, which gives power to our reappropriating it.

Bessy D., I've decided, is more or less the opposition leader. Yes, I think it's time now for us to talk about *sides*, about a division in the group. As we might have predicted, the other side has been formed by a lack of the experiences most of us have had, experiences that have driven us to take up this hard, heavy existence in a hostile environment, giving up all comforts of civilization for this freedom we now can't seem to agree on. Bessy D. and those she speaks for are all very young, with either minimal or no experience of the surrogate process the rest of us have spent most of our adult lives in thrall to.

Now there's an expression I once could not have used, yet we use it all the time now, so easily that none of us can remember the pain our first formulating it brought us. *In thrall.* Yes. Bessy D. herself had one year in it. One year in thrall. Already some of what she felt (I remember her talking to me about it on the trip out, so I *know* she felt driven by the same things impelling those of us who had years of it) has slipped away from her. This, I think, must account for her hedging on questions of organization and procedure. She doesn't understand the extent to which we never would have gotten out at all if it hadn't been for our group consciousness. She doesn't understand that her own realizations during that year came not only from her experiences as a lactation surrogate, but also from our articulation of dissent, our ability to imagine another way, to long for more than simple release, our persistence in seeing a larger picture than the pain of our anguish and degradation.

Last night I took Bessy D. aside to remind her of what she had said about her feelings toward that infant she talked so much about during the trip out. (Maybe it's the atypicality of her experience that's the cause for all her differences in attitude? How many of us ever had just one child to serve at a time?) But Bessy brushed aside my reminder and said I was trying to play on her emotions, that the point was that we, none of us, had to consider any of that now, that we could each go her own way and find the situation most comfortable for herself. I argued with her, of course, that if we didn't act as a group to create a new way, the old way would come to this world as well, perhaps in a new form, but still outside our control. That we knew now that if we worked together we could create something completely different, but that on our own none of us had ever been able to fight against the weight of the prevailing system. Her reply? There *is* no system, here, on this new world.

We may lose some of our original group, I see that now. Bessy D. loudly declared tonight that she will never surrogate again, will never take pay for serving such functions. Oh then you will surrogate for free? I wanted to flash back at her. The younger ones who follow Bessy D. consider us rigid, bitter, worn out. But our numbers are greater, and we are determined. It makes me sad to calculate the outcome in such terms. But I won't fool myself that everyone will be happy with the charter when it's finally approved.

5.VI.493

So, Ariel has arrived. At the evening meal she sat in the place of honor, next to Grand Mother. She brought an enormous tapestry that her parents had woven as a gift to the Daughters of Paula Boren. It's been hung in the dining hall & extends from the ceiling to the floor behind Grand Mother's chair. It has the richest shades of purple I've ever seen. We are all lavishing attention on her to make her feel welcome. But I can't help noticing, well, *differences*. Differences that it's hard to understand, or to know what to make of.

About the sleep-cocoon kerfuffle—I suppose I want to describe the incident because it makes me feel less selfish by comparison. But Daisy, when she told me about the incident, pointed out that Ariel comes from a different way of Family, one with a "higher material standard of living." (Which refers, I suppose, to that branch of the Family mating with men from outside, men with wealth.) But to get to the incident itself: Ariel showed up with a sleep-cocoon, apparently her very own. The adults in that branch of the Family don't have to share cocoons, that's how well off they are. That & their sending some of their children to another planet to be educated. But that's another story—I'm getting off track. Well when Daisy & Deborah, who handle such matters, saw it, they exclaimed, Oh how thoughtful of you! You'll have everyone's undying appreciation for cutting down the length of time between turns! Daisy says a strange look came over Ariel's face, as though she didn't understand, & then, after that, as though she had a suspicion Daisy was talking about sharing the cocoon in common with everyone else but couldn't quite believe that was what Daisy did in fact mean. By the time Daisy finished calculating what the new rotation would be after adding both Ariel & her cocoon, Ariel understood very well. & she *protested*! It had never occurred to her, she said, that anyone else might use her cocoon, cocoons were *personal* possessions, that's why she'd brought it with her—because she couldn't imagine ever sleeping in one that wasn't her own (& of course I know exactly what she meant: I still miss my own cocoon rather desperately. Hearing this story from Daisy made me poignant at the same time I felt a little malicious amusement at Ariel's shock—the same that I went through just a couple of weeks ago). Daisy informed her that in *this* household adults shared cocoons in common, period. That if she lived in this household she would live like everyone else, that here no individuals were privileged over others, for all had value in this household, etc. Daisy told me that she could see Ariel was wishing she hadn't brought her cocoon, that clearly she felt others' using it an invasion of privacy. Of course Ariel doesn't yet know what it will be like to sleep *outside* a cocoon. So she wasn't thinking of that when she was so full of distress about others using her cocoon.

Telling the story like this, I see that she & I have something strongly in common, however different we are. I'm still feeling a little sorry for myself on the score of sleep-cocoons—but reading Paula's journal has made me realize how lucky I am to have the nights in it I do have. She had none at all. & they hadn't a dome yet, either.

Which gets me to the subject of Paula's journal. I think I need to talk to Grand Mother about it. Daisy was so vague I got the impression that she'd never read more than a few entries of any of our journals. But Grand Mother's always busy. I suppose I could ask some of the other women of the older generations. Some of them know a great deal about all kinds of things. For instance, what does Paula mean when she talks about the different meanings of the word *mother*? Or about the "weight of the system"? I do at least know about the "surrogate process" as it's called, & what a "lactation surrogate" is—obscenity, is what it is. & to think that except for here on Frogmore, the "surrogate process" is everywhere!

But I have to stop. Too much to do before it's time to go to work!

6.VI.493

Exciting news: I'm invited to sit in on as many of the sessions Ariel is having with Grand Mother as I have time for. Second piece of news: Ariel, it turns out, has read *all* of Paula's journal (& other of the First Mothers' journals, too) & is willing to talk to me about it. She speaks as passionately about these journals as Grand Mother does: about how so many important things in them can help us understand what we're doing, how we're living, & how we got to where we are today.

One other thing about Ariel, & then I have to stop (since today is one of those days)—I've begun noticing the coloring in her chitinous flecks—& how breathtakingly beautiful they are. (I had a chance to look at her face a lot this morning when she & I were talking briefly with Grand Mother.) But then I have to remember that probably her branch of the Family has had extensive access to genetic technicians over the last half-century. I guess finances can make a certain concrete difference to one's life—making one more beautiful than another, giving one more sound nights of sleep than another...

But I still prefer our life in the Dome. I think it would be strange & lonely to be separated the way the people in Ariel's branch of the Family are. But as the men especially are always pointing out, we're in the minority. A lot of people in the world do things differently & have entirely other values. I guess it must bother the men a lot, then, if they're always talking about that difference. Can it be true? I never thought much about it. Maybe I'll ask Daisy & some of her generation, to see if they think it is. If so...well, I guess it makes it harder for the boys & men, doesn't it.

But now I totally *have* to go.

Excerpt from the journal of Paula Boren
20.XV.7

Stayed up most of the long Frogmore night working
with Vi and Dorothy on a draft of a manifesto the fifteen of us have spent days discussing. What we discovered (those of us who are insisting on a unified
approach), once we began working it out in words, is
that our wariness of fragmentation and our sense of
the importance of continuity derive from the fact that
fragmentation and a denial of continuity is what characterized the thralldom we all came here to escape. It's
a clumsy thought, probably because it was so hard to
get into words. Maybe we'll eventually find an easier
way of putting it. But it's important because this, we
think, is what Bessy D. and her crowd haven't understood and which they must be made to understand. The
diverse tasks involved in "producing" children that
all of us performed (and most of them were biological functions necessary to the child's very existence)
by being chopped up into discrete tasks and assigned
as such to us were degrading and painful not simply
because of the disapproval those of us who earned our
living carrying out such tasks received from society
due to the notion of such tasks being obscene, perverse,
dirty, primitive, and subhuman (reminding humans of
their evolutionary origins, of their being a part of nature at a time when humans control every aspect of
nature and are so far beyond any other animal species
in the universe), yet necessary for the perpetuation of
the species. Bessy D. argues: We were the underside of
Civilization. Doing the unspeakable necessary. *That* is
what we want to escape. To escape that, we have to insist on a new set of ethics and find new ways of living.

Most of us agree we need a new set of ethics, that we were all serving necessary but despised functions. But it goes much farther than that. It comes down to the way in which the tasks were fragmented. As Vi remarked after Bessy D. made that statement, with such a fragmentation of tasks, we had no notion of the production of a child except in relation to the child itself. And parentage is a matter of knowledge and deliberate production of an embryo—which usually amounts to knowing who one of the suppliers of chromosomes is, whether egg- or sperm-parent. (Only rarely both.) And in any case, chromosomal parentage never has anything more to do with the production of the child once the gamete has been supplied, after which all the tasks are assigned. Why do you think that is? Vi rhetorically asked Bessy D.

Even Bessy D. could have answered that one. The tasks are assigned because of the economic advantage of specialization, as well as to prevent the child's attachment to someone other than the chromosomal parent (who happens to be the paying customer and therefore entitled to making such a demand). Gestational surrogates usually carry two individuals, though sometimes as many as four, at once, and though lactational surrogates are usually only asked to feed two at most at any one time, most of the other surrogates tend to five or even more children at once. (Though this varies, depending on the financial resources of the parent. The wealthy can afford to make the surrogacies exclusive.) The net result is alienation and a reduction of function to particular tasks—gestation; lactation; hygiene; advanced alimentation; language acquisition; motor skills acquisition; cognitive development; socialization; and so on and so forth. All with strict rules and procedures (except where deviations are specified in special instructions from the client). This is obviously awful for the surrogates, but everyone takes for granted that the children of poorer parents get less attention—just as they take it for granted that the really poor can't afford to have children at all (which most people think is a good thing).

Bessy D. said she knew all that and what did it have to do with creating rules for living arrangements? Hadn't we come here to escape rules?

But these rules are of our own making, Vi shot back. Don't you see, rules will be made whether we make them or not. And if *we* don't make them, then we will be subject again to fragmentation, division, alienation. And the children we bear will automatically come to be regarded as products—even if we aren't paid to produce them—and then there will be legal questions about assigning parentage for these "products" (for which we, being the bearers etc., will be considered mere surrogates, since no parent ever serves such functions in the production of a child). Someone with greater authority will move in on us and say we don't know what we're doing, we're flouting all the known rules of the best way of producing children, obviously we're the primitives they have always said we are.

Frogmore, Bessy D. retorted, is laissez-faire. Which is why anyone comes to this horror of a world at all. *They* won't be bothering us, as long as they make a profit off the colonization of this planet.

As I've said so many times before, I agree with Vi that Bessy D. is naive. Which is why we must work everything out in first the manifesto and then the charter. The more organized, the more *legalistic* we are, the harder it will be for outsiders to claim we're incapable of civilized behavior. Once they decide we're "uncivilized," they won't allow us children at all. (And of course there's the possibility we won't be allowed, anyway, though we all know that's unlikely: one of our chief premises from the time we made our decision to come here is that they will be crying out for large-scale procreation and thus won't be interested in stopping us, provided we appear "reasonable" to their official eyes.)

8.VI.493

The thing people have been whispering about at work finally came up during the evening meal. Five of the twelve people sitting at my table work at my UAP unit. What will happen to us if they *do* start shutting down all the agricultural units? one of the guys asked. There's hardly any other work in the area outside agricultural production.

We can't let them shut down, Daisy said. We'd be at the food producers' mercy since none of us can produce food on our own, besides being stuck with having to take some other kind of job. I thought I heard there were outsiders around trying to recruit workers for the mining industry? Didn't you tell me that, Claire?

I said I had.

But we'd have to move to take mining jobs! Jon answered.

I could see it, though, I could see what Daisy was saying—that probably there will be more jobs (though whether they'd be jobs we'd want, here in the Pimlico District, is another story), but that once the food source is gone, is out of our hands, is *off-world*—why then we *would* be at their mercy in ways we aren't now. Sure, we have to pay extortionate prices for food, water, & oxygen, but those necessities aren't completely beyond our control because they're produced here, on the surface, where we live & work. When it's necessary, we can take action. It's not like we haven't done that, with success, in the past.

The picture changes dramatically when the plants go off-world, since they belong to greedy people whose names & faces we don't know, who probably don't even live on Frog-more but are just exploiters of Frogmore's vulnerability. There's something deeply scary about removing the food source even further from our reach. Maybe it has to do with what Daisy was saying when she reminded everyone of how fifteen years ago when UAP stopped producing Bole oil, a series of mass demonstrations & the boycott of particular products was strengthened by work stoppages at every UAP plant; Daisy says it was the work stoppages and software fail-ures, more than anything else, that forced UAP to resume its production. See, as Daisy pointed out, it wouldn't have been possible to pressure UAP if all their units had been up on space stations. & then there's the question of what we would do if something happened to the space stations. You have to start thinking about that kind of thing—about how a bad meteor shower could wipe out a space station. Or consider how if someone wanted to make a political move, a coup or something, against the Governor, they might hold the space stations hostage. We'd starve for lack of food, while UAP col-lected the insurance bonanza for the "natural disaster" that couldn't have been predicted.

It was a pretty dismal meal, discussing all that. We just have to hope it won't really happen. We don't *know* that it will, as Jon kept saying. The management hasn't said when they intend to close the units. You'd think it would take a long time to set such a thing up. & besides that, maybe they'll decide the risks aren't worth whatever it is they hope to gain from going through with it. But as Lupe said, no matter what the real situation is (& that's something we can't know for sure), it's clear that everyone working at our unit has got to get organized & make our concerns known to the manage-ment. & not only the unit's workers, but everyone in the area, because we're all dependent on the unit for food. (Hopefully in a non-disruptive way. It's no good doing anything disruptive, because if they catch you...well. There's no need to go into that here.) Later, if things get desperate (if we stand to lose the unit), then regardless of the consequences we will have to rally everyone we can in the area to take over the unit so they can't remove its tech.

11.VI.493

Today's a free day, so I spent part of the morning with Ariel & Grand Mother. Grand Mother talked mainly about the history of Birth-Home, especially about the history of various Birth-Home practices (most of which I'd never heard of). She described how Birth-Home came to be. Originally our women went to Pittikin (before it became a military installation) for the entire pregnancy, because the gravity there is so light. But they were too much under government control there & were treated horribly—which is to say as "surrogates" are treated. Which our first mothers couldn't stand, since they'd come to Frogmore to get away from all that. But in order to have pregnancies on the surface they had to figure out a way to make them physically endurable in the high gravity. That took a lot of time. They paid to send Chandra Spieden to Pleth to be educated in obstetrics & the prosthetic sciences & bioengineering as well. It took more than a generation before they were able to open Birth-Home. According to Grand Mother, everything changed after that. Also, at that time they realized they would need to ensure that we always had women trained in obstetrics, since outsiders are so horrible. (On Pleth, for instance, Chandra Spieden tried to talk to people who might be able to help her but found they were revolted by what she wanted to do & thought it all horrible & grotesque—some people even said it would be a crime if she managed to find a way.) & so was born the custom of many women being trained in obstetrics.

I could see how excited Ariel was about everything Grand Mother told us—I suppose it must be inspiring to find that your job is noble & comes of a proud old tradition. And yet, though few of us can take pay for such lifework, we could say that many of us carry on a lifework for which we don't get paid. Like Grand Mother. Or even like me. We all contribute, we all take part in creating our beautiful society. Even the guys (& of course we're always careful to make them feel just as much a part of the Family as we who bear the children). There must be people to do the special things we cannot do without.

Each to her own light.

Oh, a strange thing last night. Ariel asked me why I & the other women in the Family have paternal names since we make such a point of adopting the traditional ways. I thought she didn't understand the traditional ways where names are concerned. I told her Gaspel was my maternal grandfather's name and that we didn't acknowledge paternity immediately to protect against the father claiming sole parentage on the grounds that the mother was only a surrogate—thinking she didn't know this. But of course she knew exactly what the practice was and why. She was just letting me know she thought it was idiotically old-fashioned. Reading Paula's journal has made me aware of such legal issues & helped me understand (or somewhat, for I am pretty confused about it all, except when I can ask Grand Mother to explain & she elaborates, at which point things become pretty simple to understand but really bizarre) why we don't "acknowledge" (& this is a legal term, I gather) paternity until the second generation after. I have a feeling that they live in weird ways because of this. I know that though Ariel's branch of the Family has a dome, some of its members live separate from one another & only now & then comes together. They only have meals like ours once a month, & often the boys & men aren't present for them. & to think she thinks *we're* strange! I don't know what I'd do if I were to live for a while with her branch of the Family the way she is living with us. But that could never happen. For which, to be honest, I'm glad.

Nine distinct cultures can be identified on Frogmore, if one includes travelers and expatriates from advanced worlds temporarily in residence who make up between one and two percent of the planet's population. The native elites, who compose about five percent of the population, hold most of the top governmental and managerial positions on the planet. Though born on Frogmore and educated on Pleth, they have developed a culture distinct from the travelers and expatriates from the advanced worlds and suffer continually from a sense of inferiority to them and a determination to distinguish themselves from the planet's other natives. Native elite culture is, in a word, decadent.

The professional class is only about eight percent of the population, which though vanishingly small in comparison with populations of advanced worlds is average for a back-world planet. But although about half of the professional class are educated on Pleth and virtually every professional has had the chitinous exoskeletons genetically bred into all Frogmore natives removed, most professionals pride themselves on their loyalty to Frogmore and consider themselves the backbone of Frogmore's claim to being a rational and civilized society (even if one largely impoverished and lagging in the niceties and variety of lifestyles available to all inhabitants of the advanced worlds. Professional culture is both literate and engaged, as the elite culture is not.

Five of the six remaining cultures—the Mellorsians, Brainnardians, Spiedenese, Durazzoans, and Saturnans—are geographically rather socially located, and three of these speak dialects of Standard. They make up seventy-five percent of the population. The final culture is made up of members of the planet's security sector, which comes to about ten percent of the population (not including peacekeeping forces, which by law must be made up of off-worlders only). Unlike the planet's eight other cultures, the culture of the security sector is bound by rituals and rules that members are required, by oath, to keep secret. Suffice it to say that socially, they tend to consort only with one another.

—Frogmore: The CDS Fact Book

Four

NATHALIE STILLNESS

For most of the trip home, Nathalie Stillness has been unable to rid her mind of the images of the hugely pregnant women bound and braced by clumsy devices designed to keep the added weight they carry from literally killing them. When the transport's monitor shows that they've entered the Capitol District, her body relaxes, her heart beats more easily, her breathing feels less labored, simply because she knows she'll soon be "home." Finally she'll be able to think about how the new field data will relate to the previously collected materials and her three principal working hypotheses about the social organization of Frogmore's humans.

The metaphors of physical entrapment, weight, burden, and human frailty on this planet so hostile to any life not indigenous to it surround and, yes, even trap her; she knows they do, for they creep into her work no matter how consciously she guards against them. She finds it hard to stop thinking about how the weight of her brain could crush her spine, how her diaphragm could sag far down into her viscera, how her intestines, liver, kidneys, and other organs in the abdominal cavity could crush her pelvis if she even once forgot to wear the appropriate protective gear needed to survive this planet's gravitational forces. Often she recalls her shock on first learning that short of adopting the drastic bioengineering introduced in the first generations of colonists on Frogmore or the expensive high-end carbon-filament endoskeleton totally beyond her means, it would be necessary for her to utilize several strategies for adapting herself to the planet's gravity, and that if she wanted to study ordinary Frogmorians she would have to accept that she would never be comfortable on Frogmore, that her body would always be at war with the planet.

At times Nathalie Stillness has wished that she *had* acquired the exoskeletal frame the natives had adopted. But to have acquired the exoskeleton would, in her thesis-committee's opinion, have been to "go native," thus endangering the objectivity of her work. Even if that hadn't been the case, she's not sure she could have deliberately made herself so *alien*. After all, she often reminded herself, a military establishment plus a few thousand others from off-planet manage to live on Frogmore.

But, she knows now, most of those people live either in the Capitol District or in one of the other places on the planet where mag slabs have been laid deep underground. The anti-grav cling-ons worn in slab-based places do far more for her comfort than the ugly braces she will have to wear the next time she goes into the field. This trip, she'd escaped the braces, since Durazzo is an exception to the rule for most of the domes she needs to observe. In some places the braces are beyond uncomfortable; she remembers how the braces made the daytime hot humidity of Spieden all the more stifling, trapping sweat and causing chafing. Wearing the anti-grav cling-ons (in addition, of course, to the affordable amount of carbon-filament reinforcing her muscles), she almost feels "normal," at least when she's sedentary. But no. Not *normal*. Comfortable. Or, rather, almost comfortable. She's still having to take pains not to use the word *normal* to refer to Pleth, for instance. On Frogmore, at least, *standard* must not be confused with *normal*.

Half an hour at most before she's home, she thinks. And then she will sink into the buoyant fluid one of the original colonists had discovered as a sovereign remedy for the inherent vicissitudes of life on Frogmore. Afterwards, she can focus entirely on the wealth of new data she has collected and the astonishing details heightening the enigma she has uncovered. Settled in the Capitol District—comfortable, cool, entirely herself again—the enigma would neither frustrate, revolt, nor depress her. She would have the material to sift, the enigma to tantalize her. And the alienation would fade.

It always did.

The contrast could not be sharper. Both in military dress (the male a peacekeeping officer's, the female that of the governor's militia), they stand not more than a meter apart, the superior officer a pace or two ahead of the other and half a foot taller. Craving the enrichment after days of deprivation, she has the UV lamps on in her reception room as well as in the bathroom. In the brilliant light the lineaments of their arms and legs show clearly and distinctly through the mesh of their cling-ons. The native, her legs slightly behind and to the left of the superior officer's, seems a shadow of her superior, but fleshed-in with color above her neck, which marks the beginning of skin not covered with the same dark shade of gray, a shortened shadow distorted by the knobbed, ropy seams running up and down her arms and legs; her face, naked, of course, is empty of expression, as most daytime rigid-form masks are. The superior officer's face, though, expresses gravity, intense interest, purpose, suspicion—and, perhaps, a trace of impatience. He has interrupted her bath, but his face offers not the slightest hint of apology or awareness that she has been inconvenienced by the untimeliness of this visit.

Jangled from the trip, dragged out of her bath *sans* cling-ons, wearing a dressing gown and an opaque plastine bath cap, and, worst of all, with face bared, available, open to scrutiny, Nathalie Stillness folds her arms over her breasts and attempts to outstare the peacekeeping officer. "I'm not a spy," she says

and repeats her refusal to answer questions, which she assumes will involve the interviews she conducted in Durazzo.
Her ability to match his unwavering stare falters, and she
focuses her eyes on the large green plant she has been so
carefully nurturing on the braces and supports holding up its
thicker-than-normal stems and smaller-than-normal leaves.
"And may I point out that you've interrupted my bath" She
snorted theatrically. "In a civilized place it would be considered unacceptably rude behavior showing up on my doorstep
so late in the day."

She's not done, but while she's drawing breath to continue, the peacekeeping officer breaks into her diatribe. "I
don't care what you call yourself, Madam High and Mighty
Off-worlder." His sneer and derisive crudeness shocks her; on
Pleth, security officers are always obsequiously polite to her.
"You collect information; you're a trained observer. Which is
what the effort to prevent terrorist atrocities needs. Maybe,
though, when I tell you that the next train on the line you
took out from Durazzo exploded, taking out an extensive portion of pipeline and causing cave-ins for klicks and klicks up
and down the line, you'll understand the urgency that brings
me to intrude on you so *rudely*." His tone is sarcastic, and
his eyes and mouth openly display impatience. A silly phrase
floats into her head, that he wants her to know he is *not a
man to be trifled with*. As though that is what she's doing:
trifling with him.

"I'm sorry to hear that," she says. "I hope no one was
seriously injured?"

The rage that flares in his cold gaze sears her face. "Everyone on the train—estimates run to about seventy-five—
are dead. You know what happens when liquid oxygen goes."
The tone of his voice is beginning to grate on her nerves. "In
this kind of action people are inevitably killed. As the insurgents spacing well know."

She digs her fingers into her folded arms, which she presses more tightly against her breasts. An image of her own weak neck comes into her mind; her head seems to wobble precariously, its weight almost too great for her neck and shoulders to bear. The longer the three of them stand talking, the more the crimp in her neck and the knots in her shoulders tighten their grip on her. "I gather from newsfeeds that the governor has deliberately instituted a policy of mixing freight with passenger loads on trains," she says, too tired to speak carefully. The insurgents have until now avoided acts of sabotage certain to endanger human life. There have been occasional collateral deaths from the sabotage, but never so many deaths at one blow.

"She's a sympathizer!" The words fairly burst out of the native standing behind and to the left of the officer. Her face seethes with hatred.

The officer affects not to hear his subordinate's remark. "You're tough," he drawls. The tightness around his eyes and mouth, the stoniness of his jaw don't match his suddenly casual tone of voice. "It doesn't make you quiver, not even a little, to hear that the train after yours got it?" He shakes his head as though incredulous, maybe even admiring. "You *must* be tough. It doesn't bother you at all when you think how it could have been *your* train?"

She is shivering. She struggles against the loss of perspective, reminding herself of the tricks authority uses to manipulate, shake, and distort the construction of reality the individual holds, especially that of the solitary being caught off-guard, alone, without support...

The reminder infuses Nathalie with renewed confidence. It is a battle of wills, testing the strength of her perspective, her construction of meaning against his will to dissolve her stance within the gravity pulling together the vast network of *his* universe, the system of which he is a part. The matter becomes perfectly simple: she must refuse his insistence on imposing his construction of meaning on her.

Her arms relax slightly; despite her lack of cling-ons, she pulls her fatigued body into the straightest posture she ever has the energy to achieve here on Frogmore, and she forces her gaze onto his face. "So you'd like to hear about the social organization, rituals, and myths of pregnant women? Shall I tell you how they cope with the weight of placenta and fetus, of the things they eat and don't eat, of the regimen they follow at each stage of their pregnancies, of what they say about pregnancy and about themselves in that condition?" She smiles into the anger she sees coiling behind his eyes. "That's the information I collected this time. Hundreds, no thousands, of details. Of *observations*."

"What are you talking about?" His voice is harsh. "Speak clearly. I don't know academic jargon, and I'm not *interested* in knowing it."

Nathalie's smile widens. Of course. Why should anyone from an advanced society know the word *pregnancy*? She glances at the native; one look at the distaste on her face makes plain *her* comprehension of the word. "Pregnancy is another word for gestation," she says.

The officer frowns. "Gestation? So you went to Durazzo to study gestation-surrogates?" He looks baffled—and more suspicious than before.

Nathalie Stillness sighs. "Not surrogates. The natives in the outlying regions don't use surrogates. Which is one of the reasons they're so interesting to study."

His mouth twists. "You're not tough, you're crazy. And perverse." He gives her a measuring look. "I won't keep you any longer. But we will be arranging an appointment with you. To be conducted in more official circumstances."

Why, Nathalie Stillness wonders, has he switched tactics? "Before I came to Frogmore I was thoroughly briefed on my rights as a visiting field researcher," she says. "I was told that all my field observations are—legally speaking—confidential. And as I am only here for research, I in no way come under the Combine's military forces' jurisdiction."

His fingers fidget with the clasp of his weapons belt. "This is routine questioning of the sort we would put to anyone who was at the Durazzo Terminal at the time you were there." He smiles. "Purely routine, Dr. Stillness. You are compelled by the same laws of your planet of residence, which is Pleth, that pertain to any other person in the circumstances. Your status as a researcher doesn't exempt you from ordinary applications of the laws. It exempts only your field work."

She knows by the way he's said this that while they were standing there talking he received instructions to drop the hard line and take this new approach with her. Civilly, she shows them out of her quarters. The war of wills, she knows, is not over yet.

The morning after her return, Nathalie Stillness emerges from her sleep cocoon humming the most popular tune among the Durazzo women she met in the field. She continues humming it as she ducks under the shower to slough off the cocoon fluid and pulls on a pair of cling-ons. For the first time in two weeks, she feels relaxed and rested; her body crackles with as much energy as it ever has on Frogmore. She raises her arms above her head, stands on tippy-toes, and lifts and stretches her muscles to their furthest extent. The sense of struggle against gravity invigorates her; her freshness and springing energy make her feel feisty, challenging, even powerful as she swings into the exercises she neglected to perform the mornings she spent in the field. *One, two, three, four, one, two, three, four . . .*

When she finishes the calisthenics, she subvocalizes the two pitches, then *Calendar, personal: enter reminder after lunch: schedule appointment at clinic.* She needs to have her weight as well as her muscle/fat/water ratios checked. Time spent in the field always means deviations in diet, sleep, and physical activity; and deviations from routine on Frogmore tend to create havoc in her body.

Her groin tingles with excitement; her brain ferments with ideas. First she'll dress, then breakfast. And *then* she'll get started with the new material. She deopaques the closet door and finds that Ardeth has already cleaned her soiled and wrinkled clothing. Exuberantly, she dons a pair of loose lilac, coral, and gray culottes and belted tunic. The women in Durazzo may not have unveiled their deepest mysteries, they may not have explained the enigma that has been teasing her for months, but the new material will help her find her way to figuring it out for herself. She *knows* the answer is there, if only her own imagination and insight are powerful enough to see what is likely right before her eyes.

"This is the beginning," she murmurs aloud, reopaquing the closet door. "I *will* understand, I *will*."

Looking away from the screen, Nathalie subvocalizes *pause.* Again the pregnant women have fallen into talking about food production. She hadn't noticed at the time how frequently they discuss the subject. It strikes her that this may be the sort of thing Agee was hoping she would tell him. She wonders. Could someone like him even begin to consider the talk of pregnant women significant—women whom he carelessly confused with gestational surrogates, all because he could not grasp important distinctions between the social and sexual organization of standard advanced societies and that of many of Frogmore's inhabitants? His subordinate, though: surely she will have put Agee straight...

She looks again at the screen and subvocalizes the command to resume the transcript of the playback:

DIANA ELEAZAR: What kind of fools do they take us for? No one fell for it when they tried it right after the military first occupied us. Why do they think we'll fall for it now?

BETA FALLON: Their methods are different this time. Besides, it's been nineteen years since the military first got here. That's a generation. They probably think most people won't remember. But the main problem is the bribe. How can we keep people from taking it? If the outsiders give in to it—and they probably will—we all know how shortsighted outsiders are—then the whole thing will come about, one way or another.

JAN SILLERY: It's hopeless. Cheaper food is a bribe no one who doesn't work in food production will be able to pass up. And even some of the people in food production will go for it, since they'll be attracted by the higher wages in all those mines the governor keeps talking about opening.

DIANA ELEAZAR: Don't underestimate our powers of resistance, Jan. We aren't all fools. At least not in Durazzo. Around here, people who own the small-scale operations aren't going to be giving up. As long as there are people to work in them and people to buy from them we'll be resisting. And the bosses won't be able to pull off their bone-crushing blackmail if there are regions of resistance. Every single food-production operation would have to shut down before they could manage that.

JAN SILLERY: Not true. Those operations depend ultimately on materials that have to be purchased. If they make it hard enough to access those materials, the food-production operations will fail. That'll be their next tactic when the bribe is shown to be less than one hundred percent successful.

DIANA ELEAZAR: I still say it's a mistake to think they're going to get away with it. These things can be stopped—if the resistance is organized and determined enough to stop it. It's a matter of making people see their survival depends on not falling for the bribe.

Nathalie Stillness pauses playback and slips out of her hammock to prowl and pace about the poky cubicle. Why spend so much time talking about politics? she asks herself.

After a minute of pacing it comes to her: the issue passionately engages these women because it involves food and because they're pregnant. They're thinking in the long-term, generationally, because they're preoccupied with the continuity of life and are concerned with the issue of food because their bodies are at the moment devoted to nourishing the fetuses they carry. It's that simple. These women are obviously not actively involved in politics. They simply need to pass the time in talk, and what could be more natural than talking about the subject most on their minds?

She returns to the hammock. She will access the Central Library to see what she can find on conversational topics among gestational surrogates on worlds inhabited by advanced societies. It is always interesting to find the exigencies of biology (shaped, of course, by cultural structures and topoi) determining behavior. This bit of the material, though basically irrelevant to the larger themes of the project, could serve to help get her foot in the door of the long-raging controversy about instinctual traces. Nathalie Stillness has never before considered joining that particular fray, but given this new bit of material she might find herself fully launched in it. Which could be interesting—and might even attract a lot of attention to Frogmore. For which she, Nathalie Stillness, would have laid the groundwork, which every new study would then have to acknowledge...

❧

While she consumes the portions Ardeth has measured out according to the specifications of her personal dietary schedule, Nathalie accepts the incoming transmission and sends it to the printer on the assumption that it's another batch of files from the Central Library. *Word Processing*, she subvocalizes. *Religion, Thematic Elements of; Section Eight.* She glances at the screen as she swallows some concentrate, then scrolls to the end of the section. *Append*:

I'm beginning to think the practice of personally carrying the fetus may be more widespread on Frogmore than I originally thought, for I've slowly been accumulating evidence of it in places where the culture of the family domes has spilled over into the more prosperous sectors of the directed classes. To what extent, I wonder, is this a consequence of the fee-based crèche care and elementary schooling some of more socially-open domes have been furnishing for the children of people they call "outsiders"? It is an important means for the domes of acquiring SCUs, but may also have done much to disseminate their values—though only to a point.

The women I made contact with in the Durazzo Region appear to regard the custom of personally carrying the fetus conceived directly within their own bodies as the ultimate manifestation of their worship of "the natural." Conjecture: such "natural" conception, gestation, and delivery out of the same body may effectively constitute a sacrament, should the hypothesis that their worship of "the natural" is indeed the atavistic set of constructs defined as "religion" and springs from the exaggerated hardships and tenuousness of survival inherent in life on the planet prove correct. I wondered if they appreciated the irony of this, and so spelled out the inherently "unnatural" genetic engineering that had created their exoskeletal modifications (which, it is now well-documented, have never been of a uniform degree or design— one can, indeed, trace genetic lines through examining and comparing the variety of forms these modifications have taken). I then pointed out that the mechanical and electronic appliances necessary for making the gestation of a fetus *in utero* even *possible* (much less endurable) on Frogmore as well as the special surgical procedures entailed by delivery (given the difficulties created by the exoskeletal modifications)—both "unnatural"—were what allowed them to celebrate "natural" processes of birth. They insisted that these "necessary adaptations" (as every woman I discussed this with called them) allowed them to live "naturally" on a world that humans had not evolved on. As they see it, the "non-indigenous individuals" of Frogmore have a "responsibility" to adjust themselves to the planet's "nature," even to strive to discover what that "nature" is. They insisted that it is a terrible thing—a "crime against the universe," they called it—to violate the essential being, the natural ontology, of the planet. They further claim that each being in the universe has a responsibility to live harmoniously with the universe that existed before he/she/it came into existence and that to do otherwise not only violates others' as well as one's own integrity, but also is disruptive to an all too fragile order and increases entropy. *Pause.*

Something unsettling has occurred to Nathalie Stillness. She reminds herself that religions tend to be a mix of the radical and the reactionary. Bolstered by its invariable claims on the history it insists on constructing, religious organization focuses and concentrates power within authoritarian, totalitarian, and monolithic structures. Despite this inherent conservatism, however, religions are always centered on an eschatology that can only be described as radical. In the early history of humans, therefore, religions engendered violent conflicts and atrocities as each religious grouping struggled to assert its own eschatology and history. High-mortality wars had been inevitable because in asserting its eschatology and history, every organization demanded dominance and required that all other humans submit to the totalized system that constituted each religion.

If this Frogmore cult of the natural is indeed a religion, Nathalie Stillness realizes, then violent conflict will be an inevitable outcome. The incomprehensibly murderous attack on the train could be comprehended (after a fashion) if it had been perpetrated by people imbued with a religion. (How else, she wonders, explain such excessive violence?) Her sense of euphoria has vanished, replaced by restless anxiety. The political discussion among the women, then, must be understood as more than an instinctually driven preoccupation.

A religion, Nathalie reminded herself, searching for a way out, must have god, an absolute. Do the women in Durazzo? At first sight, no. But gods need not have personalities or be called by name to be gods. Consider: these women take what they refer to as "the essential natural order" as their absolute.

A religion must have an ethical system. The women in Durazzo do.

A religion must have a set of rituals: again, the women in Durazzo have those too.

And a religion must have an eschatology. Here, Nathalie sees, lies the key question: viz., have they mapped out a "destiny" that their values and historical constructions compel them to fulfill? In other words, can one detect an ideological agenda and strategies for achieving that agenda shared by the people on Frogmore who worship "the natural?"

Suppose, Nathalie Stillness reflects, I find the answer to be yes. Ought I, in that case, to warn the government of Frogmore, or even the military apparatus, of what they are up against? Someone like Agee would probably not even have heard of the word *religion*, much less be able to comprehend its meaning. And scholarly ethics...

But mass violence—mass murder!—had not been a consideration when the ethics of preserving the integrity of the Anthropological Communication had been developed.

For the first time in months, Nathalie Stillness wishes she were not the only anthropologist on the planet.

She knew it would be just this tight when she planned out her day; still, as she steps out of the decontamination chamber and switches off her respirator, it bothers her to be cutting it so close. Having a single decontamination remaining in her allotment for the current thirty-one-local-hours period means that she must go straight home when she leaves, straight home without any deviations whatsoever, for any reason whatsoever, and then she must stay at home until ten the next morning.

The image of her own fragile neck dominates her thoughts until the sight of the human attendant waiting to conduct her to Inez claims her attention. Nathalie bows slightly at the attendant and follows him into an elevator, then through the twists and turns of the Institute's corridors and hallways. At last, standing to one side, the attendant gestures her past the threshold into a darkened room filled with an enormous holo. When her eyes adjust, she spots two women seated on a rug at the edge of the holo. Their ID broadcasts tell her that one of the women is Inez.

The figures in the holo are a tangle of writhing bodies. Some of the limbs convey a sense of desperation, while others resemble sluggishly sinuous worms. The facial designs the bodies wear offer a featureless blankness, as though their faces had hatched into hard-boiled eggs. Revolted, Nathalie skirts the holo until she reaches the women, who are talking numbers. One of them waves a finger in the air, and the holo reforms to show a tall, thin observer looming over the writhing bodies.

"Inez?" Nathalie says when she realizes that neither of the women have noticed her.

Both heads turn toward her. "Nathalie! So you *did* decide you could make it, after all. Wonderful! Belle, I'll finish looking at this later, and then we can talk more. Within the week,

I promise." One of the women rises and moves toward the threshold. The day-mask she wears is one that Nathalie has never seen before. Inez stretches out her hand. Nathalie takes it, and together they walk, hand in hand, out of the room.

Nathalie blinks against the brightness of the corridor. "I'm basically a risk-taker," she says. "What's running around with one decontamination allotment compared to doing field work in Durazzo where crazies are blowing up the underground?"

Inez squeezes Nathalie's fingers. "When I heard about that explosion, I never made the connection. So that's where you were, Durazzo? I'd completely forgotten where you'd said you were going."

That's because she hadn't said. "It was the train after mine, according to the officer who came to interrogate me as soon as I made it back to the CD." Just the thought of it makes Nathalie's heart thud as though she'd walked miles in this bone-crushing gravity.

"What an adventurer you are. But I can tell by your breathing that your visit to the clinic must have landed you with a tough regimen. Maybe we should go slower? My little room isn't far from here."

"I admit I'm a wreck," Nathalie says. "It's impossible, though, to follow one's personal dietary schedule while out in the field. It simply doesn't work that way. The natives seem to think of food consumption as a very social sort of activity." Maybe even sacred.

Inez groans theatrically. "I know *exactly* what you mean. It's a variant, I believe, of what *I'm* always up against on this world. Though if the governor's circle ever *guessed* I connected their mores with those of the directed classes—" Inez gurgles with laughter. "But their horrid banquets! I no sooner get my body straightened out after going to one of them before I have to go to another! I don't know how my father's officers manage it, I really don't. Ah, here we are, right in here, Nathalie. Take a hammock, if you like. We've stopped being formal long ago, you and I. Oh, and let's remove our masks, shall we?"

They drop into two of the room's hammocks and strip off their day-masks. Inez grins at Nathalie and claps her hands together. "Oh, it's wonderful seeing you, I was beginning to wonder if you'd *ever* come back! I've so *much* to tell you, you'll never guess what I've been up to lately." Inez's lips curve into a sly, proud smile. "Take a guess," she invites.

"You've figured out a way to leave the planet," Nathalie says. She knows that of all things, Inez wants most to escape Frogmore.

Inez laughs. "No, no, nothing *that* fabulous. But still, something most people would regard as little short of miraculous."

"I give up," Nathalie says, hoping Inez won't prolong the game. Inez can be maddening in forcing one to play silly games like Guess.

"I acquired a time-tripper pelt and wore it to one of the governor's banquets." Inez all but crows her triumph.

"I don't believe it! How? How did you *acquire* it? I thought it had been decided it's impossible to catch or kill time-trippers."

"Well the person who trapped mine for me has apparently found a way. I heard about him because he managed to get a couple for some biologists who were having a terrible time trying to study time-trippers without ever having seen one."

"Alive? Or dead?"

"Dead, of course. How could one ever be captured alive? It would simply blink out into another time."

"How did he do it?" Something about this conversation is making Nathalie queasy.

"I don't know," Inez says. "I gather he doesn't want to give away his secret. So that he can keep a corner on the market, I suppose."

"But it's illegal, isn't it?"

"Yes, though given the near-impossibility of doing it, I imagine the laws exist to protect people from the consequences of carelessness rather than to prohibit acquisition proper. A lot of laws have that sort of basis."

Nathalie thinks of the profusion of images of time-trippers she has seen out in the field. "I'm not sure that's how the natives see it."

"There is definitely a taboo." Inez looks her straight in the eye. "The governor went to great lengths to keep me dark the night I wore it. And according to the general, the governor's military aide said my wearing the pelt was obscene. I was wondering if you could shed some light on the subject."

"An aide actually said *that* to your *father*?"

"He *was* taking a chance," Inez says. "But you can never tell with the general." She sighs. "Since then, though, he's been in a foul mood that as far as I'm concerned is, in its rabidity, without precedent." She sighs again and gestures madly. "But tell me what you know about how the natives feel about the time-tripper. Do they have superstitions to go along with their taboo?"

"Give me another year, and I think I'll be able to answer your question. You see," Nathalie says, dramatically lowering her voice, "I think the time-tripper may be extremely important to my study. It may even be at the heart of it."

Inez leans forward. "Do tell!"

The shine in Inez's eyes is so intense that Nathalie grows wary. She makes her voice carefully level. "Really, I'd rather not, at least not yet. Anything I might say now would be sheer speculation. I'm still at the stage of playing with ideas."

"*Well*," Inez says in that emphatic way she has of speaking. "You must tell me about it once you've got it all figured out. I'm *passionately* interested. Especially since discovering waterdance."

"Waterdance? What in the galaxy is waterdance?"

"You, the anthropologist, don't know about Frogmore waterdance?" Inez tsk-tsks. "Well, my dear, allow *me* to tell *you* everything about it I've managed to *discover...*"

How astonishing, Nathalie Stillness thinks: Inez is talking the way she does when she's just connected with a new lover. And knowing well how Inez Gauthier feels about the native population on Frogmore, for a moment she wonders if Inez is playing some new game mocking her. But no: the look on Inez's face could not be feigned. Waterdance must be exceptional if it can make Inez so passionate over something thoroughly *native*.

Frogmore is recommended only for those who relish the most extreme forms of tourism. Not only is the gravity punishing and the Scourge a deterrent to physical exploration of the surface, but the lack of universal full connection is also severely challenging and, indeed, has been known to cause acute panic attacks in those unaccustomed to widespread areas of communication silence.

Information is expensive on Frogmore and can leave the unwary traveler facing charges they have not budgeted for. What passes for full connection on Frogmore is a patchwork of private networks that individuals can subscribe to, either as a member of a particular association (or employee of a particular corporation) or for a hefty per diem fee. Even were one able to subscribe to all of the planet's networks (which, of course, few individuals can), the coverage would amount to a tiny fraction of what is routinely available on worlds with universal connection. All short-term visitors and newcomers suffer from Information Deficit Shock (IDS)—the effects of which are actually more painful when returning from Frogmore to universally connected worlds.

The traveler should also take note that due to the Scourge, interference with radio signals happens often enough to render even the strongest networks unstable. Also, personal internal systems have been known to have been wiped clean in tiny pockets of intense electromagnetic storms that appear (and subsequently vanish) without warning. Such wiping of personal systems, of course, tends to be even more traumatic than IDS. It is recommended that travelers to Frogmore conduct daily back-ups on their personal systems. (The planet's elites are said to back-up their personal systems three times a day.)

Because this lack of universal full connection impacts security policies especially, the corporations dominating Frogmore's economy have long argued that the planet's security services—or even its permanent contingent of peacekeeping forces—ought to bear the cost of implementing universal full connection. Local Frogmore governments as well as the Central Governing Authority in turn argue that only the corporations can afford to do it, since they not only are exempt from local taxes, which largely fund the planet's infrastructure, but would also be the primary beneficiaries of universal full connection. The security services, in their turn, contend that basic infrastructure does not lie in their purview and that in any case their budgets are already stretched and their major duties entail protecting the corporations' interests, not improving the efficiency of corporate communications.

—*A Traveler's Handbook to the Galaxy*, 49th edition

Five
INEZ GAUTHIER

Inez devoted most mornings to the Family's Affairs. On the morning on which the general interrupted this work to pass her a message from Hugo Gauthier, she was giving half her attention to the holo of a board meeting and the other half to the quarterly report under discussion in the holo. She paused the holo and looked up from the screen in her lap to glare at him. "So what is it, Paul. What is so important it can't wait until lunch?" Their ground rules stipulated that the general was never to disturb his daughter in the mornings.

"What else could it possibly be at this time of day?" The general spoke as snappishly to her as she had to him. "It's something largish from Hugo. Haven't read it myself; I sent it to the printer at once." He held out a sheaf of printout. "And since it's from Hugo, I assume it has everything to do with the Family's Affairs."

She snatched the sheaf out of his hand. "He's never been forthcoming in any other context." Inez did not mean this ironically, for she never paid much attention to the thin legalities by which she acquired the sort of information Hugo sent them. By virtue of being the Combine's most visible representative on Frogmore with a justifiable claim on any and all information about the Combine's Council for Developmental Strategy (of which Hugo Gauthier had been a member for the last ten standard years), the general could be sent such information with absolute propriety. The general's daughter, being the executor of both Hugo Gauthier's and the general's financial interests, in the strictest sense could not. Though of course everyone knew it likely that the general *told* her things. He certainly never sent such things in traceable forms like data files.

"Let me know if there's anything there that I need to know about," the general said, lingering beside her hammock.

"And if there's anything anybody else should know—the Intelligence Division, for instance—be sure to send a copy to Handler."

Yeah, as if she needed to be told. If there was one thing the general hated, it was being burdened with information. Whenever new officers came on staff, he explained to them that it was his officers' job, not his, to evaluate information, because he needed to keep his head "clear of the muck and mire of details" in order to "see the larger picture" necessary for the broadest sweep of decision-making. Thus he depended heavily on his aides and his daughter to "keep track of things" (as he liked to call it), to keep him "selectively informed." His aides knew well that briefings could be excruciating when the criteria for selection proved not stringent enough. So now his daughter looked up from the report she had been reading and smiled. "Perhaps you'd like to read it with me?" she said. "We could take turns reading out loud to one another."

The general left at once. His daughter seldom made idle threats.

Inez made time to read Hugo's dispatch before lunch only because she was haunted by the fear that some major economic upheaval was on the way, that some larger pattern had begun warping the fabric of the civilized galaxy that neither she nor her agents had yet noticed, and that any early warning would likely come through Hugo. Despite the vastness of the galaxy, change could come about with disconcerting rapidity, taking even the sagest analysts and strategists by surprise. Though one paid analysts to spot such patterns,

they were often as surprised by upheavals as the merest dislocated mining worker.

She began by reading the abstract provided at the top of
the dispatch:

CDS has ordered a second, larger technical team to
expand and broaden the investigations of the original
team sent to Frogmore in SY1358. The second team's
primary mission will be to assess the feasibility for
(1) eliminating the five plants primarily responsible
for rendering Frogmore inimical to humans and subsequently (2) propagating plant- and animal-forms
suitable for human consumption and nutrition, and,
should such feasibility be determined to be within a
90% positive range, to (3) map the strategy and lay the
groundwork for carrying out the elimination.

Policy Considerations: There is a consensus among
CDS's analysts that such a project could be funded
through accessing two new sources of income: (1) a selectively structured tax on exports flowing out from the
Brainnard Project; and (2) a temporary tax (that the
Combine will permit to be passed on to consumers) on
profits that will eventually accrue once the agricultural
consolidation has been achieved.

[Note: It's my considered opinion that the agricultural consolidation may be made more attractive to its
resisters through judicious linking of the consolidation
with the possibilities of (a) ridding the planet of its
permanent fog & consequent chemical poisoning; &
(b) the eventual introduction of open-field agriculture
(though should such a time actually come, the obvious
argument against such an introduction would be the
difficulty of agricultural enterprise in opposition to the
harsh gravitational conditions of the planet—an argument Frogmore natives will presumably be familiar

with by the time the question will have been seriously raised). H.G.]

Before reading the main body of the dispatch (which ran to several thousand words), Inez lay back in her hammock to consider. Not surprisingly, liquid oxygen popped first into her mind. Clearly the L.O. market would collapse without the planet's tremendous inelastic demand. They would have to ease out of that market gradually enough so that they'd be long gone by the time that particular crash hit, since to hang on and precipitously move at the last minute would enrage everyone who got burned. Determining who should eventually be let in on the secret would be tricky. But no matter who took the heat when it did go, the collapse would likely provoke a political crisis, which the planet could ill afford. On the other hand, she could begin investing in all aspects of aboveground travel, which would be *the* boom business. Business! The entire planet would be a *hive* of new business—mining in particular would suddenly become *safe*. Imagine the drop in the overhead now so onerous to the Brainnard Project, the overhead that had retarded the full development of any mining industry at all on this mineral-rich planet!

Another benefit of the elimination of the Frogmore Scourge now occurred to her. Without the fog, the insurgents wouldn't have a whisper of a prayer against the general's organization. Even better, should the Combine succeed in cleansing the planet of the Scourge, most insurgents would be won over to the advantages of subscribing to the Combine and become reconciled to the elected government's running the planet. Though so far even their best mass-propaganda had mysteriously failed to touch the insurgents ∼ Inez rather obscurely and perhaps even superstitiously suspected the fog had something to do with this determined psychological resistance ∼ once the boom hit the planet, only those insurgents with a lot to lose—the power-hungry leaders, in other words—would continue to oppose the general. And should the opposition evaporate with the fog, why then—then!—the general could leave, and *would* leave, with a lustrous reputation that would stick to his career like the densest powdering of Aurelian dust.

The pertinent question now must be the feasibility of the elimination. Undoubtedly the Intelligence Division had reports of everything the original team had sent the Council. She must access them and then, perhaps, interview the team herself—presuming it could be arranged with discretion. It wouldn't do for her to be seen later to have been in open contact with it when the Family's Affairs benefited extravagantly by fortuitously prudent investments. She would manage everything so discreetly and gradually that not a ripple would be felt in the Frogmore economy. She had, after all, managed such shifts in the agricultural connection without anyone's having perceived it. No one on Frogmore had any idea which companies, subsidiaries, and proprietaries the Gauthiers had invested in—or even if they had investments in *any* Frogmore concerns.

The tone chimed quietly in her ear. She slipped out of the hammock and stretched. Lunch now. But at least she'd have a few things to discuss, hopefully enough to keep him off the subject of Solstice Balalzalar, a subject he had managed to render tedious and boring in less than a local month, despite her own interest in Solstice Balalzalar *qua* waterdancer.

A couple of afternoons later, Sidney greeted her arrival at the Institute with the observation that Solstice Balalzalar had "set up shop" in the space Inez had offered her seven local days earlier. According to the display in Sidney's office, the waterdancer had come in that morning and hadn't yet left. "I have the final list for the next series' subscription compiled."

Sidney separated a thin sheaf from the pile of printouts heaping her desk. "Would you like to see it?"

"Later. You've made a total?"

"Contributions or subscriptions?"

"Contributions."

"It comes to a little over twenty-five thousand."

"Not great, but not bad." The net gain would at least cover a few of the workshops she had planned for the new batch of performance artists due to arrive in the next few weeks.

Inez had roughly one and a half standard hours before her lecture was scheduled to begin. She'd need about half an hour for reviewing her notes and speaking to the projectionist. Thinking of the likelihood that she'd need to go off-world in the near future, she recalled her old idea of recruiting an aesthetics specialist from Pleth to assume a permanent position at the Institute. Such a person could take on most lecture series as well as serve as consultant and perhaps guest-lecturer in Frogmore's fifth-rate university. As she considered the known benefits of disseminating aesthetic standards and experience to mass populations, she decided there was a good chance she could persuade her father to allocate peacekeeper funds for such a position under the rubric of general Communications Projects, or perhaps arrange for CDS to pay for such a slot—just as, to take one example, they had funded Nathalie Stillness's research on Frogmore's social organization.

Following her usual custom when visiting the Institute's artists, Inez entered the waterdancer's workspace without going through the formality of sounding the chime to request entry. She agreed in principle that the artists should consider their workspaces to be places of inviolable privacy but liked to think of the Institute as a community whose creativity flowed and merged without boundaries and borders—as a garden of activity cross-fertilized and nourished through free interaction among all the Institute's inhabitants.

She enjoyed chatting with the artists about their work, about their theories pertaining to their own disciplines as well as about aesthetics in general, and had accumulated a variety of theories of the arts and achieved a growing comprehension of the particular problems and controversies the artists grappled with. Far from thinking of her visits to the artists' workspaces as interruptions, she considered herself a useful sounding board, someone the artists could talk to about technicalities, someone articulate and able to stimulate in the artists a more conscious appreciation of "the broader questions." Occasionally she remembered that such "visits" contributed to her own education, but rather than feeling she was leeching on the artists' time and attention, she considered the accrual of such an education not a privilege to herself but a benefit to all future artists at the Institute.

Entering the waterdancer's workspace, Inez did not see her. Her eyes, of course, went first to the enormous tank set up and filled with a clear viscous fluid in which floated a grid formed by what appeared to be taut-straight ribbons. A manual console occupied a low table to one side of the tank. The hammock hung limp and empty. And the threshold into the dressing room had been left deopaqued, allowing her to see that the waterdancer was not in it. Turning to go, she caught sight in the mirror of a blob near floor level. She stopped to stare, then saw the body she had missed noticing because, wearing beige cling-ons and lying flat on the wood floor with limbs outstretched, the waterdancer's body had effectively been camouflaged. Inez advanced a step; irrelevantly she thought of how she would like to put wood floors in all the rooms of the Commander's Residence and how she regretted the general's decision to economize in certain areas when he had had the Residence designed and furnished. "What splendid timing," she said, staring down at the dancer's closed eyes and naked face. "I've caught you in a rest period!"

Inez wondered if the dancer was sleeping, but then detected a slight ripple of movement in the face, mostly a tightening of the muscles around the mouth. Solstice Balalzalar opened her eyes. After a few blank seconds she said, "Were you speaking to me just now?" She sat up. "I heard your voice, but not what you were saying." She looked dazed.

"Oh, you were sleeping. I had no idea." How could she have? One did not expect people to sleep out in the open, lying on the floor completely unprotected from the environment.

"No, I wasn't sleeping. But I wasn't precisely conscious." She got to her feet.

Watching the dancer, Inez realized what had been nagging at her. On both the other occasions she had seen her, as well as now, she had been missing the transmission of the dancer's ID. Why, she wondered, would Solstice Balalzalar be suppressing her ID? One did so in certain public situations where one would prefer to remain anonymous. But what possible reason could the dancer have for suppressing it here in her own workspace? Or, for that matter, at the Governor's Installation?

"What state is it you're referring to?" Inez said. "Not precisely conscious, but not sleeping, which rules out being focused. Were you doing some kind of meditation?"

"I don't mean to be rude," the dancer said. Her eyes flicked over the patchwork of daytime clothing Inez wore. "But are you in some way connected with the Institute?"

Taken aback—unable to remember the last time anyone had asked her for her credentials, which it seemed to her was what the dancer, albeit obliquely, was doing—Inez locked eyes with her. "You don't remember me?" she finally said. Much as she wanted to support the dancer—even to the point of ignoring the latter's rebuff of the general, which had, after all, generated quite a bit of discomfort in her own personal life—she found it difficult swallowing this degree of rudeness to her personally.

The dancer stared at her with a measuring yet puzzled look in her face, until the dark gleaming eyes widened and the pale thin lips parted. "Oh," she said. "I tend to forget you people assume everyone is connected." She held up her left hand so that Inez could see the thin strip of band implanted on the inside of her wrist a millimeter or two from its sharp knob of bone.

Inez gasped. "I had no idea!" Solstice Balalzalar bore no obvious traces of an exoskeleton, she spoke standard as though she had been raised in it, and her manners boasted an ease and casualness that almost anyone in the governor's circle might envy. Despite her head-hair (which some natives clung to even after having been connected), she gave the impression of being as civilized as any native of Frogmore could be.

"The implanted band is adequate," the dancer said.

Inez drew a deep breath: how absurd she felt announcing her own name! "I'm Inez Gauthier," she said.

The dancer half-smiled. "Yes, of course. And now I will, in the future, recognize your voice. I just hadn't heard enough of it before to remember."

Every encounter with Solstice Balalzalar seemed fraught with awkwardness and strange pauses and uninterpretable undercurrents. And despite the waterdancer's easy manners—manners of the sort Inez found attractive, since most people tended to be intolerably stiff and rigid and self-conscious around her—something in those manners disturbed her. An ironicalness, perhaps? Or indifference? It was as though this woman were making the barest effort to play the game, while holding herself aloof.

Gritting her teeth against the embarrassment ~ no, she would *not* admit to embarrassment, though her awkwardness and self-consciousness approached that wretched plebeian state ~ of having announced her own name, Inez expected the dancer (as a sort of balm, perhaps?) to make a graceful remark conveying appreciation of being furnished with workspace here at the Institute. The general's daughter had never yet met a Frogmore artist who hadn't been gratified by and enthusiastic at the opportunity and honor such distinction bestowed. But the waterdancer failed even to *mention* her privilege, much less acknowledge Inez's generosity and graciousness for having granted it to her.

Inez oscillated between perplexity and dis-ease on the one hand and anger on the other. For a split second she considered walking out of the workspace and ignoring Solstice Balalzalar forevermore. Then the impulse passed, overridden by curiosity and the desire to penetrate the waterdancer's peculiar barrier. And yet, really, she could not allow such rudeness to slide by entirely. Therefore, she chose to speak ironically: "I dropped by to tell you that if there's anything the Institute can help you with, not to hesitate to see Sidney Wickham about it. She's always busy, but however large or small the issue, she is the one who ultimately gets things done around here."

Solstice Balalzalar's face registered not a trace of awareness of irony. "I'm not certain I know who she is," she said indifferently.

"She has pearly gray eyes," Inez said in her next-to-frostiest tone of voice. "Noticeable within any day-mask."

The waterdancer rubbed her thumb over the implanted band. "Oh yes. I talked to her yesterday."

Another awkward pause ensued. Inez took a few steps closer to the tank and the massively buttressed platform, which reared almost a meter above her own head, on which it sat. "You use the grid for practice?" she asked at random.

Solstice Balalzalar came and stood beside Inez. She gestured at the manual console on the low table nearby, which she presumably needed because she wasn't connected. "It's a little complicated to explain," she said. "The temporal and spatial placements in the dance must be precise because of all the things besides my own movement going on in the tank as the dance unfolds. I begin the choreography and basic design in my imagination, conceptualizing it more or less hazily. Then I go to the console and process my conceptualization into images I can see in a scale-model holo. It's usually at that point that I begin sharpening and refining my conceptualization. When I have something ready for mockup, I have the image produced in the tank. All the while, from the time I begin processing my conceptualization onto the screen, it is all elaborated within the confines of the grid system you see in the tank now." Solstice Balalzalar turned her head toward Inez; the latter drank in the excitement that had transformed the waterdancer's face from mask-like placidity and remoteness to glowing warmth and animation.

"That's what you were doing when I interrupted you? Conceptualizing a new dance?"

"Yes. I'm still in that first stage with this new work. But later, once I've sharpened and defined the conceptualization, I return to that state to learn the dance."

"*Mentally* learn it? To memorize it?"

"Neurally. I simulate it. My muscles and tendons actually rehearse the movements, though without incurring the strain it would cost my body to learn and practice it outside the tank."

"Incredible!"

The waterdancer laughed with pleasure; her eyes sparkled. "Not really," she said. "It's a logical solution for me. Pilots, for example, are trained using that method before they ever go near the real thing. It would be too expensive, you see, to do it any other way."

"You invented this method yourself?"

"How many waterdancers do *you* know of?"

Inez laughed a little, embarrassed. "Until I saw your performance, I didn't know that such a thing as waterdancing existed."

"As far as I know, I'm the only one who does it." Solstice Balalzalar shrugged. "It's a natural for this planet, though, if one is interested in dance."

"I understood from the governor it was some sort of traditional art-form peculiar to Frogmore."

The waterdancer's face subsided into remoteness. "When I was a child I saw free-fall dancing when my family vacationed on Holliday. I cried when I saw it. Because it was so beautiful. And I wanted to do it myself. So I used to try simply to dance expressively." She half-laughed. "But between my exoskeleton and the gravity..."

The waterdancer turned away from the tank. "Seeing myself in the mirror, I despaired at my grotesqueness. Expressive dance became a sort of obsession I could indulge only by watching holos. So when I went to university on Pleth, naturally I began to follow up my obsession, even after I discovered that professional dancers all start their discipline in early childhood." The waterdancer seated herself on the floor, her arms stretched out behind her with palms pressed flat on the wood surface, taking some of the weight of her body.

Inez turned from the tank and stared down at her. "You attended university on Pleth?" The dancer's story grew stranger and crazier the more she heard. Most of her assumptions about Solstice Balalzalar seemed to have been wide of the mark.

"Not one of the best," the waterdancer said dismissively. "You must know there are tens of thousands of universities on Pleth. My Family would never have been able to afford to send me to one of the better ones, even with my CDS stipend. Apart from figuring out a way to dance on Frogmore, my other main purpose in going to Pleth was to change my body. To acquire internal artificial reinforcement and phase out the bulk of my exoskeleton." She smiled self-mockingly. "I still feel ambivalent about it, but I knew I had to do it if I wanted to create the kind of dance I found so moving."

Inez sank down onto the floor a meter or so from the water-dancer. As her fingertips stroked the grain of the faux wood planks, her eyes strayed over the dancer's body as though in search of residual exoskeletal traces, and then withdrew in confusion as she realized (again!) that Solstice Balalzalar wore only the beige plain nickel-threaded cling-ons. "CDS gave you a stipend to study dance?" she said. "What dancers did you work with?"

Solstice Balalzalar's mockery shifted direction. "Of course CDS didn't give me a stipend to study dance." Her voice acquired a sardonic edge. "I was to get further training in education. I was a teacher. Perhaps you know how that system works?" Inez nodded. "So it made sense to everyone for me to go to Pleth for an advanced degree. And no, I never did study with any dancers. I watched a lot of dance. And I found out about simulation-learning and gravity and fluids and all that sort of thing."

Inez tried to take it all in. "How long have you been doing this?" she finally asked, gesturing at the tank.

"Four Frogmore years." Solstice Balalzalar's raspy voice grew oddly weary. "Long years. Out in the Fidalgo Archipelago. I found a few people there to help me."

"Your attendant is one of them?"

Solstice Balalzalar looked blank. "My attendant?"

"The woman who attended you the night of the performance. I saw her in your dressing room when we talked with you afterwards."

A look of surprise crossed the waterdancer's face. "You mean Sadora?" She laughed. "You must mean Sadora. She isn't my attendant, you know. Sadora Lumni would never be anyone's attendant."

"The governor's protocol officer said she was your attendant."

Still smiling, the waterdancer shook her head. "That was the only way I could get her in. Security is so spacing tight in the Governor's Installation. No, Sadora Lumni is my intimate friend and artistic collaborator. We're inseparable."

Inez felt as if she had been slapped. The words and the tone in which they were spoken had a firmness and solidity about them that threw her off-balance.

As if to rescue her from an awkward moment, her voice of reminder warned her that she had only three-quarters of an hour before her lecture. She got to her feet and made her goodbyes. One positive thing at least had come from the encounter: by getting the waterdancer to talk about her method, she had managed to break an ice she had begun to think infrangible.

Travelers to Frogmore should be prepared for not only higher food/lodging/air per diems but also frequent decontaminations and the need for medical counsel and services that will not be available on the planet via personal system. As mentioned elsewhere in this chapter, the poor choice of networks available to individuals on this planet has allowed the domination of most services that are routinely functions of licensed software by monopolies that have instead created institutions for administering these functions.

Thus, medical counsel and services have been monopolized by institutions that operate by regulation of "medical guilds." These medical guilds require that all medical counsel and services be mediated by human beings (regardless of the fact that the latter are merely relaying to the consumer of their services what the software shared by all guild members has told them). The personal software the traveler arrives with will, unfortunately, be inadequate for addressing the problems and conditions particular to sojourning on Frogmore. And it is earnestly advised that medical counsel be taken at regular, frequent intervals in order to avoid serious damage to the traveler's heart muscle and immune system and less acute but sometimes more chronic damage to other organs. (We recommend for the first few months at least twice a week; thereafter, once a week.)

Legal counsel has similarly been institutionalized, and the legal system as a whole, though its purpose is to adjudicate the laws legislated by the local and central governments, functions under guild regulation that operates largely independently of the governing authorities that write the laws they adjudicate. We urge travelers not to rely on the software on Frogmore law they've acquired off-planet: such apps will be at least 25 years out of date (due to guild regulations on exporting information outside the guild) and vague on judicial procedures.

—*A Traveler's Handbook to the Galaxy*, 49th edition

Six

ARIEL DOLMA

Ariel Dolma to Livvy Kracauer
14.VI.493

Dearest,

Admit it, you're wondering whether I've lost my mind, sending you a letter. The truth is, I need to be able to speak freely to you without letting the rest of Paula's Dome into the conversation, which in this place is impossible to do in a screen chat. You may have noticed the other night when we chatted that I was constantly being interrupted. (Or maybe you didn't—maybe you thought I'd been sniffing something that made me change the subject mid-sentence every few minutes. Trust me, I haven't sniffed anything since my arrival. As far as I can tell, no one here has ever bought a vial of anything in their life.) See, constant interruption is the norm here. No one seems to need privacy. Hmm. Do you suppose that might be the result of everyone here's having been raised collectively in one big crèche?

The situation makes me sorry I don't have full connection—though I suppose that if I *did* they wouldn't have me here, even if I paid them ten times the fee for my board and instruction. The whole idea of talking head-to-head used to freak me out. My mother has always claimed she did it for her job, but I'm starting to think that at least part of the decision must have involved social considerations too.

One of the things I started to tell you when we were chatting is that the sleeping situation here is dire. The dome has appropriated my cocoon for the duration of my stay here, for common use in a pool shared by all the adults. Yes, you read that right. (The children, at least, each have their own.) Not only will I get to sleep in a cocoon only two nights in seven, but it will usually not even be in my own cocoon when I do—and sleeping in fluid that numerous other people have slept in. (Because of course the fluid doesn't get changed often. Gross, no?) And so I'm sleep-deprived. Which is making me cranky—not a good thing to be when you're meeting new people who are just waiting to pounce on you for putting a step wrong.

Of course, we can still do some chats, too. I don't suppose anyone hearing us talking about life "outside" (as they think of it here) would understand half of what we might be saying. I think only a handful of people here have been to the Capitol District, much less attended even a year at FCU. I just need a way to let you know what's going on at my end.

In case you're wondering—worrying, more like—Durazzo, where I'll be working when I finish this stage of my training, is a much more comfortable place and not at all isolated the way this dome is. Granted I'll need to spend a lot of time in the birthing dome, but Durazzo is a proper (if smallish) city. Believe me, if I thought it was at all like this place, I'd probably be considering taking a job in a clinic on Holliday, even though that would mean I'd probably not be able to live on Frogmore anymore and that we couldn't live together unless you decided to take a job up there too. You did like what we saw of Durazzo when we spent that weekend there last year, right? Dearest Livvy, I'm only going forward with the plan because I think we can both make a life there. Remember that!

Sorry—I've been complaining a lot, I know. I don't *want* to be boring. Just for balance, you should know that it's not *all* bad here. The "Grand Mother," as they call Dana, the person who runs Paula's Dome, is a smart, fascinating person. The best part of my days are spent with her, discussing philosophical and ethical issues that matter tremendously to the women I'll be attending. This is the part of my training that differentiates me from the other midwives turned out at FCU. (I know you don't totally get the stuff beyond the physiological challenges that Frogmore's gravity poses, but trust me, it's complicated.) I already knew some of this from studying the journals and chronicles of a few of the original settlers, but this woman carries what seems like five centuries of theory and practice around in her head, like an encyclopedia stored in supplemental memory (which capacity I've always envied you, you know).

A distant cousin of mine, known as a "First Daughter" (who is in fact the Grand Mother's actual granddaughter), sits in on these lessons. She's utterly clueless and is always coming out with uninformed questions. I don't really mind, though, since the Grand Mother's answers often serve to clarify points I'm vague on or make generalizations I hadn't yet been able to articulate for myself.

It's getting late, which means I'd better try to sleep now. I miss you so much, sweetie.

A.

Ariel Dolma to Livvy Kracauer
20.VI.493

Dearest,

Thanks so much for "playing the game" as you put it in your (rather brief) letter. I think that's an apt characterization for our—what is it? Not subterfuge, but, let's say, our resourcefulness in creating a space where we can be private. And of course, as you said in our chat right after you read my letter, there's no reason we can't still do frequent voice chats, even if you'll probably be doing most of the talking.

I'm feeling pretty good because I got to sleep in a cocoon last night, and also because the Grand Mother today talked about the difference between the "biannual ritual calendar" and the calendar of rituals observed by individual pregnant women over the course of their pregnancies. Because I was raised by a Daughter of Suzanne and attended day school in Suzanne's Dome, I'm familiar with the major ritual celebrations of the biannual calendar. (They all have to do with various natural cycles particular to Frogmore's native flora and fauna, as I'm sure I've told you before.) But there's much about it that went unexplained. I vividly recall how, often, when I asked one of my insistent "why" questions (having always been one of those pesky kids most teachers dread getting saddled with), I was put off with "that is not for idly curious little girls to know, Ariel." Well today I learned that the ritual calendar is biannual rather than annual to mirror one full gestational cycle of the time-tripper. Sweetie, I had *no idea.* In fact, I had no idea that anyone knew anything about the biology of time-trippers, much less the particulars of their reproductive physiology.

Obviously a large part of this instruction is intended to deliver the message that so-called outsiders' sources of knowledge are inferior. You do know that I can't tell you more than this, I hope. I'm sworn on my honor as a midwife not to divulge what I'm learning to anyone not officially approved by the Matriarchs and Grand Mothers of the domes. I can say, though, that when I asked why this knowledge of the time-tripper is unknown to outsiders, the Grand Mother replied that outsiders always strip particular bits of information of their contexts in order to render the context invisible, a process that often results in significant distortion. And destruction of context, she gently reminded me, is anathema to anyone wishing to live in harmony with the planet.

That rendered me momentarily speechless. I just looked at her. She raised her eyebrows and stared at me for a long

moment, perhaps waiting for a rejoinder. When I didn't produce one, she said, "Can you deny that the ecology of Frogmore is delicately balanced?" And of course, I couldn't. And
then she said, "The people who govern the outsiders' world
have made no secret that there are parts of that delicate ecology that they're eager to destroy. What do you think they
would do if they acquired small chopped-up bits of information about the time-tripper that they then used without
reference to its larger context?" I had to concede the point.

The weekend's coming up, and that's when I miss you
most. I appreciate your wanting me to join the weekend game
remotely, but it's just too difficult to pull off while living in
the dome. It's not that they don't game here—they do—but
again, interruptions. (And of course they'd think me snotty
for choosing to play remotely rather than play with them.)
A.

Ariel Dolma to Livvy Kracauer
24.VI.493

Dearest,

Please let's not fight. I'm sorry I cut off our chat so
abruptly. I felt constrained, because of the privacy thing, and
thus frustrated at being not able to explain properly to you.
Please, can't you compartmentalize these cultural differences? That's what I do. (I learned to do it young, because of
attending day school in Suzanne's Dome.) Please accept that
there are certain things that won't make sense to you but
that I need to accommodate myself to and treat respectfully
if I'm to pursue my chosen career. I thought you understood
that. Though maybe I was a bit too confident that that part
of myself needn't come between us.

Perhaps it would be best if I didn't try to share parts of
my instruction with you. Not in the spirit of holding back,

but more to keep those cultural differences from coming between us.

My heart is yours.
Ariel

Ariel Dolma to Livvy Kracauer
27.VI.493

Dearest,

I've read your letter four times already—I almost have it memorized. I was already feeling good from our chat, of course, so it's not because I need reassurance. I think my compulsion to keep opening it up and reading it again is because of a feeling it gives me, strangely more powerful, strangely more intimate, than our chats could ever be. Whenever I think of it, I'm surprised, because the only thing more immediate than chatting is being together in the flesh, touching. I have some theories for why this might be, but they're too crazy to divulge in writing. I'll just say that every time I read your letter, a delicious space opens inside me that holds just you and me, making your letter a sort of magic that I can summon up just by reading your words to me.

You are a wonder, Livvy.
A.

Ministry of the Interior,
Frogmore Central Governing Authority
[Dossier: Inez Gauthier, File #37421]
CONFIDENTIAL
Report from G. Emphala, 26.VI.493

Having performed the quarterly assessment of the current group of off-worlders sponsored by the Inez Gauthier Institute, I see only one as potentially troublesome: Ainsley Hillith, who styles herself a "textual artist." The file on her that OC has made available to me notes that she is widely recognized on Janniset, has won numerous awards (though her audience is tiny), and is an "opinion-maker" on Pleth, where she holds a permanent position from which she is currently on leave. The question of her possible motive for accepting a residency at the Institute raises an orange flag. Reviews of her work characterize it as "edgy"; the PFI officer's assessment in the file is that Hillith is critical of the way Peacekeeping Forces are being deployed on Frogmore and helped foment outrage (on Pleth) against the Combine's Anacondan policies. OC has put her under level-4 surveillance.

I recommend assigning a status of Cautious Watch to Hillith, to be upgraded to Concerned Surveillance should she make contact with anyone on the DOI's Watch List.

Note: IG threw a party for her on her arrival earlier this year and has included her on most of her guest lists since then. To all appearances, IG considers AH a cultural icon, and her residency at the Institute a symbol of its success. I strongly advise that any surveillance of AH be carefully managed to avoid IG's awareness and possible interference.

Seven
INEZ GAUTHIER

Major Cleveland's shoulders, the general's daughter lecherously observed with surprise, rivaled even her father's, which many persons (not all of them sycophants, either) declared to be nonpareil. She passed the vial of *Spice of Life* back to the major and watched him inhale, wondering why she was noticing this only now.

Major Cleveland returned the vial to her, and she noticed that his fingers carefully avoided brushing against hers. *Hands off.* Perhaps that's why she had missed the magnificence of his shoulders under the tight, sleek, black uniform. Hands off the general's officers. Hands off so eyes don't see? Although she knew that wasn't quite right, since she often feasted her eyes on the bodies of the general's officers, the thought amused her, and she chortled discreetly in her throat.

The major gave her an inquiring look.

"I was just noticing," she murmured, glad he couldn't see her naked face, "how well your uniform suits you—even over the cling-ons—and how ridiculous by comparison the natives look in a similar uniform. The enlisted more so, of course, than the officers, but the native officers, even those without an exoskeleton, really do look ludicrous in it." Inez looked pointedly at Lieutenant Emphala, one of Major Cleveland's native advisors on loan from the Governor's Militia, chatting with the Minister of Culture and Education and Ainsley Hillith, whom Inez had brought to the Institute from the glittering scene on Janniset where her fame had first been made.

"The peacekeeper uniform was definitely not designed for the froggie body." Major Cleveland snickered. "They do try so hard, though, that one must give them some credit. They can hardly help what their ancestors did to them. Their feelings on the subject are eloquently attested to by the fact that most of them shed the exoskeletal mutations the first chance they get."

"Not all of them," Inez said, barely suppressing her irritation at his using that abominable slur in polite company. "Just as not all of them give up their clumsy and inadequate wrist implants" Like Solstice Balalzalar. Which Inez found absolutely maddening. "I'll never understand why this planet is so backward about connecting. That's what always makes it such a pain re-adjusting to a fully-connected life when one returns to civilization."

"And not only that," the major said. "It makes our job here all that much more difficult in several respects. It certainly makes Hobgood and the Minister of Communications' task that much harder."

Inez recalled that the governor had recently appointed her number-seven-offspring Minister of Communications. "If the governor wanted to do something about it, she could." The payoff in technical data alone would be worth it to the planet's economy. But one could argue with the governor till one was blue in the face, and it wouldn't change her mind.

"She can hardly legislate personal connection," the major said. "Barely a fifth of the population of Frogmore can afford to pay for it."

"But surely those who can afford it could be made to see why they *should* connect."

The major sighed. "It's a cultural thing, Madam. Something to do with the embattled mentality they developed in the first centuries here when conditions were so harsh and they had no other way than the exoskeletal-mutations route. The only ones who think of full connection as essential are the ones who've gone to university on Pleth and had the visible exoskeletal mutations removed and acquired internal reinforcements—which, as I understand it, serves as a sort of rite of passage to adulthood. While the froggies who never go off-world, never have the outward signs of the mutation removed, have a sort of inbred alienation." He shrugged his magnificent shoulders. "Which is something I can't seem to get Hobgood to understand."

Inez ignored both the offensive slang and the disparaging reference to the general's propagandist and went straight for the breech he'd opened.

"There's much we don't understand about the average native of Frogmore," she said. "Their peculiar values, the reasons for their resistance to the benefits of civilization, even their social organization. I'm still astonished when I think of their structures of family reproduction."

Major Cleveland's eyebrows pulled together; he opened his mouth, perhaps to protest the intrusion of such a disgusting area of life into civilized conversation. But Inez smoothed on, cleaving the dust nebulae and minute debris junking the void around them with the ease of a Type IX Quantum Starcruiser. "I've a friend doing research on the natives' social organization," she said. The major's eyes snapped into alert, dispersing the cloudy residue of *The Spice of Life* so instantly that Inez knew her subtext had registered despite her deliberately casual tone. She smiled ~ her mind's eye envisaged the gold and lavender sprays shooting across her design: but then she knew *Subduction* well, she had worn it dozens of times over the last three years ~ in pleasure at the major's comprehension (but then he *should* be sensitive to subtlety, else he'd have no business being the general's chief intelligence officer) and continued. "Her work will be of immense, perhaps immeasurable value to CDS and, more specifically, to the General Staff, once it's completed. Not that I mean to denigrate the efforts of your people, Major; the general extols the Division of Intelligence."

The major mustered a faint (rather frosty, actually) smile and bowed.

"But your people are focused on the immediate, the practical, the specific," she forged on. "You haven't time or resources to study the underlying individual psychological and social psychological structures that make the natives tick. Most of the natives, I mean, of course," Inez amended as Lt. Colonel Legs passed into her line of vision. "But the point, Major, is that so much will become clear that you'll finally have a broader *context* in which to place the nitty-gritty facts and details of your analysis." Inez let loose another gold and lavender smile. "Context, yes. Context is everything. Don't you agree, Major?"

The major again bowed. "Oh most definitely, Madam. One can hardly formulate analysis without it, can one?"

She nodded vigorously: such a gesture, at least, he would comprehend unambiguously. "Precisely," she said. "Precisely. And it will be Nathalie Stillness who will uncover the structures, the mentality—shall we even go so far as to say the Weltanschauung?—that will brilliantly provide not just the Intelligence Division and even the propaganda specialists but the Council for Developmental Strategy itself! with this marvelous new context." In a burst of exuberance she threw out her hands to both sides, intimating a magnificent embrace not only of Major Cleveland and the rest of the room but of the entire planet as well. "Imagine understanding what the insurgents are up to, Major!"

The major made an ambiguous sound in his throat. "Ah, pardon me, Madam, but I thought it was obvious what they are up to?"

Inez heaved a great sigh. "Oh, Major!" she said in a scolding, how-greatly-you-disappoint-me-you-whom-I-expected-better-of tone. "Oh, Major, surely you can *not* be confusing superficial impulses with the more deeply seated cause!"

Judging by the tension now apparent in the major's jaw, she understood that she had annoyed him. She should have tempered her playfulness, she saw, for he might now out of malice make her squirm when she pressed him on the second point.

"Far be it from me to embrace the superficial, Madam," the Major said not quite through his teeth. "I might point out that Major Banebridge's staff has a sufficiently deep understanding of the froggie mentality to bring about absolutely total cures. Some of the insurgents initially placed under his Division's care have subsequently proven to be among our best native advisors." The Major's gaze traveled across the salon to rest on the redoubtable Major Banebridge (the very sight of whom sent shivers snaking up the general's daughter's spine). "Unfortunately, we cannot place the entire native population of Frogmore under his Division's care." He looked back at Inez's design. "Still, one cannot accuse *him* of being superficial. His very accomplishments prove he understands native psychology more than adequately."

It struck the general's daughter how consistently her father's officers' faces resembled one another: all had that same sharply cut, well-shaped aesthetic severity about them, though one could never accuse them of adopting identical visages that were doll-like in their uniformity. The general, too, had at some point acquired such a face. Inez had never asked her father about it, but as she considered this phenomenon, it occurred to her that probably they did it because they knew their faces must always be visible and clearly individual. Only in the most civilized worlds did commanding officers sanction their staffs going masked or design-dressed. And how many officers ever had the privilege of serving on worlds that had no need of peacekeeping forces?

Inez shifted and recrossed her legs. If she couldn't recline on a couch or lie in a hammock, she preferred sitting on rugs with bolsters, but chatting with an officer, such informality would never do. "I'm puzzled, Major," she said in her clearest, most straightforward voice. "I'm puzzled that you regret that the *entire* native population cannot be made to undergo the radical therapy practiced by Major Banebridge's Division. I really cannot imagine the governor appreciating such a sentiment." Touché, she thought, for his persistent usage of that offensive shit-slinging slur she had for nine years been haranguing the general to ban.

Now the major did speak through his teeth. "I'm sure you understand that I was only talking rhetorically, Madam. We are, after all, here to support the governor and her lawfully elected government."

She *had* gone too far. "I do apologize for ragging you, Major." She landed a brief touch on his impeccable sleeve. "I appreciate the fact that you're one of the general's most responsible and thoughtful officers. I'm afraid *The Spice of Life* tends to have a rather, ah, mischievous effect on me." She forced a smile, certain that by now the major would recognize the spurt of lavender and gold for what it signified. "No, in fact I never would have brought up Nathalie Stillness's work if I hadn't felt you would find it, when completed, both useful and interesting."

A slight flush tinged the major's cheeks. He achieved a stiff smile, however, and coughed with painstaking politeness behind his hand. "I'm sure you're right, Madam. I certainly don't mean to exaggerate our grasp on the native mentality."

Inez inclined her head. "I understand perfectly, Major. And certainly I don't mean to underestimate your grasp. I think we were probably haggling about two separate categories of understanding. You and all my father's officers are naturally concerned with upholding law and order and turning violent, destructive persons into responsible, law-abiding citizens.

With *civilizing* them. That is, after all, the ultimate objective of CDS. I do appreciate that, Major. What I was trying to get at, however, has to do with our coming to understand this very alien *culture*. Which of course CDS would never dream of trying to *alter*. We all of us appreciate the distinction between civilizing a world and destroying its culture."

The major's eyes were beginning to glaze over. Good. He had sunk into boredom and inattention. Now would be the time to launch her first strike. "Of course," she went on, shifting into a brisker, less droning tone as she again re-crossed her legs—*wake up, Major, it's time to pay attention!*—"it is rough for a scholar to be stranded on this planet, for the duration, practically alone, going out into the provinces doing field work in barbarous conditions her body was never intended to deal with. But Nathalie Stillness is, fortunately, highly dedicated and disciplined. That much discipline and dedication you would find a credit in any officer under your command, Major." Inez sighed loudly, hoping he would hear it. "But as though all the natural difficulties are not enough, I'm afraid your people have been harassing her, Major. It would be quite a loss to my father's mission were she to be-come so demoralized as to need to leave. I would really hate to see such a thing happen. And I know the Council would be most disappointed."

"*Harassing* her, Madam? I really must take exception to such a characterization," the major asserted in a toneless voice. "All my officers are well-trained professionals. And it is a matter of the firmest policy that CDS scholars in partic-ular—not to mention anyone who is so responsible and dil-igent and devoted to the Public Good as to come here from the comfortable life of ease and stimulation and pleasure to be had in any advanced society..."

The major sucked in a deep breath and, apparently at a loss as to where he had intended his sentence to go, aban-doned it and started a fresh one. "As I say, Madam, we in the

Intelligence Division have a keen appreciation for the integrity and responsibility of CDS-sponsored scholars. We have the utmost respect for them." He paused to stare at Inez's design, as though trying to penetrate it. "I'm afraid, Madam, that I must conclude your friend has exaggerated, or confused my officers with, perhaps, the governor's."

The major, Inez observed, looked quite stern—except for his eyes, which remained devoid of expression, empty almost. "Agee," she said. "A lieutenant, I think. Yes, that's the name. Lieutenant Agee. Three times now he's gone bothering her."

The major sat up even straighter (if that were possible). "I will look into the matter, Madam," he solemnly assured her. He would, too, Inez thought. She had sufficiently driven home her point to make it unlikely he would allow himself to forget the matter. On the other hand, he would undoubtedly make her pay when she introduced the second thing on her mind.

"So here you are, Inez." The general, standing behind her, dropped his hand onto her shoulder. "Major," the general added, and Major Cleveland bowed. "You two have been monopolizing one another for some time, I've noticed." The general spoke in that edgy voice he had been using constantly for the last week. "It must be an absorbing subject, whatever it is."

She knew very well why he was taking this suspicious tone with her, just as she knew he knew she would not be playing around with Major Cleveland. "We were discussing Nathalie Stillness, General," she said in her lightest, most butterflyish voice. "I've been explaining to the Major how important her work is for the Council. And how highly we regard her."

Would he take her cue? She watched the major's face for any giveaway he might let slip.

"Ah yes, Nathalie Stillness. Brilliant, of course. The Council knows how to pick them. But not the sort of person one would wish to be stuck with in a last-ditch life-support raft. A little too dry for my taste."

Her father loathed Nathalie Stillness. But the general had made the point with Major Cleveland: she could see it in the major's face.

"How *are* things going, Inez?" The general's fingers dug into her shoulder for emphasis.

She interpreted this question as a chivvying for her failure to attend personally to the guests. "Captain Deaver is doing a *marvelous* job, General, as he always does. Except that there haven't been any servers this way with all those lovely herbal grasses I so adore."

"The Minister of Culture and Education was asking after you—told me he felt he shouldn't interrupt your tête-à-tête with Cleveland here." The general's voice grated with a much nastier tone than his merely edgy one.

Clearly her father wouldn't budge until she'd broken off the conversation with Major Cleveland. Such a pity, for it meant she'd have to go through the entire social grind with him on yet another occasion to get the biology reports out of him—unless, of course, she flung ordinary caution to the winds and asked the general to requisition the reports for her. Getting things so directly out of him might not be illegal, but such practices, when exposed to the disagreeable scrutiny of disgruntled, fault-finding eyes, presented a negative appearance the Family did well to avoid.

Inez rose to her feet and bowed to the major, who also rose and bowed to her. On to the Minister of Culture and Education, she prodded herself—only to realize with surprise that she actually preferred relatively unpleasant conversation with Major Cleveland to inevitably tedious but innocuous conversation with the Minister of Culture and Education.

Such was the life of a general's daughter.

When the guests had gone, Inez linked arms with her father and took him to his personal quarters. Predictably the general suggested they share a vial of *Midnight Song*, his favorite nightcap. She added that she wanted a good massage, too, so rather than taking their usual hammocks ~ at this hour of night she could usually wait for her sleep cocoon, so far superior to a mere massage couch ~ they stretched out on the pair of couches arranged at a ninety-degree angle with their heads at its vertex.

"I'm miserable," the general said before taking his first good whiff of the vial.

Inez inhaled before answering. The oak-casked brandy flavor of *Midnight Song* had always appealed to her even more than its crasser effects. Long after completing the inhalation she could taste the brandy as though she had taken a big mouthful and was lingeringly rolling it around on her tongue. "I know, Paul," she murmured. "I wish you would leave it to me. You're out of your depth. She's different. *Very* different. Not like anyone you've ever been involved with before."

"No woman has ever made me wait this long," he complained. "Except that greedy bitch, what was her name? The one who wanted that aviation-tech stock first. By the time we were done, she cost me big-time."

"Only because you were willing to pay."

"And she wasn't worth it, either."

Were they ever? "Don't try to offer Solstice Balalzalar stock or even SCUs. That kind of approach would only put her off. Believe me. She's too sophisticated." Having said that the waterdancer would not be tempted by financial gain, Inez wondered: how could she know such a thing? Solstice Balalzalar had been amazingly candid, true, but her candor left one unsatisfied. As though something important had been omitted. Or as though what she had said weren't true. Could her entire autobiographical spiel have been a story? Why else would the waterdancer have been so forthcoming after having shown herself to be remote, aloof, and (supposedly) uninterested in plugging into valuable connections? But she had spoken so naturally. And that look of passion that had come into her eyes when she had begun talking about her method: surely that hadn't been feigned?

But what was a person educated on Pleth doing living in the Fidalgo Archipelago? It made no sense! Even stranger, though, was her declared "ambivalence" at getting rid of the horrid exoskeletal modifications she had begun life with. And the implanted band! Why not simply connect? Surely she could afford it!

"Do you want more of this or not, Inez?"

She lifted her hand over her head and took the vial from her father. "Will you agree to let me see if I can manage her?" she asked before inhaling. If the general pressed her, the waterdancer might be forever lost, *qua* dancer. The waterdance *itself* might be lost. Whereas the general's interest would be transitory. Not that he would see it that way.

He took the vial back. "I don't know what you think you can do. It's *me* we're talking about here. It's *me* I want her to be attracted to." The general snatched a deep, hissing breath that sounded fantastically greedy to his daughter's ear.

She exhaled. "If you leave her to me, I can get her to start coming around here. She's not used to our kind, Paul. She's led a sheltered existence. But she's ambitious, which will offer her a reason for connecting with me. Back off a bit and come on a little less obviously. Not everyone chooses a sexual partner on first sight." The general always did, but she wasn't about to let him get away with taking himself for the standard.

"All right," the general said after he'd exhaled. "I don't suppose I have anything to lose. But don't dilly-dally. This whole thing is getting on my nerves. I feel rejected, you know. Among other things."

The general's daughter pressed her lips together to keep from mocking his petulance. *Be nice to him. It could be you in such a state sometime, too.*

Could it? she facetiously queried herself.

She had to do her best to soothe him since otherwise he'd interfere with the waterdancer and maybe even drive her back to that backwater ~ imagine, she interrupted herself: a backwater of a backwater! ~ never to be heard of again. Which would be a loss. A terrible, desolating loss.

Anyone who even attempts to talk about a movement for Frogmore's independence soon runs aground on CDS's control of the discourse on Frogmore's status. CDS denies that Frogmore's relation to the advanced worlds is that of a colony and claims that, therefore, it is nonsense to suggest that Frogmore is not already independent. Here is the statement that has appeared in *Frogmore: The CDS Fact Book* in every one of its last 150 editions: "Frogmore ceased being a colony in the one-hundred-twenty-first year of its colonization, when the Colonial Settlement Corporation ceased its activities on Frogmore and the planet became a member world of the Combine." We reject this simplistic statement.

We also reject CDS's similarly simplistic and disingenuous assertion that like any other member world, Frogmore may leave the Combine at any time, if it so chooses. *May* is the operative word, here. *May* is a fiction, since CDS policies have rendered it virtually impossible for Frogmore to do so. The cautionary example of a world that has been attempting to leave the Combine is Arriga, which has been engaged in violent revolution (which CDS characterizes as "civil war") for twenty years now. Arriga was once numbered among the "advanced worlds" (a term of CDS discourse unthinkingly adopted by most Frogmore elites). It has been so eaten up by its bloody war that its standard of living and levels of productivity have reduced it to "backworld" status.

Frogmore, of course, already has "backworld" status. The stakes here are different. It's instructive to consider Frogmore's attempts at nonviolent, gradualist reform. It has been less than five decades since Maurice Nsazi, governor during the second great rising in the Capitol District, attempted to enact reforms that would enable Frogmore to begin the process of acquiring the institutional autonomy necessary to become an independent entity. Among the significant changes he attempted to enact was the development of a credit and banking system located on Frogmore, independent of the Standard Unit of Credit that is controlled by CDS and is virtually universal (except, significantly, on Evergreen) throughout the Combine. Another change he attempted to make was the subjection of everyone on the planet to Frogmore's laws—eliminating the exemption that off-worlders with citizenship on the "advanced worlds" enjoy, on the assumption that they should be judged by the laws of their own lands adjudicated by the judiciary of their own lands. Neither of these changes stood after Governor Nsazi was implicated in a corruption scandal (in which none of his fellow conspirators were named or brought to justice)—a scandal that could be effortlessly generated for just about any member of Frogmore's elite.

—Frogmore's Destiny: A Manifesto for Independence

Eight

MADELEINE TAO

"The defendant will rise and approach the bench." Madeleine Tao intoned the ritual words in her most neutral and formal tone.

Elliott Tracy stood, moved around the defense table, and advanced with heavy, jerky movements, his fists jammed into the pockets of his shorts. The chitinous spalls marking his naked face glittered an iridescent bile green. He looked both angry and terrified. When he reached the outer boundaries of the bench, he thrust his head back and lifted his eyes to her day-masked face. Madeleine held his gaze with steadiness of purpose.

A wave of cold, impersonal tension seemed to flood into the courtroom as Madeleine read out the list of charges and counts Elliott Tracy had been convicted of. She had spent days reviewing the forty-seven hours of testimony, as well as all the specialists' evaluations of the defendant. The spate of violence that had recently begun to characterize actions of the insurgent movement now made the matter of sentencing far more critical than at any time in Madeleine's career. Because erring in the direction of leniency could mean a later loss of life, most judges now inclined toward handing down the harshest sentences at their discretion. Madeleine suspected that in doing so, most of her colleagues had conveniently wiped the significance of Total Therapy from their consciousness.

A few months past she had received a letter from her district supervisor advising her to sentence all those convicted of disruption to Total Therapy. His letter argued that those who resort to violence begin with disruptive activities, and that since violence is so abhorrent to civilized society, measures must be taken at once—while the problem was still controllable—to stamp it out. "It is well known that violence is a disease of virulent contagion," he wrote. "It spreads and proliferates as easily and rapidly as the Scourge of Frogmore reproduces and disseminates itself."

The violence worried Madeleine. But the district supervisor's letter notwithstanding, she was determined to continue following her instincts with each individual defendant. A check of the recidivism rate among those she had sentenced had bolstered her self-confidence. The district supervisor had not responded well to the reply she had sent him, but he had not interfered with her, either.

Madeleine began by stating the statutory minimum. "Elliott Tracy," she intoned. "You are hereby sentenced to a fine of one hundred SCUs. In view of the grave threat your offenses pose to the Public Good, this Court requires that you undergo such Limited Rehabilitative Therapy as the Therapy Team to be subsequently named by the Court deems necessary and desirable." The defendant's eyes widened; his breath gushed out of his body in an explosion that appeared to shake his entire body. "In addition you will pay all costs of said therapy, and all court and police costs incurred on account of your offenses, as well as the damages that have been proven and assessed before this Court to the following parties: Henry Rosaldo, a private individual; Arnaud Hydroponics, Inc.; and Howard and Layton Employment Contractors. You may choose to make arrangements with the bailiff to pay said charges by installments at five percent annual interest over the long-term, but must in that case remain on Frogmore until such time as you have completed payment for the amount assessed."

Madeleine stared hard at the defendant, who no longer seemed to be paying attention. "The Court hereby warns that should the defendant fail to meet any of the conditions of this sentence, or should he again be found in violation of the laws of whatever place he is in residence, whether on the Planet Frogmore or elsewhere within the Combine's sphere of jurisdiction, he shall be remanded to state custody and required to undergo Total Rehabilitative Therapy." Elliott Tracy shifted from foot to foot. Madeleine pressed her lips together. They never seemed to pay much attention to the caveat implicit in the sentence, the caveat that with one single infraction they would face Total Therapy, the fear of which obsessed most defendants from the time of conviction to sentencing.

Madeleine nodded to the bailiff and opaqued the barrier. *We do the very best we can do, which is all anyone can ask for*, the Deputy Minister of Justice always said in the orientation meeting at the outset of each new term of service on the bench. Madeleine tried to take comfort from the words, but following a sentencing, they seemed meaningless. That evening, the defendant and his family and friends would be feeling elated. But tomorrow, she knew, the defendant would be sobered at finding himself in the hands of the Therapy Team to which she had assigned him. The idea that the specter of Total Therapy could—when it had been avoided—produce a cause for elation at such a grave time in a person's life troubled Madeleine, troubled her deeply. But she had never been able to think of an alternative to this system, nor had anyone else. *We do the very best we can do, which is all anyone can ask for.*

"I've only spent one night in it so far, so I can't say for certain that it's the best I've ever slept in, but the way I bounced out this morning, *bursting* with energy, every *muscle* in my body relaxed and easy—" She shrugged. "I can't claim to have gotten that kind of performance from my old sleep-cocoon. Over the last year I've been so dragged out every morning that I've had to start the day with a soak in the tub." The woman's design pulsed a steady rhythm of pale yellow splotches spewing over its deep pink ground.

"Anaconda, hunh," the man with the chlorophyll-green goggles said. "Not many starships come to Frogmore from Anaconda. Anaconda doesn't really have that much in the way of consumer goods, does it?"

"They're known for having the top specialists in sleep-cocoons in the *galaxy*," the pink design insisted. "And I know someone who had a new state-of-the-art massage couch coming in on the same starship. Really, in the future I'm looking to *them* for all my domestic environment furnishings. Janniset may be the most sophisticated world in the galaxy, but that doesn't mean they've got a corner on state-of-the-art furnishings."

"Jannisetians probably get their furnishings from elsewhere and sell their domestically produced stuff to backwaters like us," a woman who had just drifted into the conversational knot remarked. "They like to work it that way. Janniset then benefits handsomely."

"All I know," the pink design said, "is that for sleep-cocoons you simply can't do better than those made on Anaconda." She looked at the woman who had made the cynical remark about Janniset. "I've just acquired a new sleep-cocoon from Anaconda. A friend of mine visiting from Bullfinch's World told me about hers. On a planet like Frogmore, especially, we need the best sleep-cocoons we can get. There's a terrible bias, though, in the products available, since no advanced worlds have serious gravity to contend with."

"I agree with you entirely!" The other woman leaned forward, her hands gesticulating with excitement. The red, ornately set stone in the ring she wore on the middle finger of her right hand blazed with a simulated fire that held Madeleine's gaze like a magnet. "I've always said—"

Madeleine wrenched her gaze from the gaudy bauble and stalked away from the knot. There must be decent talk somewhere in the room, she thought as she continued to drift from knot to knot, encountering one insipid conversation after another. She sifted through the clutter of nearby IDs until she located one she knew she'd like to connect with, then headed for the knot from which it seemed to be emanating. First copper- and silver-threaded patterned cling-ons, and then sleep-cocoons. Surely Solange would have found a knot discussing something less tedious? As she passed the knot in which her host stood, Madeleine heard him gushing. "I do hope everyone adores this new custom as much as *I* do. I'm told that Inez *always* entertains without food, keeping the consumables to the so delightfully simple minimum of herbal grasses and inhalants. I know the first time I went to one of her parties I thought it a brilliant solution to the absurd awkwardness of *banquets* and all the—"

Passing out of earshot, Madeleine suppressed the wave of irritation threatening to take her over. Name-dropping had to be expected, no matter what the cultural and social background of one's interlocutor. But this insanity of worshiping planet-jumpers did not have to dominate Frogmore mores and structures. Hardly anyone in the governor's circle remained free of the taint. General Gauthier's arrival had started the trend, and then, later, his daughter's had accelerated its dissemination. Even the off-world residents before the general's arrival had mostly been people dedicated to the same things to which she, Madeleine Tao, had devoted her life. She knew very well that behind the seeming frivolity of Inez Gauthier's life-style lay a serious threat not only to Frogmore's own values and culture but also to the steady progress she, Madeleine Tao, and others like her had effected. But to talk about such a subject out loud had become socially unacceptable, and if done in the presence of anyone from the governor's circle—the Deputy Minister of Justice, for instance—could sometimes be interpreted as a threat of subversion or even sedition.

"The ones committing the acts of violence are all very young, under thirty-five," Victor Searle was saying as Madeleine joined the knot. "That suggests to me that something in particular happened to their generation to make them susceptible to this alien way of going about things, making them willing to consider violent means to disrupt the Center."

"Oh, we *know* what happened to that generation," Imogen Alençon said. "What astonishes me is that everyone misses such an obvious connection! Only *after* the arrival of the peacekeeping forces did *real* violence enter the picture. Gauthier's presence has polarized most dissenters, has inflamed and radicalized the insurgents."

"That's bullshit," Searle said. "The dissenters were headed for violence already, which was the sole reason the then governor requested peacekeeping forces from the Combine! She wouldn't have called them in if violence hadn't already been implicit in the situation! No, the informed consensus is that Governor Vedovi's terms in office can be characterized as moderate to the point of timidity. In fact, Vedovi's ultra-cautiousness is why Kundjan was elected in the first place. That's a matter of historical *record.*"

From her ID broadcast, Madeleine acquired the information that Imogen Alençon sat on the faculty at the Frogmore Central University and specialized in political theory. Searle, Madeleine thought, would wipe the floor with Alençon if the latter persisted in supporting such a whacko hypothesis for explaining the recent escalation of violence among youth.

But Agatha Minsk leaped in before Alençon could attempt to counter Searle's point. "I think it's a matter of increasingly muddied blood. Do you realize that more and more instances in which suspects' blood is found to be highly muddied at the time of arrest have been turning up in the cases of violence that have reached the courtroom?" Minsk glanced at Madeleine, as though for confirmation, then continued. "Last month when I came across the fifth instance in the last three years of an insurgent-type testifying that she had deliberately allowed herself exposure to the atmosphere to the point of intoxication, I decided it was time to do a statistical survey of forensics done at the time defendants were taken into custody. And what do you think I found?" Minsk crossed her arms over her chest and gave both Searle and Alençon beady looks, shifting her yellow-goggled eyes back and forth as though loath to take her eyes off either of them.

"That's a red-herring," Searle said with obvious impatience. "It doesn't help to look at *symptoms*. Their consistently muddying their blood is a symptom on the same level that their use of violence is a symptom. But what *I'm* asking is what in the galaxy is the *cause* of this generation's engaging in behaviors so alien to civilized society—which, *pace* Inez Gauthier, we've had on this planet since we first settled it?"

"I think *I* can speak to the larger problem," Solange said. Madeleine smiled. She had been waiting for Solange to trot out her demographic hypothesis.

Searle waved his hand. "Oh, Solange, not your same vague old garbage again. Trust me, it doesn't bear on the subject. You're just so infatuated with your hypothesis that you want it to explain *everything*!"

"You're so charming, Searle, when you're patronizing," Madeleine murmured into his ear, knowing that of the others only Solange would be able to hear her remark.

"And you, my dear Tao, will soon become too judgmental to handle working on the other side of the bench again."

Solange's elbow jostled Madeleine's arm. "Pay no mind to this collegial bickering," she advised Minsk and Alençon. "This is what happens when one sees too much of the same people year after year. But my hypothesis, which Victor has done his best to prejudice you against before you've even heard it, explains several disturbing patterns, including the upsurge in violence. We're all so familiar with Frogmore's demographic trends that most of us fail to draw certain connections from them. Perhaps the most significant thing that's happened on Frogmore in the last century has been the population growth. During the first century of Frogmore's settlement, the population took off, from immigration as well as from birth rates extraordinarily high relative to the rest of the civilized galaxy. And things were pretty unstable. And so the original peacekeeping force hung around for most of the century. But then both the population and public order stabilized—until about thirty or forty years ago, when the ruling elite engineered a new surge in births. Madeleine and I have reason to know a bit about what was going on, because both of us took a lot of flak for raising only two children. The intended population explosion—for Vedovi, of course, had the beginnings of a massive expansion on her mind—was incredible." Her design pulsated with spurts of dark purple. "Well, what result could one have expected but unrest and violence, when most women were raising seven or eight children each?"

Solange snorted, and Madeleine knew she was thinking of the government's campaign to persuade women educated off-world that personally undertaking gestation would have no stigma attached to it—a lie, of course—all because enough surrogates could not be recruited for carrying out so many births. Nursing and post-nursing surrogates had been in such demand that the costs had been prohibitive for most women. The judiciary system had been strained, for they'd hesitated to raise salaries that would pay for such costs while knowing full well that the system could not function with men only unless it replaced human labor with machine labor, which everyone had agreed was not a desirable solution for Frogmore. Even if they'd agreed to let off-worlders take such jobs, they'd never have been able to attract qualified candidates without better compensation and reimbursement for all the out-of-pocket expenses of immigration. The most pressing issue had been the need to preserve the profession's monopoly on judicial and legal services. Allowing AIs to supplement their ranks would have been the thin edge of the wedge. Humans, after all, played few roles in the judiciaries of any of the most developed worlds.

"But my principle point," Solange said, "is that the violence obviously has a lot to do with these unprecedentedly large family sizes and the consequent effects on those raised in such crowds without the usual nurturing supports our generation had the advantage of being raised with."

Searle made a comical gesture at Solange. "You see, ladies, she has an ax to grind. She still resents being asked to…" he hesitated, then, lowering his voice, delivered the risqué punchline, "personally undergo gestation!" Searle turned to Solange, and Madeleine wondered whether Solange was feeling embarrassed. Most people would, but Solange, given her habitual frankness on the subject to Madeline, might not. "It's obvious, Solange, that you can't be objective on this subject. I can hardly blame you, of course, for resenting the policy of those days. But don't you think it's time to put it behind you and get on with Real Life?"

"No, no, Victor," Alençon said. "Rousseau's point makes sense. And doesn't necessarily contradict what I was saying about the presence of the peacekeeping forces having a bad effect on our youth. No, your hypothesis is very interesting, Rousseau." Alençon nodded at Solange. "But can you tell us *why* Vedovi pushed such accelerated expansion? Namely, what motivations did she have, and who else supported that direction for Frogmore?"

Madeleine sighed: she could see where Alençon hoped to go by subsuming Solange's hypothesis within her own. "We all understand, and have always understood," Madeleine said softly and precisely, "that Frogmore does not exist in a vacuum, is not an isolated world."

Alençon bowed.

Gah. The woman's in love with irony, Madeleine thought. She forged on. "Frogmore made that choice four centuries ago. If at any time it chooses isolation, the Combine will not stop it from doing so. Whatever else one may say about the Combine, one cannot accuse it of coercion."

Alençon laughed. "Not *violent* coercion, certainly," she said. "But there are other, subtler forms of coercion that CDS has never scrupled to exert over us. It's plain that Vedovi was CDS's woman. Far more so than Amanda Kundjan is."

"I don't see what any of that has to do with these violent young people deliberately intoxicating themselves," Minsk complained.

Madeleine looked at her colleague—whom in her annoyance with Searle and her desire to argue with Alençon she had entirely forgotten. "No, no, Minsk," she said, "we must take Alençon's argument seriously. I would like to ask her one or two things."

A bluish-tinged pink suffused Alençon's design. "Ask away, Judge." She bowed—*again.*

"Professor," Madeleine said and bowed to Alençon. Let her decipher that, Madeleine thought. If we must play silly games as we attempt serious discourse, then so be it.

"Question Number One. Are you insisting on regarding all manifestations of social disruption, whatever their *direct* causes, to be interpreted as epiphenomena of Frogmore's, shall we say, colonial status? Or are you claiming some more direct relationship—which was, in fact, the impression I got from what you originally said a few minutes ago about violence being a response to the presence of the peacekeeping force. Because by your second set of statements, one must then simply interpret the presence of the Peacekeeping Force as yet *another* epiphenomenon." As Madeleine spoke, Alençon's design lost all its pink and shifted into a brilliant deep indigo splashed with shiny black patches. "You do see what I'm saying?" Madeleine said. "That you can't place your catalyst in both categories of explanation at the same time?"

"Tao," Searle said without giving Alençon a chance to respond, "when you get so abstract on us you surely must know we can't understand a word you're saying." He leaned forward and stage-whispered to Alençon. "It's all right if you don't understand her, Imogen. When she talks like that, none of us do. Our Madeleine does get a bit dense now and then."

"On the contrary." Alençon's tone was crisp. "I understand precisely Judge Tao's point." She bowed yet again. "I'm afraid you've caught me in a bit of sloppiness that I can only excuse as carelessness in the heat of debate." A slight tinge of pink edged into the shiny black patches of her design. "And certainly I should make up my mind, shouldn't I. Or rather, I should rephrase my argument. Yes, I think that is really the point." She scratched along the edge of her design. "I think my hypothesis would be better stated by regarding our larger colonialist structure as a sort of inexorable context in which these more specific events and effects are worked out. The general's arrival here with the peacekeeping force, for instance: in the context, one would understand such an event as it relates to the expansion Vedovi pushed onto the planet as a result of influences the larger context were working upon her. But at the same time, that event—the general's arrival—must be seen now, in retrospect, as having provoked this new element we're talking of, namely the violence that has come to mark opposition to the peacekeeping force."

"Not only to the peacekeeping force," Searle said when Alençon paused. "These people are opposing our entire structure of government. Which includes not only the governor herself, but the very office of governor, right down to the electoral procedures we employ. You're failing to take the *scope* of the opposition into account, Imogen." Searle's eyes glittered behind his yellow-tinted eyepieces. Did he, Madeleine wondered irrelevantly, wear that particular shape and style of eyepieces because they were a replica of the ones the general had lately been holo'd in? "The opposition attacked Frogmore's constitution long before the governor requested peacekeeping troops. It simply grew more visible once the peacekeeping troops arrived, because only then had attention begun to be so directly focused on the opposition."

Alençon shook her head. "You are trying to force me into quibbling points with you, Victor. Points you and I have argued on other occasions. First, the opposition before General Gauthier's occupation did not attack the constitution per se, but the way the governor was failing—in their view—to abide by its provisions. Second, the opposition was always visible. And it is the general, and the governor's reliance on the general, that has become more visible, not the opposition." She snorted. "I imagine that if we were to circulate this room we'd find from one-fourth to a third of all conversations to include some discussion of either one or both of the Gauthiers. And other planet-jumpers as well. The Gauthiers have made certain sorts of interests and attention *fashionable*. They've brought out the worst in Frogmore society."

With that, at least, Madeleine could agree. "Inez Gauthier has promoted a dangerous frivolity and a pervasive trivialization of the most significant problems facing Frogmore," she said.

"Oh I really must dispute that," Agatha Minsk said. "Inez Gauthier has brought the Arts to Frogmore. We no longer have to hang our heads when we go off-planet for not knowing who, say, Arturo Belizaire is. When our children go to Pleth now, they're not plunged into a bewildering sophistication that stuns them for the first two years of their stay there. If *that* is frivolity, then I'm for it!"

Alençon's mask flashed a sequence of gaudy colors—chartreuse, purple, cerise, aqua, orange, lemon—that Madeleine guessed signified amusement; she envied Alençon's design for its wit. "What a terrible thing it would be not to know who Arturo Belizaire is!" Alençon cried. "Perhaps we'd better name a mountain or a region after Inez Gauthier in solemn appreciation for all that she's done for us poor benighted souls! Wherever would we be without her?"

Madeleine couldn't help smiling, but when she saw the darkness in Minsk's design, her amusement drained away. "Without Inez we'd still be wearing day-masks in the evening and no masks during the day," Madeleine said. "Which is rather hard to imagine now, isn't it."

"Some of us still wear day-masks in the evening." Solange jerked her coral angora-capped head at a knot in which three such persons stood talking to two others more conventionally garbed.

"Yes," Minsk said in an acerbic tone of voice, "and *some* Frogmorians retain their exoskeletons even when they have the choice of internal reinforcement."

Alençon gave a slight nod. "It's partly a matter of pride and partly a matter of principle, since only those of us who can afford to go off-planet and cough up enough SCUs to pay for internal reinforcement have such a choice. Some people don't like the sort of distinctions that inevitably come to be drawn when such privilege is exercised by the elite."

"I see that *you* don't sport an exoskeleton."

Alençon sighed. "I hadn't thought yet about such things when I was attending university on Pleth."

"And now—if you had the choice to make?" Madeleine said, curious to know what was going on in Alençon's so busy mind.

"I really don't know. How could I honestly say?"

Alençon practiced a level of honesty one had to respect, for all her anti-Combine opinions. Still, though Madeleine did not consider herself a Combine partisan, she understood what they had to work with. For all her seeming reasonableness, Alençon was probably as dangerous—perhaps even more dangerous—than the violence-using insurgents.

Madeleine excused herself and headed for the antechamber. It had been a long day, and the morning would bring the start of yet another case. Such conversation could be stimulating, but in the end it was the day-to-day work that counted. Which was why, of course, Alençon and her dangerous opinions could be tolerated.

Frogmore's time-tripper, as it is erroneously known, is without doubt the most mysterious of Frogmore's unique flora and fauna. This aquatic mammal prefers to live in salt-water (though certain subspecies have been found in freshwater rivers and lakes). Its name derives from its characteristic "blinking out" of the space it occupies only to appear, within nanoseconds, elsewhere. This behavior was verified by radio-tagging several specimens, using a remote-controlled dart gun. The most jumps recorded by that method have to date been three, after which time an electromagnetic pulse has rendered the tag useless. Whether the pulse emanates from the time-tripper or nearby mistflowers has yet to be determined.

The time-tripper received its name when the first explorers of some of the planet's coastal areas noticed the creature, hours later, blinking back into the same space it had occupied before blinking out, a space the observers had staked out with cameras. They concluded that these creatures had the natural ability to time-travel.

In fact, the time-tripper's instantaneous travel is due to its capacity for quantum entanglement, which humans use to transfer information between worlds. It has so far been impossible to capture a live time-tripper for study, and deceased time-trippers have yielded little useful information for explaining this capacity. Several leading biophysicists have expressed a strong desire to make an in vivo study of the creature and have argued that doing so might well revolutionize star travel. But live capture—and retention of the specimen after capture—would seem to require finding a way to neutralize the very capacity the biophysicists wish to study.

—Enoch Fulmer, *A Star-Hopper's View of the Galaxy*

Nine

INEZ GAUTHIER

"Madam?" Elgar's eyes, framed by the egg-shaped holes in his pin-striped day-mask, blinked frantically. "That stock has been doing exceptionally well, and its prospects remain strong and bright. While P.A.T.... " Elgar shrugged. "Frankly, even with the new mining projects creating greater demand, anything to do with air transport is going to have problems in the long run."

"Don't argue with me, Elgar." Inez maintained a neutral tone of voice. "The proceeds from the sale of those holdings should at the very least purchase me a controlling interest in Pemberton." Elgar's eyes and mouth looked disgruntled rather than suspicious. Excellent. "And if you choose your time well, you might even be able to buy up most of Pemberton's stock—if, that is, you can get the current stockholders to sell." Inez tapped her finger on the screen she held in her lap. "But since an appreciation of timing is in the skill-set I'm paying you for, I'm sure you won't have any difficulty pulling it off."

Elgar sighed. "Very well, Madam, if you insist. But you will lose a substantial sum of SCUs on the deal." She was paying Elgar an enormous salary with a hefty annual hardship bonus for living on Frogmore. But he seemed to have a hard time remembering that he was getting paid to carry out her orders rather than to enlarge the Family fortune. It often seemed to her that he identified her interests so closely with his own that, emotionally anyway, the Family fortune seemed in some way to be *his* fortune. And since she seldom told him the reasons behind the orders she gave, those orders tended to make him anxious.

"Just *do* it, Elgar," she said. "Do it and forget about it and let *me* worry about the lost SCUs."

Elgar bowed. "I'll notify you when I've chosen my time and ask you then to confirm—"

"Don't bother," Inez said. "Simply notify me when you've finalized the arrangements so that I'll know exactly how much of Pemberton you managed to get for me."

Elgar bowed again, and she sent him away. She had already instructed her agent on Janniset to headhunt someone who would be able to manage the expansion she planned for Pemberton. The entire process of acquiring Pemberton and imposing a new direction on it should take no more than a local year, giving them ample time before the biologists would be ready to move on the Scourge, and in the meantime they could be given all Rosario Mining Limited's transport contracts, thereby justifying as well as paying for the expansion.

The reports looked good; they'd finally figured out the problem with the methods the planet's very first technical team had tried before the first settlers were brought in. CDS wouldn't take that kind of risk on an inhabited planet unless the odds against failure were negligible.

Inez sank into her hammock and reveled in a moment of euphoria. It wouldn't be long before this world's problems were cleared up. And then she and her father would be *gone*.

The instant she entered the room, not even waiting for her to take her place at the table, the general said, "Cleveland finally came up with that background report. I spent half the morning poring over it." His lips pursed. "I can tell you straight off I don't like the sound of it." He heaved a big sigh, one of the biggest yet of all the great sighs he had let loose over the last local month.

"Background report on what or whom?" his daughter asked as she settled into her chair.

The general glared at her. "On the dancer, of course. Who else would I be talking about?"

Inez removed her day-mask and laid it to one side of her place setting, taking care to position it exterior-side up. "What exactly is it you don't like the sound of?"

The general's breath puffed out, and his large hairy hand resting on the table near his water glass fisted. "There are any number of things that leave one with plenty to be disturbed about. For starters, I'd like to know exactly what that woman has been up to out in the Fidalgo Archipelago for the last four years!"

Inez spread her napkin in her lap and signaled the human supervising the mechanical servers to have the soup brought in. "Besides fulfilling her teaching obligation? Isn't it obvious?" The service door deopaqued, and the servers entered. "Surely you don't think it's possible to create that sort of art-form without devoting a great deal of time and effort to it? I imagine she's been working herself crazy. There's precious little else to do in such a backwater."

The server bearing the tray stood behind the general's chair as the other served the general. "Just where do you think the insurgents come from, Inez?"

She snatched a quick gulp of water before answering. So the general's frustration had taken a new turn. "What possible reason can you have for suspecting Solstice Balalzalar of being an insurgent? I've never before heard that simply living in the wilds was enough to cast suspicion on a native." A server set a frosty glass of soup before her.

The general lifted his glass to his lips and sipped, and his daughter did the same. Citrus, she noted, dominated the soup's creamy vegetable flavors. The cook, it seemed, was experimenting on them again. She expected her father to grumble about such adventurous fare, but apparently he wasn't noticing what he was consuming, for as soon as he had swallowed his first gulp he said, "What kind of idiot do you think I am?"

Inez stared with pointed inquisitiveness at him, for whenever he directed such exasperated rhetorical questions at her, she found it a struggle not to answer it seriously.

"Cleveland did such a thorough job he even sent off to Pleth to see what *they* had on her during her years at university."

Inez lifted her glass to take another sip. "And?" she queried before drinking.

"And," the general said, his fist near his soup glass again clenching, "it seems that she was involved with some pret-ty subversive characters while on Pleth. She has the profile of someone who can be expected to turn up as a troublemaker. As Cleveland himself noted at the end of the report."

Inez dabbed her napkin to her lips. "Perhaps I'd better take a look at it," she said.

The general harrumphed. "Yes," he said, "perhaps you should. Perhaps you should know what kind of person you are sponsoring."

She knew her father well enough to suspect that something in particular had so aggravated his frustration that he had embraced this interpretation solely to whip himself into anger against the dancer. She took another sip of soup. Perhaps it would be best if the general lost interest in Solstice Balalzalar. But would he? Or would his interest simply channel itself in another direction? And might not that direction interfere with Solstice Balalzalar's practice of her art? The general's daughter glanced at her father and wondered what had set him off. He had been fairly calm over the last local week, seemingly content to accept her management of the situation. Maybe now she could get him interested in someone else? But then she remembered. "I almost forgot to tell you," she said.

The general lifted his broody eyes from his soup to his daughter's face. "Tell me what?"

"I'm expecting Solstice to be at our event tonight."

The general's face paled. "Oh," he said. "I had no idea."

So he *was* still interested. "Just don't be all over her," she said. "Be as casual as you can. And I suggest you wear a design without eyepieces revealing your eyes so you don't have to worry about her catching you staring at her."

The general pushed away his half-full glass. "Is she going to dance?" he asked.

Inez decided she liked the soup. "No. I think it would be best to involve her socially with our kind of people. And she can't really do that if she's always performing at such functions." How else combat the dancer's indifference to them? Once she became a part of their social world, everything else would follow. No one—except perhaps Nathalie Stillness—who had become a part of their circle could resist any degree of intimacy either she or the general might offer.

"Can't we have the next course?" the general asked. "This soup is an abomination. The cook has obviously slid back into considering us lab animals here for him to test his filthy swill on."

What a pity. Inez would have liked to have introduced the new soup into their *cuisine ordinaire*.

En passant, the general's daughter overheard one of her guests remark to the knot he had just joined, "Inez is wearing diamonds on the toes of her shoes!"

"Diamonds!" another guest exclaimed. "On her shoes?"

"Diamonds," the man confirmed. "On the *toes* of her shoes."

Inez, gliding out of earshot, smiled. She had been hearing the same commentary all evening. It might be fun to order pairs and pairs of shoes, each with emeralds, rubies, opals, or topazes variously sewn onto their toes. The list of jewels could go on forever. Diamonds one night, garnets another, sapphires the third, zircons the fourth...always on the toes of her shoes.

Abandoning the canons of *politesse*, Inez grabbed Ainsley Hillith's arm. "It's wonderful you could come, Ainsley! I'm dying to introduce you to these *biologists* that arrived on the shuttle this morning—I knew they would be coming, only I simply didn't expect them so soon—but they've just pulled off the most *stunning* sort of work it's possible to imagine! I suppose in such instances biologists must feel like Supreme Artistes! Think of it, they've been seeding some basically disagreeable-to-humans world—not far from here, actually, which is why they arrived so much earlier than I'd expected—anyway, they've been seeding this planet with a variety of species, *all* of which they themselves created in their lab. Isn't that *fabulous*?"

"I can hardly wait to meet these Supreme Artistes," Ainsley said politely.

But hold on, Inez said to herself: Ainsley's reply might be facetious rather than polite, for while Inez had been speaking, her design hadn't responded *in the least*. Or had *Sense of Wonder* so sabotaged her sensory interface that she simply hadn't been attending to changes that had actually been transpiring in Ainsley's design all along? Inez noticed how tightly she was clutching Ainsley's arm and loosened her grip. "Ainsley, am I boring you?" she said, honestly curious.

Now Ainsley's design *did* shift into motion. "Inez, really! You ask the most embarrassing questions."

Inez sighed. "The trick is to not be embarrassed under any circumstances, Ainsley. That's the trick of living in society."

"You know me," Ainsley said. "I'd rather *not* live in society."

"Maybe at heart you're a recluse. But you wouldn't be able to produce the kind of art you do if you actually *were* a recluse. Which is why you need me to drag you out of your workspace into the world." Anyway, Ainsley *did* like moving in the best circles (as she had done back on Janniset). She only pretended to be a hermit for her artistic persona.

Ainsley sighed. "All right, Inez. Lead on to these power-freaks."

"Maybe I should find another vial of *Sense of Wonder* to properly prepare you for the introduction," Inez said. "Your enthusiasm is overwhelming me."

"Oh," Ainsley said with that infuriatingly knowing inflection. "That explains everything. How long ago did you sniff that garbage, anyway?"

"Ainsley, Ainsley, your ascetic streak drives me *wild!*" Ainsley claimed never to inhale anything even mildly psychotropic. But how else, wondered the general's daughter, could she have gotten her father into a decent mood but to share a vial of something really powerful with him?

"You can hardly call me ascetic, Inez. It's a matter of discipline. Of keeping my head clear. I intend to work tomorrow morning, not spend a couple of days off my stride because I craved the short-lived wackiness an inhalant like *Sense of Wonder* can give one."

"Oh don't remind me," Inez moaned. Pulling Ainsley farther into the room and aiming straight for one of the biologists' knots, Inez brightened. She could introduce Ainsley to Solstice. Solstice would have heard of Ainsley and would probably like her. They both had that remote aspect to their personalities, so perhaps they might understand one another. Unless Solstice would find the biologists interesting? But given Ainsley's attitude (reminding Inez that often the practitioners of art and science did not mix), this seemed doubtful.

❧

"I've sent out the announcement," Inez said into Nathalie Stillness's ear. "Let's go in now ourselves."

"You mean the announcement of the performance in ten minutes?" Nathalie asked, lurching along so jerkily, it seemed to Inez, that she spoiled the swan's glide Inez had programmed herself to move in.

They crossed the threshold into hazy reddish light swirling with wisps of near-cloud. The performance to come had taken them nearly two days to set up.

"Those things you're wearing?" Nathalie queried. "Are they—"

"Diamonds," Inez interrupted, for she had begun to tire of the comment.

"Diamonds?" Nathalie repeated, sounding puzzled. "What diamonds? Aren't they...*feathers*?"

Inez released long silvery peals of laughter. "Yes, yes, I'm wearing feathers, Nathalie!" she cried between spasms. "So do you like my feathers? Actually, it's a blend of angora and feathers. And it's so, so sensual, Nathalie. And soft, soft, all over my body." Over cling-ons, of course. She touched her free hand to her breast and stroked the soft downy feathers. Leave it to Nathalie to ignore the diamonds and zoom in on the feathers. But that's why the woman was an anthropologist. Her powers of observation far surpassed those of that fool Cleveland.

Shapely shoulders were not everything.

All the Frogmorians would be purchasing feathers. *They* could not run to gems on their shoes, but they'd be thrilled to spend their last SCU on frippery like angora and feathers. Consider the instance of the time-tripper pelt—they had ignored what had been outside their means to emulate. Cheap imitations would be tacky, and one had to give them credit for so thoroughly comprehending that. Yes, Nathalie had an astute eye, Inez thought in a burst of affection, sliding her hand up Nathalie's cling-on covered arm to curve around the anthropologist's shoulder.

The floor seemed to tilt. Walls sprang up before and to one side and behind them, leaving them only one direction in which to move through the smoky red atmosphere.

Nathalie moaned. "Why didn't you *warn* me you put psychotropic junk in the air in here! You know I don't do drugs! And I left my respirator with my cape!"

The walls fell away from them. "Holos," Inez said. "No drugs."

"But I'm dizzy!"

It was their view of the room, not anyone's head, that was spinning. And the floor rumbled, as though at any second it would collapse and the underworld swallow them up. Deep musical tones too slow to hear but so powerful they thrummed through one's body, making the floor shake and rumble, tickled the bottoms of Inez's feet, penetrating the soles of her shoes. "I'm glad," she said to Nathalie, "that it's the room and not me. For a few seconds there I was worried! Tingling ears can mean any number of things." It occurred to her, though, that some of the effects might be interacting with *Sense of Wonder* and that what she and Nathalie were each experiencing might be different. For a few seconds she regretted not having a clear head. "This is their first performance since arriving on planet," she said.

"I *hate* this kind of thing!" Nathalie wailed. Her design pulsed a pattern in dark scarlet and surly purple-tinged black.

If only Nathalie knew how well her design matched the atmosphere of the room. But, Inez reflected further, it wouldn't matter if she did. Nathalie simply didn't appreciate the finer pleasures of life. Or *any* pleasures of life, for that matter. "Nathalie," she said, shaking a chiding finger at the anthropologist. "If you'd simply let go now and then and allow yourself some pleasure, you might be surprised at the beneficial effects on your overall existence. Instead of robbing your work, it would *enhance* it. Why—"

"Stop preaching at me, Inez." Nathalie sounded cross. "You know I don't like this kind of thing. In fact, I don't like parties in general, but—"

"Okay, okay, " Inez said hastily. Every time Nathalie came to a party, her hand had to be held, she had to be taken personally to someone she might like talking to, because if she weren't, she simply wouldn't come again. Period. Nathalie was worse than Ainsley Hillith that way. So why did she even *bother* with Nathalie? She was too intoxicated to remember, but there was a reason there somewhere.

"Where are we supposed to sit?" Nathalie asked. "I don't see any bolsters, and the floor's behaving so weirdly that it's not at all clear it's even safe to sit on."

"The lights produce that effect, dear," Inez said, almost absently. For an idea had occurred to her: she would fix up Nathalie with one of the new biologists! The biologists were of course suffering the torments of the void trying to adjust to the gravity after having lived almost constantly in near free-fall for who knew how many standard years. And from what they had said (and one of them had slyly hinted his interest in seeking partners), they had been living in a group with less than fifty individuals (all biologists and engineers) for several standard years. The prospect of living for a time on a world populated by millions of humans both excited and disturbed them. One woman had confessed she didn't know how she was going to manage so much "stranger-contact." As for Nathalie ∼ part of her problem, Inez believed, was rooted in the sexual abstinence she had practiced since her arrival on Frogmore ∼ what could be better than a good varietal round of partnering? It would stir her blood and cut through the physical sluggishness she was always complaining about.

Inez caught a faint tinkle of bells and wondered if it had been in the background all along. Her eyes seemed to be perceiving more, too, for she suddenly saw that the room held dozens of people through which thin veils of transparent wall—another holo effect, she assumed—cut in crazy zigzag patterns, sometimes right through whole persons.

"So it's going to be one of *those* kinds of things," Nathalie grumbled.

"What fun," Inez said. "I haven't been to such an atmosphere-manipulative event since my last trip to Janniset. It's like getting a heady whiff of civilization!" The ceiling zoomed down on them; the floor thickened into a dense black morass; the red fog cleared to reveal stark chrome and white walls, and the vibrations and tinkling of bells ceased so abruptly that the air felt strange on her face and like a rushing torrent in her ears. The harsh white glare raining down on them from the lowered ceiling ~ Inez imagined she would be able to touch the ceiling if only she could lift her arm above her head ~ revealed people crowded all around them. Looking at those nearest her, she saw, in the harsh glare, the edges of their designs, the inevitable result of lack of specialized skill that usually passed unnoticed in the softer lighting used in most evening settings.

When an abrupt dislocation threatened to knock her to the floor, she threw her arms out in her struggle to keep her balance. The drug? she wondered uneasily until she saw others doing the same. She opened her mouth to speak to Nathalie, only to gasp for breath, burdened with a sense of immense gravity and an odd pressure in her ears pressing inexorably against her body. All around her people collapsed to the floor, first to their knees, then sprawling in untidy horizontal messes. Inez, too, succumbed, toppling onto Nathalie, who groaned at the additional weight of Inez's legs on her own.

The room, still pressured, blacked-out without warning.

Seconds later, illumined by lights shifting through a range of shades of green, a vivid scene appeared, floating above them. Simultaneously the air thrummed with a rhythmic thumping Inez identified as a simulated heartbeat. Lying on her back ~ Inez knew Nathalie to be lying beside her only because her own arm barely touched a bit of cling-on-encased flesh she knew must belong to the anthropologist ~ she stared up at the tableau of figures (wearing only cheap, nickel-threaded cling-ons) loosely shackled to one another, the large looped chains connecting them an electric shade of green in sharp contrast to the subdued light suffusing the figures. After a few seconds she saw that the chains themselves were pulsing with light in synch with the heartbeat, a thudding that increased in volume, filling the inside of her head and beating through the floor as well as in the air above and surrounding her. Mesmerized by the pulsing of the chains, she noticed that two of the figures had put their backs to the others, entangling themselves in the chains—now pulled taut between themselves and the others in the group—wrapped around their waists, while two others had begun physically struggling with one another—to what end, she had no clear idea, for they seemed to be struggling to get their own bodies to work against the gravity pinning everyone outside the tableau to the floor—each toiling to direct aggressive gestures at the other.

Watching their struggle made Inez's arms ache and so enervated her that she could not imagine ever being able to scrape her body off the floor to stand and walk. After what seemed an interminable time, the two who were struggling sank to their knees, then slowly collapsed into a crumpled heap—all the while they continued assaulting one another. Inez had to will each breath before taking it, so effortful had even her passive, sprawling state become. The heartbeats, she realized. The heartbeats had gotten faster and heavier. Perhaps that explained why she felt her own heart's effort to have become superhuman, almost beyond what little strength remained in her body.

Something, a movement or shift in the lighting, made her look away from the struggling, barely moving mass the aggressive pair had become and see that the fifth and sixth figures were involved in an elaborate form of partnering—or rather, a miming of partnering in the same way the other pair were miming aggression. This miming left her cold, almost literally chilled; her reaction intensified when two perfect crystalline tones faded in, swelling into a sound of unutterable sublimity, so powerful that it resonated in every cell of her body, just as the heartbeat around them had become her own heartbeat. Tears started in her eyes and spilled over her cheeks, where, trapped under the design, they rendered her uncomfortably aware of both the design's presence and the discomfort of salty moisture on her face. The sound—two tones formed into one split sound—bore a terrible gaping hollow within, a windy chasm that for its duration cast her onto a desolate ice-rimed plane of windswept barren rock with a slate sky that vaulted impossibly high, an infinity speaking of the void one knew existed but could never perceive with one's senses.

Riven by that hollow beauty, Inez longed to tear the design from her face. But she lacked the strength of will to lift her hand even as far as her neck. She blinked through tears and saw then how the partnering had become so much a captive of its chains that one of the figures seemed to be strangling in their pulsing squeezing suffocating grip as its body arched for breath—while its partner continued as before, oblivious to the other's death throes. Inez understood death to have come when the green of the figure shaded almost into black while the chains twisted around its neck shimmered ever more brightly, as though feeding on the death. The partner froze, then launched itself onto the dead body. The force of its movement in turn yanked the aggressive pair closer and pulled the two isolated figures—still standing—backwards, crashing down onto the others.

For a long moment the pile of bodies writhed. The exquisite sound faded as though the wind soughing through the central hollow, shooting through the axis of a perfect cylinder of ice, had begun to lull, then die into absolute stillness— while the heartbeat sped faster and faster as it grew fainter and less perceptible to the ear. Finally, the lighting dimmed to a muted yellowish green, leaving only the chains clearly visible, the pile of bodies distinguishable only sporadically as a limb momentarily separated itself from the mass of parts.

A sickly horror seeped into Inez, a horror so suffocating it seemed to cling to her skin like the unclean film of unimaginably vile sludge and filth.

Without warning, the tableau vanished, and the room shifted back into its original foggy red state. The walls and floors slid and whirled, but she hardly minded when (after a period of shock during which neither she nor anyone around her stirred) she found she could move her arms and legs and realized that her breath now came without hindrance and her heart was beating without that terrible wrenching strain that had made her doubt she would survive the event.

"I have to get out of here, Inez," Nathalie said as she and Inez struggled to their feet. "I'm afraid I'm going to be ill."

"Shall I call an attendant for you?" Inez asked with alarm. The idea of anyone being sick in public made her own stomach queasy.

"No, no," Nathalie said, "I'll be all right once I—"

"Inez!" a male voice Inez recognized called from a few yards away. "Hey, that was *fabulous*, Inez! Absolutely first-rate!"

"Don't look at him," she said into Nathalie's ear. "Cut him dead. He's got some gall. I thought I told Deaver to prune him from the lists." It infuriated her that this native would be so brash as to barge in on her privacy without invitation, as though she were just anyone. She recalled now how it had been clear even at the time that his only reason for partnering her had been his eagerness to call her Inez. To spread the word that *he* had partnered *Inez*. Hah. He'd been such a boor that if she hadn't been so experienced it would have put her off partnering with men forever. At least she hadn't removed her design for him. He'd never be among the few to whom she had given knowledge of her face.

"I don't mean to be monopolizing you," Nathalie said. "This kind of thing just isn't my scene. It's not like our sitting somewhere quiet and chatting. I mean, this is your party, and all these people—" She waved a hand. "I've gotta go," she concluded. "The sooner the better."

"I'd much rather be off in a corner somewhere discussing the work of Alexandra Jador of Pleth with you." Inez could not seem to shake the chagrin that little creep had made her feel. *I must remember to tell Deaver, to make it explicit I don't want that man crossing our threshold again under any circumstances.*

Nathalie said, "That sounds lovely, Inez, but I don't know anything about Jador's work. I'm an anthropologist, not a philosopher."

"Nonsense, you're too modest," Inez said. And in the expansive moment of expressing the largeness of her generosity of spirit, she felt the poisonous dart fall harmlessly to her feet.

"In any case, I do think I should go." Nathalie gestured toward the threshold, visible now that the red fog had begun to disperse.

Inez felt unutterably weary. And bored. Yes, she hated to admit it, she was bored at her own party. "I can't blame you for deserting me. I have to agree that these events are a terrible bore." She linked arms with Nathalie, and they began moving toward the door. Most of the people who had come into the room for the performance (including the boor) had already gone.

"Oh come on, I'm sure you enjoy your own parties," Nathalie said. "You seemed to be having a good time when we connected a little while back."

"You mean I'm intoxicated," Inez said. "The sad fact is, it's necessary to get up before these events so that I can even bring myself to make an appearance. You have no idea, Nathalie, what it's—"

She stopped short at the sight of Solstice Balalzalar sitting on the floor, her back propped against the wall only a couple of yards from the threshold into the next room. Solstice sat alone—without Lieutenant Fortunato, whom Inez had assigned to assist her since the dancer, having only the wrist implant, would otherwise have no way of connecting—with a starkly naked face. The only other persons at this party not wearing *something* on their faces were the general's officers. What could possibly have possessed Solstice to behave so?

"Oh, look," Nathalie whispered. "That woman over there is going naked-faced. Is that what you're staring at, Inez? Who is it, do you know? I can't seem to read an ID."

"Look, Nathalie, I'm going to have to abandon you now. You understand, don't you? There's obviously some kind of problem here—"

"As I was saying before," Nathalie said. "I'm ready to leave. I—"

"We'll meet sometime next week then," Inez said, not taking her eyes off Solstice, who seemed oblivious to the two of them loitering not far from her. She squeezed Nathalie's hand. "Have a safe trip home," she said. Nathalie said something in return about the party and then moved to the threshold.

Inez drew a deep breath ~ she wished she could clear the drug out of her system instantly ~ and walked over to where the dancer sat. "Solstice," she said, staring down at the dancer. She searched for an opening as she realized it would be awkward to start off by demanding the dancer's reason for dispensing with her mask. "What happened to Fortunato?" she asked instead.

The dancer looked up. "Inez? That *is* you?"

"Yes, it's me."

"I sent him away." Her dark eyes glittered. Inez wondered what inhalant the dancer had chosen to ingest. "I mean, what's the point of having someone like that glued to one's side?" She shrugged. "So I ditched him once he told me about the performance."

"You saw it?"

"I saw it." She lifted her day-mask from the floor. At least, Inez thought, she hadn't ditched the day-mask, too. "Very clever, but a little cheap, I think."

The thought of how many SCUs that performance had cost her distracted her. "Cheap? What do you mean?"

The dancer got to her feet. The long, belted tunic she wore looked strange on the dancer's body: as though she weren't used to wearing clothing. "Cheap because it extorted a calculated emotional response from the audience. I don't like that kind of manipulation. It worries me. And sometimes it bores me." The dancer frowned. "I realize this isn't polite, but I don't think I can hold this kind of conversation when I can't see the other person's face." She half-laughed. "I guess this isn't the kind of setting in which one tries to hold conversations, though."

Inez bit her lip. Obviously merely drawing the dancer into their social circle would not be the solution. "I don't think you're giving it much of a chance," she said. "As a matter of fact, people do have real conversations at these affairs, but it's a question of knowing who is likely to be having them and connecting with them." She refrained from pointing out how the dancer's stubbornness about the wrist implant put her outside ordinary channels. "Which is what I hoped Lieutenant Fortunato would be able to help you do." She had told

Fortunato to introduce the dancer to Ainsley and all the other artists and performers present.

"I don't fit." The dancer had given "not fitting in" as a reason for declining all previous invitations.

"You aren't used to us yet," Inez said. Some of her anxiety lifted when Solstice lifted the day-mask to her face and attached it to her cap.

"I like your feathers," Solstice said. "They look wonderfully soft and light, as though they're floating just above the surface of your body, so unlike the way they grow in real life." The dancer's hands dropped from her mask.

"Touch if you like," Inez said as she suppressed a shudder of horror at the day-mask. The mask's glossy black surface was absolutely smooth except for holes for the eyes, nostrils, and mouth.

Solstice leaned forward and touched the feathers covering Inez's thigh. "Lovely," she said, her raspy voice low and soft. "You're attracted to the natural coverings of other living creatures."

"Oh," Inez said, remembering the time-tripper pelt she had been wearing the first time she had seen the dancer. "Yes, I suppose I am. Furs, feathers, pelts..."

"Just imagine," the dancer said, stroking the long silky feathers, "another species liking to wear *our* natural covering. Human hair and skin. I wonder how we'd feel were we to encounter such a species and then see them take up the habit."

"What a horrible thought!" Inez shuddered. "None of the alien species we've discovered—" She broke off as a particularly gruesome image of a giant bird dressed in a human pelt came into her mind. *Sense of Wonder*, she reminded herself. It's *Sense of Wonder* doing this to me. Uneasily aware of that shiny black mask throwing back a reflective flash at her, probably from her own design, she forced a laugh. "But I *do* see your point, Solstice. So you're a protectionist?"

Inez tried to remember exactly which political types Cleveland had reported the dancer to have been involved with during her years on Pleth. But staring at that shiny blank surface, only that one particular fact—the one that had the general so upset—came into her mind, conjuring up images of the dancer caught in the ugly embrace of a half-human creature. A chitinous carapace covered the backs of many natives—it was not outside the realm of probability that one covered Sadora Lumni's back, too. How could the dancer—so obviously moved by beauty, so tremendously moved that she had had to *invent* a dance-form for a world so physically inimical to dance—how *could* she be *that* attached to a native? Or was she? Perhaps Cleveland's people had misunderstood.

"Inez," the general's voice said into his daughter's ear. Always interrupting, always coming up from behind...

"Deaver tells me the governor's number-two is about to depart and says you aren't taking messages, so he came to me." The general cleared his throat; his daughter surmised from his pause that he had just seen the black day-mask. "Off by yourself again, you're the only one left in this room—except...who *is* it you're talking to? I can't make out an ID."

Something about the way he'd been staring at the dancer made her suspect that he knew exactly who it was behind the mask. She shifted to include her father in their grouping. "This is Solstice Balalzalar," she said, knowing she ought to be able to think of a way to throw the two of them together. Everything felt out of control; she knew the drug must be impairing her, for she felt a bit wild, as though parts of her might begin flying off on random tangents and she might say anything that popped into her head, however false or whimsical or indiscreet. Usually she didn't have this bent a reaction to *Sense of Wonder*. "I think I mentioned to you she has a band implant in her wrist? Solstice, you remember the general, I think." She had meant to sound dry, but cringed at the sarcasm she heard oozing out of her voice. *Look at those shoulders, Solstice. Can you pass up shoulders like that?* But the thought of Sadora Lumni again came into her head, supplanting the joke, making her skin crawl at the thought of someone like the dancer being intimate with such grotesquerie.

"Oh," the general said. "I had no idea." His voice had gone hoarse, and Inez saw that behind his royal blue eyepieces his eyes were riveted on the dancer's mask in manifest fascination. *How can he stomach looking at that mask?* "I'm so pleased you've come, Madam." He bowed deeply. "I hope Inez has made you welcome? Is there anything we can get you?"

The dancer bowed slightly in return. "General," she said.

After an awkward pause in which he waited—in vain—for more from her, he said, "Forgive me for interrupting, Madam, but this will only take a minute. Inez," he said, turning to his daughter. "You can't let the governor's number-two go without speaking to him at least once. He specifically remarked to me that he hadn't seen you all evening." His fingers dug into her shoulder, perhaps with the frustration he must be feeling over his lack of traction with the dancer, crushing her lovely feathers. "I gather hardly anyone has."

Why must they expect this of her? It should be enough that she gave them stimulating entertainment and one another's society. Inez unloosed a martyr's sigh. "Very well. I'll seek him out and say all the proper things before he goes." She had just had a business meeting with him three local days ago. It wasn't as though she hadn't seen him in months. But the natives had their little hang-ups, didn't they. "Solstice, you could of course come along," Inez said. Most artists would recognize an opportunity when offered one and would seize it with both hands. She already knew enough of Solstice Balalzalar, though, to know she would decline the invitation. "Or you might join my father and me for a nightcap. Truly, I'll only be a couple of minutes."

"Thank you," the dancer said, making another bow, aimed this time at both of them, "but if I'm to make my usual start in the morning, I'd better be going."

"Must you really?" the general said.

"I must, really," Solstice said.

"I would be the last person to quarrel with such discipline. I honor you for it, Madam." He bowed. "I hope, though, that you'll allow me to escort you to the antechamber?"

The dancer bowed again, and the general's daughter held her breath. Would Solstice be rude to him? But the dancer extended her arm to the general for him to take—an unlooked for grace that surprised Inez—and murmured, "You're most polite, general."

As the three of them left the performance chamber—now lit by plain yellow light that revealed the clear plasteel platform hanging from the ceiling—Inez wondered whether Solstice had meant her words to be sarcastic. They had sounded merely dry. But then the dancer had a gift for subtlety and understatement, even when being rude—which, in Inez's judgment, was most of the time.

Ask just about anyone who's never actually been to Frogmore to describe their impression of it, and they'll likely say that all the people there wear respirators attached to small canisters of oxygen strapped to their bodies and skin-tight patterned fabric over all of their skin except their faces and walk around in a dense, stinky fog. Oh, and that they sniff drugs all day and party a lot, to forget the horror of being there. The reality, of course, is something else. I suppose the reason for such impressions has to do with the lack of available views of landscape on Frogmore. The most one can ever see is a fragment of a view, which one gets when the Scourge is on the thin side or the wind is strong and capricious. The holodramas purporting to show Frogmorians on Frogmore are all set indoors, showing beautiful bodies in revealing cling-ons lounging languidly in recliners, massage couches, and hammocks, sniffing vials, and having hot, languid sex.

Yes, people who live in the Capitol District all wear cling-ons. They're essential for living a relatively normal existence. But one's choices for having sex on Frogmore are somewhat limited, unless you're in superb physical condition—or wear cling-ons during sex. (Needless to say, all cling-ons are made with easily openable and sealable slits to accommodate necessary bodily functions.) But skin contact tends to be an important part of the experience, depending on one's sexual psyche, and so many people find sex while wearing them less than satisfactory. What many people do, though, is take the shuttle up to either Holliday or Pittikin, the planet's two largest and most stable moons. Holliday teems with resorts offering cheap one- or two-night package deals, and that is where most Frogmorians go to have sex. Pittikin is more up-scale and has super-tight security (requiring screening a week in advance) and is home to most of the planet's health-care facilities.

On advanced worlds it's almost impossible to guess any person's age, provided they're past thirty standard years, even when their face is not masked. Frogmore's gravity, however, levels a fine on the faces of long-time residents of Frogmore; granted, Frogmorians, excepting military personnel, go decently masked, thus sparing everyone the sight of the damage. But the gravity also tempts long-term residents into poor posture, which also, over the years, leaves its mark on bodies. Beauty, on Frogmore, is, with few exceptions, only for the young.

— Enoch Fulmer, *A Star-Hopper's View of the Galaxy*

Ten

NATHALIE STILLNESS

Personal Journal Entry. Insert time and dates, standard and local. Append: I woke this morning with a head full of irony. Inez's parties generally provoke intricate, melancholy theories of decline, degeneration, decadence. Last night's, though, offered an apotheosis of the genre. *Shell. Mark text here for later query: "apotheosis" or "exemplar"? Append:* Again I recall Alsiedre Chavez's remarks more than a standard millennium ago, delivered as she set forth on anthropology's first transgalactic mission, reprinted as the introduction to her foundational text, *Anthropology in the Galactic Age,* from which I quote here to refresh my memory: "We will in all likelihood come full circle one day, probably not in my lifetime. But regardless of whether anthropology will again claim the privilege of studying a virgin indigenous population, our discipline will rediscover its previous state of purity." Of course Chavez used the signifier *purity* with more than a little irony. "Perhaps the day will come when the notion of applied (or, as some of my colleagues have it, *creative*) anthropology will seem quaint, or (more likely) a lower yet necessary function of those in the discipline lacking the brilliance required for the theoretical work without which past anthropological studies would have been nothing more than anecdotal collections of quaint ethnographies, myths, and customs. The resurgence of anthropology as a legitimate scholarly discipline will depend largely upon the extent to which the human drive to populate other worlds manifests itself. However swift and easy transgalactic travel might become, worlds will nevertheless remain units in isolation from one another. Therefore, although all such worlds (unless intelligent alien species are discovered) would be inhabited by humans sharing a common stock and cultural background, the enforced singularity of individual worlds will undoubtedly produce a heterogeneity such that anthropologists will again have alien (and possibly primitive—for we have no idea what effect to expect following separation from the father-culture in primitive rugged settlers' circumstances) cultures to study. This cycle may take millennia to achieve, but I am convinced it will occur if humans continue to explore and colonize space. That applied or 'creative' anthropologists themselves may exercise influence on how such new cultures develop is simply an irony our descendants will appreciate as they begin excavating these neo-primitive cultures."

I think I can construct a compelling case for including not only the Frogmore elites, bureaucracy, & business sectors in my study of the Frogmore primitives, but off-world culture as well. They impinge upon one another strangely but intricately. I originally intended to avoid any consideration of the elites in this study. But now that I've realized that all Frogmorians are inherently distinct from other humans, it's become clear that the "primitives" can't be considered in isolation. Unlike many off-worlders, Frogmore elites maintain close contact with their children (and in many cases personally raise them), children who are born with the adaptations that so markedly differentiate them from all adult elites as well as off-worlders. Only when the elite children go off to Pleth does their difference become strictly internal. However discontinuous consciousness may be, however continuously reconstructed memory may be, each elite adult carries consciousness of that difference within—a consciousness that obviously must become acute when interacting with their children. The repeated warning to keep my perspective "politically neutral" rings in my ears—but surely any consideration of the mixing of the elites with the primitives and the sharp conscious contrasts between them must drag the political into my study. How else see Frogmore as a complex whole?

The off-world people (specifically the Gauthier contingent) exercise an enormous effect not only on the Frogmore elites but also on the day-to-day existence of the people I originally determined to study. If, then, I need include that influence in any account I make of the Frogmore primitives' social organization, it hardly seems fair to omit consideration of influences—if any—in the other direction.

Until last night this line of speculation waxed nebulous & inchoate. *What* influence on the Frogmore elites? I have very little contact with them at all, & that which I do have has always taken place within the social contexts set up by the Gauthier contingent. Now I glimpse some dim glimmer that I want to pursue. Unfortunately last night I was in no fit state to do so: I lost my observational stance, as sometimes happens in Gauthier-produced social settings. Perhaps I should be both general (at the risk of vagueness, but in order not to get bogged down too greatly in detail) & specific (in order not to be swallowed by the vagueness I've found such a hindrance in thinking about this area of the work).

Any discussion of this nature must, alas, start with Inez Gauthier. She is my key & to a large extent (because it is through occasions constructed by her that I have a chance to make any observations in this area at all) determines the parameters of this discussion. I say "alas" because Inez is singular, & her position within the planet's social organizational texture prominent, not to mention the more obscure areas of her input into the world's economic & political affairs, an input she veils from view & that one less acute than I would not begin to guess at, for she consciously cultivates an image of being frivolous—though her ambivalence at allowing this image to stand sometimes provokes surprising slips—& of her only "serious" interests being "high culture"—namely, the arts: her "passion" in life, which (she constantly informs one & all) motivates her every waking moment & "compels" her to "bring Frogmore into the light of civilization" through a wide-flung promotion of "high culture."

For an example in which this "cultural" influence she exerts carries with it obvious economic consequences, cf the instance in which she deliberately introduced the fashion of variously decorated & cut wrist-ribbons. When I asked her how the Frogmore elites had been able to adopt this particular fashion in imitation of *her* having adopted it (i.e., explicitly asking her how they had gotten hold of such items), Inez obliquely let fall that she "had known" an entire shipment of such wrist-ribbons had come in with her own & that certain retailers had them in stock, whereupon the elites' requests for these items at Frogmore's most fashionable shops, such requests had of course been met. Needless to say, I took this to mean that Inez herself had planned well in advance of her actual adoption of the wristbands for this particular fashion to take hold—& had probably profited financially from it.

As for the indirect influences she exerts through her relationship with the general: who can say? The nature of their relationship has always been unclear to me, though the fact that she remains on a planet she insists she loathes simply because she "can't" leave on her father's account suggests depths her rather flippant attitude toward him camouflages. It would perhaps be more useful to have a more representative person assuming such a critical role in my understanding, but my lack of access to the elites makes this, for now at least, infeasible. Therefore, I must constantly remind myself of the need to take Inez's singularity into account whenever I extrapolate, & also of the skewed perspective I must necessarily start from in this area of the study. (I seem to have admitted here that this will, indeed, form a part of my study: but I imagine my committee might have something to say to *that*. Therefore I must be careful to keep some sort of separation so that the entire study itself need not be blighted should the committee insist on my excising all references to non-native persons from the finished published work.)

It's important to note that Inez adopts an arch, playful (perhaps "cynical" might be an appropriate adjective?) attitude toward this influence on the elites. When I first began talking to her, she brought up a patent instance of this influence that occurred shortly after her arrival here. General Gauthier & the peacekeeping forces had already been here for several local years & had become well-entrenched & thoroughly accepted by the Frogmore elites, who have learned to think of the general as their insurance policy for keeping things the way they like them. Thus any resistance Inez might have met from the elites would have been due to circumstances other than resentment of who she is. Apparently as a joke (she confided in me that when she arrived the planet horrified her, she considered the elites primitive, all affective ties she had remained behind, & that she had perpetrated her joke as an amusement for her correspondents back on Pleth & Janniset & Evergreen—&, I suspect, for her father), Inez told the elites she met that dueling was the latest fashion on Janniset. The elites took her seriously & adopted the fashion as their own. Even after they discovered Inez had been punking them, they continued this fashion, & now there are places where one can go to carouse & engage in (or watch) it. [Cf my personal journal entry six local months ago when Inez took me to a place called Mongo's. On this occasion Inez was asked to judge a contest but decorously declined the honor.]

She has introduced a variety of customs & fashions, sometimes things she has herself invented, sometimes things she has brought back with her from her short trips off-world. The Frogmore elites almost invariably copy her. She frequently mocks their customs & mores, & when one of her innovations passes an invisible boundary of what they will tolerate, they simply ignore it. It's my opinion that Inez consciously pushes at that boundary, not merely because she so despises Frogmore culture, but perhaps because she is frustrated when they choose to ignore rather than confront her. She once described Frogmore culture & mores as "a phantom impossible to grasp." But she fails to distinguish between the Frogmore I've been working on and the elites' Frogmore. *Her* distinction has largely been whether or not the Frogmore individual has shed the exoskeletal adaptations. If they have, they are elite & attempting (mostly unsuccessfully & gauchely) to imitate civilized manners. If they haven't, they are too benighted even to recognize civilization when they see its products. [Cf Inez's response to Frogmorian childbearing customs & the matrifocality widespread (even among most elites) throughout the planet.]

But let me pursue an incident that called itself to my attention last night. We had just finished experiencing a highly manipulative performance piece, the sort of thing that leaves one limp as a dishrag & hating one's society, culture, & self. Inez is occasionally attracted to nihilism, so I can't say I was exactly surprised to see such a performance at the C's Residence. We were on our way out of the room back to the main salons when someone rudely & familiarly called out to Inez from a distance. This made Inez furious, & she ignored it. But something about the incident got me to thinking about a certain sort of feedback. I've been mainly talking about Inez's influence on Frogmore elites. But it obviously works the other way too. When I first met Inez, I was put off by certain attitudes she displayed. But I began to realize that some of those attitudes had to do with the very things she criticizes the Frogmore elites for—their extreme hierarchicalism, for instance, & the formality that goes with it. Well, she herself has adopted some of those attitudes (& living in the bosom of the military surely doesn't help, either). In advanced societies where everyone is connected, it's unthinkable to invade another individual's privacy. One sends out a tendril & only approaches on receiving a positive response. But on Frogmore the entire thing is perverted, at least among the Gauthier contingent (& I imagine also among the elites Inez knows, who make up the bulk of those natives who are connected). Instead of applying the privacy rule universally, Inez uses it in tandem with the hierarchical attitude as a method of keeping her distance—that is, *peers* (among the elites) approach one another at will (without invitation or sending out tendrils), with the privacy barrier working in favor of superiors. Hence at her parties, very few people can approach Inez without committing a social solecism. Whereas *she* may approach whomever she likes. & so this works downward.

Inez seems unaware that she's adopted some of their values. But it's clear a feedback loop (an unequal one at that) is at work here. I wonder how she would adjust to ordinary advanced society? I rather think she's forgotten what the social conventions are. As for the stunts she uses to distinguish herself from the Frogmore elites (last night she wore shoes with diamonds sewn onto the toes), such things would probably be ridiculed by members of any advanced society, just as the insistence on titles & formalities & other manifestations of hierarchy would be found gauche & second-rate.

Now, as to the other incident, the one which I think is probably causing Inez some dissonance (& therefore discomfort). Let me preface my discussion of it by saying that it took place after the performance, at the outset of which, due to the bizarre spatial, visual, & audio manipulations worked upon the audience, I had sensations of hallucination & disorientation similar to those produced by psychoactive stimulants. My first suspicion was that inhalants had been released into the air—such an extravagant & expensive & decadent gesture not being beyond Inez's means, either financial or ethical. But Inez assured me not drugs but lighting & sound effects plus a brief neutralization of the mag slab's force in that room were responsible for the effects. Then followed the

depressing, sleazy, nihilist piece, after which that man ver-
bally accosted Inez. A few seconds later, as we approached the
threshold to one of the adjoining salons, I spotted a woman
sitting on the floor against the wall (yes, the *wall*. It didn't
bother her in the least that it was an electronic barrier she
had propped herself against) with a totally bare face. Up until this point I'd seen very few naked faces at the party, all of
which belonged to military officers. For some reason their
faces never look *naked* the way civilians' do without masks or
dress-designs. This woman was clearly a civilian.

One part of me felt queasy at seeing that naked face. But
another part of me felt an incredible relief, as though I were
looking at something fresh, positive, sane. I can hardly describe it, but I realize now that it had something to do with
having just been dunked in the worst sort of slop civilization
is capable of producing—not to mention the rawness of that
unpleasant encounter between Inez & the man she refused to
recognize. & so we come upon this woman sitting on the floor
with her face bare—*& no ID broadcast!* My first thought was
that she was a native, & not elite. But then, looking at her, I
realized she had no exoskeletal adaptations that I could make
out (though since, unlike the less confident of the elites who
feel the need to display their backs & other areas often heavily marked by the adaptations, she wore clothing that concealed all of her back—which I wouldn't have been able to
see anyway, since she was seated against the wall—as well as
her arms & neck & shoulders. But I could see that her legs
were smoothly muscled under the plain nickel cling-ons she
wore). Inez didn't take her eyes off this woman for a second.
She didn't even look at me as she essentially dismissed me.
Since I'd already been saying I had to leave, I could think
of no reason for hanging around. Transfixed: yes, that's the
word. The barefaced woman had her transfixed.

For now, I can only speculate (but I hope on my next
meeting with Inez to get a bit more data from which to

work). My guess is that this woman is not an elite & so not the type of Frogmore native Inez is used to. She wore her naked face too easily, for one thing. Who else could carry that off (besides military officers)? Elites are too worried about the question of their civilization & sophistication. They'd *never* go naked-faced except in some extraordinary situation, which this clearly was not (given the woman's remarkable self-possession). I don't see off-world types doing this, either, though it's possible—since, after all, I detected no sign of exoskeletal adaptations. But I think it unlikely (unless there's some mystery that justified her concealing her ID, but in that case why go bare-faced?). Therefore I must conclude that this woman was of Frogmore's directed classes. Question one: How did she shed her exoskeletal adaptations? Question two: How did Inez come to invite her to a party? Question three: What could Inez possibly make of such a cultural confrontation? All the natives I've contacted in the field would have found last night's party totally bizarre & discursively incomprehensible. I can't imagine natives ever feeling comfortable wearing a dress design much less a day-mask.

During the return trip home last night I began fantasizing the idea of Inez among such women—on their turf. *But couldn't imagine it actually happening.*

I suppose a more pertinent question is what effect being among those women in the field had on *me*. Does it make me see Inez & her following with different eyes? I think it does. But there's no fear of my succumbing to the Going Native Syndrome. Their religion, their appalling childbearing practices, their sprawling, unlimited procreation revolt even as they fascinate me. (I must be honest in this journal, that's the point of keeping a *personal* journal.) Yet the contrast with advanced societies & the standards of civilization itself leaves me dissatisfied. No, the correct word here is *dissonant*. I'm out of synch. Hopefully once I return to Pleth I'll be able to readapt to the academic life: after all, I ordinarily wouldn't

be engaged with an Inez Gauthier, but with academics more
like myself. This type of subcultural conflict would engage
me were I exposed to Inez Gauthier in any place. *Close personal journal.*

Nathalie Stillness slips out of her sleep cocoon while subvocalizing the command for her morning music. After exercising she will shower & presently sip the breakfast Ardeth
will bring her. & then she will get down to work tracing the
household patterns of the directed classes of Durazzo.

Most of Frogmore's industry is in the gas-extraction and mining sector; the bulk of the planet's exports are metals, gems, and gas. But the Spieden region, most of which is an archipelago of islands and an expansive marshy delta of the Great Imbyino river system where the mainland morphs into sea, is home to a range of crafts that utilize some of the planet's other natural resources, including the clay found on the islands, which is highly prized and desired by potters throughout the galaxy. The Combine's regulation of trade, however, makes it prohibitively expensive to export either the clay for off-world use or pottery made from it, since export licenses are too costly for any but the largest corporations to purchase, and import duties on goods from Frogmore are usually about five times their purchase value. Many species of shellfish in the delta yield beautiful dyes in a variety of shades of purple and green. Spieden's potters use these dyes, of course, as do the weavers of Saturna. The famous silk textile industry on Evergreen also uses these dyes (which are far more costly than the silk itself). The animal fibers used by Saturna's weavers are produced in Mellors, but Saturna's weavers also use plant fibers, and these too are products of the delta.

Examples of Spiedenese pottery can be found in museums and private collections on Evergreen and Janniset. I own two pieces myself, but I was allowed to keep them only when I made a deposition promising never to sell them. The visitor to Frogmore will be astonished at how inexpensive Spiedenese pottery is in situ. The remuneration for such crafts is so poor that most potters and weavers must also have a day job to survive.

—Enoch Fulmer, *A Star-Hopper's View of the Galaxy*

Eleven
INEZ GAUTHIER

Inez bowed at Stavros, her crew, and the security team Glance had chosen for her. Remembering the tidbit of gossip the latter had confided to her, she flicked a second look at the crew, wondering which one was Stavros's lover. A hardware specialist, according to Glance. But they all wore flight fatigues, which made it difficult to distinguish maintenance from operations. To Inez's eye, none of them seemed likely.

After strapping in, she took a screen from Zagorin. "Feel free to sniff a calmer," she told her attendant. *She* had no worries. They'd be less endangered flying to the other side of the planet via suborbital flight than they would had they been dropping in on the Governor's Installation.

Shortly after everyone in the cabin finished donning their headgear, Stavros announced the final countdown to liftoff. Inez shifted her seat into a horizontal position and closed her eyes. Listening to the countdown, she fingered the anti-nausea hypo she carried in her pocket. But Stavros and her crew managed the liftoff so smoothly that she suffered discomfort only from the slamming force of that initial intensification of gravitational pressure it took to break free of the planet's gravity. Most other pilots—in her experience—created such turbulence, erratic motion, and out-of-synch vibrations that liftoff could make one shuttle-sick for the entire suborbital flight.

Once they reached cruise-phase, she directed her headgear to transmit to Lieutenant Glance's. Handler had revealed yesterday that Glance would likely be leaving the general's staff in six local months because his current tour of duty would be coming to an end and Glance had said he intended to request a transfer. Inez planned to persuade her father to recommend Glance for promotion to captain. Glance performed essential functions to near-perfection. Even should his replacement prove as sharp, personable, and savvy as Glance, it would take many local months before he or she would settle in to a reasonable performance and probably a local year (if ever) before achieving Glance's level of efficiency. And all *that* would be assuming Glance's replacement did not suffer the Fresh-to-Frogmore Syndrome so common among off-planet persons newly arrived from advanced societies.

She gazed out the window. Below lay the planet—in theory. All one could see of Frogmore at any time from any vantage point was the Scourge. One had to take on faith that the planet existed. Instruments constantly produced holos and a plethora of statistical facts about the planet, but without the confirmation of one's senses, those facts and holos had a fictional air about them. As though the universe were playing "Let's pretend there's a planet named Frogmore. And on this planet..."

"Lieutenant Glance," she said, her view-starved eyes feasting on Pittikin's shimmering reddish glow. "Captain Handler told me yesterday that your tour of duty is up in six local months."

"Yes, Madam. The matter has come up for discussion because it's necessary to plan that far ahead in order to secure a replacement before I go."

"A replacement." The general's daughter sighed. "I don't see how anyone could replace *you*, Lieutenant. I don't think you appreciate how completely the general depends on you. And how fond both of us are of you. It will be a sad day for us, your going."

"Thank you very much, Madam. I have to admit I've never worked for anyone like the general before. He's such an inspiration."

The general's charismatic charm had always been re-marked on by his officers. He often pointed out to his daughter that by delegating most of his authority—except that of making the most important decisions, of course—he left himself free to exert a stronger personal influence on those in his command as well as most of the governor's circle. For a moment she conjectured that perhaps ∼ her speculations grew rather mischievous ∼ the general had taken to mumbling suspicions of Solstice's being a subversive because in his experience insurgents and dissidents alone seemed able to resist his charm. *How* could *Solstice Balalzalar resist such shoulders????*

She said, "If you go, Lieutenant, things will fall into a sad mess. So many matters—I doubt we could begin to enumerate them completely, we take them so for granted—just so many aspects of our affairs depend on your unique combination of expertise and tact, the two essential qualities in a superior ADC. Take the routine matter of test scores. How will someone new to the planet understand that blood chemistry is not necessarily more critical than performance scores? Or even know about which pilots have that intangible something that make them peculiarly able?" She heaved another sigh in the hope that Glance's headgear would pick it up. "I imagine that if you desert us, the general will be bogged down in endless quibbling over details for a long time to come. Details *matter*, Lieutenant—I imagine you know that better than anyone—but details, as we all know, hamper the effectiveness of a commander-in-chief when they become too prominent a feature of the landscape."

"It is likely, Madam," Glance said after a pause Inez interpreted as one of defensive regrouping, "that my replacement will come two local months before my departure. Which is why I need to file my request at least four local months in advance of the actual date of departure."

Which gave them two local months to work on Glance—providing, that is, they could dissuade him from an immediate filing of his request. "I'm confident you'd do your best to help your replacement pick up the exigencies of the job. But even so, Lieutenant, I'm afraid we'd be *lost* without you."

She hoped that by persisting in the use of the conditional rather than the future tense she would subliminally persuade him to consider the matter as yet undecided. She sighed again. "I suppose we should have expected you'd want to leave. This planet is hardly a plum assignment. I know, though, that the record of your tour here will stand you in good stead in your future career. Of that there can be no doubt." Had she laid it on too heavily? Or had she been too subtle for him to understand her promise of loyalty rewarded?

"Oh, Madam, I would never say I've regretted my posting here, except maybe during those first six local months when my body was making the adjustment. Working under the general has been a privilege!"

He paused, and Inez wondered if he was as overcome with emotion as he sounded.

"In f-fact," Glance stuttered, "well, Madam, I'm half-undecided about leaving. I mean, obviously there are easier places to be stationed. But the kind of situation on this planet, well, it's rare. And the general—well, how often does a junior officer like me get to serve under someone like General Gauthier?"

"Oh, Lieutenant," the general's daughter exclaimed. "Almost you give me *hope* that you won't desert the general! All I ask is that you give it some thought. Don't jump to a hasty decision. *Take* the two local months you have, to *think* about it. Will you do that for me—and for the general?"

"Oh...well, of course, Madam. Of course I can take my time thinking about it. Well, you know, it never occurred to me..."

Inez smiled. She could do a lot in two months, especially if she mobilized the general. And once she had the general mobilized, Glance wouldn't stand a chance. *Captain* Glance, for sure. And when his promotion came through, he'd know he'd made the best decision.

Inez had to prompt her sleep-dazed attendant. "The mirror, Zagorin."

Zagorin stumbled to the panel and opened it, revealing the full-length flat mirror Inez had had installed on the shuttle. She removed her day-mask and, before replacing it with the nondescript mask, checked her appearance one last time to make certain she had eradicated every possible clue to her identity. She started by scrutinizing her plain ivory silk cap, the numerous golden triangles dripping from her (concealed) earlobes, the gold-threaded black cling-ons, the indigo and gold silk tunic tied at the midriff with matching elbow scarves and briefs scanty enough to pass for something a Frogmore elite might wear, and the padded cloth boots. The accouterments Zagorin would carry for her looked standard for an elite. If anything gave her away, it would be a verbal slip, though she expected her voice—when doing business utterly unlike her social voice (of which she had often heard imitations)—would form a major part of her disguise.

Satisfied, she attached the plain ordinary business day-mask, removed the anti-nausea hypo from her pocket and replaced it with several hypos each of glucose and caffeine. She turned to Zagorin and Glance. "I'm all set. You have that plainclothes escort ready for me, Lieutenant?"

"Yes, Madam," Glance said. He looked nicely self-conscious. "And they've already inspected your transport and declared it satisfactory."

"Excellent." Inez gestured for Zagorin to precede her and muted her ID broadcast. Before following Zagorin into the lift, she inclined her head at Glance.

"I'll be receiving reports every quarter hour, Madam," he replied.

Glance's communicativeness suggested a great deal to her. She would have to speak to the general that very evening. Individuals so needed to be appreciated.

Because Inez had decided only at the last minute to attend the meeting in person, they had to travel from the shuttle base to the meeting's location via pokey ground transport. No way would she entrust above-ground transport to crew she didn't know. She used the time to review the strategy she had devised with Vashon, the agent who usually represented her at this board's meetings. She didn't lack faith in the agent's shrewdness, grasp, and manipulative abilities; she simply could not trust the agent with confidential data that might be drawn upon to great advantage in this critical meeting.

She'd always monitored UAP directors' meetings in real-time. Of the other directors, she had met Lieutenant Governor Andrew Aberdeen perhaps seven times in the last nine local years, Philippa Radclyffe three or four times, and five other directors once or twice. The rest may have been introduced to her, but she had no memory of ever having met them. If they guessed her identity it wouldn't be because they recognized her, but through subtle deductions from what she revealed that she knew or could accomplish.

"Though Jack Carter, being the CEO, is chair, Madam," Vashon said, "you'll find that Commander Bukharov dominates the meetings."

Inez scrolled through her data on Bukharov: a retired starship officer, he owned twenty percent of UAP and had interests in the LO market as well as in transport. She pulled a hypo containing a mixture of caffeine and nicotine out of her pocket and applied it to her neck. Getting up in the middle of the night in order to make a meeting on the other side of the planet certainly had its drawbacks. But it was better than holding such meetings in the Capitol District. Worlds at Frogmore's stage of development tended to clump their top management in one geographical center—until they learned the price of such centralization. "We won't let Bukharov dominate this one," Inez said. "What do you imagine his position is going to be on UAP's transfer strategy?"

It might come down to the two of them duking it out over which transport companies would get the bulk of the contracts. Though Inez owned more stock in UAP than Bukharov did, he might have other directors lined up to take his side. Should she have contacted him earlier and agreed to split the contracting down the middle? But what he didn't have—and wouldn't be prepared for (any more than he'd be prepared for her pushing any particular transport company)—would be an interest in a human resources management corporation.

"On the issue of whether to transition all the units at once?" Vashon asked.

"That's primarily what I meant."

"I think he might be willing to go along with the more cautious approach. I doubt there will be much of an argument over that. A radical approach would tax the shuttle transport facilities of the planet to the breaking point."

And Bukharov in particular would no more want to spread those contracts over the five different companies than she would. "On the other matter of delicacy," Inez said.

Vashon anticipated her. "I'm to let the Lieutenant Governor offer the services of the Governor's Militia before proposing that we request assistance from the general," Vashon said.

They had already discussed the strategy in detail. Agents often spoke for their principals, even when the principals themselves were present in the flesh. On the assumption that

Vashon had already established certain lines of communication, they would begin with Vashon speaking. But part of her reason for attending the meeting in the flesh had to do with certain intangible effects a principal's presence might have. Throughout the meeting she would have to be vigilant for moments in which it would be optimal for her to take a hand in it herself. If she and Vashon had been accustomed to attending meetings together, they would have had a definite advantage in being able to play out more subtle strategies with their dual presence. But Inez would not risk attempting anything fancy. She didn't know Vashon well enough, and she had a great deal at stake.

"At last," Inez said as the transport halted and its doors opened. She switched on her respirator and stepped out onto the pavement. Shagg led the way into the antechamber, and they each submitted to the decontamination procedure in turn. A pair of UAP personnel awaited them as they exited decon. Their ID broadcasts identified them as executive assistants to Jack Carter.

They greeted Vashon first, and then Vashon introduced her to them as "my principal, Madam Smith." Everyone had to exchange bows, of course, and then Inez allowed herself to be conducted into an elevator.

No one would ever guess from the appearance of the place that it was a corporate headquarters. Dingy, drab, barely functional, the corridors and elevator so bored her that she could not help but stare at the human scenery so obligingly shapely and vivid. Both executive assistants wore the minimum of fabric over their brightly colored, black-veined cling-ons—to show off the smoothness of their musculature, of course, while revealing an alluring vista of thighs, hips, buttocks... Just as well that UAP didn't waste SCUs on tasteless or poorly situated art. Would they retain this building when all their units had been transferred to space stations? Or would they sell or abandon it?

Glancing into the large, open workrooms they passed, Inez couldn't see the building as anything but temporary, the kind of place that could be evacuated at a moment's notice without a twinge. Flimsy, dingy, uncared for: one would never see such a place on Janniset or Evergreen. Even the lowliest employees in advanced societies would complain that the place was cursed with poor vibes, while their managers wondered how they could be expected to get work out of personnel in a place so carelessly depressing...

They rounded yet another corner—the woman of the pair in the lead, her body swinging along as easily as if she strode Pittikin—and Inez considered requesting a slower pace. She'd have to try to sneak in a shot of glucose before the meeting started, veiling her neck with her elbow-scarf if necessary. The fatigue came, she knew, from the interruption of her established metabolic and circadian rhythms. If she had to she would intake more powerful stimulants, but only as a last resort since they would soon leave her wasted.

The assistant halted the procession outside an opaqued threshold. "This is the conference room. Two of the directors haven't yet arrived. Would you care to use a private CS before going in, Madam Smith?"

Inez bowed. "Lead on."

And so the assistant, leaving her male colleague and Vashon behind, again headed the procession. The assistant's ceremonial demeanor amused Inez. Here we have the quintessence of Frogmore, she thought. I must remember to tell Nathalie Stillness about it.

The plan Jack Carter's First VP laid out for the directors would divide the units into four groups and shift one group of units at a time. That, he informed them, would be the most cost-effective method and would assure that at least half of their units at any given time would still be in production.

The directors seemed pleased with the plan as the First VP unveiled it.

Vashon raised an issue the First VP hadn't named as a possibility much less addressed as a potentially serious problem. "How will security be handled? Even supposing the first group of units can be removed without incident, how will you shift the others once word gets out that the process is actually going forward?"

Up and down both sides of the table Inez surveyed the directors' averted gazes and fidgeting hands. Standing at the head, to the right of his seated CEO, the First VP fiddled with the laser pen he'd been using to point to particular bits of the holo (now depicting the interior of one of the new orbital stations UAP had made leasing arrangements with). The First VP bowed to Vashon, then cleared his throat. "We have a competent security contractor, Madam. I will be meeting with their rep well in advance of the first shift, at which time we will work out a strategy for assuring there will be no problems of *that* sort. We will of course have the standing teams beefed up, in case some freak mishap occurs. But all discussion with our security contractor must wait on our settling the strategy and logistics of the shift itself."

Inez made her move. "Is it possible," she asked after going through the procedure of being recognized by the chair, "that this board can be so naive? According to figures provided to me two local days ago by Jack Carter's office, few of our workers have allowed themselves to be recruited by the mining industry reps we invited in three local months back. Second, we've suffered disruptions at our units over the last three weeks. And third, I ask that we recall what happened when Farraday Liquid Oxygen Supplies shifted its much smaller operation to a space station last year. I hardly think it alarmist to take the potential for violence in this situation seriously."

"Violence?" Jack Carter said. "There isn't a history of violence among our workers, Madam Smith." He glanced at the First VP. "What was the nature of these recent disruptions? I don't recall hearing of violence."

The First VP bent down and spoke with his lips millimeters from Jack Carter's partially exposed ear. "No," Jack Carter resumed when his First VP had finished whispering, "there was no violence. Just speech-making and placards and chanting at the main entrances of the units." He bowed to Inez. "I would remind you, Madam Smith, that violence on this world is limited to certain regions. Perhaps we should take special precautions for the units in those areas, but otherwise I think such concern misplaced."

"In any case," the Lieutenant Governor said, "we can alert the Governor's Militia to stand by in the remote case that they *are* needed."

The time had come to roll out her heavy artillery. It would be ticklish, since she couldn't say outright (considering how many natives were sitting around the table with her) that the Governor's Militia might simply fan the flames, given the primitive, violence-prone methods it tended to use. "Apparently I am the only one in this room familiar with the study made by General Gauthier's intelligence division when CDS first contemplated arranging for orbital stations to be made available to Frogmore industry." Inez glanced around the table, but not one person's gaze met hers. "As I recall, a synopsis of that report is furnished to every corporation when they make inquiries about leasing space on the stations. Surely our CEO has read this report?"

Jack Carter fidgeted with his stylus. "I recall looking over the synopsis. But we *did* decide to go ahead on the assumption that the displaced workers would be recruited by the mining reps, did we not?"

"Precisely," Inez said. "But the recruitment hasn't worked out as well as we'd hoped, has it. How many local weeks before the first shift is scheduled to take place? Just under four, isn't it? And less than fifteen percent of our workers have signed up. Unless you think they'll rush to do so at the last minute? I don't see it, myself. Considering the distances most workers will have to move to take new jobs, I'd think they'd want to allow themselves as much planning time as possible. Workers prefer to be as secure as they can. They don't like risks and upsets and instability." What Inez could *not* reveal to them was what Cleveland's informants had said about talk in the units since UAP had publicly announced the "eventual" shift of its operations to the space station. So far as the public knew, the shift lay in the hazy undetermined future. But once the ten-day notice had been given, the future would rush upon the displaced UAP personnel. Surely these fools who called themselves directors must see that their meager plan would inadequately safeguard the smoothness of the transition?

"Now look," said the Lieutenant Governor. Once he had their attention, he cleared his throat with noisy ostentation. Inez had to work not to roll her eyes. "Even supposing there's violence—and I can't say I can picture it—I gather, Madam, you come from off-world, and thus have a rather exaggerated notion of what the people of Frogmore are like—but in any event, let's suppose it *does* come to pass that there's trouble. There's no reason the Governor's Militia can't handle it. That's what they're there for. For keeping the civil peace. I don't see any need for us to involve General Gauthier. Which is not to say I don't appreciate the general's professionalism—I know we *all* appreciate what his very *presence* on Frogmore has accomplished. But I see no need to blow this situation out of proportion. If you think our workers will cut up at the shift, well think again about how the sight of the general's peacekeeping forces would affect them."

Almost everyone at the table had become absorbed in their screens. As Inez considered which of the Lieutenant

Governor's points to attack first, she wondered who had called up what data.

Retired Commander Adam Bukharov took the floor. He, Inez noted, boasted broad, rocky shoulders that rivaled even the general's. "Madam Smith seems to be working on the basis of more information than any of us currently have. Obviously she wishes to protect her sources, and we can't fault her for that. I'm thinking that maybe we should act along lines suggested by her cautionary note. For instance, investigating what's going on within the units themselves. And, certainly, to consider possible ways we might diffuse the situation."

How unfortunate, Inez thought, that the argument had already taken on the outlines of a native versus off-world conflict. If she had let Vashon handle it—but of course that hadn't been possible since Vashon didn't know what she was up to here—that perception wouldn't have taken hold. "There are other possible expedients beyond relying on the brute superiority of peacekeepers or militia," Inez said, taking back the floor. On any other world—especially those that enjoyed universal connection, but even on less civilized worlds, where holos could always be used to good effect—the population would have been gradually prepared for the shift, the public would have been eager for the change because they would have learned to appreciate the long-term benefits that would accrue to *every*body. Here, though, the governor had chosen to ignore CDS's advice—the governor being in too much of a hurry to see the orbital stations utilized and new industries on the surface consequently encouraged, and the business community being unwilling to make the investment it would have taken to lay the proper groundwork. "I'm not suggesting we expect trouble because the people of Frogmore are prone to violence. No, I'm not suggesting *that* at all."

But of course, Inez thought, the people of Frogmore *were* remarkably prone to violence because of their spacing perverted birth- and rearing-arrangements, mention of which was taboo. She rapped her knuckles on the table. "While I think Commander Bukharov has made excellent suggestions, there's one more line I'd like to propose we follow. About a decade ago Anaconda shifted a sizable portion of its industry to its moon. At the beginning they had some problems, but a few enterprising souls conceived the idea of forming a corporation for, shall we say, taking up the slack. They cushioned the displaced workers for a time, offered them a number of options, and then helped settle them into new niches. We have such a corporation on Frogmore—the Allied Human Resources Management Corp. I suggest we have their agents at our units when the announcement of the closings is made. That way the workers won't be quite so desperate and angry at the time of the closings—they'll see a way out. Possibly AHRM will be able to place some of them locally, thus giving hope to the others; possibly AHRM will be able to make arrangements with new ventures and connect our displaced workers with some new unit needing personnel. But my point is, in the confusion of the moment the displaced workers would be less likely to react precipitately with AHRM there to cushion the blow." She paused, then said, "And by the time they understand that they will in fact have to relocate, we'll be long gone." That was blunt, but its appeal was vast and unlikely to incline them to writing her off as either alarmist or naive and would make them see her for the realist she was.

"I take it, Madam Smith, that you're familiar with this AHRM," Philippa Radclyffe said.

Inez bowed acknowledgment of the dryness of Radclyffe's comment. Was the dryness intentional, or merely an effect of the feathered owlishness of Radclyffe's day-mask? When the eyes watching her blinked, she wondered if Radclyffe knew how exactly like an owl's the blinking made her eyes look—or if Radclyffe had ever even *seen* an owl in the flesh. "I do happen to know a bit about it," Inez said.

"And, it seems, about everything else as well," an unidentifiable voice from the lower end of the table muttered.

"Considering the lack of success in recruitment the mining people are having," Retired Commander Bukharov said, "I think it worth our while to give AHRM a shot. It would put another string to our bow, as it were." He nodded at the CEO. "What do you say, Jack?"

Jack Carter absently tapped his finger against one of the two pink patches spotting his pastel blue day-mask. Finally, he said, "We'll make inquiries, check them out, hear their terms. If it looks no-risk to us, I don't see why not. Unless anyone is seriously opposed to adding this, ah, string to our bow?" His sandy-lashed gaze traveled around the table.

"I think we should demand a cut of AHRM's profits on the deal if we do," Fiona Nordstrom said.

Inez grinned. It didn't matter to her much either way which company got the most profit out of it, though AHRM did have a margin to watch. She sat back and let the discussion continue without contributing again. She judged that this part of the meeting had gone well. The rest she could leave to Vashon to handle. Bukharov would be easy to manage on the subject of Pemberton's share of the transport contracts. But she would stay and see it through, just in case some new brilliant initiative occurred to her along the way.

On the return flight Inez lay with her eyes closed, trying to relax. She sniffed a calmer, but her thoughts circled around the meeting, over what could have been handled better, over whether the transition would be difficult (for if such displacements politicized the directed classes, the losses would be far greater than any physical damage they sustained, whether the other directors realized it or not). She had been so taken up with other matters lately that she hadn't realized until the day before what they likely faced with UAP's shift to the orbital stations. If only the governor had agreed to the campaign CDS had laid out, the refrain repeated itself in her head. If only the governor...

How easy it must be to be a general, she thought. Like playing dress-up your entire life. Analysts to do your thinking for you. Aides to generate your initiatives. Governors to tell you what to do (in the properly deferential manner and tone of voice one accords to galaxy-class shoulders, of course). While all *you* have to do is look convincingly competent, authoritative, and well-intentioned.

"I'm so *sick* of being here!" she exclaimed.

Zagorin's sleepy voice came over her headgear. "Madam? Was there something—"

"No, No, Zagorin, forget it. I was just talking to myself. Go back to sleep."

Memorandum [confidentiality level 3C]
From: Counselor Daniel Sayles
To: Members of the Standing Working Committee for Frogmore
Re: New Report Evaluating Strategies for Frogmore's Development

The team of analysts assigned to evaluate current strategies for Frogmore's development have submitted their report on current and future strategies to the Select Counsel. As members of the Standing Working Committee for Frogmore, you will be granted access to the full report, if you wish, for the next sixty days (standard); your deputies and personal assistants will not, excepting those already cleared for confidentiality level 2A. I will here summarize the team's key conclusions.

The chief problem for a planet like Frogmore is that initial colonization requires a reasonable-sized population of engineers, logistics managers, robotics specialists, etc., few of whom would agree to be recruited if required to separate from their families for the ten or so years their services are needed. As a result, urban enclaves become a necessary part of development. Urban enclaves, of course, always take on a life of their own, since the services they need for maintenance require a wide variety of workers and businesses. Once settled, such workers usually do not leave. Moreover, the bureaucracies that develop to run the urban enclaves naturally generate an agenda of their own—always involving expansion of the population with all that expansion entails.

After five centuries, Frogmore has a population it cannot support. Relatively little human labor is needed for mining, and mining constitutes the primary area of export goods the planet has to offer.

The ideal Frogmore would be one stripped of most of its population. Our goal, then, must be to find ways to encourage emigration from the planet, preferably to newer frontier planets that have undergone terraforming and are ready for settlement. Once the planet's population is reduced by 80%, peacekeeping forces can be withdrawn, and Frogmore will become the resource planet we originally intended it to be. The need for reduction of the population, then, must shape all our current and future projects for Frogmore, until we have succeeded in this objective.

Twelve
CLAIRE GASPEL

1.VII.493

Today Grand Mother told me that this year on Commemoration Day I would be the one to speak to the young ones about our history & would also be narrator in the time-tripper pageant. Talking to the young ones—well, that doesn't seem so difficult. (How many times have I heard such talks myself?) But narrating the pageant before the entire assembled Family of Paula's Daughters: that's something else, even if there *is* a set script to follow. Grand Mother pointed out that she & Mother have always taken turns seeing to these tasks (of course Mother isn't always around—like this year, she's had to miss celebrating Commemoration Days with the whole Family whenever she's been at Birth-Home), which are among first daughters' duties, & that it's time now for me to share such duties with them. I'm glad Commemoration Day is a couple of months off yet. I need time to get used to the idea. I guess I'll eventually take all the special aspects of being a first daughter for granted, but at this point everything is still new.

2.VII.493

This morning Ariel & I talked a bit about Commemoration Day. She's convinced she'll be among the midwives who'll be staying on at Birth-Home. They celebrate Commemoration Day at Birth-Home in a very special way,

Ariel says. They do a selection of readings from the journals of first daughters (not just from Paula's first daughters, of course), & they have their own, *special* time-tripper pageant. It's never as elaborate as the ones done by Families, but it's got distinctive aspects to do with fertility, pregnancy, & the mother/child bond. It makes sense that the celebration is different for the women at Birth-Home, especially since the women there must be so careful about the food they ingest.

Anyway, I've decided that before composing my speech to the young ones I need to do a lot more reading in the first daughters' journals. Maybe I can tell the young ones something they haven't heard in past Commemoration Day talks. I have to keep it simple enough for the youngest to at least partially understand, though.

Time for sleep now. I'm totally wiped out, and tomorrow's going to be one of those long, exhausting days.

3.VII.493

The outside world is disrupting us. I don't think I ever realized the extent to which the Family is connected with the outside world. There's life here in our dome, & then there are our outside jobs. Which most of us have. We go to them & do the work, but then we come home to the Dome, & outsiders fade to unimportance. Of course those of us who go to the same workplaces exchange gossip, remarks, comments—all the while knowing that none of that is *really* important. They're boring, tedious, but necessary hours that we don't allow to take over our lives.

Daisy is big with I-told-you-so—after all, we've been talking for weeks about the possibility of UAP actually shutting down. But until now, it's been mostly rumors & speculation. Sure, those mining people were hanging around the plants trying to lure us away from our UAP jobs without management ever doing anything to suggest they minded the mining people's tactics. Sure, we've been hearing about how the government wanted to move agricultural production to the new space stations. But even so, it seemed so distant—& just speculation. After all, the presence of those mining people wasn't *proof* UAP was going to shut down our plant. But now we have only *ten days'* notice. & so everyone's in an uproar. Not only are there a couple dozen Family members working in my UAP plant, but there's also this other question, the one we argued at dinner a few weeks back, the question of what the consequences of having all agricultural production restricted to the space stations would be. Of what would happen to us as consumers.

Daisy's now saying we should have planned ahead, we should—centuries ago—have taken up agriculture as a Family project so that we'd never have been dependent on outsiders for food. All that's very well & good to say now, but it doesn't help. We don't have an agricultural project, & we don't have any idea of how to start one.

It's been a horrible day, & it's late. We're going to have a big meeting tomorrow night. A strategy meeting. To decide what to do about this mess.

There must be *something* we can do. Our Family can't be completely torn apart, can it? It would be horrible to think we'll all end up living like Ariel's branch of the Family. & what about our dome?

4.VII.493

Can't sleep. Too much on my mind. The meeting tonight made everything so clear. *Too* clear. Oh how I wish tonight were a sleep-cocoon night! When I'm *this* tense, it's hopeless trying to relax my body through sheer will.

The stakes are high. If we engage in massively disruptive actions, then we put our selves on the line. The warnings sent out by UAP & the Executive Regional Manager are explicit. Maybe they couldn't wipe or even wash all of us, but when you calculate as an individual, you're tempted to think of it as a sure thing simply because it *could* happen, it could be your own self that is taken. But on the other hand, as Daisy argues, there's the matter of the community's survival. Things have been tough enough, & what we have to lose, while it may be insignificant (if our worst fears turn out to be unfounded) in comparison with getting washed or wiped, could end up starving us—literally. & would break up our dome & thus destroy everything the daughters of Paula have struggled so hard for. Even a slight constriction (Grand Mother's phrase) would seriously hurt us—we haven't got much margin (again Grand Mother's phrase).

Ariel's begun to understand: I could see that by the way she sat so quietly at the meeting, her wide eyes moving from face to face. Several times I caught her staring at me. As though she saw something different, something new to her perception.

I'm wracked by terrible fear, I admit it—sometimes at the thought of the mass action my muscles begin to shake—I do mean shake, not little tremors or minor trembling, but great shivering convulsions in my legs, knees, thighs, arms, neck. My stomach burns, & the heavy lump in my throat makes it impossible for me to eat. Others are so courageous—they talk with passion about taking a stand, but calmly, as though there is nothing any rational person would have to be afraid of. Take Alma & Lelia—they looked so magnificent standing up & speaking about guarding the future & not letting the managers displace & break us, talking about how the managers have always despised us & looked for ways of forcing us to conform to *their* ways & *their* values. (When Alma talked about "their values," Grand Mother snapped back that they *have* no values.)

But I've got to sleep. Tomorrow will be a long day. & perhaps if I sleep I'll wake fresh & free of fear. More than anything, whatever decision we take (& I think I know what it will be, since almost everyone who spoke at the meeting expressed a preference for facing immediate personal danger to the draining inertia of lengthy anxiety while waiting for the most dire things—the slow disintegration of the Family—to happen). Ridding myself of fear & anxiety & cowardice would mean more to me than almost anything I can think of. Oh how honest I'm being in this journal... & the thought occurs to me that should I be taken & my brain wiped, this cowardice of mine will be the last (& nearly the only) thing my descendants (you who are reading this journal in our future—should we have a future) will know of me.

Somehow, having written that last sentence, I know what decision I will make, what vote I will cast at the meeting tomorrow night. Perhaps now I'll be able to sleep.

Excerpt from the journal of Paula Boren
12.XVI.8

Pittikin, for all its low gravity, is beginning to seem the most oppressive place in the galaxy. Oh, I know very well that our lives on Delphi were worse. And I know that probably the others, toiling on the surface not only to help support us but also to make a start on those projects that will make us a viable permanent community, are undoubtedly having a far rougher time of it than any of us (whose only toil is the physically easy labor we've contracted to perform in exchange for air and food). Though the Frogmore government claims to be footing our total bill with funds from CDS, it won't agree to pay outright for certain necessary items but instead puts us further in debt—this time to it, rather than to the spacing Colonial Settlement Corporation. But it's not our *physical* state here that's so terrible. Though I wouldn't go so far as to say we have an actual morale problem, we *are* under psychological siege. Because though we've made it clear we are different from the other pregnant women on this moon (the government isn't wasting time, either, with its reproduction projects—of which we, strangely enough, are counted as one), we are still in an equivocal situation. Our treatment is subtly different from what it was on Delphi—and an improvement, too. (Except from the medical people: they treat us the same as they always did: or so those who have been through pregnancy have said—fortunately my contact with medical management wasn't anything as extensive as that the gestational surrogates had to endure.)

But it's the others who treat us differently—the managers and the safety enforcers. They have made a point of keeping us away from the gestational surrogates. *Entirely* away. Though we know they are being housed somewhere near us, we never see them. We occasionally hear mention of them. But we are considered perverse—and a possibly dangerous influence. They don't *say* we are a dangerous influence (though they tell us in thousands of ways how perverse we are at every moment we're with them—which is a lesson to Bessy D.), but it's clear that's what is in their minds. All the surrogates on Pittikin are under contract, brought here in large numbers because there's a planet here to be filled. Most people think that because it's work that's widely despised it must pay well. But because of the need to keep population levels stable and the division of labor into specializations that allows each surrogate to manage multiple pregnancies or infants simultaneously, it's really only on developing worlds that surrogates are in high enough demand that it's possible to make a good, steady living. A lot of us fall into it accidentally, as a stopgap measure when one's career choice proves a dire mistake. I gather that a number of affluent people decided to emigrate to Frogmore precisely so that they could have unlimited numbers of offspring, making it the perfect place for surrogates to flourish. The first time I heard this I didn't believe it, for what person, however affluent (and the truly affluent surely don't worry about the extra taxation for offspring that they have to pay on advanced worlds), would want to divide up their resources among a large pool of claimants? But a couple of weeks ago I overheard a discussion between my supervisor and his supervisor that opened my eyes. With a "reasonable amount" of credit and a lot of offspring, it will be possible for affluent people to spin themselves some pretty powerful webs. Education, my supervisor was told, is key on planets like Frogmore. Those educated on Pleth will be in high demand, and since Frogmore is so difficult for unaltered humans to tolerate, there won't be that many ambitious types willing to come to Frogmore just to get a good job. Apart from which, my supervisor added, there's nothing on Frogmore to attract anyone. The upshot is that the government is in a hurry to begin populating the planet. How else develop something that could be called an economy?

For some reason that conversation sticks in my mind, I suppose because I'm becoming more and more aware of how, though the situation *seems* wide-open, certain structures are already in place. Which means, I think (or so Dorothy argues), that we need to grasp what these structures are and how we can carve out our own niche—rather than simply fling ourselves up against them, with the result of pointlessly dashing our brains out. It's a different way of fighting, but isn't it, after all, what our initial strategy of coming here to Frogmore was all about?

Is it pregnancy and the low gravity that makes me feel so light, so giddy, so unanchored? We bounce around up here, occasionally getting a chance to peer up at the Scourge-shrouded planet that is now our home... and feel totally at the mercy of these managers. But we're not at their mercy. We could be—if we allowed ourselves to be directed and managed. Perhaps it's the medical management that makes us feel helpless?

We'll have to find a way to do without their expertise. We'll have to develop our own medical resources. It will probably be a generation before we can get out from under their management, but it's clear now that that's essential—if we are to be our own managers.

6.Vll.493

Must catch up on everything that's happened. First, the momentous meeting: we decided before taking "mass action" (Daisy's phrase—she's taken it from the Bole Oil Situation of fifteen years ago) to investigate the one thin hope for finding employment to replace job losses if UAP does dismantle the unit. We'd all seen the holos in the antechamber inviting "displaced personnel" to a free "consultation," but we'd ignored them. First of all, the name alone (one of those outsider terms, I think it's called Allied Human Resources Management Corporation) put us off. Second, you can never tell what you might be getting into with "consultations" when the holos give you no information except to offer those creepy slick blandishments the outsiders are always using on one another. You just know it's going to be awful, a sort of trap you walk into, alone (they insist you go in by yourself & not "in groups"—they specifically said there were "individual" appointments only), & you never know how they might manipulate you with their tricky techniques (especially when you're in their clutches all by yourself), what they might talk you into doing. Worse, sometimes places like that do a kind of "psychosocial screening" so that if you aren't like all the other outsiders (as none of us ever are, not even the guys), there's no telling what might happen to you as a result of failing their tests. Because of all this, none of us paid any attention to the holos. But then we started noticing that a lot of the outsiders working with us were undergoing consultations, & some of them were talking about how these consultants had a solution to their "displacement situation" & how they thought they'd probably come out of the deal in a better situation—especially if food were to get as much cheaper as the government said it would once all the agricultural production was being done on the orbital stations.

It took over an hour to decide who would be the "individual" to go through the "individual appointment." It would have to be somebody strong, somebody who'd be able to stand up to pressure. As Daisy argued, we needed to find out what we're up against, since these consultations were making a lot of the outsiders we work with unwilling to do anything to stop UAP from dismantling the unit. In the end we decided that Muthis should go. Muthis is one of those people who has a strong stubborn streak. She's soft-spoken and quiet, she smiles a lot, she's pretty accommodating in general. But on certain things she can't be budged—which is what everyone started whispering during the discussion of which volunteer should be the one to go.

So today after our shift we all waited for Muthis in the antechamber. When everyone else from our shift had gone & we were still there, waiting, the militia (who've been there since UAP announced their intention to terminate us all) began harassing us—thinking, I guess, that we were going to make trouble. When we tried to explain that we were waiting for Muthis to finish the consultation and that we needed to wait inside because the van isn't air-tight against mistflowers, the militia demanded that we be ID'd & ordered us to submit our bands to the scanner in the antechamber—which we'd all already done when we'd come off our shifts. We pretended not to understand that they wanted to ID us for another reason than the usual, which after a few minutes got them really heavy-going. But Muthis was expecting us to be waiting for her when she got out, & though none of us said this out loud, we were all probably thinking she might seriously need us when she did finish the "consultation." I know I was thinking that. In the end, we got the militia to allow one of us to wait in the antechamber for Muthis. It was either that or get into something nasty & heavy with them, which we could not have won. So Paul—without discussion—stayed. Everyone knows how close the two of them are. & Paul has a good head on his shoulders & has never attracted notice from any outsider. (Or so we thought—though after what Muthis told us later about the consultation, it's not clear anymore what an outsider may notice or think they know about any of us.)

We ended up waiting in the van for more than an hour before Muthis & Paul showed up. When they did, Muthis looked dazed. As we drove back to the Dome, Muthis talked—not telling us everything (since she was going to have to do that at the meeting so that everybody could hear), just her general impressions & certain details that were particularly awful. Like the consultant's mask & cap (for me caps have always had that creepy feeling about them, since you can't help having an idea about what is under them, apart from baldness—& going by the remarks others in the van made, I guess I'm not alone in feeling that way), & Muthis's having to submit her wrist band to being scanned the entire time she was there (to "read" her physiological responses, is what we guessed was the point), her having first to wait in a little cubicle with nothing to do but stare at the walls & the scanner, & then when seeing the consultant having to accept a drug (the consultant claimed Muthis was "too anxious" for them to "talk") & lie on a strange couch that kneaded her skin &

vibrated & sometimes seemed to be sticking needles in her (also supposed to "soothe" her "anxiety").

The experience sounded horrible. But Muthis wasn't pressured into agreeing to anything in particular—at least not that she knows of.

During the meeting we learned the following from Muthis:

(1) The consultant has a name for us (which means that this is how management-type outsiders must refer to us): we're called ACCMs—for Anachronistic Collective Cult Members. That's how the consultant kept referring to us to Muthis.

(2) There are certain "personnel cluster-spheres" that are closed to ACCMs—first & foremost being any job that requires being "connected" (their word for having the brain-implant that connects individuals to the big "communication-information" networks). According to the consultant, fewer people will be needed to run the agricultural units on the orbital stations because, once certain alterations are made in the production mechanisms, the mechanisms themselves will function more smoothly since there won't be all the "special problems associated with the Frogmore surface." But more important (according to the consultant), the units on the orbital stations will need people who are connected—since UAP isn't willing any longer to deal with manual terminals, she said. That it's simply too inefficient. & that UAP is using the opportunity of this move to streamline their operations.

But we who "refuse full connection" (us "anachronistic types") can not only not get work with UAP, but also must realize that many other jobs will be closed to us because of our "handicap" (of not being connected).

(3) The consultant told Muthis that she couldn't promise to find her a job within commuting distance of our dome, but that she would try. In other words, she essentially told Muthis that anyone signing a contract with them would be taking their chances.

206 ✖ L. Timmel Duchamp

(4) Once you sign a contract, you're stuck with accepting a job from them—you're allowed to refuse a total of three before they can force you to take any old job they want to stick you with. While you're waiting for them to find you a job, they promise to lend any funds needed for living expenses, & if the job requires relocation, for moving & resettlement expenses (at a rate of four percent interest per quarter). The only give in the contract would be their agreeing to our refusing full connection on moral grounds.

So it's obvious that this management corporation has no solution for us. But as is also becoming clear, a lot of people at the plant (more than half, now) have either taken jobs with the mining corporations who've been recruiting, or signed contracts with this management corporation.

So we voted at the meeting: (a) to send a delegation (we're going to try to get others from the plant to join us) to go to the Executive Regional Manager's office to demand that he do something to keep the plant here; (b) to coordinate efforts with all the other domes (but this will take too long, since we have less than six days before the plant will close); & (c) to try to get other domes involved in taking action against the UAP plants in their areas, as well as to plan our mass action at the plant. A few people are worried about our taking such strong action—all the terminology that Muthis tells us is used to categorize us is pretty frightening. So there were a few people arguing that we should just accept it & find a way around it. But there are eighteen of us employed at the plant, which adds up to a considerable proportion of our total income. & apart from that, there's the angle Daisy keeps reminding us of—namely the importance of keeping agricultural units on Frogmore, in our local communities.

All this is nerve-wracking—but exciting, too. Everything that's happening seems almost as important & immediate as all that happened in Paula Boren's times (well, that's an exaggeration—but our way of life does seem to be under attack in a way it's never been before). We absolutely cannot let our dome be broken up, we all agree on that, totally. & if the eighteen of us can't find work within range of the dome, then the dome *will* be broken up.

Excerpt from the journal of Paula Boren: 18.XVI.8

New pieces of the puzzle have come to us: we've discovered two things more about the surrogates. First, there are only gestational and a very few lactation surrogates—for the infants are taken to the surface almost immediately after dropping. (We *must* find other ways of describing these processes. Every time the obstetrical staff comes among us, the tone of their voices when they refer to various processes and states makes me cringe. So that I almost hear those tones when we use the same words.) Second, none of the surrogates do any other sort of work—unlike we who work to pay for certain of our expenses. It struck us when we first heard this, and Bessy D. and a few others grumbled. But when we realized what it meant, and the reasons for this particular distinction, we experienced a collective relief. It means they—the government and the managers—don't consider us surrogates, or even like surrogates! (I wonder if *they* realize that? The management and the obstetrical staff insist that there's little "real" difference between us and the surrogates, beyond what they call our "perversity"—and of course the obstetrical staff know we've all been surrogates of one sort or another.) The ostensible reason that the surrogates aren't working is that they're already considered to be working just by being pregnant. And they're all under contract. Even so, it took some doing to make Bessy D. see the implications of it all.

Interesting, isn't it, how such a simple thing can make me feel so much better. I have the sense now that we're already established in the Frogmore scheme of things, that as long as we're careful, we'll make it. And once we can get rid of the need for dealing with obstetrical staff who see the entire phenomenon as a production process they're overseeing, the way I'm having to sit at a terminal for five hours a day overseeing the smooth functioning of the chemical baths assigned to my management during that shift, we'll be set. (One of the obstetrical people made a similar analogy, scoffing at us, saying that what we were doing made about as much sense as producing single items of food individually.)

Time for exercise class now. The lightness of the gravity, though a pleasant change from Frogmore, will sneak up on us if we're not careful. Those who were gestational surrogates on Delphi keep talking about what a wonder it is being pregnant in such low gravity, so I suppose our conditions (apart from the obstetrical staff we have to deal with) are absolutely ideal.

8.VII.493

Yesterday I & Grand Mother & three other women (one of them very old—Violet Chang, to be specific) went to the Regional Center to talk first to Pimlico's Representative to Parliament, & then to the Executive Manager of the region (who wouldn't see us on the grounds of being too busy to see people without appointments—after which someone with a fancy title representing the Manager spoke with us instead). I've never seen so many strange masks & caps & other such things that it seems all management people wear. What, I kept wondering, do they need to hide? The way their eyes peer through the little slits in their masks gives you the feeling of being secretly watched. & then when they do look at you directly & meet your eyes, it's weird, not like the way eyes ordinarily meet. I suppose it's because they're so shielded by those weird pieces of plastic & fabric hiding all the rest of their faces. (Usually you can see part of the mouth, but not always.) The effect is eerie.

Our effort was pointless. They lectured us on how much Pimlico would benefit from "the many changes lying in our near future" & talked about "the need to adjust oneself" to changing ways & so on. Grand Mother called the outing (when she described it at the meeting after dinner) "a necessary exercise in futility"—arguing that now that we had publicly made our dissent known, we would have a better chance for dealing with the outsiders' structures later on. (Since like me no one else asked her what in particular she meant by that vague phrase "later on," I assume that whatever is going through her mind is too scary for the rest of us to handle right now. Which may be okay—as long as Grand Mother continues to guide us to wise decisions.)

But something else surfaced at the meeting. There are five people (all of them, except for Gary Lyman & Will Park, under twenty, which is to say, as Grand Mother pointed out in response, none of them have had children) who intend to join the Anti-Combine League. After Grand Mother described our reception by the politicians, Allie Dutton stood up & made an impassioned speech urging all of us to join the Anti-Combine League, arguing that our way of life would be destroyed whatever we did, that the best we could do would be to try to pull down the government in order to re-establish ourselves afterwards. She said that we had to stop UAP from taking all the agricultural units off the surface & that the only way to do that was by joining with the Anti-Combine League. That our "feeble mass actions" would inevitably end in many of our brains being wiped, which would effectively cripple our dome. That as long as we were going to risk brain-wipe we might as well do "truly effective" things, not simply wring our hands in public as we implore UAP to allow the plant to remain. (Which isn't what we're planning on doing, anyway. But Allie got so carried away with her own rhetoric, there was no stopping her once she started.)

First Violet Chang & then Grand Mother gave stern lectures on the subject of violence—insisting on the sacredness of life as the foundation of the Family & reminding everyone of our collective obligation not to increase entropy on this planet. Gary asked how we could be talking about *principles* when *every*thing was being taken away from us, that principles were fine when people were allowed to follow them, but that the Dome was in danger & didn't we realize how little time we had left?

The five of them won one more recruit to their side, another guy. They said they would be leaving the Dome soon, once they "made contact with" the Anti-Combine League. Which must mean they haven't done anything about their intentions yet. Which, Ariel whispered to me later, might mean they won't go as far as they say they will, since they'd be joining an organization of outsiders, which wouldn't be at all easy.

As for Ariel herself, she sometimes seems almost as upset as we are, though of course she can't be. She never has lived in a dome, & her father & uncles are all, essentially, outsiders (though she doesn't call them that). & most of her branch of the Family have other sorts of jobs, too.

But now I have to do some work—Grand Mother this morning remarked that it's more important than ever that I finish my teaching preparation courses. I'm not certain why she thinks this, but I didn't ask—I have a feeling she'd just have given me one of those long looks & told me to think about it & figure it out for myself.

9.Vll.493

My head is buzzing with the argument I just had with Ariel. I don't know if we'll be able to sit at the same table at the evening meal without upsetting everyone else.

It started when I scolded her for talking to Allie Dutton & the others who say they're joining the Anti-Combine League. She snapped at me: It's none of your business who I talk to. So I explained to her that it was all our business, that people were ostracized for good reasons only, that we had their welfare as much at heart as the community's. & how did she think I felt, anyway, blocking Allie Dutton, who I'd grown up with? Of course Ariel has no notion of what peer-bonding is, since she grew up without a peer group.

They're not children, Ariel came back; that tactic might work with individual children, but not with a group of adults who have come to a reasoned decision. They're adults & they're plural—& thus able to reinforce one another in the face of total ostracism. Ostracism will only further polarize them since by ostracizing them, we disable all communication. After a few seconds of our glaring at one another, she added, "The practice of ostracism is barbarous. & if I were the one being ostracized, I wouldn't care about what anyone who was ostracizing me thought about me."

This only points up how much of an outsider she really is, if she can seriously believe she wouldn't care. But then her branch of the Family live in that weird isolated way with sexual couples in separate residences. So I patiently explained to her about how children learn right from wrong by the way the rest of the Family reacts to their behavior. & how in this part of the Family each individual *does* care what the rest of the Family thinks of her or him.

Then Ariel got into a side-issue, about how since none of them had ever been to Birth-Home, it was difficult for them to understand the injunction against increasing entropy.

(She, of course, having done her apprenticeship at Birth-Home, was trying to win a few points off me by bringing this up.) I countered by saying that although I hadn't been to Birth-Home yet, I understood the injunction perfectly well, that it's something we've been taught to respect in numerous ways since birth. "It's harder for the guys," she argued next. But of course she was thinking about the weird situation of men in *her* branch of the Family, who're mostly outsiders, since they have a tradition of genetic sex selection.

Oh this is upsetting. It makes me so mad. & *frustrates* me. I mean, you can talk & talk & talk to Ariel, but certain things just don't get through. Which makes you feel as though you might as well be talking to yourself. Things are bad enough without these sorts of falling-outs. But I guess it's at times of crisis that people do fall out. I suppose it has something to do with everyone being so tense & anxious & easily frustrated. Still, who is Ariel to judge us like that?

We stopped speaking to one another after I warned her that people were going to lose patience with her if she kept on consorting with that crowd, that if she weren't careful she'd find herself ostracized, too. Her face went into an ugly sneer when I said that, & she *laughed.* & said that it would suit her just fine if it meant I wouldn't be lecturing her all the time. I don't know which of us turned away first, but neither of us said another word after that.

Why does she say I'm "lecturing" her? Is explaining the same as lecturing? Clearly she doesn't understand, and so needs me to explain these things to her. If she understood, she'd agree with me. Obviously. Well, maybe Grand Mother can talk some sense into her.

Everything changed when General Paul Gauthier and his peacekeeping forces arrived. In private, Amanda was relieved. To that point, her sole defense against the workers' rebellions had been her militia, but that was a double-edged sword. A significant faction within the militia had allied itself with a noisy, energetic contingent of young elites who had started a movement to depose the governor in favor of a militia-supported dictatorship, calling for (yet again!) Frogmore's independence. A purge of the militia, ordered by Amanda but organized and facilitated by Orsino Cleveland, the general's top intelligence specialist, rid the militia of officers advocating independence either publicly or privately, and over the next five local years, Gauthier imposed professional standards on the militia. The militia still retains a reputation for thuggishness, but incidents of abuse have become the exception rather than the rule.

From the moment of his arrival, Paul Gauthier exercised a powerful, peculiar charm over the governor's circle. He has the gift of making everyone who meets him feel extremely intelligent and engaging. It is rumored that he has partnered every woman (but none of the men) in the governor's circle, but that is patently a gross exaggeration. It is widely believed that Amanda and the general have partnered more than once during security conferences on Pittikin, but I rather doubt this myself. My own question about the general is whether he's a pretty figurehead, or smarter than he lets on. I change my mind about this every time I see him.

—*Frogmore's First Circle: Life in Amanda Kundjan's Circle*, by Madam X

Thirteen
INEZ GAUTHIER

Inez paused mid-bite. Of course: she should have seen it by now. If the fog were eliminated, the planet could handle an *enormous* population influx. In fact they'd *need* such an influx for the boom. Although the natives reproduced at fantastic rates, even they couldn't begin to provide for the planet's prospective needs. Suppose she formed a corporation for setting up a program for immigrants—first attracting and recruiting them, then making the necessary structural adjustments to their bodies and bearing their transport costs... The influx would help neutralize the influence of the insurgents and, with proper handling, be a civilizing force on the natives. All the while the possibilities for profit would be unlike any other business opportunity (short of the projects she suspected CDS had going on that world they were getting ready to populate, the opportunities of which they had cut her out of—for which she could hardly complain, given the advantages they allowed her in the case of Frogmore).

"Inez! Are you even listening to me?"

Snapping back to attention, Inez realized she had a mouth full of food apparently not yet masticated. Nodding at her father, she resumed chewing and swallowed without registering just what it was she had been eating. She had broken their little rule about meals again. "I'm sorry, Paul," she said with a contrite smile. "What was it you were saying?"

"You were daydreaming, weren't you," the general said. "About that native boy, I suppose. What's his name again?"

"Guilty as charged," she said ruefully.

"Your mind seems to slip into the gutter awfully easily these days, woman. And you have the nerve to accuse *me* of mooning and lusting unreasonably!"

"Isn't there a difference? After all, I have mine in the bag. I'm simply *anticipating* a little. While you have no idea what she would be like were she to have you. What kind of basis is that for fantasy?"

"The only basis possible." The general stared down at his plate. "But in fact I *can't* have a decent fantasy about her." He stared at his daughter and blinked. "Every time I daydream being with her, she comes on polite and cold. She's even turned my own imagination against me!"

"Maybe your unconscious is trying to tell you something."

"What can I do? Have you figured her out yet? What *is* it she wants? What is it she *sees* in that—that *froggie?*"

"She doesn't see what you see, that's for certain. Which may be part of your problem." Silently she added *and my problem, too.* In the past, the general hadn't found it necessary to understand or "identify with" any of the objects of his desire, even the long-term ones. Wasn't the point of "objects" simply to acquire, use, and otherwise manipulate them as opaque matter one needn't trouble to "understand" unless one wished to? Solstice Balalzalar, however, would not constitute herself in that nicely objectified way for the general's pleasure. Somehow, Inez thought, she had to wrench his attention away from Solstice. But how?

She watched her father chewing and chewing and chewing the bite of Lanike flour wafer and goat cheese spiced with the pungent Evergreen grass they both liked so well. His chewing struck her as dogged. The general had a stubborn streak in him, and there, really, lay the rub. His stubbornness had made him dig in and take his obstinacy of purpose for persistence of desire. Childish, of course, but understandable. She recognized that tendency in herself.

The general dabbed his lips with his napkin and threw it onto his plate. "I've had enough. Let's have the fruit later. Perhaps after a stroll in the garden?"

"Lovely." Inez produced another smile. Someday this place would have a *real* set of gardens. But by that day they themselves would be long gone. This thought so cheered Inez that she linked arms with her father and told him what handsome shoulders he had. The general squared said shoulders and thrust out his chest. "And you, my dear," he murmured, "have the finest aesthetic perceptions of anyone I've ever had the honor to meet."

His daughter laughed. Were she to contradict him, she would be undermining her own flattery of him. Anyway, she liked him to feel good, and if such flattery warmed him, then she was happy to give him such pleasure.

That night, her sleep-cocoon rocked her gently within its buoyantly aquatic warmth, Inez leaped and soared through the corridors of the Commander's Residence. She understood that the scientists had found a way to negate gravity, to deny Frogmore's excessive mass. She flew without the awkwardness of unaccustomed free-fall, now and then pushing her hand against a wall to accelerate her inertial push or guide herself around a corner. As she flew, her spirit expanded and spread, streaming behind her unbound, its free flow delighting her with the abandoned ecstasy of omnipotence, aggrandizing her with the knowledge that she ranged outside any bounds of custom, language, or environment. No one, nothing, could impede her flight.

Turning the corner, she glimpsed in the distance another body in flight, its legs and arms thrust out on the horizontal plane. Something about the sight of another human provoked the desire in her to catch it. To see, perhaps, who it was. Or maybe simply to grab an ankle in playful demonstration that she had caught whoever it was, a little tweak that would give her a fresh surge of delight, an additional proof of her omnipotence.

Steadily she gained on the figure before her, and as she drew close she saw the strong, beautifully arched, round-heeled foot, the bony muscular ankle, the curving flow of calf, all shapely under their burgundy cling-on skin. For a long while, it seemed, she sailed close behind, just out of touching distance, her right arm stretched to its limits, ready to grasp the tantalizing ankle or toes or sole less than a meter beyond her reach. One part of her registered her inability to make out the sex of the figure or to move her eyes past the alluring curve of calf, as though a hidden strand of will stubbornly prevented her from wrenching her eyes from these corporal members of an otherwise ethereal image, forbidding her to look more closely upon it.

Without considering what she was doing, she opened her mouth to call out to the figure. She had no idea what she might say, only that she must speak words to it. But instead of speech, a bone-achingly hollow sound streamed out of her mouth, a sound of such empty beauty that it pulled hot salty tears from her eyes. Against her will, she listened to the sound and discovered she had no idea how to stop it, for even when she closed her mouth against it, the sound continued rising out of the well of her body, vibrating in her throat, humming in her belly, resonating deep within each and every bone in her body, compelling her to perceive how many bones laced her body, bones oh so achingly lonely, bones that would not keep still, bones that, however small and fragile, would no longer remain silent... The sound swelled, and she grew conscious of it echoing around her, bouncing off the walls floor ceiling, the force of its reverberations rattling her chattering teeth, though never in dissonance to that pure hollowed-out void of fullness that soughed so unbearably in her ears.

For a flash of moment—most of her attention preoccupied with the sound, her streaming eyes barely functioning,
having lost track of the toes, sole, ankle, calf that had so se-
duced her—as her eyes flitted wildly about in pursuit of the
invisible sound—she glimpsed a head turning to look over its
shoulder at her. But as she realized this and strove to pull her
attention from the sound, the figure vanished without trace,
and she found herself flying alone, surrounded and perme-
ated by the terrible beauty she could not bear, contained by
walls, ceiling, floor, floating aimlessly along the corridor, going nowhere.

Inez woke with wet cheeks, her heart heavy, desolate,
lost. The cocoon rocked her and whispered to her and gently
comforted her back to sleep.

"What?" Inez said, thinking she could not have understood.
"What did you say?"

"I *thought* you'd want to know." Sidney's pearly eyes,
gleaming within the thin crescent cutouts in her sleekly
feathered mask, watched Inez with keen attention. "She's
packing up. To leave. She hasn't said why, so I assume her
reasons have nothing to do with the Institute itself." Inez
could see enough of Sidney's mouth to perceive a distinct up-
ward curve of its lips. "Because I assumed you would prefer
that she remain, I asked her if there was anything we could
do to persuade her to stay. But she said no, and thanked me
for the Institute's having given her the workspace."

Which was more, Inez reflected, than Solstice had ever
said about it to *her*. "She hasn't left yet, I hope?" She itched
to be off to the waterdancer's workspace.

"No. I've been monitoring the antechamber."

Would Solstice have simply gone without a word to her?
She accepted that Solstice was rude and careless of the social graces, but simply to pack up and leave without a word

surpassed mere rudeness. A thin flame of anger burned in her—but feebly. Though she *wanted* to be angry with Solstice, her stomach's leaden lumpishness—why *had* she eaten a Lanike flour pastry fruit compote-filled tart for dessert, anyway?—overwhelmed her with an anxiety she could not analyze or comprehend. She recognized the sensation, of course, but found it a little odd. She hadn't experienced so much anxiety since her last trip to Janniset.

The dancer's tank had been dismantled, and translucent barrels of the fluid it had contained had been arranged along the long back wall of the workspace. At first Inez did not see Solstice; but as she made one last visual sweep before going into the space's privacy area, Solstice spoke. "Is that you, Inez?"

She whirled. Still she did not see Solstice. But then, out of the corner of her eye, she caught the movement of the hammock and looked directly at it. "Yes," she said. "It's I. Sidney's just told me you've been packing up to leave." Her voice, she realized, betrayed a hostile note she hadn't intended.

"I'm just about finished. But I'm so exhausted with shifting those spacing barrels around that I had to have a rest." *Solstice's* tone of voice, to Inez's ear, conveyed indifference.

"I'm a little surprised," Inez said, then bit her lip as she heard the querulousness she so hated to hear in her father's voice now permeating her own. "You didn't mention anything about this when I saw you the other afternoon." Yes, she thought, that had come out better: now she sounded merely peeved at being the last to know. In an effort to get a firmer grip on the situation, she looked around for a place to sit. But Solstice had already rolled up her mat, and neither the barrels nor the pieces of disassembled tank would be comfortable or safe perches.

"It's time for me to go." Solstice swayed in the hammock, her eyes apparently on the ceiling. "I knew I'd have to in the fairly near future, but everything speeded up yesterday because of an unforeseen expense. So..." One hand lifted and waved in a gesture that conveyed the same sort of attitude a shrug would have done. "Here I am."

The neutrality of the waterdancer's voice so grated on Inez's sensibilities that for a few seconds, as she considered a scathing remark about the dancer's apparent lack of concern to make contact with her before leaving, she missed the allusion. But even as she turned over a selection of facetious remarks in her mind, the words *unforeseen expense* echoed in her head and impelled her to take two steps closer to the hammock.

"You have a credit problem?" Inez said, almost beside herself with irritation. Her anxiety vanished under an onslaught of anger. "Why in the spacing fuck didn't you *tell* me? Why didn't you ask me for help, instead of just packing up?"

Solstice abruptly sat up and let her legs dangle over the side of the hammock. "Your eyes are blazing like the topazes in your earrings, Inez. I think I'm a little puzzled at your anger? *Is* it anger? It's so hard to tell when you keep your face covered all the time."

Inez yanked the day-mask from her face and tossed it across the room, telling herself she didn't care if it smashed. "Of course I'm angry!" She longed to let herself go. "What the spacing fuck did you expect?"

Solstice tilted her head to one side. Her eyes—looking infuriatingly curious—met Inez's glare without flinching. "But you really are upset!" she marveled.

The words only stoked Inez's rage. Her fingers found the flow of one of her elbow scarves and began twisting and tugging at its fine (but strong) silk. "While *you* are amused." Saying this further fueled her anger, since she knew such remarks could only lose her face.

"I don't think *amused* is quite the right word," Solstice said in a voice too earnest to be believed. "*Fascinated* might work. Yes, I think I'm *fascinated* that you would feel one way or another about it. You strike me as a rather indifferent sort of person, over all."

Inez stalked to the far end of the workspace to fetch her day-mask, which had fallen near the barrels of fluid. She should have kept it on her face. Well, she'd asked for it and should have known better. She had finally discovered one person on this planet even more of a bitch than herself. She knelt on the floor and stared at the mask. For a few seconds she clenched and unclenched her fists and concentrated on relaxing her jaw and pressing her anger to the side, out of the way until she could afford to let herself go. For half an SCU, she'd allow the waterdancer to walk, she'd wash her hands of Solstice Balalzalar. But even as she trembled with the violence of her anger, that gnawing leaden sensation returned to her, and her anxiety was back with a vengeance. She couldn't let the dancer go. It had nothing to do with her father. She had no real notion of what it might be—*Intuition, perhaps? Intuition that this woman may be one of the most talented people I'll ever encounter? Or is it something else? Something I haven't yet any idea of except unconsciously?*—but knew only that she *had* to keep the dancer here in the Capitol District, at the Institute, creating powerful, original art that represented Frogmore as no existing art did.

After perhaps half a standard minute, Inez retrieved the day-mask and got to her feet. She turned back to the hammock without re-covering her face, certain that it conveyed nothing of what she was feeling. "You'd have to be a fool not to have understood that you could tap me for financial assistance," she said as she moved to within a meter of the hammock. "It never occurred to me you hadn't understood that." She stared at Solstice's almost blank face. "And I believe you did understand. You're playing some game of your own."

Solstice said nothing, only continued to watch her. "Perhaps you'd like an arrangement somewhat more specified? A regular income, for instance?"

Solstice slid out of the hammock to stand with her arms folded over her chest. "I don't understand you people," she said. "Understanding requires some familiarity, of course. But even with certain things staring me in the face, I find it difficult to believe. All the time I lived on Pleth I expended an inordinate amount of effort trying to decipher the meaning of things people said and did. But never once did I run into an instance of this. Of course people do tend to be private about such things. Still, it never crossed my mind that even among your kind, daughters would ever do such things for their fathers."

Inez's face burned. It's not embarrassment I feel, she insisted to herself, but *rage*. "That's a sufficiently ambiguous statement that it could mean almost anything," she said, speaking in a low voice, the better to keep control of herself. "But if you're suggesting my only interest in you is to induce you to partner the general, you're wrong." She forced a smile to show her scorn for the waterdancer's insinuation but suspected she had achieved only a twitch of a grimace, so unnatural and twisted did her mouth feel.

Solstice moved a few paces away. After a few seconds of staring at the stacked pieces of the tank, she turned and said, "There's nothing I want from you. I originally thought it might be interesting to work here, to spend time in the Capitol District, to see if there were anyone here—" she waved vaguely toward the corridor door— "I might be able to collaborate with. But that didn't pan out. And anyway, I'd from the beginning decided I'd leave once I had exhausted the fee the governor paid me for that performance you saw. My unexpected expense merely hastened the process." Solstice proffered an easy but remote smile that left her eyes as distant as they usually were. "I've no desire to stay on."

"What about the new work? You *must* stay! I can see that it's performed everywhere. I can even arrange a tour for you all over Frogmore, and a long engagement on Holliday if you'd like! You must stay!"

Solstice's smile vanished. "I don't have to do anything. And I certainly don't have to stay here."

"I can do so much for you!" Inez held out her hands, palms open in a gesture signifying either generosity or supplication (or both). "Whereas if you go back to your dreary little islands out in the back of the back of beyond, you'll spend your entire life in oblivion and eventually will have to give up your work altogether! What is the *point* of creating art if no audience ever experiences it?"

A long pause ensued. Finally Solstice said, "Why does it matter so much to you whether I go or stay? That's what *I'd* like to know."

Inez bit her lip. "I don't know myself. Only that it *does* matter." She continued to stare at Solstice's face even though she hated having yielded her those words. She urged herself to leave, to wash her hands of an obviously bad situation ~ *what the spacing fuck am I* doing, begging *this woman to stay?* ~ while another part of her wished she had introduced Nathalie Stillness to Solstice, or at least given Nathalie the report on Solstice Cleveland had provided her with so that Nathalie could have explained *some*thing about this mentality so (painfully) alien to her.

In the lengthening silence Inez sought a new tack to adopt and recalled her intention to persuade the waterdancer to take up teaching her art-form to other dancers here at the Institute. "You said you hadn't found anyone to work with here," she said. "What about teaching? I had intended to ask you to consider offering instruction through the Institute, but hadn't yet gotten around to it. Surely teaching is the best way of finding others to work with?"

The waterdancer produced another smile, but this one she clearly intended to be chilling. "Maybe you know why I decided there was no one here I could work with?"

"No, I don't. There are a lot of dancers here from off-world. They aren't very good dealing with the gravity, but in more reasonable conditions of gravity they are all superb dancers. It seems to me you'd have no trouble finding first-rate people to dance with you."

"To dance *with* me?" Solstice queried with a sarcasm Inez could not fathom. "They're interested in ripping off my techniques, and that's about all. Their interests are as far from mine as it's possible for them to be and still be in any way connected with the aesthetic movement of the human body."

"*How* are they different?" Inez shot back as she tried to penetrate what Solstice was talking about. "Give me a specific example, something I can understand."

The waterdancer shook her head. "I can't think of anything I could say that could get you to understand what I'm talking about. And if you *did*, you'd probably want to turn me over to one of the therapists your kind have blessed this planet with."

The hostility of this—though the waterdancer's voice had retained its usual detached tone—not to say its injustice, took Inez by surprise. "I can't believe you can accuse me of such a thing!" She fairly sputtered with indignation. "I who have been standing here trying to persuade you to accept my support!" Resentment, hurt, desire to lash back, all fought a battle for dominance. "And!" she cried as she recalled the first part of Solstice's extraordinary attack, "And! It's not exactly flattering to discover you think I'm stupid, to boot!"

"Hardly stupid," Solstice said with another of her frozen tundra smiles. "Stupid isn't the best adjective for people whose conceptual apparatus differs from one's own. As for my so-called accusation—" She took a few steps sideways, running her index-finger along the glass-smooth surface of one of the pieces of tank. "There are only a handful of people living on this world who can afford to be indifferent to the psychiatric practices the Gauthier presence has made so prevalent." The waterdancer stared fixedly at the piece of tank she was fingering. "If anyone is found to deviate publicly so much as a jot from your Combine standards, then it's off to therapy for them." Solstice looked up. "The real twist of the knife, though, comes from the ambiguity of what those standards for 'normal socialized survival-oriented behavior' are. How, for example, does one decide who is truly survival-oriented and who isn't?"

"None of this has anything to do with why you think you can't work with the other dancers at this Institute." Inez's voice was now as remote and frosted as Solstice's eyes. "I've never mixed politics and art. I won't be so fatuous as to claim that what the peacekeeping forces do—and I naturally don't agree with your assessment of the effect they've had on this planet—as I say, I won't claim to be without connection to the peacekeeping forces, since my only reason for living on this world is my father's presence here. But I *never* mix politics and art, as I say. And I'm not in the least interested in *your* politics." She smiled coldly. "In fact, I'm quite certain your political opinions would bore me to death. No one's asking you to implicate yourself politically. Which is why your accusation is particularly and egregiously obnoxious." The fool apparently thought her differences of political opinion more important than her art.

"Now look who's considering whom stupid," Solstice flashed back—showing the first evidence of heat Inez had been able to detect. "Not only are you someone who knows inside-out the connections between art, credit, and politics, someone who understands well what functions an institution like this Institute of yours serves on a world like Frogmore, but you actively promote a repulsively blatant brand of politics, even in your capacity as the planet's foremost social butterfly. To take just one obvious example: that nauseating piece of banality you offered at that party you invited me to. It was nothing more than crude propaganda." Solstice edged a few steps closer. "And yet you can stand there and claim you don't mix politics and art!" The dancer was nearly shouting, startling Inez into the realization that Solstice's voice had been growing in volume and her eyes had become black, flaming pools of anger.

No wonder she won't have anything to do with Paul, Inez thought. She's completely insane on the subject of politics. Obviously she hates him only on principle, since she doesn't actually *know* him. The dancer's open and hot anger allowed Inez a sense of control. It puzzled her a little that she wasn't simply walking out of the room, that rather than a compulsion to wash her hands of the dancer, she felt instead a slight elation at having broken past a barrier that had been stymieing her. And Solstice's calling her "the planet's foremost social butterfly" amused her, though she knew that logically it should not. Don't laugh, she warned herself. Don't laugh at her rage. Laughing at Solstice now would irrevocably push the dancer to the wall.

Holding her mouth firm, curbing her desire to laugh and mock, Inez said, "I hadn't the faintest idea in advance of what either the content or the form of that performance piece would be. I *never* exert influence on the artists I support. And if you think I subscribe to the nihilism of the piece they did at that party, you're dead wrong." She shrugged her shoulders and held her hands out in a *what-will-you?* gesture. "I'm the last person to advocate censorship of art, you know." She smiled tightly. "And the very idea of putting an artist like you into therapy turns my stomach. That would be the ultimate in censorship, don't you think? I doubt you'd retain any interest in creating your waterdance after having been subjected to it. So I'm the *last* person who would ever hold an artist's politics against her." Inez flicked a glance at the piece of tank over which the dancer constantly moved her finger. "Unless, of course," she said, "the politics interfered with the art. In which case it would be boring." She bowed to the dancer. "As I agree that the piece performed at my party was. Obvious political messages can *only* be boring." Inez produced one of her light social titters. "I find politics under most circumstances boring. Bad enough to put up with in the contexts my father necessarily brings me into contact with, but in art it can be only tedious."

The dancer moved away from the pile of tank parts. She stopped short, a meter from Inez, and stood with her arms folded over her chest.

The plain cling-ons, the head hair, the wrist implant, all these are symbols of the dancer's politics, Inez realized. She thinks such symbols of protest significant—as though such personal choices could matter to anyone but herself and others like her.

"I picked too obvious an example," Solstice said, her voice now as cool and detached as it had been at the outset of the conversation. "The infusion of politics into art—or rather I should say the *con*fusion of the two—runs deep and is for the most part too subtle for most people to see." Her gaze locked with the general's daughter's, and the latter felt a tendril of curiosity—charged with an odd, seemingly out of place frisson that puzzled her as much as the curiosity did—pluck at the new construction of Solstice she had hastily assembled in her need to meet the situation.

I haven't the faintest idea of what is going on here, least of all inside me, Inez thought, inflating her tinge of curiosity into full-blown surprise.

"Political attitudes and positions," the dancer said, "underlie everything we do, say, or think. It's impossible for art to be *pure* of politics—that is a word you'd use, isn't it? *Pure* art? Unpolluted by dirty, grimy real-life politics?"

"Oh," Inez exclaimed with relief. "I see what you're getting at! You're referring to the basic *philosophical* issues that have always dogged aesthetics. I've been interested in these matters for a long time, myself. Are you familiar with the work of Alexandra Jador of Pleth?" She grew excited—she hadn't guessed she would *finally* have someone to talk to about Alexandra Jador of Pleth's work! She rushed on before Solstice could reply. "But of course you are, if your conceptualization of your own work is so thoroughly engaged with a consciousness of these problems. And I can see how *frustrating* it must be for you to attempt to communicate with simple ordinary dancers on this subject. No *wonder* you feel they wouldn't be able to appreciate what you are doing, that they would simply reduce it all to a matter of technique to be applied any way it occurred to them to use it." Inez smiled. "I suppose that explains why I felt your work was so much *deeper* than the others'. Really, Solstice, you *must* let me support your work. Given your obvious sense of political commitment, surely you have an obligation to go as far as you can with your dance and to reach as large an audience as you can. I *assure* you I wouldn't *dream* of interfering with anything you might choose to do!"

Solstice had an odd expression on her face, an expression Inez could not read. Its enigma lay in the dark, shining opaque eyes, a flicker in them, perhaps, or a slight shifting in their placement in the dancer's face as though her facial muscles had gone slightly awry, the eyebrows a little off, and now that Inez looked closely it seemed that the mouth and nose, too, had taken positions unfamiliar enough to make their behavior marked, though not decipherable. How, Inez wondered, would such subtle facial movements be interpreted by a first-rate design, say *The Deliberate*?

"You don't understand at all," Solstice finally said.

"I can believe that," Inez said. "Which is fine with me. It will give me something to work on. I'm always in need of stimulation, especially of this sort, which is all too rare. But at least I do have a notion that something is there." She smiled at the dancer. "Which, you must admit, is *some*thing."

Solstice's eyebrows drew together—that much Inez could make out—to express, perhaps, skepticism, or even puzzlement? After a long pause, Solstice said, "The question for me is just how far my accepting what you like to call *support* would compromise me and my work. Obviously it would have some effect. Whereas if I return to my archipelago oblivion I'll know myself to have escaped unscathed."

"I'm not used to thinking of my support as a source of corruption," Inez said. She stared down at the day-mask in her hand and fiddled with one of its adherent seams. "But I repeat, I won't interfere. And I can give you as much exposure as you'd like." She looked at the dancer. "There it is. An offer of virtual *carte blanche*. I can't remember ever having offered anyone as much."

Solstice moved back toward the stack of disassembled tank parts, then pivoted to face Inez. "I'll consider it," she said.

"All right," Inez said. "It's a shame, though, you waited until your tank was all in pieces." The weight of the dancer's being packed and ready to go would tell against a decision to stay. Still, what an offer! If the dancer refused it... If the dancer refused it, she would have to wonder what extraneous factors were playing into the decision that the dancer hadn't told her about. She could, of course, find out. Inez moved toward the threshold. No, that way lay something ugly, for using such methods on Solstice would—even should she never become aware of them—tinge their relations with something that would spoil whatever it was that so intrigued and drew her to the dancer.

At the threshold Inez turned and bowed. "If you still choose to leave, please don't go until we've talked again." When Solstice did not reply, Inez pressed her: "Will you agree to that, Solstice?"

The waterdancer sighed. "Yes, Inez, I'll tell you my decision in person—that *is* what you're asking?"

Inez smiled wearily. "Thank you." She deopaqued the threshold.

Out in the corridor she realized she hadn't replaced her day-mask and quickly fitted it over her face. I must be crazy, she told herself. I must be out of my spacing mind...

Frogmore Central University, the only institution on Frogmore permitted to be designated a university, originated in the second half of Frogmore's first century as a vocational school, intended to provide the necessary education and training for skilled workers who could not afford even two years of education on Pleth. In its first decade of existence, the school offered courses in applied mathematics, the mechanical arts, computer-coding, robotics maintenance, midwifery, nutritional design, occupational health and safety, cosmetology, methods of policing, etc. The school began certificate programs in its second decade, through which a variety of remedial courses in the basic letters, arts, and sciences found their way into the curriculum. As often happens with institutions on developing worlds, mission-creep set in just a generation after its founding. By Frogmore's third century, the school had become, de facto, a college, and by the middle of Frogmore's fourth century, was proclaimed, by the governor, to be a university with four discrete colleges.

Worlds other than Pleth are not, of course, permitted to host universities independent of Pleth's regulations and governance. When the Combine demanded that this university be returned to its original status and function as a vocational school, Frogmore's governor called a plebiscite (only the second of the three ever held on Frogmore). Ninety-five percent of Frogmore's voting citizens expressed support for Frogmore Central University. The Combine rescinded its ban. Frogmore Central University remains the only university in the galaxy not located on Pleth.

—Frogmore: The CDS Fact Book

Fourteen
ARIEL DOLMA

Ariel Dolma to Livvy Kracauer
4.VII.493

Dearest,

Everyone's in an uproar here! So I really really need to
write, especially since for the last few days I've had little time
to myself. (You could probably tell that from the brevity of
our chats lately.) Before the uproar broke out, I never had the
time because I was working so hard—doing a lot of reading
of past matriarch's logs, directives, and analyses, to supplement this phase of my instruction. All was going well with
this, and I was even enjoying myself, when disaster struck.
I at first mistook it for a serious snafu rather than the disaster it is, partly because this dome works so differently from
my mother's home dome, and partly because I didn't at first
grasp its global implications.

Paula's Dome, as you've probably understood by now,
isn't at all like Suzanne's Dome. It keeps itself as separate
from the rest of the world as it can, which means that its
internal economy works without reference to SCUs. It needs
SCUs, of course, in order to purchase inelastic goods and services that it can't produce for itself. Its SCU revenue mainly
comes from wages paid to members who hold low-level jobs
almost exclusively outside. Eighteen members hold jobs at
the UAP plant in Pimlico. They've all been given notice that
UAP is shutting down the plant—permanently—and shift-

ing it to an orbital station. The loss of this revenue stream is bad enough, but it turns out that UAP is moving *all* of its plants off-world. UAP, in case you weren't aware of this, produces about 90% of the agricultural staples consumed on Frogmore, meaning, of course, that the company will have a greater ability to leverage its monopoly from off-planet than it already has (which is, of course, considerable). In the past, according to the folks here, collective pressure has repeatedly kept UAP from "sucking blood from a stone"—i.e., keeping prices of basic (as opposed to "luxury") goods affordable.

Everything seems turned upside down. Ordinarily the people living in this dome behave as though the outside world is imaginary. (Even the ones who work "outside.") Suddenly, the world outside is totally real—and a concatenation of unknowable, hostile forces bent on crushing all good and decent people. Well, maybe that's an exaggeration. The Grand Mother has a fairly clear, calm notion of life outside Paula's Dome and certainly doesn't think of herself and her people as powerless. In some ways, though, the others are strangely childish. Claire especially. Even though she's only a few years younger than I am, it's been increasingly difficult for me to think of her as an adult, which in the dome's terms, she is.

I'm so tired! So I'll say goodnight now, dearest.

A.

Ariel Dolma to Livvy Kracauer
6.VII.493

Dearest,

The mood is calmer, I'm happy to say, even though confirmation has come that possible alternatives for employment of those being terminated would require moving to another region—or acquiring full connection. (Of course that's the reason all the people working outside the dome here can hold only low-level jobs.) Both of these conditions are deal-breakers for members of Paula's, of course. (Which I'm sure you've figured out, given that the real reason I've avoided acquiring connection is because the stance of every Family dome except Suzanne's is that members who acquire it must leave.)

The reason the mood's better is that the dome has drawn up a plan (thanks, I have reason to know, to the Grand Mother's refusal to be panicked into handwringing despair). For all that, I don't think the plan will do anything other than stave off panic; unless they have stronger political juice than I'm assuming, they have no leverage with UAP to speak of. Actually, I suspect that the Grand Mother is in the process of planning for that contingency. (Someone has to!) Having said that, I must admit I admire their insistence on attempting to force UAP to stay rather than simply trying to work around the sudden drop in revenue. It seems to me that they have so much to lose that common sense would dictate their seeking assistance to help tide them over until they find alternative sources of revenue. (Though of course a part of me wonders why they don't adopt at least part of Suzanne's Dome's strategy of opening their childcare crèches and school to "outsiders," at least to the extent that most of the other domes do. Even as I know what most members' answer to that would be.)

I have only a few weeks left before I'm scheduled to go to Durazzo to begin my practical internship. I understand why the Grand Mother's attention must go first to this crisis, but I have to admit the possibility of my not being able to finish my instruction with her before I leave concerns me.

One cool thing was that after the meeting tonight, people brought out their guitars, tambourines, and drums and lifted their voices in song. (I heard two songs I hadn't heard before, one of which was a ballad about time-trippers that I'm determined to learn before I leave.)

A.

Ariel Dolma to Livvy Kracauer
7.VII.493

Dearest,

When we chatted earlier, you sounded confused about the differences between Suzanne's and Paula's. The thing is, Violet's is the closest of the other Family domes to Suzanne's, while Paula's is more like Bessy's (if you can recall what I've said about those other domes). When I started my studies I wondered right away why Suzanne's was so different—so open. I assumed it must simply be that the Daughters of Suzanne Waters had cultivated a culture of tolerance and even openness over the course of its history. But now that I've had so much exposure to the journals of the founders and the histories of the Families, I think it has to do with the implications of their reproductive arrangements. (I'm trusting this isn't too much information for you… If it is, just stop reading here.)

The key difference, I think, is this: in Suzanne's, members choose to have mostly female children. (I've never mentioned this to you before, since it's a pretty loaded subject—and because I haven't yet made up my mind about whether that tradition will affect me. Shit. I've never even asked my parents whether they selected my sex or left it to chance.) Selecting female births was actually the practice of the founders, though the insularity and resulting conservatism of places like Paula's would suggest that they, not Suzanne's, is truest to tradition. They're not.)

Because they have mostly female children, members of Suzanne's tend to seek mates outside the Family. Of course this wasn't always true. For the first few decades they mostly recombined ova, with occasional sperm donations from men who weren't interested in Family life. Eventually, though, as most of the other domes opted to begin having male children (because, I think, Frogmore had stopped importing most of its labor), Suzanne's encouraged its members to bring mates from other Families into the Dome. Over the last century, Suzanne's began providing childcare for non-members and accepting day pupils in its school (which considerably enhances its revenue outlook). Over the last 30 years, many members have begun to mate outside the Families altogether and, in some cases, form life partnerships and establish households outside the Dome. Many of us—going back more than a century—have been educated at FCU—and hold demanding, careerist jobs. (Like my mother.)

It's always amusing (in an irony-rich way) to have people in Paula's ooh and ah over the weaving I brought as a guest gift, only to be taken aback when I explain that my father and his workshop assistants produced it, and not my mother. See, everyone here knows that Suzanne's produces some of the finest pieces of textile arts on the planet, and since they know I belong through my mother and that my mother chose to mate outside the Families, it never crosses their minds that it's my father, not my mother, who is the primary weaver. So then I have to explain how my father was a day pupil in the Dome when he was a child and how he not only met my mother there but also learned to weave with one of the Dome's top masters. (That's not at all amusing, since after the first telling it became tedious to recount.) I also have to explain that my mother's fine salary helps subsidize my father's workshop. Well, you know that, so I don't have to explain it all over again to you. What I'm saying is that most of the people here can only think in terms dividing the world between Families and "outsiders." Can you imagine trying to explain some of things you have to deal with in your job to them? As far as they're concerned, all "outsiders" have the same interests and beliefs about how to live in the world.

Hmm. I can't help but think that that conceptual division is one of the primary obstacles they face in dealing effectively with this crisis. It frustrates me, but also makes me sad, because I don't see how this crisis can end well for Paula's, no matter how bravely they act.

A.

Ariel Dolma to Livvy Kracauer
9.VII.493

Dearest,

Another meeting last night, at which the Grand Mother and a much older woman named Violet Chang reported on their conferences with Pimlico's Representative to Parliament and a flunky for the Executive Regional Manager. It came as no surprise to me, of course, that both of these politicians declared themselves all in favor of UAP's move and recommended that Paula's Dome get with the program. Much outrage expressed at the meeting, of course. Which was fine with everyone, until one of the displaced workers got up and made a powerful argument for joining the Anti-Combine League. She pointed out that if the Dome went through with the mass actions they thought their only recourse, they'd end up brain-wiped, which would result in damaging the Dome. Four other members then joined Allie (the one who'd made the impassioned argument)—using considerably more inflammatory language. The Grand Mother and Violet Chang, who were alone on the dais, then lectured everyone on their obligation, in all their collective actions, not to increase entropy on Frogmore. One of the older members arguing for joining the Anti-Combine League then said—and I quote here, because his words have gotten stuck in my mind: "Principles are fine when people are allowed to follow them. They're meaningless when they result in our own destruction." That won another adherent to the cause. Perhaps because of that, Violet Chang proposed that the six be "excluded" until they "came to their senses." A voice vote followed, in which the "Ayes" were louder than the "Nays."

I didn't understand what "excluded" meant (it's their official word for ostracized) until this morning when Claire scolded me for talking to three of the excluded (which I did last night after the meeting broke up). We got into an acrimonious argument that ended abruptly when she threatened *me* with ostracism and stomped off without allowing me to reply.

You're probably wondering if I've lost my mind, sympathizing with people who feel driven to join the Anti-Combine League. I've never been a radical, and I don't suppose I'd ever consider joining it myself, but I do think the situation needs much more discussion than it's getting around here. The six make some excellent points that need consideration. The refusal to hear them reminds me of how when we were kids we'd stick our fingers in our ears to keep from hearing something we didn't want to hear. Part of me thinks, only in Paula's. It would never work in Suzanne's, I'll tell you that. Anyone ostracized there would simply leave, since the membrane between Dome and "outside" is so permeable.

Gah. It's their spacing isolation that's making them feeble! Why can't they see that?

I'm so riled up over this I can't concentrate on the work I should be doing. This is another of those times when writing a letter to you is vastly inferior to being able to chat freely. A.

Ariel Dolma to Livvy Kracauer
10.VII.493

Dearest,

I'm making a holo describing the situation with UAP and the Families in general and Paula's Dome in particular. I know this is a lot to ask, given this kind of work is what you do all day long, but would you help me with the editing? You've dinned it into my head that the editing is often what makes good material do its work, and that no editing or poor editing can sabotage even the most powerful stuff. I know it may be too late to make a significant difference, but I feel as though I must try—using the kind of methods I've been trying to tell people here are more effective than physical protest.

I hope it goes without saying that if you can't or don't want to do it, I'll understand perfectly.

A.

Ministry of the Interior, Frogmore Central Governing
Authority
[Dossier: Inez Gauthier, File #37414]
HIGHLY CONFIDENTIAL
Report from G. Emphala, 3.VII.493

Pursuant to concerns raised by Sargent N. Ponte (Doc #J664-67-223-4901 and Doc#J664-67-223-4901A) about visiting scholar Nathalie Stillness, I've accessed her already thick PFI file, which includes a considerable volume of audio and video files as well as three background checks drawing extensively on background checks conducted by the CDS division of Grants & Fellowships. CDS has consistently assigned Stillness a green status, as has PFI. The latter's interest in her is due strictly to her close association with IG and frequent in-the-flesh contacts with PG, extending even to private lunches with both.

Ponte's concerns focus exclusively on Stillness's potential, through her scholarship, to shape off-worlders' impression of and views on Frogmore's culture, which Stillness apparently sees as distinct and unique to the planet. According to Ponte, Stillness's perceptions are largely due to her focusing exclusively on the ACCMs living in separatist domes. Such a focus can only warp off-worlders' perceptions of Frogmore and give them a disgust of aspects of Frogmore's culture that have developed as adaptive responses to Frogmore's particular conditions. My perusal of Stillness's PFI file persuades me that this could pose a serious problem after Stillness has returned to Pleth and published her findings. Off-world information about Frogmore culture has until now been highly generalized, except where it has focused on the Capitol District. Stillness is well enough regarded by CDS to be perceived by them as a potential asset, contingent on the "right circumstances."

I recommend altering NS's status to that of Loose Canon and strongly advise that her movements be restricted to the Capitol District.

Fifteen
MADELEINE TAO

Jordan Winters jabbed his fork into the cold vegetable tart he had chosen for his entrée. His vigor, Madeline thought, lately had a savage edge to it. "Getting to be about that time again for you, isn't it, Madeleine?"

She sucked a sip of puree through her pretty glass straw, then answered in the affirmative, adding that she would be glad to be shed of her criminal judgeship. "There's a reason our rotations last only two and a half years," she said dryly.

"Sometimes I wish the assignments lasted only a year," Solange Rousseau said in a plaintive voice. "Sometimes I think I can't bear yet another day of the same depressing work."

"I keep wondering, instead," Jordan said, "whether it wouldn't be better for each of us to find our niche and stay in it. To consciously specialize. Has it never occurred to you that one might be constitutionally compatible with only a certain number of jobs? That some people might make great defense lawyers but lousy criminal judges? Or that one might make a better criminal judge than a civil one?"

"That's been tried," Madeleine said. "And what's clear is that we're all part of the same system, we're all striving for the same goals and values, and the more we cross-fertilize our careers with diverse experiences, the better overall view of our goals and values and the workings of the system we'll achieve, with the consequence that we're better able to serve society than we would be were we to develop narrow partisan biases."

Solange's eyes beamed approval. "Absolutely!"

That feathered cap Solange wore: where had she bought it?

Solange said, "The rule that one must have served at least one round as a criminal defense attorney and another as a criminal prosecutor before serving on the criminal bench displays eminent sensibility. Otherwise how could a judge comprehend the bases on which to assess a case? Or have any idea what lies behind the presentations of the defendant?"

"Granted a certain amount of experience is useful, perhaps even essential for particular functions," Jordan said. He lifted an impressively large bite of tart to the wide oral-orifice in his day-mask. "But surely an internship during which one serves various functions in order to acquire experience would suffice." He slid the bite of tart into his mouth without losing any of it along the way. There was something to be said for having such a wide orifice in one's day-mask, even if it did look undignified.

Madeleine said between sips, "A rigid hierarchy would develop were one to place certain jobs—judgeships, for instance—above others. You can imagine how such jobs could come to be rated—and what a debilitating effect such a ranking would have on the legal system as a whole. We'd be open to the same sort of corruption and demoralization rife in most of the governing authority's bureaucracy."

"I take your point," Jordan said. "But to be frank, I'm getting more than a little tired of being shuffled about every two and a half years. Where our assignments are concerned, geographical location is the only real choice we're allowed."

"True," Madeleine said. "But it means one doesn't have a chance to get stuck in a rut." She caught a look from Solange and offered a shrug that Jordan, concentrating on his tart, missed. She and Solange had just the week before discussed her ambivalence about leaving the criminal bench when her term expired in five months. She felt nearly burned out by the emotional toll it had taken on her, but, given the newly radical—almost Draconian—attitude of the district supervisor's letter urging all disruption convictions to carry sentences of Total Therapy, she had begun to think of herself as one of the few lone holdouts against a dangerous tendency sweeping the legal system. Madeleine knew, for example, that Jordan subscribed to the notion that if Total Therapy were prescribed in all cases of disruption, the rising incidents of violence would be eliminated.

Madeleine often argued about this with Jordan, insisting that such reasoning so tightly defined the problem of violence and refused consideration of the possible unintended effects of such Draconian measures that only the most specious notion of logic could maintain it as a valid syllogism. But the panic so many people had lately succumbed to had erected a barrier that no amount of logic could penetrate. And so she had—for the moment, at least—given up on Jordan. Two years earlier it had been Madeleine who had succeeded to Jordan's courtroom and chambers while he had gone on to representing plaintiffs in tort and social civil suits. He made no secret of his desire that his next assignment return him to the criminal bench, or of his conviction that he was perfectly suited for it.

Just answer me this, Judge. How many brain murders do you think justifiable in the name of maintaining your government? The defendant's attorney had moved to have the defendant's remark struck from the record, but one could not somehow strike such remarks from one's memory. This one in particular persisted. Surely most of her colleagues—whether during their time on the bench or representing defendants or prosecuting them—carried similar remarks in their heads? Or *did* they? Could it be possible that such remarks served only to deepen Jordan's conviction of the need to eradicate the sickness of violence through harsher sentencing?

"Have you heard the news?"

Roberta Dumas, wearing a plain pastel day-mask, was standing beside Jordan. Her hands fluttered with excitement.

"What news?" Solange said sharply.

Dumas bent forward, until her face was only inches from Jordan's. Jordan leaned away from her, his mouth tight with distaste. She spoke in a loud whisper, her eyes darting from day-mask to day-mask. "They finally tracked down all the details in that holo-substitution case, including how and where it was made and the identity of the ringleaders of the gang who made and distributed it."

A pity, Madeleine thought, that they didn't have a more appropriate word than *distributed* to use for the gang's flagrant insertion of their libelous piece of propaganda in place of those previously scheduled and paid for. *Distributed* rendered their crime a prank or joke, which it definitely was not. Such holos, especially when illegally foisted onto the public, did special damage to preadults, who were vulnerable to that sort of bravado in the first place and the violence of that sort of presentation in the second.

"It's about time," Jordan said. "I was beginning to wonder about the wisdom of entrusting the case to the Governor's Intelligence Service." Jordan shoved his empty plate into the center of the table and activated the disposal. Dumas started to speak, but Jordan ran on without giving her a chance to finish whatever she had begun to say. "Who knows how many copies are still floating around. The spacing thing keeps popping up after how many months now since they seized the ones they *then* claimed were the ringleaders?"

"You'll never guess who one of the ringleaders is," Dumas said before anyone else could speak.

"You mean it's someone we know?"

"Or at least know *of*."

"Are you going to tell us, or do we have to guess?" Madeleine asked irritably when Dumas failed to go on.

Dumas's glittering eyes met Madeleine's. "It's the daughter of Brian Maslin and Henrietta West."

They all gasped and murmured their shock. After the first flash of surprise receded, a wave of cold rippled over Madeleine. One always had that fear. That it could be one's own child. Henrietta West had once been a colleague, was one of their own.

"Just imagine, the daughter of people right up there at the top," Dumas half-whispered. "The daughter of a minister and the governor's Chief Legal Counsel. It makes you think almost *any*one could—"

Jordan interrupted. "Where did you hear this? Surely they're trying to keep it quiet?"

"My office booked her," Dumas said. "And you know they'll never keep a thing like that quiet."

Solange said, "I wonder what will happen."

Jordan's head turned sharply towards Solange. "What do you mean? What else *can* happen but that the girl goes on trial like any other disrupter caught in the act?"

"It's more than a single instance of disruption," Dumas said. "I gather they uncovered a large-scale conspiracy involving a couple dozen people. And they caught her in the act of producing another holo of the same ilk as the first one."

Madeleine removed her personal straw from the empty soup glass and wiped it with her napkin, then shoved her soup glass and napkin to the center. She could remember meeting various of West and Maslin's progeny over the last few years; one of the daughters had been Holland's classmate in secondary school. If someone were to ask her to swear absolute certainty that neither of her own children had gotten mixed up in disruptive activities, could she honestly do so? She rose and bowed to her colleagues and headed for the administrative wing. No, of course she couldn't. Reasonable certainty, yes. But then Henrietta West had probably thought the same, too, poor woman. She was fortunate, she supposed, that she had only two children to worry over and thus less of a chance statistically to suffer the kind of agony Henrietta

West must now be going through. *How many brain murders, Judge?* How insidious language could be. Total therapy was *not* "brain murder." Still, Henrietta West's daughter would not be the same person afterwards. Not murder, no. But there would be loss, most definitely, and mainly for the girl's parents. It was they who would suffer most. Jordan, Madeleine knew, would say that was as it should be, since the parents had failed the Public Good. But it seemed otherwise to Madeleine, who had always understood her children as beings of independent mind and will. But then Jordan...was Jordan.

It's Pleth, of course, Madeleine mused as she waited outside Roland Lawrence's office. They come back from Pleth angry. Not all of them, of course. And not all of them that angry. But most of them dissatisfied, ambivalent—both loving and hating Frogmore, loving and hating everything the most advanced societies had to offer. Critical of everything they lay eyes on. Finding fault. Taking their first jobs, they needed to learn to accept the limitations they worked under, learn to set goals in the long-term and midterm as well as the short-term. To let love carry them forward, beyond anger and frustration. To learn to be *constructive.*

Lawrence's doorway deopaqued. A man dressed from his feathery cap to his linen-shod toes in a strictly matched gray and red ensemble appeared on the threshold and bowed to Madeleine. "Judge Tao."

Madeleine bowed back. "Special Administrator Lawrence."

"Please." Lawrence swept his arm back into the room behind him. "Do enter."

Lawrence's office boasted an impressive expanse of floor space. Madeleine recognized the holoscape of Lake Farragut on Pleth, an impersonal choice lacking in originality. Had he formed an attachment to Lake Farragut so powerful that the judgment and aesthetic taste with which an education on

Pleth must have imbued him had been brutally and mindlessly overrun by sentimentality?

She took the chair before Lawrence's desk, and Lawrence seated himself behind the desk. Silently she reviewed what little she had been able to learn about him after he had requested she meet with him. He had spent fifteen years on Pleth acquiring three advanced degrees in law (constitutional, commercial, and diplomatic); had served for four years on administrative and advisory panels of the Frogmore Greater Legislature; and had worked three years for the governor, serving highly classified functions. Staring across the desk at his gray and red day-mask, she grew uncomfortable as she noted that some sort of fine mesh over the eye-holes prevented her from seeing his eyes.

"So," Lawrence said. "It's my understanding that your current term of rotation will be coming to an end in five months."

"Yes, that's correct," Madeleine said. "Judging by past experience, I should be receiving notification of the new assignment within the next month or two."

Lawrence pulled open a drawer and rummaged about in it. "Yes, yes, I suppose that is so." He lifted his hand from the drawer and shoved a long, thin chew-stick into his mouth, then closed the drawer. "Yes," he said around his teeth-gripped chew-stick, "yes, I gather that is the usual procedure." His head tilted to one side, and Madeleine wished she could see his eyes. Surely he must be staring at her, but how could she establish eye-contact when all she could see was that annoying gray mesh? He lifted his hand to his mouth and removed the chew-stick. The bright threads in the red cling-ons, she realized, were really silver.

"I have a proposition to make you, Judge," he said abruptly. "I'd like you to consider taking up another line of work when your current term of rotation is up. I appreciate of course what utterly valuable work you are executing in your current capacity, work I have on the best authority you have been tirelessly dedicated to." He put the chew-stick into his mouth and gnawed at it for a few seconds before continuing.

Madeleine waited. His resorting to the chew-stick in her presence argued either incredible arrogance or infantile foolishness. Yes, one knew that many many people depended on chew-sticks. But they usually indulged in private, *never* in a professional setting, for what were chew-sticks but instruments of a surreptitious vice that betrayed fundamental psychical insecurity due to inadequate care by the surrogates who had tended one in infancy?

Lawrence yanked the chew-stick away from the oral orifice of his day-mask and heaved an ostentatious sigh. "The truth is, Judge, that I can't tender this proposition to you without your taking an oath of secrecy." He stabbed the air between them with the chew-stick. "The classification of the data involved is far above that covered by your current oath."

"I see." Madeleine hadn't been expecting this, and it threw her off balance. Did she want to hear more? She had no problem with the principle involved in oaths of secrecy, but she could imagine being informed of things she would rather not know. "I'm wondering," she said, "what you think the chances are that I'd leave my current work for the job you're proposing to me. Obviously you've learned a few things about me."

Lawrence, twirling the chew-stick in his fingers, sighed again. "Frankly, I hadn't thought of it that way. In considering divulging the data to you, my main thought has been your desirability for the position."

Madeleine stared down at her hands lying pointedly quiet in her lap. After a few seconds she looked at his day-mask. "You understand my discomfort?"

"Yes, yes, and appreciate it—oh vastly! Which rather underscores, don't you know, your suitability for this job." He harrumphed in his throat. "But I'm afraid, Judge, that I really couldn't predict whether you will take the job or not. It's unusual enough that..." He shrugged.

Madeleine thought for a few seconds. "Very well. I'll take the oath."

Lawrence pushed a screen toward her. "There's the coding data you need."

"Absolute secrecy? Or may I discuss any part of it with responsible persons?"

"For now let's say absolute secrecy. Unless you accept the position." Lawrence lifted his chew-stick to his lips. "And then we can work out what is to be said to whom, since given the nature of the position...well, you'll understand when we get to it."

Madeleine subvocalized the correct sequence and, when the oath had been messaged to her, assented to it. She pushed the screen back toward Lawrence.

He removed the chew-stick from his mouth and smiled. "Excellent. Now. The situation is basically this: CDS has asked the governor to set up an advisory board for them, of which I've been named Chief Regent. The board is to be made up of regents who will oversee the work of what we are for the moment calling "settlement cadre," whose task will be to set up and initially staff a government for the planet Aureole, which CDS intends to begin settling as soon as our board is ready to go." His fingers drummed on the desk. "It's an exciting venture. As a regent, your task would be to recruit and supervise a cadre of legal and judicial experts who would draft a constitution and legal code for this planet and set up all the necessary administrative institutions it will need to function in a civilized fashion."

Madeleine frowned. He was considering *her* for such a position? "But I know nothing about constitutions and have no administrative experience whatsoever."

"Ah but you needn't be a constitutional expert to carry out this job, Judge. Oversight: that's the key. I myself have some expertise in that area and would obviously be able to assist you in accessing the appropriate expertise for that area of your operations. But you *do* have experience in administration, whether you realize it or not. And more importantly— this is the thing that has drawn our attention to you—you have an instinct for crafting creative procedures that respond to the exigencies of the moment. You do realize why you've been tracked almost exclusively in the Criminal Section for the last twenty years, don't you?"

It occurred to Madeleine that the current district supervisor would be unlikely to concur in this judgment of her performance; only last week he had sent her a note pressing her to reconsider her sentencing in the Elliott Tracy case. "You've taken me completely by surprise," Madeleine said. "I don't know where this planet is. I'm not even sure I've ever *heard* of it. I've no idea why CDS wants to settle it, or why, wanting to settle it, they would ask *Frogmore* people to take such a critical role in establishing the new world's institutions and political, economic, and legal trajectory." The entire proposition struck her as ludicrous on its face. Since when did CDS ask people it considered backwards to be the "settlement cadre" of a new planet?

Lawrence waved his chew-stick with a disconcertingly graceful movement of his wrist. "Aureole has special problems." A small holo appeared, floating a few inches above the surface of the desk. "That is Aureole, there, the golden-pink one. It looks that lovely shade of golden-pink when seen from its second moon. It's not that far from Frogmore. Which would be one rather positive feature for our handling things there." His mouth smiled, unmistakably, at Madeleine. "But the special problems, you see, have to do with its mass. Its gravity is only a fraction slighter than Frogmore's. CDS has learned the necessity of taking into account the significance of such a factor for every aspect of life on a planet. Unlike Frogmore, it has no permanent fog, though its weather is not particularly pleasant. It has seasons, you see. And extremely cold poles, and a torrid equatorial belt. And there's still quite a bit of geophysical activity in certain areas. But it's even richer than Frogmore is in minerals. Which is one of the reasons CDS is so interested in it."

Madeleine stared, mesmerized, at the tiny golden orb tilted on its axis and the even tinier orbs circling it. "And the other planets in its system?" Madeleine asked, curious about the other five bodies circling Aureole's sun.

Making a disgusting sucking sound when he removed the chew-stick from his mouth this time, Lawrence said, "Ah, the other planets. Yes, well, that would get us into some of the myriad considerations CDS is concerned with. CDS is hoping, of course, to find an explanation rather more, ah, readily acceptable to the public than its real reasons for pre-ferring Aureole to its companions in that system. One strong reason, of course, is its mineral wealth, since the primary reason for settling a planet pertains to its potential for gen-erating wealth." He gnawed for a few seconds on the chew-stick before continuing.

Madeleine, still staring at the holo, waited patiently without speaking. He must know he would have to level with her before she would even begin to consider taking the job.

Lawrence loudly cleared his throat, and Madeleine jerked her attention from the holo back to his day-mask. "It's a bit complicated," he said. "Of course you are aware of CDS's anx-iousness to mine Frogmore's minerals. And that the Scourge has made that so difficult that they've been rather disappoint-ed in the yields to date. It's to be hoped that this new proj-ect in the Brainnard Mountains will mark a change..." His voice trailed off, and he fiddled with his chew-stick. "But, ah, there's more involved than the mining. You see... Well, one consequence of the advanced state of civilization that may not have occurred to you—" a mirthless, teeth-baring smile flickered within the confines of the day-mask's oral orifice—

"since Frogmore doesn't enjoy the full extent of civilization as it's currently known, is that certain levels of, ah, expectation are raised almost universally. Not so much on Frogmore, as I said. On this planet we aren't all connected, for instance. While on at least half the civilized planets—and on all the most advanced—every individual *is*, no matter their socioeconomic status." His fingers resumed drumming on the desk. "Though of course the standard of living of those of the lowest status on a planet like Janniset, say, or even Pleth—as you may recall, Judge—is considerably above that of our most average citizens on Frogmore. A simple fact of life and wholly understandable. Someday Frogmore, too, will be among such planets..."

Lawrence sighed. "What I am trying to say, Judge, is that there are those who may be described as, ah, cultural malcontents. And the Combine has learned through long experience that such individuals are best suited to undertake the adventure of settling a new planet. Getting off to, ah, a fresh start. Exploring a new world. Free of the usual more odious comparisons such discontented and frustrated individuals tend to indulge with such deleterious effects. And of course there may be those on Frogmore, too, who might be induced to expend their energies on civilizing a new world rather than engaging in destructive activities such as blowing up power stations and passenger trains, to take two of the most striking examples lately before our eyes."

Madeleine sat up very straight. "Are you telling me this is to be a prison planet?"

"No, no, oh certainly not!" Lawrence spluttered so precipitately that Madeleine wondered at his readiness with the protest.

"I don't think I understand," she said. Except, she thought, that obviously this planet was to be used as a dumping ground.

"It is not to be used as a prison. And we will certainly not allow demonstrably criminal individuals to emigrate to Aureole. No, what I'm trying to say is that because of the planet's considerable gravity and its obvious lack of any civilization at all—such that everything would have to be begun there from scratch—few people from the civilized worlds will want to emigrate unless the financial rewards are so lucrative that its discomforts could be overlooked. But that, you must understand from Frogmore's situation, is impossible: how could settlers be promised enormous wealth when the planet will cost so much to make habitable, to settle, and the investment for developing an industrial capacity be so excessive?"

Lawrence laid down his chew-stick and leaned forward, apparently (for Madeleine could only imagine the behavior of his eyes) staring at her over the astronomical holo. "No, Judge, what I'm saying is that the only people likely to be emigrating to Aureole are those driven by their own peculiar needs and dreams and illusions. As was the case with Frogmore's settlement, I might add. People who have bones to pick with civilization. People who are filled with the romanticism of pioneering a new world, of adventuring into the hitherto unknown. Your insight into such mentalities and experience with the harshness of daily life inevitable on a planet like Frogmore even five centuries after settlement is, I think, CDS's chief reason for wishing Frogmore expertise to make up the settlement cadre."

He still wasn't telling her all the truth. She might not be able to see his eyes, but his body language signaled evasiveness. And something about him—his words? his manner? his inscrutability?—chilled her. Yet there was something tempting, even intriguing about "starting fresh."

"We wouldn't be expected to remain there permanently, would we?" she asked, appalled at the thought of leaving her home forever.

"No, no, of course not." A purring note in his voice suggested her question pleased him. Perhaps he took it as a sign of serious interest?

Madeleine drew a deep breath and stared at the mesh covering the eye-holes of his day-mask. "To be frank, I don't know what to say, Special Administrator Lawrence. I'm profoundly devoted to Frogmore. I'm not certain I want to divert my energies to a new cause."

Lawrence's lips thinned, then twisted. "So. We arrive at another level of candor, Judge: let me say that it is our full expectation that this settlement of Aureole shall be, ah, highly *beneficial* to Frogmore. Which is not to say that the settlement of Aureole is expected to be a failure. On the contrary. We intend to recruit the best talent possible to keep from repeating old mistakes." His head turned, presumably to stare at the holoscape of Pleth, and his fingers retrieved the chew-stick from the surface of his desk and returned it to his mouth.

The quiet in the room grew tense.

"I must have some time to think about this," Madeleine said.

"Of course," Lawrence said, removing the chew-stick from his mouth. "Of course. This is one of the most serious decisions of your career. I understand completely, Judge. Already you see that this job would be a challenge beyond anything you've ever faced." He gently cleared his throat. "It is the people for whom challenges are stimulating, invigorating, and seductively appealing that we need as Regents. People who are in every sense of the word *creative*. People like you, Judge. Which is why, I trust, you *will* give my proposition serious consideration."

"If I have questions—"

"But of course, feel free to contact me about anything that comes to mind. I'll do my best. Though of course 'most everything lies, ah, *ahead* of us in this project, unpredictably so since the future will be ours to make."

Is the man a megalomaniac? Madeleine wondered as they stood and bowed across the desk at one another. Crossing the threshold out of his office, she realized that he had told her little about the job (including its salary), little about what CDS was up to. So little, in fact, that she felt they had been juggling imaginary balls in the air and she had just agreed to take the balls home and practice.

"May I," Holland asked, "wear your *Insouciance?* Several people have told me that Henny Ousmane has said she's going to challenge me tonight. And I always feel so, well, *above* it all when I'm dressed in *Insouciance.*"

"Yes, of course you may," Madeleine told her daughter. "But try not to get drawn into anything too outrageous, all right?"

Madeleine hated this ridiculous persistence in dueling. She had never understood its initial popularity; that it had hung on and become so highly stylized baffled her. On the other hand, it absorbed certain energies of the young people (especially those newly returned from Pleth) that might otherwise have taken even less constructive forms than the silliness of dueling. Some people went so far as to argue that it gave young people insights into interpersonal relations and power-manipulation, ingrained into them an almost automatic civility and grace of face, and sharpened their wits and quickened their thinking. Madeleine was not so sure. But as long as Holland persisted in embroiling herself in dueling and complained routinely and even mechanically about her supervisors in the Department of Health and Hygiene, Madeleine could be certain she was not growing disaffected, as happened too often with other young people within the first three or four years of their return from Pleth, after their enchantment with the smoothness and delicacy of their new bodies had worn off.

"I'm certainly not going to back down from an outright challenge," Holland said, her eyes flashing with indignation at the thought.

"Well don't you egg the situation on," Madeleine said. In addition to Holland and Henny's tendency to push at the boundaries of the acceptable, their friends and acquaintances would be doing their best to provoke them—all in the interests of entertainment, spectacle, and the creation of new stories of derring-do to flourish when others described extraordinary duels *they* had witnessed.

"Oh, Mother. Be nice or I won't lend you my new feather wristbands."

"What kind of feathers?" Madeleine asked, quickly checking Holland's wrists—only to find them bare below the cling-on line.

Holland grinned. "They're exquisitely soft, very small, sleek feathers of several lovely iridescent shades of aqua, rose, lavender, gray, and lilac. As soon as I saw them I thought of your gray and lilac cling-ons, and when I got home I checked and found they matched perfectly."

"And, I suppose," Madeleine said, smiling back, "they go well with your rose and lavender."

"But of course! I only said I'd *lend* them to you, Mother."

"Not quite," Madeleine said. "You said that if I weren't 'nice' you *wouldn't* lend them to me."

Holland bowed. "Touché. You'd make a rapier-quick duelist, did you know that?"

Madeleine groaned. "Of all things in the vast wide galaxy, all I'd need is a duel."

Holland laughed. "Stranger things have happened, Mother. But I have to dash if I'm to dress myself in *Insouciance*."

Madeleine sank into a hammock with a vial of *Day's Done* and checked her personal mail. She found a letter from

Bryce, which she shunted aside to read later, as well as a holo
he had two months earlier told her he would be sending by
Slow Transfer. She had been waiting for the holo's arrival
with trepidation, for it would finally reveal to her whatever
new thing it was that had generated so much excitement in
her previously indifferent-to-the-galaxy son. He had said he
couldn't explain it very well himself, but that the holo of a
lecture-demonstration he had attended would tell her "everything" about his "new understanding."

Madeleine lay with her eyes closed and let *Day's Done*
relax her. Had such constant exposure to young people in
trouble skewed her perceptions? Could it be that any other
parent with the same children would enjoy absolute confidence in their dedication to the Public Good? That none of
her colleagues expressed the sort of fears she felt for Holland
and Bryce did not indicate they didn't have them, for she
herself never breathed the faintest suggestion of her fears,
even to Solange. And the fact was, from the time they left
for Pleth to their first years of reassimilation to Frogmore,
young people had to deal with a series of major changes that
came at them in rapid succession.

What, Madeleine wondered, if she decided to take the
job Lawrence had offered her? Would Holland and Bryce go
with her? It hardly seemed likely. And if they did not go to
Aureole with her...

"No," she said aloud. "No, I trust them. It's not that." No,
it would be a question of how to keep the family together.
Bad enough Bryce being on Pleth. But for her to leave Frogmore would amount to desertion. Her mother and sisters
would do everything they could to make up to Holland and
Bryce for her absence, but...

Madeleine opened her eyes and stared at the ceiling. She
knew the folly of dwelling on the case of Henrietta West's
daughter. If such things were going to happen to Holland or
Bryce, they'd happen whether she was here or not. She had

done her best to form their characters, to inculcate high moral standards in them. Whatever path they chose would be guided by their characters, values, and standards. Therefore, Madeleine reasoned, she must not allow her fears to influence her decision. She should instead spend her free hours accessing the data to which Lawrence had secured her clearance and determining the issues at stake for her in particular and Frogmore in general, and make her decision on that rational basis.

"Well, Mother, what do you think?"

Madeleine ordered the lighting amplified and scrutinized Holland's neck and hairline. "You're well dressed," she said. "You've a better hand than I have when it comes to applying designs." Holland often assisted her, but after the first few times that Madeleine had assisted her—how many years ago now?—Holland had refused all help beyond the final inspection she insisted be rigorously critical.

"And so I shall be absolutely insouciant this evening," Holland said. "Soon no one in our circle will even dare to challenge me."

"Hubris," Madeleine murmured, though with a surge of pride as she thought of who that circle Holland so easily referred to comprised. No, Holland would be fine, she enjoyed life too much to jeopardize her position and status.

Holland blew Madeleine a graceful kiss and minced out of the room in one of the styles of walking that fashion circles attributed to Inez. Madeleine reached for another vial of *Day's Done*. She would take a little more relaxation and then consume her evening meal while she read Bryce's letter. And then—since she had promised to meet her mother for an early breakfast—she would have a bath and go to sleep (a habit which she, unlike Holland, seemed to need to indulge on a regular basis).

Virtually all Pleth-educated elites subscribe to belief in a mythological object that signifies one of the most intransigent obstacles to Frogmore's independence. This mythological object, designated "fragmentism" (as practiced by "fragmentists") serves the function of a slur, in which a simplistic labeling of individuals, groups, or ideas asserts mastery over something they have dismissed as unworthy of consideration. To put it another way, the label "fragmentism" is an ideological object that dismisses wholesale the cultures that are organic to Frogmore. Because these cultures have grown out of Frogmore's unique environment, the modifications that allow human sustainability in that environment, and the social formations particular to Frogmore's economic, demographic, and physical conditions, they have diverged from the vaunted homogeneity of the societies of the so-called "advanced worlds."

Pleth-educated elites assume, without question, that the "standard" of "advanced worlds" should be the goal toward which Frogmore must aim. Deviation from this standard is, for them, "backwards" and is what, they imagine, makes Frogmore a "backworld." Anyone who defends the multifarious cultures native to Frogmore (native, but not indigenous, since humans are indigenous to only one world in the galaxy) is, by their reckoning, a "fragmentist," for "fragmentism," they believe, is an ideology espousing the fragmentation of Frogmore into ever smaller, more separate "tribes." Heterogeneity, for them, is tantamount to the reversion to primitive tribalism.

Governor Amanda Kundjan: "All terrorists are fragmentists. And although not all fragmentists are terrorists, those that are not are potential terrorists and implicit allies of all terrorists." In another speech, she further declared: "Fragmentists hate civilization. Their ultimate objective is to eliminate it from this planet."

To this we say, if heterogeneity is the enemy of civilization, civilization is the enemy of every nonhuman species of life in the universe.

—*Frogmore's Destiny: A Manifesto for Independence*

Sixteen
INEZ GAUTHIER

Inez fussed at her design dresser. "No, no, that's not right. A sensor somewhere along my right cheekbone is chafing me. Do something about it, or after a couple of hours of irritation I'll be ready to kill."

The design dresser sighed histrionically, but unpacked the molding in order to make the adjustment. "If you would only consider switching to neural responders, Madam, your comfort would always be assured."

"I'll stick with the sensors, thank you." Only a fool would want their most immediate neurological responses to emotional stimulus exposed (in however disguised a fashion). With the sensors only the actual muscular and blood-vessel responses in one's face—which as far as Inez was concerned contained quite enough spontaneity beyond one's control— would direct the responses of the design. Even if one never wore the same design twice—as even she, who had her own personal design specialist, did—one still had to contend with others' eventual deciphering of the design's patterns (except, of course, for the most complex interactions of patterns and colors), which after a few hours even mediocre observation could usually achieve.

"Inez!"

"Don't stop," she warned the design dresser when the general entered the room. "I want to get this over with." She needed a few quiet minutes with Little One before she could take it upstairs. Though it hadn't been around many people, it had imprinted so well that she was confident it could handle the noise and bustle of the party. Supposedly the Sweet Things had been programmed for even tempers and calm dispositions.

"Inez, are you even listening to me?"

"No," she said, "I'm afraid I wasn't. What are you doing here, anyway? I thought you were going to be in the salon when the event started."

"And you aren't even finished dressing!"

"What is it?" Her father had been such a pain all day that by the end of dinner he had exhausted all her available sympathy. She had even given him a part of her afternoon, so pathetic had he been. But now—well, it was too bad that seeing Solstice perform last night had caused him so much pain. She had to pity his frustration and wretchedness. But for how long must this agonizing go on?

"Do I look all right?" the general asked. "What do you think about the feathers? Do they go with the carved jade studs?"

"We have such different taste, Paul," his daughter said wearily. "Did you ask Deaver? He usually knows about these things better than I."

"But everyone knows your taste is the best on this planet," the general whined. "Come *on*, Inez, admit it: you don't like the combination, do you."

"Is that all right, Madam?" the design dresser half-whispered.

"It feels fine. Go ahead and finish the application."

"Do you *mind*, Inez? Do you think you could give me just one spacing minute of your attention? Or would that be too much for a father to ask of his daughter?"

Silently, she counted to five. "All right, all right. If you really want to know, I think the combination looks gauche and inept. Like something someone in the governor's circle would think the most supreme elegance."

The general's design clouded into a mottled gray. He almost always chose to go with the neural responders—so greatly did he rate his personal comfort. "So you think I should do what?" Hostility made his whine querulous. "Remove the studs? Or the feathers?"

"The studs," the general's daughter said. "Get rid of the studs. Go without studs entirely unless you have some tiny tiny pearls. Or diamond chips. No, not diamond chips, even *they'd* be too much."

The general heaved a sigh. "All right, Inez. If that's what you think. But you know, I—"

"Why the *fuck* did you come in here bothering me if you didn't want me to tell you what to do?" The design dresser took several steps backwards, and Inez realized that she had jerked her head and swung her arm out for emphasis.

"Message received," the general said in his most dignified baritone. "I'll see you upstairs—soon, I hope."

His daughter bit back a retort about how she would have been nearly finished dressing by now if he hadn't barged in and forced his inane anxiety upon her. "Sorry," she muttered at the design dresser, gesturing him to step forward. "Let's get this thing finished, shall we?"

The design dresser bowed and resumed his work with tongs and spatula. Inez glanced over at Little One and noted the serenity of the Sweet Thing's eyes. If Little One could take a shouting match without so much as a quiver, the event would be a piece of cake. She had so forgotten the Sweet Thing that she hadn't even triggered its neural manipulators. Perhaps they had made the things just a little stupid? But that would be all the better. The intelligence with which the creatures had been endowed would be perfect for pets: certainly no one would mind that they lacked the smarts to get upset when emotions in the humans around them ran high. They'd be a *success fou*, once the distribution had gotten under way.

She smiled, then noted in the mirror the lovely streaking triggered in her design. Whatever taste she had she knew she hadn't gotten from *him*—fortunately, for herself...and for Frogmore, too.

That little whisper she'd caught shortly after entering the salon disturbed her. *Look: Inez's design is showing some nose!* The feathers were fresh enough and still ongoing, yet by now old enough that she knew she could introduce something else, especially in such a different genre, as it were. But showing nose in the design—well, she hadn't noticed the innovation when she'd told the design dresser to try *Strong and Silent* out on her. That's all she needed, a design novelty she couldn't make as much as half an SCU on, upstaging the launch of Sweet Things.

"Danilla," she cooed to the governor's Number-Four-Offspring.

Danilla bowed. "I love the decor. It's so *soothing*."

Inez realized she hadn't sniffed a thing since going to bed the night before. Thinking she'd offer to share a vial with Danilla, she felt around in her pockets—and found nothing. *It's all that fool's fault for barging in and disrupting my routine.* She stretched her mouth into a smile, confident that the sourness of her smile would not mar the lovely streaking the smile must be triggering in her design. "Thanks, Danilla, but I can't claim the credit for it. I suspect Captain Deaver found someone clever to do it." She wouldn't *want* to claim the credit for it. She herself would describe the decor as funereal rather than soothing. *Soothing.* Hah. Danilla was probably being tactful. For a native she had fairly reasonable taste.

"Ah, the priceless Captain Deaver." Danilla gestured extravagantly. "Mother could use someone like him on her staff."

"She does all right with Bath," Inez said with considerable dryness. Deaver managed things adequately, but not to perfection. In her opinion, Lieutenant Glance far outstripped Deaver, but of course Glance could not do everything. More importantly, of everyone on his staff, the general considered Deaver nearly indispensable. But then Deaver's tact exceeded his intelligence.

"Tell me, Inez, if you don't mind my curiosity: what *is* it? In that sling you're wearing?"

"What, this?" she asked, staring down at Little One, whom she'd been stroking since leaving her quarters.

"Yes—if you don't mind my asking?"

Inez moved closer to Danilla and took her hand from Little One's head so that Danilla could get a better look. "This tiny creature is called a 'Sweet Thing'—and is a lovely soft cuddly critter that has the most delicious purr you can feel, even through your clothing."

Danilla bent to get a closer look. Inez lowered her voice and spoke as though confidentially. "A friend on Evergreen, feeling sorry for my exile here, designed it for me. One couldn't have an ordinary pet, you know, on Frogmore, because of the gravity. But my Little One weighs scarcely more than a kilo—as you might be able to guess from the flimsiness of the sling cradling it." The general's daughter touched the filmy silk holding Little One close to her body. "And so these Sweet Things my friend designed are wonderfully comfortable in Frogmore's gravity. Truly they belong on this planet." She lightly touched the crown of Little One's head. "Aren't you, Little One?" she cooed in the voice she had used to imprint the Sweet Thing.

"May I touch it?" Danilla's design had grown positively effusive. She touched her fingers to Little One's face. "Ooh, all that fluff is like swan's down!" Inez only now noticed that Danilla was wearing a swan's down bodice. "Oh, what a lovely feeling, is that its purr I'm feeling?"

Inez subvocalized the order for stimulating Little One's pleasure center. Almost instantly the creature responded with those small murmurs she found so delightful. "Yes, that's its purr, isn't it *charming*?" Inez said softly, wanting to give Danilla a good chance to hear Little One's vocalizations.

"Oh, how precious, how *sweet!* How lucky you are to have a friend to give you such a sweet little thing!"

"Would you like one of your own?" Inez asked. "I could ask him to send you one, too."

"Oh, Inez! How charming of you! I'd *adore* having one of these sweet little things! And if the gravity is all right for them—oh! I'd *love* such an adorable creature," Danilla gushed. "I've always envied off-world people for their pets. But *this* one, well! I've never seen anything like it!"

"But of *course* I'll have my friend send you one." Inez scanned the vicinity to see who else might be around whom she might interest in acquiring a Sweet Thing. Estine Gael, yes; the Minister of Culture and Education, perhaps; the general, irrelevant; Colonel Legs, probably not…

"Inez," the general hissed into his daughter's ear. "Why in the great spacing void did you tell Deaver to let a holocrew in? I just made an ass of myself yelling at him about it and then had to endure the embarrassment of his saying 'Oh but I assumed *Madam Gauthier* had spoken to you about that.' Don't you think you might have bothered to discuss this with me first?"

Seeing Danilla edging away with her usual resort to Frogmorian etiquette on occasions when an off-world person behaved with an indifference to courtesy bordering on rudeness, the general's daughter sank her fingernails into her father's feathered wrist. "I believe you know Danilla Kundjan," she said in an acidic tone of voice.

"I apologize for my intrusion, Madam Kundjan," the general said loudly enough for Danilla to hear.

Danilla turned in time to see most of the magnificent bow that the general swept her. She glided two swan's steps toward the general, bowed, and offered her wrist. "General," she murmured deep in her throat. "How lovely to see you." Her design had deepened to an intense purplish blue.

Neural responders, Inez thought—and realized that Danilla must be sexually attracted to the general. She glanced sidelong at him and saw that he had taken her advice and dumped the jade for tiny seed pearls.

The general rose gallantly to the occasion: "My pleasure entirely." He lightly touched the proffered wrist with the tips of his fingers.

"Inez has just been promising to give me one of those sweet little creatures like her own," Danilla murmured to the general in that same throaty voice so unlike her usual robust timbre.

"Hmm?" The general's bubble-eyes swiveled to stare at his daughter's design. "What's that you've been promising, Inez?"

"Oh, that's right, the general hasn't met Little One yet, has he, darling," his daughter cooed to the creature as she removed it from the silk sling.

The general made a sound of disgust. "What is that *thing* you're holding?"

His daughter lifted her pet to within a few centimeters of the general's design. "General, meet Little One," she said in her usual social voice. "Little One," she crooned, "this is the general. Who I *know* is going to love you just as much as I do."

"Oh really, Inez." The general retreated a step.

"Oh, but I think it's precious," Danilla cooed, caressing the creature Inez still held close to her father's design. "Don't you think it has the sweetest, most sensual purr, General?"

"Would you like to hold it for a minute or two?" Inez asked Danilla.

"*May* I?" Eagerly Danilla reached for Little One. "Oh," she said and drew back. "Will it be, ah, continent?"

Inez trilled laughter. "But of course. Little One is absolutely discreet. That's the wonderful thing about having one's pet specially designed. Little One is *never* incontinent."

She held the Sweet Thing out to Danilla. Gingerly Danilla took it.

"Estine," Inez called when she had identified the woman passing quite close. Estine Gael paused, looked their way, and moved toward them in what Inez guessed was meant to be a Borillian Sashay but came off as a twisty mince. This would be the tricky part. "What a lovely effect," she said as she daringly reached out and brushed her fingertip over the lacy-gold brooch nestled in the band of feathers circling Estine's throat just at that stretch of skin between the base of the design and the top of her exquisitely patterned cling-ons (often left awkwardly naked by those who liked showing off their cling-ons).

"Do you like the feathers?" Estine asked a trifle too eagerly. "I was told they're peacock feathers. My dress-consultant showed me a holo of peacocks, which apparently are indigenous to—"

"Oh, I know what peacocks are," Inez said. Not only did this sort of conversation bore her, but she knew very well that the feathers could not possibly have derived from a peacock. "I've seen them in the flesh in the Alameda Wilderness Preserve on Evergreen."

"Estine, have you seen Inez's darling little pet?" Danilla said, saving Inez the bother of calling Estine's attention to the Sweet Thing. "It's so soft, so *darling*," Danilla cooed. "Aren't you, Little One?"

She held Little One out to Estine. "Touch its fur, it's so *downy*."

Estine bent over Little One and smoothed her fingers over its fur. "Ooh, what *is* it? I've never seen anything like it!" Estine put her design right up against Little One's face. "Aren't you sweet," she half-whispered to it.

Inez signaled Deaver to bring on the holo-crew. "It's a creature designed especially for Frogmore's gravity and climate," she told Estine. "A dear friend of mine so thoughtfully concerned about my loneliness on Frogmore had this creature designed for me. And thus sent me Little One to keep me company. And such lovely soft *cuddly* company, too," she purred.

"And Inez has promised to give me one," Danilla said as Estine exploded into exclamations of wonder and envy.

Out of the corner of her eye Inez noted the holo-crew discreetly moving in on them (subjects they'd likely been longing to get near for the entire time the four of them had been knotted together).

"What friend are you talking about, Inez?" the general asked.

Inez observed her father unconsciously shift his stance and square his shoulders into a posture that enhanced his already considerable manliness. She said, "Oh, someone I grew close to on Pleth." She would have to launch a diversion that would stifle his inopportune curiosity.

"Oh, Inez, I'd do *any*thing to have one of these darlings for my own," Estine exclaimed as she took Little One from Danilla.

The holo-cam had undoubtedly caught the exclamation, for how could it have resisted zooming in on that little piece of fluff the two natives held between them, especially considering the lavishness of their billing and cooing over it? Though Inez remembered how excessively people in advanced societies could behave with their pets, she had not expected someone like Danilla Kundjan—ordinarily so cool, so concerned to present the properly detached façade appropriate to utter sophistication—to so forget her appearance and image as to be making kissing sounds for the sake of that little piece of fluff (adorable as it was) that she had so reluctantly relinquished to Estine. "Oh dear," Inez murmured. "I really don't know…"

Estine understood at once. "But of *course* I'd be willing to pay *any* expenses," she said in a rush. "Its cost of production, transportation, and all that." Her design pulsated with bursts of brilliant iridescent colors, among which Inez thought she glimpsed a trace of neon. Estine pressed the Sweet Thing to her neck. "I hate to put you to so much trouble, but I'm so attached already to your precious little darling—"

"Then I'll ask my friend to send you one, too," Inez interrupted. "Since he sent me Little One as a gift, I really have no idea, though, of the expense. Perhaps I should have him contact you directly?" The less she had to do with arranging sales, the more likely she would succeed in keeping her association with the business of importing and marketing Sweet Things dark.

Danilla's fingers lighted—and for a few seconds lingered—on Inez's arm. "Do you mind if Henry and Valentina join us?" she whispered into the general's daughter's ear. "I'm sure they'd just hate to miss meeting your Little One, and—"

"But you must invite them over at once," Inez said in a rush of apparent generosity.

"Inez," the general spoke directly into his daughter's ear. "What the fuck is going on here?"

The general's occasional acuity amazed his daughter whenever it made an appearance. "I'll tell you everything later, Paul," she whispered back. "But in the meantime, do you have anything sniffable in your pockets? I forgot—"

"Are you out of your mind?" he said. "There's a holo-crew not three meters away, and you're suggesting we—"

"Don't be absurd. How long do you think I'm going to go on standing here like this?" She would allow just a few people (and of course the holo-cam) to get a good look at Little One, and then she'd drift off in search of the biologists she'd specially invited to this party and share a few vials with one or two of them. Word about Sweet Things would travel swiftly, and because only a few people would actually have seen Little One, both curiosity and desire would spread like wildfire.

As Henry Poljai and Valentina Nsazi approached, Inez reached out to take Little One back from Estine Gael. A jewel nested in the fluffy crown of Little One's head, she decided, would be exquisite. Restored to the sling at her breast, Little One throbbed with its deepest purr. Inez considered what sort of jewel it should be—and almost crowed with pleasure as the inspiration came to her: Little One's jewel could change every evening, in accordance with the jewels she herself happened to be wearing on the toes of her shoes. It would be charming—and distinctive, for no one in the governor's circle would be able to imitate her.

Observing the general moving off arm-in-arm with Danilla, she grew positively sanguine. Certainly Danilla was a cut above most of his lovers. Perhaps the governor's Number-Four-Offspring would accomplish what none of the recent one-night-stands had been able to do. Life might yet metamorphose into a bed of roses.

Arriving at her usual hour the next morning in the breakfast room, Inez found her father already at the table. Concern for the reasons behind this behavior swallowed the spurt of irritation the sight of him this early in the morning provoked in her. "Good morning, Paul," she said, gesturing the server to pour out her third cup of coffee of the morning.

The general rubbed his bare face and halfheartedly glowered at her for a second or two.

"You're up early," his daughter remarked. He rarely breakfasted this early, except for the weekly Staff Breakfast Meeting and occasional breakfast meetings with the governor or certain of the governor's officers.

"Got a busy day today."

Inez told the server she wanted Schedule F. "I trust you slept well?" she said to her father.

"Are you going to leave that thing on through the whole meal?" The general growled. "It's as ugly as a naked native face."

Inez removed her day-mask. "So you didn't sleep well."

"Of course I slept well," the general snapped. "How would one not sleep well if one slept at all?" He sipped from the tall glass of juice he had only half-finished. "Just didn't sleep long enough."

"Ah," the general's daughter murmured. "Danilla, I presume?"

"Then you presume wrong."

"I could have sworn she was interested."

"Hmmmph. Since when is interest on one side sufficient to get something going?"

"Oh," his daughter said. "Oh, I see. It hadn't occurred to me..."

The general heaved a great sigh. "It's ridiculous. I'm sick of this. But I can't *concentrate* on anyone but that spacing dancer of yours."

Of mine? Hah! "What about taking a nice long leave?" she suggested. "You're due for one, they can't turn you down if you request it. A nice long leave on Janniset or Evergreen, time to relax, time to get everything to do with this bone-crushing planet off your mind? We could go together. I have to go to Janniset myself as soon as one little matter is taken care of here. I'm sure that's your problem, Paul, more than unrequited infatuation." She thought of adding that he had never fallen into unrequited infatuation before, that he wasn't the type to do so, and that obviously he'd been on Frogmore too long.

"I can't do it. Things are too tricksy. I can feel it in my bones, the way things are simmering, as though they might at any moment explode."

He had been saying that same thing for two local years. "Surely Colonel Farquhar, Major Cleveland, and the governor's officers can collectively handle anything that might flare up. They're not total incompetents, Paul. And besides, you could zip back here at the first hint of trouble. A full battery of contingency plans have been worked out."

"Are you trying to claim I'm not needed here?" the general demanded in a voice that had shifted from hostility to petulance.

"Of course not!" The impasse with Solstice had made him touchy. "What I'm saying is that when situations flare up, there's a first by-the-book response that is only *then* followed by more on-the-spot decision-making, which is where you come in. And you know that you could be back here in no time, since the Combine would certainly keep a galaxy-class starship standing by for just such an exigency."

The server entered and set a large cup of Lanike Porridge with fruit before the general's daughter.

"Ugh." The general's naked face contorted into a grimace. "How you can eat that *slop*, Inez, is beyond me."

"You have such delightful table manners when we take meals alone together, General."

"Excuse me, Madam."

Inez turned with surprise to face her personal attendant, standing behind her chair. Inez had assumed it was a server, not Zagorin, standing there. "What is it, Zagorin?"

"It's that creature." She cleared her throat. "I mean, Madam, your, ah, pet."

"Yes? What about Little One?"

The general snorted.

"It seems to be upset, Madam. It's been making a lot of awful, ah, noises, ever since you left to go to breakfast."

"Really? It should be, well, just *sleeping*."

"It's far from *sleeping*, Madam. Unless," Zagorin added with a twinge of that Frogmorian sarcasm she now and then liked to deploy, "it's having a nightmare."

Inez sighed. "Very well. I'll return to my quarters to see about it when I've finished my breakfast." When Zagorin paused just this side of the threshold and hesitated uncertainly, Inez said sharply, "Is there anything else, Zagorin?"

The attendant bowed. "No, Madam. But it *is* rather, ah, noisy."

"I'm not going to interrupt my breakfast. I'll take *care* of it when I'm *done* here."

Zagorin bowed and departed. Her unhappiness was plain.

"By the way," the general said. "You said last night you'd explain about that creepy little beastie, whatever the void the thing is. But you never did."

"All right, Paul. If it matters so much to you, I'll tell you the real story." She glanced around to assure that they were indeed alone. "The creature, called a Sweet Thing, is something I want to market. And that's all. So don't hassle me about it. Don't make cracks about it. And don't whatever you do wreck my cover story."

"What a crackbrained scheme, Inez. You'll probably lose every SCU you've invested in it. If that's the way you're hoping to preserve the Family Fortune, I have to wonder—"

"Stay out of it, Paul. Believe it or not, I know what I'm doing. I won't make a fortune on Sweet Things, but I'll do well. Trust me."

The general guffawed in disbelief. Obviously it was one of those mornings—as his staff would no doubt soon discover. "Sweet Things," he scoffed. "You're out of your mind!"

At this, his daughter threw down her napkin and snatched up her day-mask. "I don't tell you how to handle your business, so don't you tell me how to handle mine." She rose to her feet.

"Well we both of us know now who had the bad night, don't we."

Inez stalked away from the table without replying.

"Have a lovely day, Inez," the general called after her.

She paused on the threshold to look over her shoulder at her father's now positively cheery face. "Up yours, too, Daddy Dear," she said through her teeth.

The general boomed his heartiest laughter as his daughter strode past the human server who had arrived with the next course of her breakfast.

Toward the end of the afternoon Inez checked with Sidney to make sure that Solstice Balalzalar had not yet left for the day, then set out for the dancer's workspace, to catch her before she did. Earlier Sidney had mentioned that Solstice had lately been bringing Sadora Lumni into the Institute with her, and it now occurred to Inez that she might find Sadora Lumni with the dancer this very afternoon. The thought so disturbed her that by the time she reached the dancer's space, she had worked herself into a tangled knot of anxiety that, when she recognized it for what it was, aggravated her irritable mood.

But entering Solstice's space, she found not Sadora Lumni but several off-world dancers sitting with Solstice on floor mats, talking. All but Solstice wore day-masks. "It seems to me that it's simply a matter of practicality," one of them was saying when Inez crossed the threshold. "And that constraints imposed on the practical possibilities make it nearly impossible if not totally unlikely for certain creative strains ever to be developed."

Inez stood just inside the threshold; a couple of heads turned her way, but since they knew who she was from her ID broadcast, this brief flurry of attention did not interrupt the discussion. As she listened to another of the off-world dancers put forth a similar comment to the previous one, she wondered if Solstice would recognize her despite her day-mask. This sort of difficulty, wholly unnecessary ~ Inez had offered to bear the cost of full connection if the waterdancer were willing ~ continually manufactured situations of ambiguity and inconvenience, producing wrenching spurts of anxiety as relentless and inevitable as it was needless. "And of course," another of the off-worlders said, "quite apart from their exoskeletal adaptations, the basic size and shape of most Frogmore natives is aesthetically unsuited to the Dance. Your shape is quite exceptional among Frogmorians, Solstice."

Solstice stared hard at this discussant's day-mask. "Aesthetically unsuited?" she said. "I don't think I understand just how you've come to formulate such a judgment. The only thing I can make of such a statement is to conclude that you find us Frogmorians too ugly to look at to be interested in watching us perform with our bodies." Was she just being ornery? Inez wondered. Hadn't she said she'd undergone surgery to make her body more aesthetically suited to Dance?

"Not ugly," the interlocutor ~ Inez identified him as Florian Farah, whose group's performances on Frogmore had been so abysmal that their tour had had to be canceled ~ hastened to say. "That's not at all what I meant. But you must admit there's a certain physique, a certain shape and grace and physio-elegance appropriate to the Dance. This has been recognized throughout the millennia of human history. And again, to be practical, the dancer must have a supple, *expressive* body. Yes," he said, his voice suddenly eager, "that's *precisely* the point: one's body must be *expressive*. Forgive my bluntness, but I don't see how a short squat body knobbed and gnarled with the oddities of exoskeletal adaptations can possibly be *expressive*."

Solstice shrugged. "I must confess I still don't see your point. But then I grew up with such bodies all around me. And, frankly, they express a great deal more to me than off-world bodies do." She smiled faintly. "I'm often baffled by my interactions with off-world people. The whole time I was on Pleth I felt I never understood ordinary body-language." Her smile broadened. "In my desperation to learn how to

communicate with the non-Frogmore people surrounding
me there, I intook dozens of books on the subject." Solstice's
smile faded. "But what I suspect you're saying has more to
do with a certain fixed prejudice I constantly encounter in a
myriad contexts." She lifted her hands and extended them
away from her body, palms up. "It's that nasty little thing
called 'standard,' isn't it. Always there's some *standard* by
which all value must be determined, by which the acceptable, the good, the true, the beautiful, the appropriate must
be measured. It doesn't surprise me to find it dictating to
dancers what they think dance can—or, in your case, perhaps, *should*—be." Solstice dropped her hands back onto her
knees; she glanced at Inez, then stared down at the floor.

"That's not it," another of the off-world dancers said.
"I don't think that's what Florian—or any of us—is saying.
When you talk about a *standard*, you make it sound horribly
offensive. Just as our talking about *ugliness* would be horrid, too." She sighed. "But standard*s*," she went on, heavily
emphasizing the plural, "that's something different, something *necessary*. As dancers we *have* to have standards, just
as artists in any discipline as arduous as Dance must have
standards. You don't deny *that*, do you?"

"Basically you're saying you can accept my work only because I happen to be closer to physical standard than other
Frogmorians. And because I've devised a method for dancing
on an otherwise undanceable planet, as all of you put it."

Inez realized that bringing any more dancers to Frogmore
would be pointless—unless she could get something going
with Solstice, some sharing of her method with off-planet
dancers (a prospect that seemed increasingly unlikely the
better acquainted with Solstice she became).

"Look," Florian Farah said. "I think what's happening
here is that you're taking this personally, and there's no need.
We all admire you. I thought we'd made that clear!"

"Why would you think I take your chauvinism personally? I thought we were having an abstract discussion about dance?"

"But it's *you* who are refusing to keep it abstract," Allie Sherr said. "You've been accusing us of chauvinism, accusing us of ascribing ugliness to all Frogmorians."

"I give up," Solstice said. "As far as I can make out, you *do* consider the Frogmore physique ugly. All of you claim that anyone with the average Frogmore body—a body suited to this planet as well as any human body *can* be—you claim that the average Frogmore body more or less defiles dance, that the Frogmore body is not *expressive* enough to be appropriate for dance." She shrugged. "I don't see how I can take such pronouncements as anything *but* chauvinism."

"It's *you* who are chauvinist," Florian said. "Is it *our* fault if the average Frogmore body isn't suitable for the Dance?"

Inez—still standing near the threshold—slipped out into the corridor. She would come back later, when they had gone. Such talk troubled her. It did no credit to either side, and it confused her. Solstice would have none of them, that much she comprehended. But why, *why* Solstice insisted on dragging them—all of them—into such depressing and even embarrassing talk baffled Inez.

Nightlife on Frogmore is a largely sedentary affair, with the exception of a few venues that cater to the youth in the upper levels of the directed classes in the Frogmore Central University area of the Capitol District, which feature social dancing (for which possession of an exoskeleton is pretty well necessary). Most nightlife involves lying in hammocks or even recliners in small private rooms, sniffing intoxicants or sipping wine, chatting, and watching other people do the same by way of the monitors provided in every room. A protocol exists for making contacts with individuals in other rooms; the hallways serving these rooms tend to be high-traffic later in the evening, with some patrons partnering up, others leaving one party to join another, and whole parties joining other parties. All establishments are required to close at 2 a.m. Parties have been known to continue out in the streets—usually ending in protective custody, since extremely intoxicated individuals tend to ignore the risk of prolonged exposure to the open air or lose track of just how long they've been exposed.

Another set of venues are devoted to networked drama gaming (with or without VR gear). And finally, I should note that Frogmorians are addicted to comedy. Clubs serving audiences hungry for comedy can be found in the South Bank neighborhood, coming and going quickly, perhaps because the form on Frogmore is fad-driven. Off-worlders should be advised that Frogmorian humor can be elusive, even in those routines relying on physical slapstick. Humor really does not travel well across the galaxy.

The Inez Gauthier Institute for the Arts offers high culture events featuring art installations, music, lectures, and theater. Artists and performers are usually visitors in temporary residence on the planet. Its permanent art collection is quite good, as is its occasional exhibit of Frogmorian fiber arts; these are open to the public most mornings.

—*A Traveler's Handbook to the Galaxy*, 49th edition

Seventeen
INEZ GAUTHIER

Only after Inez finished watching the Late Evening Edition of the Data Network's Update Holoview Service did she go to her father's quarters to join him in their usual nightcap of *Midnight Song*. She went happy in the knowledge that the data networks were giving the UAP shift little coverage and carefully placing that coverage within the context of Frogmore's burgeoning economic renaissance. (Naturally the release of a CDS report forecasting a new wave of development and prosperity had helped immensely in establishing this context.) UAP's first T-Day lay only three days away.

So far they'd had only a few minor incidents and that foolish spot of theft in the Mellors Region. (How could the thieves not have been aware that the signals the stolen equipment—most of which was slated to be sold since the bulk of it could not be used on the orbital stations—transmitted would be run to ground in no time? The thieves and their families would spend most of the rest of their lives paying for the expense of retrieving the equipment as well as for their therapy, proving yet again the futility of theft.) Otherwise, the transition seemed to be running smoothly—due mostly, Inez believed, to the intervention of AHRM.

Her father—already sprawled in his hammock—had had his design removed and exchanged his clothing for a lavender silk dressing gown, which he wore over his cling-ons. "You look comfortable," she said, noting that certain absence in his face.

The general's eyes popped open; for a moment the stare he leveled at her remained blank. Then the slackness of his face vanished, and his eyes fixed on Little One. "Fuck it, Inez. Did you have to bring that wretched monster with you? You know I can't stand the thing. Some people may find those outlandish eyes and all that fur—" the general's mouth twisted with distaste— "appealing, but the very sight of it makes my flesh crawl. The thing is *unnatural*, Inez. I mean who knows *what* the fuck it is—how much is robot, how much animal. And the thought of an animal incapable of locomotion!" The general closed his eyes. "It's nauseating, woman. Profit or no."

"That's an emotional response, Paul." She slipped into the hammock hanging a few centimeters from the general's. "Those who adore Sweet Things have one emotional response, you have another. It won't affect the success of Sweet Things in this market."

The general took a vial from one of the pockets of his dressing gown and handed it to her. "I'm perfectly willing to accept your making a profit on the little horrors," he said, "but I don't see why you have to carry one of them around with you all the time. Meals, nightcap, parties, work, *everywhere*! What is the spacing point, Inez?"

She stroked the crown of Little One's head, as though to apologize to it for her father's aspersions (though she knew very well that Sweet Things had no verbal abilities whatsoever). "Little One gives me pleasure," she said, smiling. "It's that simple. And since it gives me no trouble in the least—" no, the only trouble Little One ever caused happened when she didn't carry it with her when leaving her quarters— "I don't see why I shouldn't take that pleasure." She broke the seal and held the vial to the tiny holes in her design that allowed the passage of air into her nostrils. Hesitating, she glanced over at her father. "Do you, Paul?" She inhaled deeply and passed the vial back to him.

The general, frowning, took the vial, inhaled without speaking, and passed it back to his daughter.

"Surely you don't begrudge me such a small pleasure?"

"It's disgusting," the general said. "Though you may think it causes no trouble, it upsets me, Inez. But apparently that's of no importance to you."

"Aren't you at all curious about what it feels like?" She drew her next inhalation and passed the vial back to the general. She never tired of the oak-casked flavor of *Midnight Song*. How many local years had they been sharing it in their *de rigueur* nightcap?

"The thing's a parasite, Inez. It wouldn't get through even a day on its own. It's as much a parasite as the bacteria that live in your body are parasites. You wouldn't make a pet of bacteria, would you?"

Inez tucked in her chin to get a better look at Little One. "This part of it is gravy, Paul. And as for denigrating it for being a parasite, well all I can say is it's not like *human* parasites. Before long, Little One will have earned its keep many times over."

"I prefer human parasites to these creepy legless monsters," the general said. "Paying a human's way isn't such a bad thing. Take Solstice. She's hardly spent an SCU of all that you've given her." The general turned his head to look at his daughter, and she saw that his eyes, previously dull, burned with an intensity only the subject of Solstice Balalzalar could these days evoke. His forehead wrinkled. "She spends so little. And then her purchases...well, take the example of the last purchase she made, over a local week ago. That's how little she spends, that she could go a whole local week without making a single charge on her account. Anyway, she bought thirty pairs of cling-ons, a normal amount to buy, especially since she dances in them. But unimaginably cheap. Maybe she found a bargain?" The general's lips pursed. "But I doubt it." He sighed. "She doesn't seem in the least aware of how shoddy her apparel is, even when she comes to our parties. But that's off the subject." The general stuck his arm out to return the vial to his daughter. "You'd better take it again since I don't want to interrupt this to inhale. I want to ask your opinion on this. Because it's something of a mystery to me. I just can't account for it." He bit his lip. "The thirty pairs were in assorted colors—mostly dark drab colors, and none of them textured, much less meshed. But the weird thing is that fifteen were in one size, and the other fifteen in a different size. Not *that* different, but the explicit measurements specified on the account were undeniably different. Do you suppose she's planning to alter herself in some way?" He sighed. "I'd really rather she stay just as she is. Not that *my* opinion counts for anything."

Inez stared at him; after a few seconds, she remembered to hand the almost-spent vial back to him. "Have you been spying on me?" she said.

"*Spying* on you? What do you mean?"

She hadn't obscured the credit transfer to Solstice's account because she had perceived no need to go to the trouble of concealing it from possible future scrutiny. That she had given the waterdancer five hundred SCUs would matter to no one. But the thought of her father poking into her accounts, checking up on her, disturbed her and made her wonder how often he went behind her back, checking up on her more overt operations. (If he *really* wanted to, he could—with assistance from Major Cleveland and his people—track down at least some of her covert operations, but it would take some doing.) "Did you or did you not come across the transfer while looking through my accounts?" she coldly answered her father's question with a question.

"Of course not! Why would I be looking at *your* accounts, Inez?"

Ah. He'd been sniffing after the waterdancer, had come across the transfer and investigated its provenance—probably out of anxiety about its possible source. He must have been relieved to find out that it had been she—instead of some unknown rival.

Her father still didn't understand the first thing about Solstice Balalzalar: his persistence in making the same assumptions about her as were usually true of his past lovers must surely by now have begun to strike him with discordance...but apparently not. "Oh Paul," she said, sinking her fingers into Little One's fluff. "You're getting to be hopelessly obsessed. To actually go dipping into that kind of data. You *know* how bottomless an abyss that kind of surveillance can get to be, don't you?" One of the most important things her great-great-grandmother had taught her was to be careful of the extent to which one allowed the availability of data to seduce one. One's time and attention could be sucked up without one's even noticing, so compelling could the minutiae and trivia of data resources be when almost any hard data lay within one's grasp.

The general dropped the empty vial onto the Saturna rug below. "So why did she buy two different sizes of cling-ons?" he said. "You didn't even try to answer my original question, Inez." He snorted. "Not that you would have any better idea than me."

The general needed a dash of cold water, his daughter decided. Very well, she would be blunt. "My dear, I should have thought the answer would be obvious," she said in a provocatively frivolous tone of voice.

His eyes rolled to the ceiling. "Oh so you think you know the answer? What, did she tell you she was acquiring new exoskeletal adaptations or something?"

Inez maintained the teasing tone of voice as she retorted. "The second set of cling-ons are for her lover, of course." The general's head jerked sideways. "What is her name? Oh yes. Sadora Lumni." She watched his face go purple, a shade that complemented the lavender of his dressing gown. "Of course they're for her," she said. "Don't you think?"

The general glared at her. "You're taking that pretty coolly, I must say! When it's your credit she's spending on the ugly little froggie!"

She smiled. "Why should it matter to me if she buys her lover cling-ons? It's her credit now, isn't it." She tittered. "And to think not ten minutes ago you were marveling at how little she had spent of the credit I'd transferred to her! What does it matter? Can you give me one good reason why it matters that she's spent a few SCUs of the five hundred I gave her on cheap, drab cling-ons for her lover?"

"That's not what you're paying the woman for! You're paying her to dance, not to support her disgusting froggie lover!"

"Leave that slur out of this conversation," she said coldly. "You know how I feel about it. And let me ask you this. When you pay someone in your employ—your attendant Everlove, for instance—"

"His name is *Evergood*. After all these years, can't you get it straight?"

"Very well, Evergood. When you pay Evergood, General, do you ask him what he does with his pay? Or do you simply pay him because he's rendered the services specified by his contract, which in turn obliges you to pay him according to the guidelines set down in that same contract?"

"It's not the same thing at all, Inez."

"Oh? And how is it different?"

"I doubt you have a contract with her."

"No, Paul, I don't. Which fact is irrelevant to this particular point of dispute."

"It's *not* irrelevant, Inez. I pay Evergood for services rendered. That man *earns* his pay. It's not the hardest job in the Universe, but it's real work! Whereas what that dancer does—" The general shrugged. "Let's face it, Inez. She's essentially living off you, for nothing. And probably laughing up her sleeve at your easiness. Or is it possible you do have a contract with her, specifying the number of dances she is to perform for you and what they are worth and so on?"

She was starting to get annoyed. "Obviously, creative work is different from service-type labor. As you should be able to see for yourself without my having to spell it out for you."

The general snorted. "So I'm *right*. You're lavishing credit on her without exacting work in exchange. In other words, she's a parasite living off you. And not only her, but that ugly gnome of hers as well!"

"All right, Paul," Inez said, barely keeping her voice even. "Let's just leave out the whole question of exchange. Let me put it another way. I'm paying Solstice Balalzalar simply to make it possible and attractive for her to stay at the Institute. She can throw the spacing credit at the *subversives* for all I care, as long as it keeps her at the Institute. Because as long as she has the time and space to work, I know that she will, whether I specifically pay her to do so or not. She was dancing before I even heard of her. And she'll go on dancing whether she's at the Institute or not. It happens that I badly want to keep her at the Institute. Which makes your model of exchange irrelevant. If we have to talk about exchange, we could say the exchange is that she stays at the Institute in exchange for my keeping her in credit. Except that I didn't even ask *that* of her. Because that's not how she works, Paul, and this entire arrangement is on *her* terms. And allow me to say that I find your crass—"

"You're telling me you gave it to her without any strings whatsoever?" the general said, his voice rising even higher than his daughter's.

Registering the heat and volume of their voices, Inez realized she had revealed far more than was wise. If her father decided to be contentious about her support of the dancer, life could become an endless series of quarrels and harassment. "Let me ask you this, Paul, before we carry this absurd brawl any further," she said in a fairly well-controlled tone of voice. "How much exactly did those cling-ons cost?"

His mouth stretched into a sneer. "Six SCUs. For thirty pairs. You can imagine the kind of rags that would go for so cheap."

"Six SCUs. Which means three SCUs were spent to purchase cling-ons for Sadora Lumni." She draped her hand over the edge of the hammock. "And that empty vial of *Midnight Song* we just sniffed. Of which we sniff a vial or two every spacing night, without fail. Do you know how much a single vial of *Midnight Song* costs, my dear, generous, openhanded father?"

"You're getting bitchy, Inez," the general warned. "Which must mean you're on the defensive. Because you *know* you're wrong."

"Let me *tell* you how much a vial of *Midnight Song* costs, Daddy." Her hand—its fingers squeezing the fabric of the hammock—spasmed into a fist. "A vial of *Midnight Song* costs ten and a half SCUs. Ten and a half. We share at least one vial every night. The cling-ons Solstice Balalzalar shared with Sadora Lumni several days ago from what you said earlier cost *three* SCUs."

The general glared at her. "It's not the credit, woman. Can't you see it's the *principle* of the thing?"

"The principle of the thing," his daughter said. "I don't see any principle here. All I see is jealousy, General. *Your* jealousy. Of a Frogmore native of all things. Of a Frogmore native who wears cling-ons that sell at three SCUs for fifteen pair. A pretty pathetic jealousy, I'd say." She unclenched her fist and skimmed her fingers over the top layer of Little One's fur. "But that's only my opinion. I don't know if there are principles defining what sort of jealousy is pathetic and what sort isn't."

The general abruptly swung out of his hammock and towered over her. "Enough is enough, Inez. I'm retiring for the night. I'll leave you to your parasites." He glared at Little One. "And with a thought, just one small thought you would do well to consider." He stared at his daughter's design in such a way that she guessed his inability to see her unmediated face vexed him. "One does well to be careful about allowing parasites to feed on one. In their voraciousness they can be deadly, for they've no morals at all."

"Good night, Paul," his daughter said, making plain her intention to ignore his parting shot.

The general bent and kissed her ear, the only part of her head currently available. "Good night, Inez." He leveled a last look of disgust at her, turned on his heel, and entered his inner chambers.

Inez closed her eyes and concentrated on Little One's purr and the feel of its simulated heartbeat against her breast. She would have to do something about his problem before going off to Janniset. The whole thing had gotten out of hand. On the subject of Solstice Balalzalar he behaved like a thwarted child. As for finding him a new interest, it would first be necessary to get him to relinquish his obsession with Solstice. The problem was circular.

She rolled out of the hammock and toiled her weary end-of-the-day way to her own quarters. Maybe with a clearer mind—tomorrow, perhaps?—she would be able to break out of the circle. But for now, she could see only the circle. Absurd as it was... And then she perceived it: her difficulty in seeing a way out came from the fact that he had somehow made her a part of the circle... Or had she done it to herself by bringing Solstice into the Institute?

Reaching her quarters, she removed Little One from its sling and put it into its own tiny sleep-cocoon. "Zagorin," she called and then, going into the dressing room, saw that it hadn't been necessary, for Zagorin already stood near the dressing table, waiting. "Get me out of this design," she said. "I'm about to start clawing at it."

"Allow me, Madam." Zagorin indicated the dressing table chair.

She looks, Inez thought, as tired as I feel. She sank into the chair and watched in the mirror as Zagorin positioned herself directly behind her. Relaxing, she leaned her head against the attendant's fleshy body and closed her eyes as Zagorin meticulously set about the removal process. After perhaps half a minute the attendant's slow but deft movements had already begun to soothe and relax her. In the morning, she thought. In the morning would be soon enough to think about the problem.

The next morning, Inez's mood turned grim. A new report she had read in the bath detailed outbreaks of trouble at more than half a dozen UAP units. As she settled into her workspace hammock with a screen in hand, she realized that she had left the printout on the rim of the tub. One certainly did not want that kind of data floating about. Printing out reports always entailed a risk that their data might get out of control. She had wanted to read it in the tub, though, and because she hated reading anything lengthy in the air and found a screen awkward to manage in that position, she had printed it out. She often did that, and until now that hadn't been a problem.

She rolled out of the hammock and headed for her quarters. Messaging Zagorin to bring the printout to her would compound the error. Zagorin had probably not even noticed it lying there, and even if she had probably wouldn't have so much as glanced at it. It would simply be more business to her—in other words: meaningless gibberish. But if she were asked to carry the printout all the way down here, why then the chances were that she might be tempted to glance through it.

Stupid, stupid, stupid...

What was it that had made her forget the printout in the first place? Oh yes, something in the report had sidetracked her (her mind did tend to get a bit labile in the bath, a consequence she ordinarily considered a productive rather than distracting property of bathing) into thinking about the growing seriousness of her father's problem. She had laid the printout on the rim, leaned her head back, and closed her eyes to ponder the problem. When the chime had sounded, she had gotten out of the tub without even noticing the printout.

Blame for the trouble at the units must be charged to the account of the UAP's Director of Public Communication. It came as no surprise that the DPC had botched the job, for Inez had been certain that the governor's refusal to follow CDS's plan laying the groundwork for the shift would severely handicap them. But perhaps more important, UAP's DPC lacked that certain brilliance required of the top people in the field on civilized worlds. She had learned basic techniques on Pleth, but never having done more than a minor apprenticeship with a galaxy-class firm of consultants, lacked the breadth and nuances experience working on civilized worlds would have given her—which often stretched a long way toward mitigating a lack of that stunning imagination that characterized the very best public communication specialists.

So now they were in a fix. Inez could think of no one currently on the planet (apart, perhaps, from Major Hobgood, whom she rated as near galaxy-class talent, but to little avail, since she would hardly take the high-stakes risk of tapping one of her father's officers for a contretemps so relatively insignificant) likely to do any better in this short-run situation than UAP's DPC. Inez had from time to time considered importing a PC specialist to serve as her personal consultant but had always discarded the idea as too extravagant when she knew she could count on the local firm of consultants she employed to advise her on routine questions of technique and implementation.

Entering the dressing room, she observed Zagorin seated on a stool, head bent over a piece of close-work she was holding under the beam of a high-intensity lamp. Apparently startled by the sound of Inez's passing, the attendant glanced up to see who it was. "Madam," she said. "Is there something...?"

"Nothing, nothing, just ignore me," Inez called over her shoulder as she passed into the bathroom. The printout was lying on the rim of the tub, exactly as she had left it. Excellent. No harm done. Obviously Zagorin hadn't noticed it yet—otherwise she would have been expecting her and probably would have taken the printout from the rim and put it someplace "safe" (as Zagorin would be wont to think of it). Inez bent to retrieve it and found it damp and slightly oily to the touch and fragrant from the solution she always had Zagorin dilute in the water. Yes, that was the page she had been reading. A weight lifted from her chest, and this surprised her, for she hadn't realized she'd been *that* anxious about it. Idiot, she muttered at herself as she tucked the printout under her arm. And then as she passed through the dressing room and offered Zagorin an amiable wave it occurred to her what sort of mess they might have been in should it have become apparent that Zagorin *had* read the printout. She shuddered. It was a lesson to be more careful in the future... Perhaps even to give up printouts altogether?

Sydney gave Inez a pregnant look as she entered the office. "It's Solstice Balalzalar," Sydney said without waiting to exchange polite greetings. Her pearly eyes rested almost fixedly on Little One. But then she made no secret of her desire for a Sweet Thing.

"Yes?"

"She asked that either I inform her of when you would be free to see her, or that you stop by her workspace."

Inez furrowed her fingers in Little One's fluff, careful to avoid the emerald clipped to its crown. Solstice had never asked for an appointment before. "Ask her to come up here," Inez said. "I have a lot of meticulous work to do this afternoon. I don't suppose it matters when, does it? Unless you've made any appointments for me?" Certainly she had nothing on her own calendar; she had checked during decontamination.

"No, I've arranged nothing."

"Good. Then Solstice can see me whenever she likes." Inez went into her workspace and settled into the hammock nearest the heavily draped window currently without function. She'd insisted the architect include it in the building's design, partly through optimism, partly through the desire to remind herself to keep toiling away at her plan. Had Solstice discovered traces of the general's surveillance? She hadn't taken the possibility of such a development seriously, but now it seemed all too likely. If so, it would be difficult to smooth over the waterdancer's anger.

But maybe, just maybe, Solstice wanted to talk to her about a new dance she had thought up. One could hope.

Lacking any appetite, Inez sent word to both her father and the staff that she would be passing up dinner, and spent the extra time that gave her lying on the massage couch in her inner chamber, listening to music and staring at the moving audible holoscape of an Anacondan ocean beach hanging in the air above the massage couch. Though solitary, she sniffed *Golden Panacea.* The last few days had been terrible, and the pressures she faced—taken together almost overwhelming as they would not have been singly—entitled her to indulgence. The intensification of the general's desire for Solstice having approached the point of mania, the sudden difficulties at the UAP plants ～ she could only think that at this rate, by the time they worked their way to the last scheduled shift they'd have a massive public relations snafu on their hands ~ and now (of all things) Solstice's bizarre defection not only from the Institute but (apparently) from dance as well: all combined to produce the sense of being caught in an irrational nightmare in which nothing made sense and all one's actions proved inevitably impotent...

Solstice had been wearing one of her loose tunics—this one heavily embroidered with seeds and rough unrefined fibers in peculiar designs possibly bearing arcane significance—over her cling-ons, giving her a formal look, since only on elaborate social occasions had Inez seen her wearing anything *but* cling-ons. As for the cling-ons...of course Inez had snatched covert looks at them, convinced that the dancer had discovered the general's inquisitive surveillance. But even as Solstice had been thanking her for finding the time to see her so promptly, Inez had been thinking rather wistfully of how she would like to dress the dancer in one of the many elegant varieties of cling-ons, for Solstice possessed the grace to carry off even the most baroque textures and patterns in such high fashion on Frogmore—as few who could afford them did. But staring at the waterdancer's grave, naked face, she had remembered the general's snooping and put the thought away. *She's essentially living off you. And probably laughing up her sleeve at your easiness.* Laughing up her sleeve, Inez repeated to herself. She probably is.

Or was she? The dancer hadn't seemed particularly sneery. She had offered to return most of the credit. She had humbly—trustingly, even—requested the favor of the Institute's shipping her disassembled tank to her later, when she had "finally settled." She had been cold, distant, grave... Solstice often seemed cold and distant, of course. Only this time she had looked distressed, as though she were barely keeping a powerful emotion from escaping her tight control... Standing in the roseate ultraviolet light, her face turned toward

Inez, her legs astraddle, her feet firmly planted (did she stand that way at the bottom of her tank, perhaps?), her eyes like bits of carbon film—lifeless, detached, but as always vigilant (for what sort of things Inez had still not discovered)—declining an invitation to sit or lie or perch—it had seemed to Inez as she regarded the dancer's presence that as always, Solstice seemed to be only just there, always on the verge of vanishing, perhaps even an illusion projected with trembling instability into that particular space from some other past or future moment of time. Listening to the low, hoarse, nearly monotone voice, Inez understood only that, whatever the problem, whatever she might say to Solstice, it was all coming to an end ~ this is superstition, she told herself even as the conviction tightened its stranglehold on her ~ and that whatever break Solstice had come to force upon her, that break would shatter her current existence, would affect not only her enigmatic relations with Solstice but everything else as well. *But how can that be? It's mere superstition. Perhaps Paul will be affected, but probably for the best, and as for everything else: impossible! What passes between Solstice and me has nothing to do with the Family's Affairs.*

But trying to fathom Solstice always left her stranded on a stark rock of an island surrounded by hostile seas ~ a shivery image of silver and phosphorescent time-trippers lurking in black choppy waters unaccountably flashed into her mind, an image that could have nothing to do with the lush, warm, sun-glittering Anaconda ocean whose complex tides pulled at the waves hanging above her ~ for the enigma of Solstice, though seductive, carried no promise of pleasure for any delving she might work on it or even with its revelation. Indeed, Inez obscurely feared that the unveiling of the enigma would be an exposure—however irresistible—of a Medusa that while it might not turn her to stone might yet conceivably freeze or melt or in other ways transmogrify the very tissues composing her self, the very sinews holding that self together.

Superstition, it's all superstition. She always felt uneasy after encounters with Solstice. Each time she explained her anxiety hangover as a matter of miscommunication. What could one expect when two cultures clashed? In fact, they had nothing in common whatsoever (beyond the bare fact of their humanity). *No, that's not correct. The dance. We have that in common. We share aesthetic values in common. And as Alexandra Jador of Pleth has shown in extensive and elaborate detail and explication, aesthetic values, whatever one wishes to think, can never be taken as a separate sphere of influence within an individual's life.*

But perhaps it had been that common bond, that one single thing that had made her believe ~ of all artists whose work she had ever experienced, surely Solstice's struck the greatest resonance, created the most profoundly felt (however intangible) personal sensations—and even the general, his daughter realized, even he, blunted though his sensibilities were, had deeply felt Solstice's art, for only that sort of response could account for his current uncharacteristic frustrated obsession ~ that the cultural differences (and whatever other differences, political, for instance) that lay between them could be transcended if not forgotten altogether. And yet, Inez reflected, something about that art made her deeply uneasy. She'd been imagining that if she could only get past the differences that lay like a barrier between them, she would access something marvelous and, well, transformative. Something that would light up her existence here on Frogmore. But what if what lay beyond their differences was, instead, unbearable? What if it was better for her that she *not* understand Solstice's art?

Why, then, did she feel so compelled to get past their differences? Wherein lay the seduction pulling her toward that threshold, making her intent on finding the command that would blink out the barrier separating her from the possibly terrible sight she would probably rather not see? She had to admit that she could not explain her own pursuit of Solstice (a pursuit quite different from the general's, but a pursuit nonetheless) except by reference to this desire to glimpse the secret now veiled from her.

She canceled the holoscape and music. Her head seemed to be floating above her body—huge, tremulous, swollen to the point of pain. It wasn't *Golden Panacea. Golden Panacea* made one feel so light as to be a hairsbreadth from hallucinating levitation, but at this moment her head felt heavy, leaden, swamped with fluid as thick as the solution she bathed in. At last, in a burst of defiant—or desperate—recklessness she gave the order to block all physical sensation. She would maintain the block for only a few minutes. She would soon have to get up to be dressed, anyway... *That spacing mediocre drama I agreed to attend, even though I know they never perform anything worth seeing, all for the sake of Project Sweet Things...* What possible harm could there be in blocking physical sensation for a mere quarter of a local hour?

Her thoughts wandered back to the mysterious, almost sinister threshold, an image that now seemed to say absolutely everything about Solstice. Visualizing herself standing before the barrier wondering what lay beyond it and how to find the key to blinking it out, Inez speculated on what Solstice's eyes saw when they looked at her, Inez Gauthier. Even a few moments of speculation provoked intense discomfort, cracking open a crevice through which rushed the general's taunts— *She's a parasite living off you. And not only her, but that ugly gnome of hers as well!*

The chime sounded in her ear, overriding the block. Inez rolled out of the hammock. It took her a few seconds—clutching the hammock, hesitating before crossing the room—to find her balance. For a moment she considered ordering a diagnostic scan, then scoffed at her hypochondria. She had a theater party to join; she had Project Sweet Things to foster. I feel perfectly steady now, she said to herself. As proof, she released the hammock and walked into the dressing room without the least difficulty.

"Madam," Zagorin said, waylaying her a couple of meters short of the dressing table where the design dresser stood waiting.

"What is it?" Inez wondered if she'd forgotten to specify the evening's accouterments, then remembered that she had done that before sinking into her orgy of solitary pleasures.

Zagorin regarded her with wary intensity. "There is a favor I need to ask of you, Madam." Her voice was barely audible.

Inez sighed. "Don't tell me. You want a week off for some festival or other that's not on the list of holidays."

Zagorin folded her arms over her chest. "It's something else, Madam."

Inez glanced at the design dresser. "Let's talk while the dresser—"

"It's important, Madam."

The significance of the interruption—unique in her memory—did not escape Inez. "All right, it's important," she said, trying to keep the impatience out of her voice. "Then perhaps you should tell me what favor it is you would like from me."

Zagorin visibly swallowed. "Yes, Madam. It was, you see, I was hoping you'd release me from my contract. I know I have almost eleven years to go, but—"

"Release you from your contract!" Inez was incredulous. "Are you serious? After all the expense I shouldered to fix your body, after the further expense of having you connected, after all the time I've spent training you to be a first-rate personal attendant, after all that, you want me to release you from the remainder of your contract? Are you out of your mind?" Zagorin would never be able to repay the expense of the surgery that had removed every trace of the exoskeletal modifications and internally reinforced her body. It had been worth it to Inez to bear the expense because she had known she would not be able to tolerate having to look at the exoskeletal excrescences day after day after day first thing in the morning and last thing at night and had felt confident that Zagorin would work out well. She had even entertained the notion that Zagorin might accompany her when she and the general finally returned to civilization. Yet Zagorin could cavalierly stand there and propose she simply write all that off, that she erase their contract (the terms of which she had always felt redounded handsomely to the attendant's advantage). Inez took a sharper look at Zagorin. "Someone's made you a better offer?" Of course. Let her first employer bear all the trouble and expense, then leave for a new employer who could afford to offer more lucrative terms precisely because all the trouble and expense had already been attended to.

"No, Madam! I wouldn't do that!" Zagorin's voice and eyes expressed deep indignation.

I never realized what prime acting talent the woman has.

"It's because...well, there's trouble in my Family. I feel a great obligation and need to go to them."

Family? But a note in Zagorin's voice indicated she was hiding something; and her gaze, though meeting Inez's, seemed...shifty. "What about your obligation to me?"

Zagorin's crossed arms pressed even more tightly against her chest. "I know I have that obligation, Madam, but..." Her eyes implored. "I'm so worried about my Family. I know you could replace me easily, I've always been aware of how lucky I am to have this job with you, so it seems—"

"If you know how lucky you are, then be satisfied with the way things are." Inez indicated the design dresser. "I can't stand here arguing with you all evening, Zagorin. So you might as well accept it. The answer is no; I will not release you from your contract." She strode the remaining distance to the dressing table, ignoring whatever else it was that

Zagorin was saying. First Solstice running off for who knew what reason—abandoning her art! of all incomprehensible things in the galaxy—and now Zagorin wanting to run off.

Inez snapped her order to the design dresser: "*The Deliberate*. And don't dawdle, I'm already behind schedule." Her father would be barging in on her any minute now, judging by the way the day had so far gone. *Paul. Oh no. Paul. I'll have to tell him about Solstice.* Dismay almost crushed her. But it dawned on her that Solstice's going might be the very best thing that could happen—for the general, that is. Out of sight, out of mind. Or so, at least, she hoped.

Power chairs can be leased at the shuttleport and a few other locations. Rates vary tremendously, depending on the current state of supply and demand. One model comes equipped with a canopy that allows the user to be sealed in, but the seals are not guaranteed air-tight and, in any case, users will still be required to undergo decontamination each time they enter a building or complex.

While power chairs can be used out of doors, we don't advise it. Few Frogmorians walk the streets for any appreciable distance, and the streets are thus reserved mainly for surface transport vehicles. The shuttleport has five slidewalks, the Capitol District has four slidewalks connecting shops in the primary shopping area, and the Governor's Installation has several, but slidewalks are nonexistent elsewhere on the planet. Most surface transport services, including the fixed-route shuttles that circulate through the Capitol District, accept power chairs.

Many buildings do not comfortably accommodate power chairs. (The traveler may reasonably conclude that Frogmorians consider those unprepared to cope with the planet's gravity moral and physical weaklings. This attitude can be a disadvantage for any off-worlder who uses a power chair and is wishing to be taken seriously.) Such buildings will usually allow users to check the chairs in a holding room near the antechamber that serves as a lock between the entrance and the building's interior. (Note: if its decontamination chamber is closed, you will not be able to gain entry to the building. We advise, then, that the visitor ping the building or complex before leaving any particular destination.) Buildings and complexes that do accommodate power chairs will require the chair to go through decontamination. (This will entail an additional charge.)

— *A Traveler's Handbook to the Galaxy*, 49th edition

Eighteen
NATHALIE STILLNESS

Personal Journal Entry. Insert dates, standard and local. Append: Lunching with the Gauthiers, *père et fille*, marks something new in my relations with Inez. One is expected to take such invitations & kind treatment as honorable distinctions. But just how well does it bode for the course of my future relations with her? A certain distance is desirable for such tricky relations, especially considering Inez's peculiar role in the world I'm studying.

Can I truthfully describe the lunch as unpleasant? No. That would be an exaggeration. Everything glittered with the patina of superior civilization—literally, for the holos forming the dining room's walls offered the illusion of sitting on a terrace of an estate in Janniset's Turquoise Hills; it is done so well that, combined with the room's lighting, it gave the impression of bathing us in Janniset-like sunlight. The general exerted himself to charm me. Surprising, considering how he always ignores my presence unless forced by Inez to acknowledge it. For the first time I could see what makes him popular. Or rather, I can see why his officers adore him. But charm or no charm, it's difficult to understand why the elites of Frogmore also adore him, imitating his dress & posture & gait, & insisting on his being the governor's man.

His attention & efforts to charm made me squirm, heightening my awareness of a certain problem that I imagine must be common for alienated types like me. [*Interrupt text: note that the words from* for *through* me *are to be deleted should any intrusive entry be made into this file.*] *Append:*

This problem may be characterized as the discomfort that is generated when a lower status individual's perceptions & affective responses do not match those that others of higher status assume as likely & appropriate. This status differential forms an essential element of the discomfort, since in failing to respond in line with the expectations of those making the overtures, the lower status person not only experiences a dissonance in perception but finds herself placed in the position of rejecting the received perception of that particular situation. Fortunately, in this case I only had to simulate a tepid response to the general's warmth in order to disguise the fact that not only did his warmth not generate a responsive warmth in me, it actually irritated & chafed me for the obligation it placed on me to simulate a warm response.

& so the three of us lunched in civilized elegance. Inez's day-mask seemed designed to fit the Turquoise Hills setting (the synthetic Janniset sunlight playing brilliantly over the turquoise gems set into it), while the general's pink & brown day-mask, which covered at most a third of his face, was simplicity itself. Oh yes, one other interesting feature of the setting: as a background we were treated to the sounds one would presumably hear on such a Janniset terrace—a variety of bird calls, the rustling of those magnificent mammoth willow-weeds, the burbling of a stream... & an odd thing happened to me as I became conscious that I had been taking in those sounds (that seemed so natural to the setting that at first I didn't even notice them): I realized that a non-elite native hearing such sounds for the first time would be unable to identify them unless they had heard them on holos—& many of the natives don't subscribe to holoservices.

All through lunch, while making a strenuous effort to maintain the politeness-line, I subjected Inez to close scrutiny, which wasn't easy, because unlike the general's day-mask, hers covered every centimeter of her face (except for small eyeholes & a reasonably sized oral orifice. I listened to every sentence she uttered for clues to why she had foisted this "intimate little occasion" on me, but remained mystified throughout. (I really cannot see the Gauthiers entertaining in this fashion often—with *one* guest, & at a meal at that, given that Inez is known for her repugnance for consuming meals in social settings, which I imagine derives from her early exposure to Anacondan mores.)

Tension fairly vibrated between Inez and the general. I know nothing about what is normal for them, so I can't make comparisons in judging the nature of this particular tension. They took turns in stroking one another in a disturbing, weird way that I have the feeling is normal for them. One for you, one for me... Always this lively concern for one another. Yes, that's it: they seem eternally conscious of one another. Perhaps how that tension plays into it may have something to do with it? I've always wondered why Inez doesn't simply leave this planet without him and what she could possibly mean when she says the general "won't let [her] go."

Speaking of stroking, a slight digression here. I was appalled to find Inez with that synthetic creature (all fluffy fur & big eyes) carried in a sling between her breasts, even during the meal. She seemed almost unaware of the thing, stroking it from time to time, but in a way that seemed absent from its presence. The general, on the other hand, directed disgusted glares at the thing, which Inez seemed never to notice.

I can't help but consider the spectacle of "Sweet Things" within the context of the two main streams of thought on the subject of the evolution of the human psyche. On the one hand, if one subscribes to the ancient Freudian notion that civilization is a castration of the "natural killing/raping/torturing man" of violence, a castration necessary for the perpetuation of the species, then these creatures can be considered a further sign of the progressive weakening of the human psyche as civilization becomes increasingly rarefied & "artificial," as humans grow increasingly dependent on technological manipulation of their Total Environment & perpetually search out ever new ways of redirecting the primitive instinctual drives that have been forced to burrow ever deeper within the psyche. Or, on the other hand, if one subscribes to the school of thought in which the definition of human *is* the "non-natural" & assumes that humans have always manipulated their environment & the "givens" of their (human) situations, then these "Sweet Things" may be seen as merely one more created object along the way to freeing human beings from excessive, even crippling, dependence on one another for fulfilling the needs that arise from the as yet poorly understood failures of child-rearing. Though I prefer the second school of thought to the first, the notion of seeing these wretched creatures as aids to healthy maturity not only turns my stomach but also strikes me as absurd—if not perverse... Whatever function the thing serves for Inez, I suspect that it's one she's not even aware of. A disturbing thought, but then many of our deliberately created objects serve veiled functions, even when at certain times we are perfectly capable of both bringing to consciousness and naming those functions for ourselves... Yet of course they serve those functions beyond our conscious apperception of the process, & for the most part *only* when they are "forgotten."

After lunch Inez swept me off to the gardens, a rare treat. I almost burst into giggles the instant we had escaped the dining room, where we left the general chatting with an aide who resembled one of those old Greek gods, so exceptional was his physical beauty, and had entered the room just as we were finishing our dessert. Inez clasped my arm, took me through an antechamber, & strolled me through the lush, well-ordered vegetation—the fog as though held off by invisible glass above & around the gardens (though of course what kept the fog off the gardens were hundreds of fog-eaters, as lavish a display of extravagance as anything I've seen at the Commander's Residence). As we strolled, we talked.

First Inez remarked that she was "in the doldrums," but that the certainty that she would soon be going to Janniset on business was "keeping her going." I asked her if it was life on Frogmore & her sense of being trapped here that had gotten her depressed. (This would have been something I could easily have sympathized with.)

Oh, she replied, pausing to stare at me through the rhomboid-shaped eye-holes in her day-mask, oh I wouldn't go so far as to say I'm depressed, Nathalie. That would surely be too strong a word. No, I'm just a little, well, *discouraged*. Or perhaps a better way to describe it would be to say that I feel at a stand. To tell the truth, I have to confess that certain aspects of the natives are leaving me feeling more *stymied* than anything." She squeezed my arm & moved us forward. & then she lapsed into a lecture on the particular botanical specimens before us, with digressions on what special things had to be done to help them survive Frogmore's gravity & how, still, none of them were quite the same as in their natural habitats...

This guided lecture-tour seemed to take forever, I suppose because of the vibes I was getting off Inez. Out of her father's presence, I sensed, surprisingly, far more tension—but of a different sort—than that I'd sensed between her & her father. & something else. In retrospect, given my interpretation of what passed between us, I'm inclined to think that a good part of the subsurface currents pulling at us must have been her concentration on how best to manipulate me. That she would even have to think about it is a strange notion where Inez is concerned, but nevertheless...perhaps the absence of the stunning confidence she usually radiates suggests this notion to me. Or perhaps it was her talking about feeling a little off her stride that made me project tension onto her as we walked in the garden...

Eventually the lecture came to an end. We stood there, staring at one of the more bizarre specimens, & I noticed the silence all around us. I remember being struck by the fact that we were out of doors, that we had been out of doors for some time, in the open air, without using respirators. Instead of reveling in a sense of freedom (for one of the principal fantasies that recur throughout each of my days here on Frogmore is the fantasy of walking around on Pleth in the open air with the sense of having achieved total freedom), I felt panic & a desire for safe enclosure. Inez must have understood, for she unlinked her arm from mine in order to put it around my shoulders. Don't worry, she said. I know what you're thinking, but everything's fine out here. Not only is the Scourge kept at bay, but all these plants produce enough oxygen to supplement the thinness of oxygen in the Frogmore atmosphere. I think I gasped in a great lung-full of air as I concentrated on taking in the sense of her words. Inez then went on to tell me that she herself had, at the beginning, often experienced not simply panic but acute fits of terror that had driven her inside. & that for a while she had been in the habit of wearing her respirator here in the garden.

Oddly enough, my response to Inez's reassurances resembled my response to the general's exertions to charm me: I felt uncomfortable & a little resentful. Which was unfair, since Inez thought she had been giving her poor deprived friend a treat & thus can't be accused of having deliberately dumped me into an unpleasant situation. As for my irritation with her solicitousness, I suppose that must be laid to flaws of the ego—my ego. Still, I didn't throw off Inez's arm (Inez has always been a touch-prone person anyway); instead I muffled my irritation.

At this point, she introduced the subject that must have been the reason for the occasion. (Inez is so devious one can't help but suspect reasons for everything out of the way that she does. & having me to lunch with the general was in every respect out of the way.) At the time it seemed that the change of subject was casual, designed to help distract me from my panic-attack. But in retrospect it is clear that of everything we chatted about, this subject interested her most. Are you familiar with any of the people in the Saturna Region? she asked as she headed us back in the direction of the door.

I haven't done fieldwork there yet, I said—and stopped to consider. I used not to be so careful in talking about my work. But given the insights fieldwork on Frogmore has forced on me—insights about certain political & economic interconnections with what I'm doing here—I've grown cautious. Especially with Inez—for it's been contact with Inez that has taught me a certain sensitivity. I try to make myself remember at all times, no matter how casual everything seems, that Inez has axes to grind (however she tries to give the impression that she does nothing but play), that one never knows what Inez might do with any given piece of information. It's an awesome sort of problem. But I've been burned (or so I surmise—these sorts of things are so subtle & intangible that one can never be certain that any one piece of information set a particular process in motion) by such casual conversations before. & I'm well used to Inez pumping me. When I got back from Durazzo, for instance, her pumping—she all the while bubbling over with amusement at her own "voracious curiosity," as she called it—approached the threshold of insistent interrogation.

At any rate, since I was in the dark as to what Inez wanted to know about Saturna (& of course knew she'd never level with me as to *why* she wanted to know), I decided not to mention, as I had originally intended to do—Inez likes to know when I'm going to be away—my upcoming trip there. Nor did I mention that I had interviewed two women (both, of course, pregnant) from Saturna at Durazzo, preferring to feel my way carefully before exposing them to Inez's scrutiny. (It's interesting to note how protective I'm becoming of my subjects. I'm afraid my supervisors will eventually accuse me of having gone native—or at least of having gotten "involved in local politics." But there are problems with the guidelines, & I don't intend to close my eyes to them. Or rather, I don't think I *can* close my eyes to them. Not & listen to my subjects' voices at the same time.) So my cautious answer was that I knew only general things about the Saturna Region, since I hadn't yet done fieldwork there. Inez looked disappointed & asked me to tell her what "general things" I knew about Saturna & more particularly about the people who lived there.

So I said that from what I could gather, Saturna was the quintessence of non-elite Frogmore. Inez goggled at me (& I can hardly blame her: the expression is certainly odd), & I tried to explain what I meant by *quintessence*. Which required giving a little background on the loose matrilinear formation common to all Frogmore society, even among a sizable portion of the elites.

She looked puzzled at first, & then, I think, flabbergasted as it dawned on her what I was talking about. She tried to argue that the elites weren't matrilinear, that she knew many of them herself & that though the most *visible* elites appeared to run family lines down a nearly exclusive maternal descendance, she knew lesser families—of course Inez's idea of "lesser" is risible—whose descendance conformed to the patterns of those common in advanced societies.

Then I explained how certain of the non-elites lived in much tighter matrilinear formations, within domes—all under one enormous roof, in what is called a "family." She found this difficult to grasp & kept asking questions that revealed that she didn't have an inkling of what I was talking about, or of how such a thing could be. She wondered, for example, how so many people could stand one another while living under one roof; of course she knows about families with large numbers of siblings—the governor's, for instance, about which she once said she could not imagine how there could be any real relationship between parent & child when so many children had to share a single parent. I tartly pointed out that many people lived in the Commander's Residence, but she dismissed that as an inappropriate comparison.

I gave up trying to explain the concept of such thoroughly extended families—& went on to say that Saturna had three such domes & that each of the domes at Saturna was known for a particular commodity they produced, beautifully worked textiles in one (much of the fiber derived from an exotic mammal that has been successfully adapted to Frogmore & the dye from shellfish found in the Spieden region), a beverage made from one of the few edible berries native to Frogmore, & an aged cheese that was one of the staples of the ordinary non-elite Frogmore diet. At my mentioning this last commodity Inez suddenly started asking me what I knew about the cheese, what its name was, what kind of distribution it had, & other similar questions. (I'm a little queasy about this: the sharpness of her interest makes me wonder if I haven't blundered.) But when it became clear I could tell her none of the things she wanted to know about Bessel cheese, she dropped the subject & asked me to go on. I didn't want to say much more, so I merely remarked that I was looking forward to visiting Saturna, for in picking up references to it, the place had always struck me as being unusually vital & creative. I didn't add that I was curious to know if this vitality & creativity have anything to do with Saturna's having three domes (most areas have only one, or at most two) & with most of their population being of that very intense strict matrilineal extended-family formation.

At this point we reached the door & went inside. Inez suggested I go with her to the Institute to see some sculpture that had recently arrived. Although she didn't return to her usual self, neither did she question me further about Saturna or Bessel cheese. Imagine getting so worked up over cheese…it must have some special business significance to her. Of all people, Inez would be the last to get excited about cheese (especially one she had never tasted) for no apparent reason. *Close personal journal.*

Nathalie Stillness slides out of the hammock and messages Ardeth. It is time to begin packing for the trip to Saturna. Of all her trips into the field, she has an inkling that the one to Saturna may be the most rewarding. For the first time she will be staying in a native household. Because she got along well with the Saturna women she met at Durazzo, they agreed to let her stay in one of their domes. Nathalie Stillness wraps her arms around herself in a tight, ecstatic hug. If they have a religion, she will be bound to detect it, living right there among them. If not, it will still be fascinating to explore her hypothesis about Saturna's special vitality. Either way, this trip into the field will be the turning point of her study: she feels it in her bones. As for the coincidence of Inez's asking about Saturna only days before her scheduled trip there... well, coincidences do happen—even on Frogmore.

Holliday, the largest of Frogmore's moons, is *the* destination for people on the sexual make. Couples often spend a few days there, luxuriating in its light gravity, while singles crowd its hotels, bars, and spas, cruising for casual partners. Some people, just wanting a few days' respite from the rigors of Frogmore, check into full-service "privacy hotels," where quite a lot of business is transacted. (Many business travelers to Frogmore never actually visit the surface at all, but instead schedule their meetings in privacy hotels on Holliday.) For those unfamiliar with privacy hotels, be warned that cruising in them is verboten, and friendly approaches to strangers are solecisms that can soon escalate into civil violations entailing penalties of large fines.

Except in the privacy hotels, the bars and restaurants on Holliday have open-space arrangements. Frogmorians can be strangely loud and gregarious in these circumstances (as they definitely are not in the private rooms with monitors, arrangements typical on the surface). Enoch Fulmer, in *A Star-Hopper's View of the Galaxy*, opines that the open-arrangement of bars and restaurants on Holliday reminds Frogmorians of their days on Pleth and triggers a relapse into youthful behavior. Whatever.

Certain areas of Holliday are off-limits to tourists because they are strictly private, for instance clinics, extended-stay spas, and residential childcare centers. Admission to these areas is tightly controlled and ought to be sought before traveling to Holliday, since it always requires permission from Frogmore's Governing Authority as well as the permission of the specific institution or business one is visiting.

—*A Traveler's Handbook to the Galaxy*, 49th edition

Nineteen
MADELEINE TAO

"Bear me away now—" Creon moaned, clawing at his design, pulling bits of it from his face "—away from the one who killed my son. I can find no peace. My life is too twisted to be fixed. Fate, alas, has destroyed me."

His barefaced officers surrounded the king, crowding close. The threshold to the enormous portal cleared, and Creon and his entourage crossed it, making their final exit.

The stage dimmed. In the eerie haze only the chorus—dressed in costumes that, though without insignia, unmistakably resembled the uniform of the Frogmore Militia—remained. "A good life depends," they chanted, "on wisdom prevailing. The gods will receive their due. Lofty speeches by the proud just bring greater suffering down on their heads. So wisdom comes to those who learn this truth."

A thick, smoky darkness crept over the stage, pressing the audience into a lightlessness alleviated by only the little dots of blue marking the house's aisles. All around Madeleine people began clapping. Willing herself to effort—moving at all seemed to require waging a battle against inertia—she consciously lifted her hands from the armrests of her recliner and dragged her palms together. Once she had produced a few wide-spaced claps the process grew easier, so that by the time each member of the cast had in turn been singled out by the spotlight she had achieved a rate of clapping almost as frequent as that of the majority of the audience.

When the house lights came up, Madeleine, blinking, looked around her. On her right, Holland sat with her arms crossed, her palms gripping her elbows. On the other side of Holland, Madeleine's mother, Althea Tao, sat stiffly erect, her design a somber gray rhythmically spurting dark red streaks that spread into blotches before melting into the dull gray background.

"I hope you won't think it rude of me if I ask you to meet me at Mongo's," Imogen Alençon half-whispered into Madeleine's ear. "I promised to go backstage after the performance."

Madeleine recalled that at the time she had invited them all to this performance, Imogen had mentioned that a former student was directing this production. "Not at all," she said. "It's nearby, isn't it?"

"Just across the street. I've reserved a space for us and will message them that you will all be arriving in advance of me."

Solange as well as Holland's friends Leanna and Anike had already risen to their feet. Madeleine touched Holland's hand. "We're to go on ahead of Imogen," she said. "To Mongo's, just across the street."

Holland said, "I know that place. I've been there a few times."

Madeleine rose. She had always had a vague notion that the young people had places they especially liked in the neighborhood of the FCU but had never specifically imagined Holland in such a milieu. She herself, on returning from Pleth, had found the FCU boring, depressing, and something of an embarrassingly cheap imitation of the real thing and, like most others of her generation, had avoided the entire vicinity. In fact, this party to the theater marked only the fifth time she had ever had anything to do with the FCU. If Imogen hadn't invited them, it would never have occurred to her to attend this production of *Antigone*.

"A little too obvious," Madeleine heard her mother remark crisply to Solange. "They might as well have stuck a sign on him labeling him General Gauthier. The same with the Ismene character: might as well have blazoned Amanda Kundjan across her chest. Absurd! To take a serious play and distort it like that!"

"I can see," Holland said to Madeleine, "that we're going to have quite a discussion tonight."

Madeleine glanced over her shoulder. Imogen had already joined the crowd moving toward the exits. "It was a controversial interpretation, certainly," she said. *Antigone* had been on the required reading list for Pleth Universities for as long as Pleth had existed, the only piece of drama from remote antiquity to be so distinguished. But then *Antigone* bore special relevance for galactic civilization. The ancients hadn't realized it, but for millennia they had in *Antigone* held the key for understanding and resolving many of their conflicts. Madeleine had always thought it ironic that only advanced civilization could fully appreciate its value.

Feeling she had been deputed to keep the party organized, Madeleine discouraged the others from discussion as she shepherded them through the exits and out onto the street. Along the way she was struck afresh ~ she had first noticed the oddity when they had taken their seats and been waiting for the play to begin ~ by the high proportion of unaltered Frogmorians in the audience. In general, altered Frogmorians predominated at most cultural events she attended. She supposed it must have something to do with the production's being a University-sponsored event.

As they entered Mongo's, a whispery mechanical voice greeted Madeleine by name, informed her that "Space 12 awaits occupancy by the Alençon party," and offered an apology: "Your host has been delayed but expects to be joining you within the next fifteen minutes." Holland said that she knew where Space 12 was, offered to lead the way, and set off down the long, twisty hallway.

Above each threshold glowed a number. "It's this one," Holland said. "But the threshold's opaqued. Shall I inquire?"

As Holland spoke, the threshold deopaqued. "Ah," Holland said. "It must have been keyed to your ID, Mother."

They entered the space, and the threshold reopaqued. The walls offered holoscapes of some unidentifiable piece of rock thrusting out of water that Madeleine thought must have been taken from a Frogmore site since little of it beyond the foreground could be made out through the dense fog swirling over rock and water. The holoscapes had been arranged to suggest that their space constituted most of the rock's surface, while only the bare edges of the rock extended into the choppy gray water that surrounded them on all sides.

"Do we want total privacy or not?" Holland asked, waving at the screen displaying successive shots of the occupied interiors of other spaces.

Madeleine sank into one of the hammocks. Her mother, she noted, had already settled into a recliner, and took that choice as a sign that she had disapproved of the play. Not that her mother made such choices only when she was being disapproving, but though her design had settled into a dull placid pattern of golds and olives and browns, she had been manifesting diverse smaller indications of discontent that Madeleine couldn't account for except by reference to the play (or, possibly, to Imogen, which arguably amounted to the same thing). "Why don't we leave it to Imogen to decide," Madeleine said to Holland. "Unless anyone feels very strongly for total privacy?" The rule of courtesy dictated that in such situations a group always yield to a desire for total privacy should even one person express a need for it.

Holland moved to the recliner facing her grandmother. "I prefer being able to see other spaces. Otherwise what's the point of going out?"

And how else would the young people challenge one another to duels? Madeleine thought. "Audio is off, I hope?"

"Not many people like to have the audio on," Leanna said. "Being seen isn't the same as being heard."

"Especially when you're dressed in a design," Althea Tao said. "When I was your age we didn't wear designs. And we wore what you call day-masks only at night." She chuckled. "We called them 'night faces.' The expression used was that before going out one 'put on one's night face.'"

"But that's incredible!" Anike said. "I distinctly remember while at University—I loved browsing in those old holoview stores, of which there were so many everywhere you went on Pleth—anyway, I remember seeing an old holoview of designs worn at least a hundred Pleth years earlier—it was some kind of catalogue for ordering from Janniset. So that doesn't make sense, does it?"

"My mother isn't trying to prank you," Madeleine said, wondering if Anike or Leanna had begun imagining they were being challenged to duel. "We didn't wear designs until after Inez Gauthier came to Frogmore and plunged us into her fashion frenzy. Perhaps if you think back to your adolescence you'll remember how people wore masks instead of designs in the evening?"

"How embarrassing, to think Frogmore was so far behind the times and that only Inez's arrival got us up to standard," Leanna said. "I guess all that happened while we were away at Pleth?"

Althea Tao said, "Embarrassing! Could it have escaped your notice that at least two-thirds of the audience wore masks tonight?" She shook her head and drummed the tips of her fingers on the end of her armrest. "To be ashamed of one's own society and culture is bad enough. But to talk about mere fashion as being a matter of standard is even worse! Fashion is always absurd! And for a developing world it's a drain on scarce resources. *Standard* simply refers to an assumption one society makes about itself and arrogantly applies to every other society!"

"That's not true, Grandmother," Holland said. "Many worlds comprise what you call a single society. Pleth, Jannis-et, Evergreen—"

"Oh look." Madeleine pointed at the server that had noiselessly rolled through the threshold and only caught her attention now that it loitered beside her hammock humming its ready tone. "I was beginning to wonder if we'd have to request service. So. Who wants what?"

The younger generation decided on wine, a beverage recently taken up by their peer group, while Althea, Solange, and Madeleine chose to share a couple of vials of *Day's Done*. "What, has Inez taken to drinking wine?" Althea sardonically queried as the server departed to fetch their choices.

Madeleine suppressed a groan. She wished she hadn't included her mother in the party: if she were really irritated it could take weeks to placate her, and in that case would be making references to the evening for years to come. When Imogen had issued the invitation and generously urged her to include family members she had thought she couldn't miss pleasing her mother with a performance of *Antigone*. Not only had Althea Tao been educated at Frogmore Central University, but as a lover of tradition she naturally had a deep appreciation for *Antigone* and had a few times in the past mentioned—with pride—FCU's tradition of annual public performances extending back for more than a century. It had never occurred to her that the production itself might be non-traditional. Madeleine tried to pull her wits together to find a way to make peace without further aggravating her mother. Although Althea Tao would consent to a certain flexibility in such social situations, Madeleine sometimes found herself in the position of being the object of a grudge that served to displace her mother's annoyance onto her.

"You'd be good at duels, Grandmother." Madeleine knew her mother would be flattered at the remark as much because it came from Holland as because of its reference to her wit. "You've got just the right touch for verbal riposte. Have you ever considered taking up the sport?"

Althea Tao guffawed. She enjoyed the idea—the fireworks in her design attested to that. Still, she offered a tart reply: "Unlike you younger generation, I've got better things to do with my time."

Holland leaned forward and tapped her grandmother's knobbed, gnarled knee. "We sharpen our wits on one another, Grandmother." Holland turned her head in Leanna and Anike's direction. "Isn't that right, Anike?"

"All work and no play means you work less efficiently," Anike recited the old adage.

Madeleine glanced at her mother and saw that she had taken Holland's hand. She had never made a secret that she preferred Holland of all her grandchildren (and probably, Madeleine thought wryly, to all her children, too). While Holland had been away on Pleth, her mother had made few visits to the Capitol District. Now she came two or three times a month—to see Holland.

"Hello, hello everyone," Imogen said as she crossed the threshold. "Sorry I took so long. Fred was excited about the performance and had dozens of questions to put to me."

"Fred?" Solange queried.

"Oh, didn't Madeleine tell you?" Imogen sank into a recliner. "Fred's a former student of mine. It's he who's directing this *Antigone*."

"Aha," Althea Tao said. Madeleine waited tensely for her mother to elaborate, but the server rolled back into the space and began distributing their orders. Madeleine agreed to share a vial with her mother and Solange and asked Leanna to trade places with her. When Imogen said she would like to join them in sharing *Day's Done* (having already ordered a vial on her own account, thus allotting a generous three vials for the four of them), they went through another repositioning, ending with the three younger women seated on cushions on the floor and the four older women all within arm's reach of one another.

When everyone had gotten comfortably settled, Althea asked, "Exactly what is it you teach at FCU?"

"My chair is in Political and Social Theory." Imogen handed Madeleine the vial. "I teach a variety of courses, mostly at the advanced level."

"What do they need Political and Social Theory at FCU for?" Althea said irritably. "Students serious about such subjects can be assumed to be going to Pleth to undertake a more in-depth study, wouldn't you say?"

"It's my opinion—and many of my colleagues share it—that every citizen of Frogmore should have a grasp of how their political system works," Imogen said. "The full and responsible exercise of democracy—and Frogmore from its inception has been devoted to the goal of full and responsible democracy—requires an understanding of power and a reasonable knowledge of how the political system on the planet is structured. How, may I ask, can the ordinary citizen participate in democracy unless she or he grasps such things?" She took the vial Althea was holding out to her. "Thanks." She held the vial to her design and inhaled deeply.

"Am I jumping to unwarranted conclusions when I take it that that mangling of *Antigone* we just saw is the result of what you call 'a grasp of such things'?" Althea demanded.

Madeleine glanced at her mother's flashing eyes ~ Althea, to whom design-dressing had come late, refused to wear designs that obscured her eyes ~ and wondered whether this contentiousness indicated mere annoyance and her usual competitive inclination to challenge others and engage them in argument, or serious disapproval or even anger. Her mother's eyes would flash in either situation.

"I'd be flattering myself if I could attribute all that Fred has so clearly understood to my teaching," Imogen said. "The performance was impressive. Eye-opening, even." Imogen turned her head to look at the younger women lying so quietly on the floor. "Do you get much of that sort of thing on Pleth these days?" she asked them.

"I've never seen anything like it," Anike said. "That play's always seemed to me the epitome of conservatism. At least that's the way it's always presented in the different contexts it's brought into. History, civics, cultural history, socio-political history. How it demonstrates something it took humans literally millennia to come to terms with, namely the insanity of the ancient values and social structures that contained built-in conflicts. How the structures of family and tribe and religion, by pitting themselves against the authority of the whole and challenging the authority of the Public Good, created inevitable and intractable conflicts. And they did, too, over and over and over again. It was like a mass mind-trap all human beings were caught in, unable to get past. Because they were so entrenched, it was as though these conflictual structures were programmed in humans from birth." Anike took a sip of wine.

"Which is why early humans always invoked nature to justify everything they did," Leanna said.

"What excellent memories you have," Imogen said in a mock-approving tone of voice. "You've learned your school lessons well. But what makes you think you can equate Creon's autocratic authority with the Public Good?"

"I didn't say they were equated," Anike said sharply. "Only the worst productions of the play misunderstand it to that extent. After all, remember Haemon's saying to his father, 'No city is the property of any individual,' and Creon's replying, 'But custom grants the ruler sovereignty.' The chorus never approves of Creon's irrational arbitrary legislation of a law that goes against the community standard. Which is part of the point. Creon's just as irrational as Antigone is. His irrationality is ego-oriented and gynephobic. Which I don't think your student's interpretation fully appreciated. If

Creon had really had the Public Good at heart, the conflict would never have arisen. He is a part of the totalitarian structures of family and religion that inspired so much violence. His assertion of paternal authority over Haemon, stressing father-son bond and absolute filial obedience— 'That's my worthy, virtuous son,' Creon says when Haemon at first appears to slavishly agree with him. 'So all should honor and support their father in everything.' At this point it looks as though one family line is to be pitted against another. For it's this that at first appears to be in opposition to Antigone's obsessive obedience to the religious honoring of her brother's body and her sister Ismene's in turn finding it necessary to support *her* despite her disagreement with her sister's defiance of their uncle."

"Instead of which," Althea Tao suddenly took up the thread, "we are given a morality play about General Gauthier and Amanda Kundjan."

"This is most interesting," Imogen said. "Can I take it that all six of you think students at FCU have no business questioning old interpretations of the canon we've all been loving and worshiping for the last void-knows-how-many centuries?"

The younger women seemed too busy drinking to reply. Solange appeared to be completely absorbed by *Day's Done* and the monitors' peeping. Althea Tao hmmphed in her throat. The question made Madeleine too uneasy to be able to answer it without first thinking it through.

"Hmmm," Imogen murmured. "This collective silence is even more interesting. I wonder what it can signify besides the discomfort and irritation of unconsidered disapproval?"

"'No one can call me weaker than a woman. And no woman will dictate to me as long as I'm alive,'" Holland softly quoted. "Those lines are at the heart of *Antigone*. If Creon hadn't been so twisted by gynephobia he w*ould* have been speaking for the Public Good, and his autocracy wouldn't be an issue. If those lines had been stressed, there couldn't have been the ridiculously strained comparison tonight's production insisted on cramming down our throats. Kundjan and Gauthier are allies, not enemies. Gauthier doesn't have Creon's power or role, and Kundjan doesn't partake of Ismene's familial and religious ambivalence. If all of Creon's gynephobic ravings had been given their full due, the production would have been laughable, for no one living on this world would have been able to see Creon-Gauthier in such a role without turning the play into a comedy. And likewise if the Antigone character had been subtle enough to comprehend Antigone's pathological fixation with the dead to the point of not caring whether either the living or herself survived. Who can imagine a sane person willing to throw several lives away over the question of burial rights for the dead?"

"I do recall the standard interpretation," Imogen said. She opened a fresh vial of *Day's Done* and handed it to Madeleine. "I think that probably all of us have a fairly good memory of what the standard interpretation is. What I'm wondering is what it is you're saying—or perhaps not saying?—about this alternative interpretation when you resort to statements about what the standard interpretation is. I wonder if what you're thinking, though not saying, is that there should be only one interpretation, that all other interpretations should be censored?"

"Who's talking about censorship?" Althea Tao grumbled. "It's more a matter of subtle slander and political agitation! Considering the current wave of violence harrowing Frogmore, I should think it would be obvious how potentially damaging this sort of performance could be. Last month in my region alone four people were *killed* because of anti-Combine terrorism. I don't say I agree with everything either Kundjan or Gauthier does, but by and large *they* aren't the problem. The real problem with these people is a lack of concern for the Public Good. These people are not only isolationists, but Fragmentists as well. And fragmentism is precisely one of Antigone's problems; it's the thing that blinds her to the whole picture. She doesn't give an SCU for anything but burying her brother. What kind of exemplar is that to hold up to naive young students, especially when such a character is explicitly associated with the governor—who never in her life was a Fragmentist!"

"Fragmentism," Solange said thoughtfully. "Now there's a loaded concept that's doing Frogmore no good."

"But it's apt," Althea said. "And if you'd actually thought about it, you'd agree with me."

"And what about the younger generation?" Imogen asked. "Do you three think it's dangerous to allow students to dissent from standard views? You're not too long off Pleth. Surely you must have definite opinions on this?"

The younger women looked at one another, then grew busy with pouring more wine into their glasses. "But it's different on Pleth," Anike finally said.

"Ah. You mean that people who attend Frogmore Central are so inferior to those who go to Pleth that they shouldn't be allowed the same educational opportunities and experiences that students on Pleth demand and expect?"

Leanna held up her hand in protest. "No, it's not a matter of *inferiority*." She cleared her throat. "Although it's true that the very best students go to Pleth these days. Now that there's financial help available for the truly bright and promising. It's more a matter of what Pleth is. Pleth is a world apart. The entire planet is given over to education and is run to accommodate education and all things academic. While Frogmore...well, Frogmore is a *real* world struggling to make it. Frogmore Central University exists within this context. And so what is permissible on Pleth isn't necessarily desirable or safe here. Surely we all agree that there are people whose lives could be adversely affected by the processes students routinely go through on Pleth."

"You sound as if you've thought a lot about this," Imogen said.

"Of course we have," Holland said. "It's such an obvious difference when one returns from Pleth. One must behave responsibly here, one must take care always to take the Public Good into account." Holland's passion surprised Madeleine. "On Pleth one can be heedless, can explore various paths as a part of one's learning experience. But here—well, this is reality. As Grandmother said a few minutes ago, people are *dying*. That's something to bear in mind."

"Well said, well thought out, Holland!" Bursting with pride, Madeleine couldn't stop herself from praising her daughter. Tiny purple and lavender stars shimmered in Holland's design. Madeleine almost laughed from the sheer delightfulness of it: this new design might very well become her favorite in which to see Holland dressed.

"I suppose it follows, then, that you think it proper that dissent should also be stifled on Frogmore," Imogen said. "As, indeed, it most thoroughly is. You would privilege Pleth, but not Frogmore. What about Janniset and the other worlds we call *advanced*? Some dissent is allowed on Janniset. They're more careful in such places about packing people off for brainwiping. Such worlds have far stricter laws regarding brainwipe than they do here. I happen to know that there's a general horror on Janniset of our quickness to brainwipe citizens. It's why people in advanced societies shudder when they think of Frogmore. Apart from everything else, the use of brainwipe for punitive rather than therapeutic purposes is a major component of advanced worlds' notions of what Frogmore and other not-so-civilized places are like. Quickness to brainwipe is always a sign of a primitive society, don't you know."

"But we *are* primitive, or at least most of the people on this planet are," Leanna said. Violence can't be tolerated—and there's no other possible response to violence than therapy that takes violence out of the violent. When Frogmore is more mature, more civilized, only *then* can we begin to talk about enjoyment of the privileges of more advanced worlds. *Then* we'll be able to handle it."

Madeleine saw that she needn't have been worrying about Holland and her friends; they had a firm grasp on the situation, and their years on Pleth had assisted them in understanding where they must all be working to bring Frogmore along to.

Imogen said, "But not every Pleth-educated person of your generation agrees with your rationalization for suppressing dissent. I suppose you are all pleased at Maida West's being caught and charged on several felony counts."

"Of all people," Leanna said, "the daughter of the governor's chief legal counsel should be expected to behave responsibly. She has no excuse for subversive and seditious acts."

"But if she'd done it on Pleth or Janniset she'd have gotten at most a fine. Isn't that correct?"

"But Frogmore isn't Pleth. Pleth doesn't *have* a problem with violence. Nor Janniset, for that matter."

"You are all of you, of course, the governor's women." Imogen waved her hand to include all six of them in the characterization. "Althea works on the regional level, the three of you work in the ministries, and Madeleine and Solange order the brainwipes. But none of you has any doubts whatsoever. You're all just as well trained and obedient as General Gauthier's officers are."

Madeleine jerked herself upright, causing her hammock to rock wildly. She gripped the edge of it and glared at Imogen. "I find your attitude offensive. Even in your silly version of that play, one thing still managed to come through, and that's the critical importance of law and order in civic life. It was the lack of good public order, the lack of adherence to the law that generated all the violence that comes about in that play, not Creon's irrationality per se."

"Obey, obey whatever the person in possession of the greatest physical force orders?" Imogen's derisive tone mocked Madeleine.

"Law is always better than the violence and selfishness of chaos," Madeleine said. Law could be repressive, yes: but think of all the evil that the elimination of law would unleash. Frogmore, fortunately, had many responsible citizens, and most of those working in law were devoted to bringing Frogmore to the point where certain restraints on dissent *could* be relaxed... Yet what of Aureole? Madeleine wondered. Wasn't the implication of everything she had learned about the plans for Aureole that they expected right from the start that Aureole would not be, in Leanna's word, "civilized"? That the sorts of people they would be settling on Aureole would be disorderly and that the purpose of establishing a legal system before settling the planet must be to make clear that law would be used to restrain the violence and barbarism expected of such settlers?

"I'm sorry," Imogen said, "that you all found the *Antigone* so odious." She half-laughed. "I presumptuously thought you'd be stimulated—and that you'd find such stimulation welcome since there's so little of it on Frogmore." She sighed and laid her head back.

"It's a matter of public responsibility," Anike said.

"I'm familiar with your argument," Imogen said, presumably to stave off further discussion.

"I do wish," Holland said wistfully, "there were even a tiny fraction as much in the way of cultural activity on Frogmore as there is on Pleth. I miss all that."

"Yeah. But that's the frosting on the cake of civilization," Anike said.

Imogen turned her head toward the younger women. "You and I, Anike, have different definitions of what civilization is, then," she said. "You want to predefine it and then add as bits of frothy decoration what I would take as inextricable from the whole. You want to make it safe and then expect some little extra but unnecessary bit of sugar to follow as reward. In my opinion that's a pretty strange way of looking at it."

"If you were correct, then there'd be plenty of artistic cultural activity on Frogmore."

"There would be," Imogen said, "but for the obstacles thrown in the way of anyone trying to engage in such activity. Look at your attitude toward *Antigone*. Or toward the renegade holomakers. You favor suppressing all such activity."

"I wouldn't call tonight's *Antigone* an artistic cultural activity," Althea Tao said. "It was nothing more than political propaganda, as most of such activities tend to be. And, may I note, no one suppressed that performance, did they."

"But you all agree that it should have been suppressed," Imogen said.

There would be *nothing* on Aureole, Madeleine realized. It would be bleak. And its bleakness would have nothing to do with whether they intended Aureole for dumping troublemakers or not. Could she face such a gray, depressing prospect? Those who planned the settling of Aureole intended to see to it that it would be civilized—going so far as to create its law and its government before even populating it. But would law and a government constitute civilization? What *was* civilization, anyway?

It dawned on her: despite Imogen's assertion that they had all predefined it, Madeleine realized that she hadn't any *idea* what civilization was. The thought made her queasy and lightheaded. Imogen had confused her, remarkable to say. It had been a long time since she'd felt so muddled.

We don't recommend camping on Frogmore, unless you simply want to claim the credit for having done so. Shelters appropriate for the non-mountainous areas of the planet are available (and even come equipped with decontamination chambers), but they are expensive, and given the availability of all-terrain surface transport, which can take you wherever you might want to go, there's little point to camping. It won't give you a more authentic experience of the planet than staying in a hotel in the Capitol District and venturing out for day trips would. It can't. Any truly "authentic" (i.e., unmediated) experience of Frogmore would send about 95.5% of humans into anaphylactic shock.

If you want to view Frogmore's "landscape," you'd do better to invest in S. Gorely's *A Glimpse of Frogmore*, an impressive collection of holoscapes Gorely obtained under optimal (for Frogmore) conditions, i.e., when visibility extends to an astounding (for the planet) 40 meters (which it almost never does).

— *A Traveler's Handbook to the Galaxy*, 49th edition

Twenty
INEZ GAUTHIER

Such lovely limbs and torso, so beautifully long, an actual genuine *waist*, smooth, flowing curves, subtle and supple, over which Inez smoothed her palm, dawdling and lingering… The immense flood of pleasure, the sheer sensuousness of it brought flashing into her mind a memory of the last non-Frogmorian with whom she had partnered. Recollecting the tight round curve of his scrotum, a surprised chuckle gurgled in her throat at the realization that non-Frogmorian bodies both male and female more resembled one another than a same-sexed body of a Frogmorian. To think of that boy that last time on Janniset while here on Frogmore floating in a bath she shared with this so ordinary (but in her own way stunning) woman made her acutely conscious of the enormity of the difference.

Inez opened her eyes to look at the long body ~ *and yet she's only as tall as I and under the average non-Frogmorian height, though here they all of them stare up into my face to see me, so short and squat are they, even those in the Governor's Militia* ~ whose subtle curves her hands could not stop exploring, and found the other's brilliant green and brown speckled eyes intent on her mask. The moment felt so extraordinary that Inez allowed it to sweep her away. "Shall we remove our masks?" she said, running her fingers along the edge of the biologist's mask and brushing them over the edges of her own.

"I'd be more comfortable," Margaret said. "Among ourselves we never wear the things." And she peeled hers from the edge of her cap and tossed it across the room.

"I would have thought living in such close quarters all the time would have had the opposite effect," Inez said, removing her own. And then she remembered what Nathalie Stillness had said about the natives who lived in domes.

"Mmmm, not at all." Margaret's fingers, moving over Inez's face, sent wild tremors streaking straight down to her pelvis. "We live in fairly close quarters, you know. We each have a tiny cubicle. Which is what we use for moments when privacy becomes an urgent need. But we don't partner in those cubicles—they're for privacy. It quickly began to seem absurd, given our working so intensely together and partnering and eating together, to be wearing masks at all."

"Sounds like one long, wild party." Inez sleeked her palm downward from Margaret's abdomen. As she slid her finger between the other's already slippery labia, a pleased smile spread over her face until, disturbed by a glance at those watching eyes, she grew conscious that her smile was showing on an utterly naked face. Reflexively she closed her eyes, to escape a degree of self-consciousness almost too great to bear.

"We accomplish a tremendous amount of work. More than most people ever manage to do while living on the surface of a civilized planet. I might almost recommend the setup for situations in which time particularly matters. But given the isolation, the bleakness, the threat of boredom, we've explored every possible permutation of the group. Ahhh," she interrupted herself.

Several minutes later she said, "I should perhaps qualify what I said about the group. One of us abstains."

"Why? It's hard to imagine one person holding out in that kind of environment and able to stand being there." Inez opened her eyes to see what the other's face was showing.

After a long pause, Margaret said, "He'd had aversion therapy to sex. He never elaborated, but I gather it was some sort of pathological nexus that—" Gasping, she broke off and never finished her sentence.

Later, as they lay on the jellique-mattress in the adjoining room in which she had arranged to project the image of a vine-covered, lattice-enclosed garden on Evergreen, Inez recalled the conversation and considered resurrecting it. She opened her eyes and stared at the patch of flesh only a centimeter or two from the tip of her nose and nudged her fingers just enough to heighten the sensuous pleasure from simple skin-on-skin contact she often experienced at such moments.

"It's such a different experience in this kind of gravity," Margaret said. Traces of respiratory stress lingered in her voice. "It gives one's heart quite a race, doesn't it. But then I'm used to very low gee."

"When I first came here I used to go once a week or so to Holliday," Inez said. She smiled at the memory of her insistence to her father after her first sexual encounter on Frogmore that she could not manage sex on the planet's surface. It had taken her a long time to make the adjustments, both physical and psychological. But at a certain point the weekly trips to Holliday with a prearranged partner began to strike her as absurd, especially since it ruled out spur-of-the-moment engagements.

"That must have been expensive," Margaret said.

Not as expensive as going to Janniset, Inez thought.

"Of course the bath and this mattress help cut down on the strenuousness of much of it. But..." Margaret half-laughed. "I guess it isn't so much that part of it as the physical stress orgasm itself causes. I can see that even using autoerotic options in a cocoon would be nearly as rough."

What a strange conversation. Frogmorians, even those who had recently been to Pleth, never discussed such things "They don't go in for group encounters much on Frogmore," Inez said when she realized that the desultoriness of her participation in the conversation had created a silence.

"I suppose our preference for group encounters is more a function of our unusually small, closed society than anything else," the biologist said. Her voice grew dreamy. "I think I had maybe one or two such encounters before. Certainly nothing that stands out in my mind. Then, on the station, it all came about, well, *naturally*, I suppose you might say. We more or less fell into it. Not as though we had sat down and said, well hey wouldn't it make sense if we did it in groups, gang? I think it had something to do with the privacy thing, the way space is allocated on the station. I mean if we *hadn't* gotten into the group scene, then there would have been all kinds of tension. Voyeurism. Self-consciousness. Resentment. Maybe even hostility. And there was sufficient cause for hostility and resentment on other, more collegial, grounds that we didn't need *social* tensions to add to the mix."

"Hmmm. Intellectual disagreements, turf-fights, things of that sort?" Inez queried, trying to imagine what issues a low-stakes bunch of biologists could have to get so worked up about.

"There are always bound to be problems when we're all required to put out unified group reports and when we're competing with one another for equipment and other divisions of our funding."

"I see." It sounded boring. Could conflict ever be truly riveting if fortunes and worlds weren't at stake? How *did* one get one's adrenalin up over who got access to which mass spectrometer (or whatever it was that biologists used)? "Then I suppose the group sex must be seen more as an escape valve for tension."

Margaret laughed. "Frankly, we see it as *fun*." She laughed again. "In fact, if it weren't for the difficult gravity, I probably would have brought one or two of my colleagues along with me. But most of the others have given up sex for the duration of their stay on the surface, alas."

Inez ground her teeth in annoyance. The off-worlder had her nerve, so coolly talking about thrusting other sexual partners on her when it had been *her* invitation in the first place that had brought Margaret into her inner chambers.

"But perhaps sometime you might drop by for a visit," Margaret said. "We're not far from Frogmore as such distances go. I'm sure you would have no trouble getting a security clearance." So Margaret—and probably the others—had taken note of how much she knew of what they were up to in orbit around Aureole. "I think we could give you quite a good time."

Margaret's tone sounded smug to Inez's ear. "I could never go maskless with so many people," she said. "I find the very idea obscene."

"But you took your mask off for me."

Margaret's fingers brushed Inez's cheek. This odd touch, again, moved her (this time quite differently), and she rolled away from Margaret—awkwardly because of the powerful undulations her movement set up within the thrumming jellique-mattress—in order to see the other woman's face. "I don't do that easily," she said. "Nor does anyone else I know." She heard the defensiveness in her voice and disliked it...but then remembered that Solstice went more easily barefaced than masked.

"You've a better face than most people," Margaret said.

Inez wrinkled her nose. "I wouldn't know much about the aesthetics of the face, except of course for military officers' preference for symmetry and regularity and boniness."

"Oh them." Margaret's voice and face—her mouth scrunched up, her eyes and brows derisive—expressed disdain. "They look like walking corpses. They look barely human."

"They are under a disadvantage," the general's daughter said coldly. How could anyone blame officers for making their faces so rigid and masklike? What other recourse lay open to them?

"There's a curious thing about faces accustomed to constant concealment that we figured out only gradually. People who never go barefaced in public often lack certain sorts of mobility in their faces—as well as show more marks of stress and anger than those who habitually go unmasked—and there are quite a few such people, you know, apart from officers I mean. Some of us worked on Mellisante, and Mellisante *teems* with Naturalist types. But to get back to the differences between faces. The unmasked face is accustomed to respond in other-pleasing ways. Masks, however, seem to make such response socially unnecessary. And yet there appears to be a critical function such facial response serves. As biologists, all of us have had extensive training in human physiology, even those of us who specialize in ecology or other fields relatively distant from human physiology, and thus know that facial gestures exert influences on both body and mind, though until we consciously began thinking about this had basically forgotten it..."

Staring at the pink- and white-fleshed carnivorous lily wafting gently a few inches from her edge of the jellique-mattress, Inez prepared to interrupt. This extraordinary conversation had to be the most obscene she'd ever been treated to in her life. Clearly these biologists living in their perverse little enclave had gone off the deep end. To actually lie there—after exhaustive and warmly friendly sex—and talk about such things came close to shocking and even *embarrassing* Inez.

"...and of course then Cernack recalled one of the techniques they use in therapy, requiring patients to express particular emotional responses facially whether or not they are *feeling* that response, not only with the therapy team and the others in the group, but in mirror sessions as well, because—"

"I don't want to hear it," Inez said, shuddering at the sensation of flesh crawling: the skin of her arms, back, thighs, and even her belly shrank and slithered, twitched and crept in horrid repulsion. The carnivorous lily looked obscene, its wafting now seeming a voracious lecherous lurching, its tiny teeth deep within its thick, fleshy petals distorting the sensual resemblance into an obscene caricature of a vulva—Margaret's vulva. Inez terminated the holo-environment and struggled against the jellique to achieve an upright posture. This woman—and probably all her colleagues as well—had gone off the deep end, to be harping on such horrifying and intimate subjects in bizarre detail. All that time spent shut up together had generated mass psychosis.

Margaret lay supine, relaxed, riding the jellique undulations Inez's vigorous movement had released. "What is it that disturbs you?" she asked, looking and sounding genuinely curious.

Curious!

"I don't find this sort of wallowing in sordid detail at all amusing." After sex on Frogmore one wished only to relax. One wished, actually, for one's sleep-cocoon—but simply to cut out like that would, Inez had always thought, be rude, graceless even. Still…in this case, pressed this far to ground, surely considerations of courtesy could be abandoned? "If there's anything you want, just message the contact I gave you earlier. And now, if you'll excuse me—"

"Wait," Margaret said, struggling to sit up. "Please. There's something I wanted to ask you."

A cynical smile broke out on Inez's face. So this woman wanted something! She really *had* sunk low. "A *favor*, perhaps?" Inez said dryly as she watched Margaret Abish finally get the better of the jellique-mattress.

"Not really, no," Margaret said, apparently stung. "I'm not asking you to arrange anything. I just need to know the best way for going about doing something that we've been finding difficult to accomplish. Since you're *au courant* with the way things work on Frogmore."

"What is it?" The thought that this woman had accepted her invitation to partner solely to get this favor pleased her in some strange, perverse way.

With laboring breath, Margaret Abish struggled to her feet. "We need to know the best way to approach the governor. To get a face-to-face meeting," she said, her hand pressed to her heaving chest.

"Why?" the general's daughter asked baldly. "Why would you want such a meeting?"

Margaret stared at her for a while—reminding Inez that her own face was still bare, too—before answering, and something in her eyes, or perhaps in the crease between her eyes, gave Inez the uncomfortable sensation of being studied. Finally Margaret said, "You know about our work on the Scourge, so I suppose it wouldn't be risking security to tell you something of our concern." She bit her lip. "You see, we have a disagreement among ourselves. An important advisory opinion was omitted from our final report to CDS because the most powerful members of our group insisted on censoring it."

Inez's attention shifted from casual to intense. "Oh? Can you be a bit more specific?" she asked in an easy voice as her body consciously adopted a relaxed manner. Should she move closer to the biologist, perhaps take her arm? No, she would wait. Margaret's face seemed to suggest she trusted her.

"There's concern about a possibly catastrophic effect of wiping out the Scourge," Margaret said in a nervous near-whisper.

"Catastrophic?" Inez repeated skeptically.

"Yes, I know, one would intuitively feel that wiping out the Scourge could be only positive for this planet." Her hand went to her throat, momentarily distracting Inez with awareness of the oddity of discussing business while standing a meter or so apart bare-faced and stark naked. And then the thought crossed her mind that without cling-ons it was no wonder they had each found it so effortful a struggle to move against the jellique. Margaret made an ambiguous gesture with her left hand. "But such things are never as simple as they seem. The problem is, we don't know what effect removal of the Scourge—such a complex stable ecology in and of itself, it's not simply one organism you know but several that interact even down to the most minute aspects of their cycles of propagation—"

"Yes. I'm familiar with their basic existence. They're also quite resilient, I understand, considering how before the planet was first settled great efforts were made to eradicate it."

"Yes. But to continue. A few of our group specialize in areas touching on climatology. None of us are climatologists. But we've all read the preliminary reports the CDS specialists in those areas put out before our group was even formed. And it seems that they were divided among themselves at the time—as we are now—about assessing the risk of this planet's atmosphere being entirely destroyed by the eradication of the Scourge. This atmosphere is, after all, unique in our experience. In general in such—"

"Am I to understand you to say," Inez said sharply, "that you want to tell the governor there's a minority opinion in your group suggesting that there's a risk factor involved that should be used to halt plans for eradication?"

"Yes." Margaret sounded relieved not to have to spell it out any further. "We think the governor should be made aware of the possibility."

"What order of risk are you talking about?"

The biologist blinked. "What order?" she said, as though confused. "Why, the viability of a livable human environment. Surely you must understand that without—"

"Of course I understand," Inez said. "I'm not entirely a fuckwit. What I want you to tell me is precisely how the odds are weighted. In other words, what *likelihood* is there that this catastrophe could result from eradicating the Scourge?"

Margaret licked her lips and stared questioningly at her as though taken aback at the response she was getting. "I don't see what that has to do with your telling me how to access the governor," she said.

Inez silently sneered. A little late to be cautious, Margaret. "My question is simple. Before I sic you people onto Governor Kundjan, I'd like to know if it's worth her time." All they'd need would be to let a few of the Fragmentist types get wind of this kind of thing to set them back a local decade or so—once nay-sayers got hold of the slightest expert opposition, things tended to get tied up indefinitely on the grounds that it was always best to err in favor of caution.

"Even if the atmosphere isn't entirely destroyed, other native forms of life and most of the existing oxygen is more likely than not to go," Margaret said. "It's not clearly understood exactly which chemical processes are explicitly dependent either directly or indirectly upon the Scourge's existence. You see—"

"What I *see* is that the odds are so minute that you don't want to tell me what they are," Inez said.

Margaret folded her arms over her tiny (civilized) breasts (so very definitely non-Frogmorian in size and shape). "You have some interest in this, don't you."

The general's daughter shrugged. "Anyone who cares about this planet has an interest in removing the Scourge. If you're talking million-to-one-odds—"

"Anyone who *cares* about this planet would be interested in preserving its atmosphere and macro-ecosystem!" The green in her eyes blazed so brilliantly that their small brown flecks all but disappeared. "And the odds are not a million-to-one, either, they're much narrower."

"Then why won't you say what they are?"

"Because they haven't been properly assessed. It's quite, quite clear that CDS pressured our team's administrators into underplaying the problem. But when has CDS cared about anything except profitable development of non-civilized worlds?"

"And you don't think they'd lose anything should the whole spacing planet go to arid vacuum?" Inez shook her head. "You haven't made a case, Margaret. I'm sorry, but I can't help you. It sounds to me as though you want to rock the boat. And since I don't know the politics involved, I can't assess your motive for doing so. But whatever it might be, it obviously doesn't concern Frogmore, and I see no reason why Frogmore should be made to pay for your political infighting." Inez made for the threshold into the bath. She grinned over her shoulder. "It was a nice try, but I'm not quite as much a bubble-head as you pegged me for."

Margaret was accusatory. "You don't give an SCU for this planet, do you."

Inez paused at the threshold into the bath and turned to face her. "I care a great deal more than you do, who barely knows this planet. While you, on the other hand—" Inez stopped herself: she couldn't tell the woman outright that she and her claustrophobically close colleagues needed therapy in the worst way. "Who knows what you're up to. I certainly don't." She entered the bath chamber. Margaret's voice pursued her, but only for the half-second or so it took the threshold to opaque.

Inez stretched out on the recliner as she waited for Zagorin to prepare a fresh bath and stared up at the sky holo she hadn't turned off when she and Margaret had gone into the other room. How fortunate, she thought, that Margaret had picked her for connecting with the governor. If it had been anyone else, even the general... She would have to take steps to make certain the dissenting biologists— whoever they were—would have no opportunity to propagandize *any* Frogmorian (much less the governor) during the remainder of their stay on Frogmore. A little chat with Major Cleveland and a meeting with the highest-ranking biologist should do the trick. All of the stock transfers she had made, the new enterprises she had initiated... No. Consider the source. Margaret had shown her insanity long before she had brought up her crazy theory about the Scourge. In fact, she had been on her way out of the room precisely because Margaret had been talking so crazily... *Clearly* the woman and her colleagues had gone off the deep end. Which, considering the kind of life they apparently led, was not all that surprising.

After finishing the morning's work, Inez made a routine check of her personal message queue and found a three-local-hours-old request for contact—marked **Urgent**—from Nathalie Stillness. As she set out for the dining room for lunch with her father and a few others ~ the general had held a large-scale conference that morning to strategize and coordinate the efforts of peacekeeping officers with the Governor's Militia and regional officials to cope with the disorder associated with UAP's shifting operations to the new orbital stations ~ Inez messaged Nathalie Stillness. Nathalie had never before used the word *urgent* in any of her messages. Recalling Nathalie's previous problems with one of Major Cleveland's subordinates, she wondered if Nathalie might be in a tight corner and in need of extrication.

Nathalie's response came swiftly, suggesting that she may have had a block prepared in order to message it as soon as the general's daughter initiated contact. <<Hi, Inez. I need assistance. Newly imposed travel restrictions are preventing me from making a trip into the field, to Saturna, where special arrangements have already been made to accommodate me. Can you help me? I'd be eternally grateful. These people refuse even to *listen* to my request for permission.>>

Saturna!

But of *course* she would help Nathalie. Margaret Abish, of course, would prefer to believe that she never did anything for anyone, but she would be wrong to believe that, dead wrong.

Inez subvocalized <Yes of course I'll assist. Who exactly is it who is denying permission?>

Nathalie Stillness replied almost instantly. <<The Governor's Militia. After three days of effort, I've worked my way up to an officer who IDs herself only as Captain Trausch. I spent all day yesterday waiting outside her office, and when I finally got to see her in late afternoon, she wouldn't let me explain. All nonessential travel into the area is prohibited until further notice, she said, and since I don't have an official order for travel in the area nor perform any "life-support function" there can be no possible reason for granting me permission, and thus no reason for her to waste her time listening to my "sad story" as she termed it.>>

The Governor's Militia would be tricky. If it had been peacekeepers it would have taken a single contact with Major Cleveland to take care of. Unless… Perhaps instead of trying to intervene through the chain of command, it would be easier just to come up with some sort of official travel order?

Inez subvocalized <I'll take care of it, Nathalie. Though it will probably take me a day or two, since it's the Governor's Militia you're up against. I'll be in touch.>

<<My thanks, Inez. I hope someday I can return the favor.>>

Entering the dining room, Inez glowed with a pleasure her mask concealed. Not even the necessity of performing the formalities with the general's guests managed to dampen her pleasure, as each bowed in turn and offered her an impeccable wrist. Already she was anticipating the payoff in gratitude that lay in the future. It felt good, knowing Nathalie Stillness would owe her.

She woke in the night, briefly, as sharp fragments of dream flew about her consciousness, their jagged edges threatening, frightening, glittering, and all the more disturbing for being elusive.

What—?

But no...these were the shards merely of dreams: fleeting, transitory, on the flip side of inexorable reality. And yet that long passage that didn't exist in reality she nevertheless recognized as a corridor in the Institute... Solstice standing with her back to the room as Inez waited ~ the dancer's head-hair was a primitive, feral cap swarming bestially over her head, her shoulder blades thrust prominently outward beneath the drab, cheap cling-ons ~ that breathless moment excruciatingly prolonged, drawn out, waiting, waiting for the dancer to turn, to show her face, to reveal herself as more than a body recognized from behind—only to discover when at last the dancer moved a face covered by a lacy white and pink confection, a glittering froth the dancer invited her to eat. Inez puzzled over the horror of that moment. While still dreaming she had wondered how she could find Solstice's mask and her invitation to consume it so horrible that she could do nothing but cover her eyes and run out of the room with a silent scream choking her throat. Awake, the horror made even less sense.

And why did all the cocoon's ministrations not banish the horror entirely?

She resorted to her sleep command. The horror, the disorientation, the heavy confusion could not stand up against such force, of course, and she plunged at once into deep, dreamless sleep.

"It's never the same," Major Cleveland said, gesturing expansively. "No matter how clever the holo and the audio—even with the appropriate olfactory track—it can only offer a resemblance that at best makes one nostalgic for the unattainable. And as for living gardens..." He shrugged his splendid shoulders and turned his face toward the general's daughter, who suddenly recalled Margaret Abish's remark about military officers' having corpse-like faces. "They, too, make me nostalgic for a more livable environment. I imagine that walking daily in this garden might in the long run be harder to take than going without."

Once reminded of Margaret's remark, Inez could not stop studying the Major's face. Regimented, iron, *disciplined* she would have likely described it before the biologist had implanted the poisonous suggestion in her mind. And certainly the *general's* face possessed fluidity, mobility, expressivity...for certain sorts of emotions. But the natural resting form molding his face ~ she supposed she must take his most unconscious moments as offering glimpses of that form ~ suggested discontent—though never stress. The general, his daughter believed, had no notion of what stress was, and she knew that except for this latest defeat with Solstice he would consider his life a success and was conscious of feeling only satisfaction with it. Whence, then, the impression his face offered of discontent? Could it be that the resting form of one's face had little to do with one's life?

"I'd hoped to get back to you last night, Madam," Major Cleveland said abruptly, "but something unfortunately came up that demanded my entire attention."

Unfortunately? Inez repressed the smile that nudged at her lips. The attempted jacking of a shuttle might be unfortunate for some people, but certainly not for Major Cleveland. The general had remarked as they sniffed *Midnight Song* that such jacking attempts were windfalls, for they guaranteed solid universal support for ensuring Pittikin's possession and maintenance of state-of-the-art armaments. And of course for those more closely participating, such incidents provided welcome excitement and challenge the daily routine never afforded. "I understand there was a bit of excitement yesterday evening," she murmured. Of course the general had had nothing to do but wait for news as the incident unfolded. The net effect on *him* had been to make him itchier than ever.

Major Cleveland offered a slight bow. "Precisely. But to turn to the matter you asked me to see to. I'm afraid your friend's only recourse will be to get an official document ordering her travel to Saturna. The Militia are adamant about not letting her in. One of their concerns is the normal one they would have for any off-world person entering such a touchy area: they want to avoid off-worlder casualties at all costs. I know the chances are minuscule that there would be such a casualty, but the Governor's Militia is a little sensitive on the subject. Second, and more particularly, they seem to wish to keep Stillness out of the area because they want no unfavorable accounts getting out. They're concerned for their reputation in the advanced worlds, and since Stillness will be *publishing* her Frogmore work—something that apparently doesn't thrill them anyway—they don't want her exposed to any situation that might open them or the people living in that area to advanced-world criticism." Major Cleveland lifted his hand to forestall Inez's protest. "Allow me, Madam, to suggest that you simply override the Militia with an order from a minister. Or even from me, if it comes to that." He half-laughed. "Though of course Stillness may not *want* an order signed by the head of the Frogmore Peacekeeping Force's Intelligence Division." He chuckled again, and she wondered at his amusement. She couldn't remember the last time she had heard him laugh.

An astonishing but instantly recognizable-as-brilliant thought flashed into her head. "I have another idea entirely, Major." She kept the excitement whirling her thoughts into fiery pinwheel profusion out of her voice. "I will travel to Saturna myself and will ask Nathalie Stillness to accompany me." She bowed with great flourish. "There should be no problem about *my* access to the region, I suppose?"

"I imagine not," Major Cleveland said rather dryly. "But are you certain you want—"

"I have my own fish to fry in Saturna, Major." She had been taken off balance, she had not asked the appropriate questions or made definitive offers...which left room for possibilities that she saw now she had to explore. Unlike the general, she could take as much rejection as the waterdancer could dish—she had no personal stake in the matter. So what would it matter if the worst came to pass and Solstice rebuffed her? She would lose a few days, but perhaps that would be a positive benefit of the trip. She needed a change, and clearly this Saturna place was nothing like anything she had yet seen on all her extensive travels.

And then she perceived another benefit. She would at last be throwing Nathalie Stillness and Solstice Balalzalar together. Perhaps Nathalie could interpret everything alien that hid so much of Solstice from view. And then, once Nathalie had explained it, she would know how to work it all out. Perhaps, she thought a bit wildly—but half-seriously—perhaps even the general's problem had a chance of solution.

And Nathalie would be grateful. To her *true* friends, she staunchly reminded herself, Inez Gauthier was ever generous and helpful.

Up yours, Margaret.

Frogmore passes as an "electoral democracy" as far as the "advanced" worlds are concerned. But this is an illusion accomplished by restricting the franchise to those who have a degree from an accredited institution of higher education on Pleth. So few Frogmorians qualify that virtually every member of the electorate holds positions of authority in either the government or in the corporations plundering Frogmore's natural resources. In short, only Frogmore's so-called elites and professionals can vote.

Probably the most influential native-born functionaries (after, of course, the governor and the governor's chief ministers) are the executive regional managers, who are appointed by the legislature for ten-year terms that are infinitely renewable. Frogmore's 41 executive regional managers (ERMs) basically serve to keep business running smoothly, finding the credit to fund infrastructure where necessary for advancing corporate agendas, and liaising with the bureaucracies of the central governing authority, including those administering its judicial and policing functions.

ERMs can't be impeached. Once the parliament appoints them, they are essentially in for life, if they wish. ERMs have occasionally been forced to resign (in all but one instance by corporations they'd annoyed). If Frogmore is to be truly independent, the power and tenure of ERMs will have to be severely curtailed. And if Frogmore is to ever become a genuine "democracy," Frogmorians not educated on Pleth must be allowed to vote for the members claiming to represent their interests and to actually sit in the parliament.

—*Frogmore's Destiny: A Manifesto for Independence*

Twenty-one
CLAIRE GASPEL

I'm remaining here in the Dome with a skeleton group of adults & everyone under eighteen. And I'm feeling absolutely useless. I didn't realize when we first began planning our mass action that I & Grand Mother would necessarily—that *is* the word people have been using—stay behind...for safety. *Safety!* I can see the importance of ensuring Grand Mother's safety. After all, she is the central pillar of the Dome. But me? I've barely begun learning the duties & knowledge of a first daughter, so why should my safety be so special? Illyrys could just as well become our generation's first daughter when she comes of age. But when I advanced that argument in the meeting, no one would listen to it! Which just goes to show I don't have much influence around here, First Daughter or not.

I'm frightened, too. My stomach is all knotted up, & I have a gnawing headache, maybe because I didn't get much sleep last night. My mind keeps straying into unthinkable thoughts but then pulling back, because I can't bear to follow them to their logical conclusion. The response from the rest of Pimlico has been disappointing. People are afraid, obviously; but it's become clear that their fear of being brainwiped is greater than their fear of losing their way of life. Or, as Daisy said last night, people outside the domes may not have a "way of life" they fear to lose as we do. They might think it's not so bad to be sent to some other part of the world, to do a new job, to be uprooted, maybe even to get electronic things planted in their brains. (After all, even brain*washing* forces that upon one.)

Grand Mother stopped Ariel from joining the mass action, too, because of her precious obstetrical skills, which we absolutely cannot afford losing. But Ariel has been able to do other things. She made a short holo (who knows how she did such a thing?—but she says it's easy & inexpensive, something she learned at University) that we're using in our efforts to persuade outsiders to join our mass action.

Oh it's nerve-wracking, waiting to hear. Tomorrow's the day they say they're moving the plant to the orbital station. Today's the last day of work. Will it be possible to occupy the facility? I don't see how. All *they* have to do is activate their repulsive shields &... No. What's the point of speculating? Perhaps we will manage to take one of the essential elements hostage...

I wish I had more faith. But this isn't like that Bole Oil Situation Daisy's always talking about. I keep going over & over how they took us off-guard. Not only the Dome, but all the outsiders living in Pimlico as well. Which was stupid of us. Anyone having read Paula's journals should have grasped the danger of not being prepared for such attacks. Instead, here we are, helpless to do anything to save our way of life.

If we survive this crisis, I swear by the memory of Paula Boren to do everything I can to persuade others to prepare so that this kind of thing can never happen to us again. I swear this as a first daughter.

Oh the care in Grand Mother's face. It's terrible to see. She feels responsible for the mess because she's never paid much attention to our relations with outsiders, which clearly *somebody* should have been doing. Maybe that's why she insisted I stay? Because she's feeling so inadequate? Not that she says anything like that. But I can see it in her eyes, in the lines in her forehead, in the dullness of her facial spalls.

Time to go check on the children I've been assigned to supervise. I'll tell them a story about Paula. Who knows, it might even cheer me up.

15.VII.493

I never imagined it could turn out like this, not even in my most negative moments. & it's all happened so fast. One minute our life is as it's been for centuries, the next minute everything's changed, threatened with destruction. Grand Mother says that the only thing for us to do is to preserve the possibility of the life for the next generation by raising the young ones as we ourselves were raised.

Which we can't do in our nearly empty dome now. Those of us left can't all be working outside to pay the costs of maintaining the Dome. The children need as many adults as remain just to see to them. & besides, even if we stayed, they wouldn't know what growing up in a dome is really like, not with the sad, sometimes eerie atmosphere it has now, silently screaming the absence of all those people who aren't here, who will never be here again. Who are not dead in the strictest sense, yet are truly dead to *us*, or rather *will* be dead to us.

I'm going to see Daisy tomorrow—those adults remaining will make as many visits to Family members as are allowed before their therapy begins, to stand by them during their trials & during this horrible period of "diagnostic procedures" as they call it.

Just talking about it makes me shake with rage, makes my jaw clamp so tightly that my teeth grind together & my head aches.

No, better think instead of what is to happen to those of us who are left. Grand Mother is in contact now with other domes, trying to work something out, which probably won't be hard, since a few other domes were involved in mass actions of their own, too.

After Grand Mother announced the news, in advance of making specific visiting assignments, Ariel asked me in a whisper if the ostracized would get visits too—implying, without actually saying, that she wouldn't put it past us to be so cruel.

Last night when we went to bed, it hit me when I saw all those sleep-cocoons—empty. It hit me that none of those who went would be coming back. *Ever.* It was then that I cried, for I could hardly bear the thought. I don't understand. I don't understand how this could happen, how they could do this to us. It's so unfair, so *immoral* to wreck our lives this way. & all those children! We've told the older ones, of course (they don't really understand, they haven't yet taken it in). But the younger ones? How explain the sudden absence of almost their entire Family?

This does no good, weeping over this entry. I have too many things to do—packing, storing things away, bracing myself for visiting the people locked away in those places of horror. I need to see them, Daisy especially—the thought makes my throat tight, the thought that I will be seeing the last of Daisy, that when my visits end there will no longer be such a person, only someone physically resembling her—but though I need to see them, I'm terrified of going into such a place. I'm afraid of seeing the horror they will be living every hour of the day & night until they have become someone other than themselves...

I must pull myself together. As Grand Mother says, we must salvage what we can. Never have first daughters borne such heavy responsibility. The very survival of the daughters of Paula depends upon it.

17.VII.493

I suppose I'm recovered enough now to try to write about it. I know that I have to. If ever anything was important enough to go into this journal, it certainly has to be my first visits to Daisy, Marcy, & Erin, who aren't allowed to see one another, which is heartbreakingly cruel. They haven't yet been sentenced to "therapy" of any degree, but they're being treated as if it's all been settled.

I knew the place would be horrible, but I couldn't have imagined *how* horrible. Daisy, Marcy, & Erin are each forced to have their left wrists attached to some sort of electronic thing *all the time*. They are made to watch holos & answer questions about them—to see what they think about them and whether they're paying attention. & they're so *scared*-looking, especially Erin. Even Daisy was jittery—& distant. It felt with each of them as though a wall of glass stood between us.

I've never thought so much about masks before. I mean, we see them at work, worn by the managers, but I always thought of that as just part of the whole inhumanness of the workplace. I suppose I knew that they—the ones who wear the masks—don't really look at our faces when they talk to us. But I really felt it in that place. I kept thinking that if that woman had her mask removed, it would be harder for her to pretend to be so neutral and matter-of-fact about what she was telling me. And if we actually stood face to face, she might even feel as though she ought to look me in the eye. But the fact is, outsiders don't do eye-contact.

Grand Mother warned me before I went to always assume myself monitored while in that place. To be careful of what I say. (This wasn't clear to me & still isn't: about what I need to be careful about. I don't understand what it is that marks a person as "crazy" & thus in need of therapy.) They allowed me only ten minutes apiece with Daisy, Erin, & Marcy. Grand

Mother says this is because the law claims to "protect" detainees who haven't yet been tried in a court of law by allowing them visits from their assigned defense counsel and one
"intimate." I saw Marcy first. She asked me about the Dome.
I had to tell her that Grand Mother was making arrangements for us to move, that hardly any adults remain now.
When she heard this, she broke into bitter sobs—which she
then tried to stop, for fear that they would drug her again for
having an "outburst." She hadn't known about the Dome, &
her defense counsel (a man she'd spoken to once, for ten minutes) had refused to answer questions about the other Family
members who had participated in the mass action. About her
defense counsel, she said that he had told her that because of
her youth etc. that if she presented herself "correctly," if she
at all times cooperated, & if she scored reasonably well on the
"diagnostic procedures," then she could probably get a wash
rather than a wipe. Marcy looked at me with terrible eyes
& made a choking sound that was supposed to be a laugh.
What does it matter? she said. In any event I won't be able to
go back to the Family. They won't allow it since they say the
Family is part of what they call "the unhealthy environment
out of which the instability developed," & I won't ever feel
the same again about the Family or the Dome—that's what
they say—& anyway will have to follow their regimen until
I've paid off the expense of whatever it is they're going to do
to me. When Marcy said that, I almost broke down. We were
both sitting at this silly table (they call it "free-form," Marcy
said) holding hands across it, & I could feel her shaking &
knew she must know that my whole body was shaking, too. I
don't think I've ever felt so frightened in my life.

Marcy & me, so close all our lives, born only a month
apart, our mothers at Birth-Home at the same time...we
were always partners when we were growing up, we did everything together. Holding hands in that awful place, I really
realized that I was losing her. & how I'd taken it for grant-

ed we would always have each other & hadn't ever thought about how special she is to me, how much a part of me she is. & she finally said—the last thing she got to say before they interrupted us—that it would be for me as though she had died. & that she wished she *were* dying physically rather than this other way, that she hated the idea of becoming someone she couldn't respect or like, someone completely different from her real self. That she didn't understand how this could be done to her except that she knew it would. & of course we were both thinking of the one person in our lives we personally knew who had had therapy, Jennifer Glade, who had been one of our crèche mothers, & who (after we were out of the crèche, but of course we still knew her then, because though she had taken on a new crèche group she still spent time with former crèche-charges) only five years ago had been taken away. We had never understood why—the adults had told us she had been taken but wouldn't talk about it.

It was while Marcy was telling me how she would be dead to us that they came in & insisted I leave. We still had five minutes left, but they said I had "upset the patient" & told me that I could either "leave the facility" or visit Erin. Those people are so frightening, the way they look at you through the slits in their masks (& of course they all wear caps covering the whole head, creepy, slithery, always reminding you of the strange things going on inside their skulls, computers inside their very brains), the way they speak so coldly & say everything in that tone of voice there's never any answer to but anger or humiliation. I was sure that if I argued with them, they would make me leave before I'd seen Daisy & Erin. & after what Marcy had said, it seemed more important than ever to see them.

So I went into another room like the one Marcy had been in, also with a silly table, & my heart felt as though it were breaking because of what I'd just realized—fully realized, I mean, because I had known, of course, but not *really* known.

& Erin was… Erin didn't even look like the same person. Her face was so strange that I don't think I'd have recognized her if I'd seen her in a crowd with other people. She blinked a lot, but that wasn't all of it. Her face looked pinched, & it twitched, & her hands twisted, & her fingers pressed into the weird surface of that table, digging in deep (making her fingernails turn white), & her eyes—at first I saw mostly all that blinking, but then I managed to see past the blinking to the eyes themselves, & I saw how *terrified* she was. She talked in a mumble, sometimes only whispering, & told me how scared she was, how she wanted Daisy, why hadn't Daisy come (instead, I guess, of me). I thought about lying to her about Daisy, but then knew I had to tell her the truth, that until it actually happened, even if it was harder for her, we had to be honest. So I told her that Daisy was here somewhere & that I would be seeing her. It turns out that she, too, had no idea that everyone who had been at the mass action had been taken. No one had expected that, it was thought they'd only take a fraction, because it was thought they couldn't handle so many cases at once. I told Erin that some of those taken had been transferred out of the area. They couldn't have taken all of us, could they? she cried, then started mumbling about how much the outsiders had always hated us & how glad they must be to be ruining so many of our lives… I didn't know what to say to her, I felt helpless & kept thinking of how it would have been me, too, if Grand Mother hadn't insisted I not go.

& then Daisy. Who looked as she always does, only very sad. Daisy didn't talk about what they were going to do to her or about how many were taken or anything like that. Instead she asked me about the children & told me the things that she thought were most important for me to know about nurturing them. Several times she said that my role would be one of the hardest any Family member would ever have, because I now had the largest share of responsibility for ensuring our Family's survival & the Dome's "reconstitution."

& that I must understand that the children were the first priority for doing this. & she also said that I must recommend to Grand Mother in her name that I put off the start of my childbearing for a few years so that I could devote all my energies to the children... As she was saying this to me I was wanting in the worst way for her to put her arms around me—to comfort me. Even so, she is the one going through the ordeal. Though *she* was the prisoner, she comforted me (who was free to leave that wretched place & return to sanity)—because she's so strong, because she's always loved me in that special way she has.

I couldn't help thinking the whole trip back how much better it would have been for the Family if Daisy had stayed at home for safety instead of me. She knows what needs to be done & how to do it. I don't know anything. Everything I do must be learned as I do it. & this in a time of extreme crisis.

I wish Mother weren't away at Birth-Home. We may not get along very well, but she would know what to do, just as Daisy does, though maybe she wouldn't do it as well as Daisy would. No one is as good as Daisy at managing the children.

20.VII.493

I've been so busy I haven't had time to write anything here for days. The children need so much attention, & there are so many other things I have to see to because Grand Mother's off to the meeting at Saturna. (She says that in her memory there never has been such an emergency meeting called, bringing together all the senior first daughters on an occasion other than the annual meeting that is held after the Commemoration Festival.) Despite my sleeping in a cocoon (we now have far more than we can use), I wake in the night from nightmares about people wearing caps & masks, sinister people in horrible bright white surroundings. & when I wake from these dreams, I feel, for a few minutes, what it must be like to be in such surroundings, constantly around creeps in masks & caps, away from anyone who knows or loves you. Alone, surrounded by enemies. That's what they are: enemies. I know I am not to say this outside the Dome. Grand Mother has warned us all about being careful with our words. But these people are our enemies.

Apart from deciding what is to be done by the domes most decimated by these mass detentions, the Matriarchs will discuss petitioning the government to spare the domes on the grounds that our way of life is threatened & that children had been planned according to careful calculations about the numbers of adults needed to nurture them & to support the Families. There is fear about this strategy—fear that the children could be taken from us on the grounds that their legal parents have been detained & thus must go with them. Violet Chang argued so before Grand Mother left for Saturna. They've done enough to us, Violet Chang said. Don't give them an excuse to do more. We've had an agreement with the government of Frogmore since the beginning, Grand Mother answered. & then Violet said that there was always the danger of their taking anyone who argued contrary to what they consider sanity to be, that if some of us tried to testify in the trials (whether or not we petitioned the government on the political grounds entailed in the plea about our Family institutions & values being destroyed), those who spoke might be taken, too, such words in our people's defense being judged crazy in the same way that those who had been taken are being judged crazy.

It's all a terrible tangle. How can anyone know for certain what strategy is best?

Ariel is talking about going home to see if her parents can do something—her mother works as a civil engineer for an ERM, while her father is an outsider & thus probably knows more about what it is best to do, as she thinks *she* does—

having spent all that time at the university in the Capitol District. Oh it's so depressing.

& now here is Illyrys, standing on the threshold, wanting me—not for anything in particular, just contact. She's frightened now she's finally beginning to take it in. She says the Dome feels haunted. "It's creepy, Claire," she said yesterday. More disturbing, she told me that some of the middle children are making up stories about what has happened to the people taken away. I must find some way to tell them what has happened without damaging them. How to do that? They are all frightened. The little ones don't know what's going on, only that things are different—& it's as though they're waiting for everything to go back to normal. I'm dreading our leaving the Dome: that will really be something since none of those under seven has ever been out of it even once. & while they wait, suspended in time, they grow anxious & ask for specific people who aren't here & won't ever be here again. We few remaining adults feel so helpless. & so tired.

It's a nightmare. I have to keep telling myself it's worse for Daisy, Erin, & Marcy…whom I am allowed to visit again three days from now, & so must. The thought of seeing Erin makes my insides twist. But I miss Daisy terribly. So though I dread the thought of seeing Erin, I *long* to see Daisy. Knowing, as I do, that she won't always be there.

Illyrys is asking if she can sit by me while I work. So I must leave this & find something for her to do, preferably with others. Maybe I can get her interested in the four-to-seven-year-olds. It might help both them & her at the same time.

22.VII.493

Packing our belongings is the most depressing thing I've ever done in my life. I keep having to stop to wipe the tears oozing from my eyes. Not only must we pack everything belonging to the Family collectively, plus our own personal possessions (as well as help the children pack theirs), but we're having to pack everything personal belonging to those in detention, for although they can't touch such things until they're either acquitted or judged rehabilitated (in which case the therapists will go through the possessions & decide if there are any that might be "unhealthy"), their things must be held "in trust" for them—i.e., placed in one of the Justice Ministry's warehouses. Bad enough to be tearing yourself away from your home. But to be packing the things belonging to someone you love who someday may again have them, but only when she's become another person—someone you will never know, someone who will no longer know and love you (or probably even remember you, either)—is heartbreaking. Because I've been more or less assigned to see Marcy, Erin, & Daisy through their trials, I'm the one who must pack their things. Oh Daisy. What do I do with the vast collection of things so many children have made for you? Should I keep the little mobile I wove for you on a handloom when I was nine, that I was so proud to give you for your birthday that year? It would be a memento not of you but of my life-long love for you. What could such mementos mean to Daisy later? Probably they are the kind of things that will be removed by whoever decides what is "healthy" & "unhealthy." But I can't *bear* to think about it. I must just do what I have to do. *& not think about it at all.*

Grand Mother told us everything—I mean the full extent of the discussion that was held at Saturna. I'm glad they've guts enough to choose to take a stand, publicly—all of us together, as Grand Mother says. Insisting on our collective sanity, our collective fitness, insisting that the government not destroy our way of life, which is supposedly guaranteed by the charter signed by the first elected governor of Frogmore way back in the first century of settlement. Some of the Matriarchs expressed fear, Grand Mother said, but in the end yielded to the general opinion. So now there will be letters

& delegations to the government at all levels, plus a special brief to be submitted in each case of the detainees.

The other thing they discussed was the fate of the domes disabled by heavy losses of adults. Ours is one of the worst cases. Grand Mother said there was some testiness on the subject, a silent accusation that if *all* the domes had done as we had, then they wouldn't have been able to detain everyone, that the scandal of these detentions would have been clearer. In our case, we are to put everything but personal possessions (& sleep-cocoons) in storage, including the collapsed structure of the dome itself, & then move to Saturna, to one of the domes there. Everyone agreed that Families must not be divided, no matter how difficult logistically this will make things (obviously since we could all be distributed over many domes, that would be the easiest answer—but a disastrous one, too: but then everyone recognizes the importance of holding Families together).

Ariel's mother & her mother's sister have come to help us. How strange they seem to me, to all of us, I'm sure. It was a shock to see that Ariel's mother wears a cap—because she has all that junk in her brain. Like Ariel they are impressively fluent in standard & read the legal documents quickly, easily. I was with Grand Mother when Ariel's mother told her that she & her sister would be willing to take a child or two apiece into their "homes" & that she knew others living outside would be willing to do so, too, if the financial hardship of keeping the Family together were too severe. I could see that Grand Mother had a difficult time not losing her temper. She so heavily disapproves of Ariel's mother (even though she likes Ariel—but then Ariel is dedicating herself to Birth-Home) that she was cold & curt to her even before she made the suggestion.

I face another visit to that horrible place tomorrow. We'll probably have moved before the visit after that—which means I'll have to train back to Pimlico for each remaining visit. We must not desert them, even if they are to be taken from us so soon.

23.VII.493

Taken from us so soon? I wrote too optimistically. Erin is already gone. Or so it feels. & Marcy & Daisy are receding. Daisy has a preternatural stillness about her. I don't mean only her speaking so little. But there's a stillness in her face. As though she were wearing a blank mask. Her eyes are remote, far away, somewhere else. Not vacant, exactly, but elsewhere. *Inside.*

What surprises me most, I think, is the differences—each of them moving away in such different directions. I wonder why that is. But then I have no idea what is happening to them—only that they are in that place night & day, without respite, surrounded by those creepy people in their caps & masks... Do they always sit at those awful tables? Daisy sits with her hands quiet in her lap—not touching the surface of the table at all, while Erin's fingers burrow into it, sunk past the knuckles, & Marcy... Marcy stares straight ahead, her palms down flat on the surface, rigid, now & then twitching as if in a burst of impatience that quickly fades. She looks tired, worn out. As though she isn't sleeping. (Don't they have sleep-cocoons in those places?) One of her eyelids twitches a lot.

Will I have to watch them change so much from visit to visit? Grand Mother asked me not to tell her about it. Nor to talk to anyone else about it. To keep it to myself—except for writing it in this book. This is the sort of thing to put in the book, she told me. The others who visit don't share their observations or feelings, either. We keep the horror locked tight inside us. Because, Grand Mother says, it is obscene & therefore not to be spoken of. Except in the journal, where all things *must* be made explicit, *must* be brought into the open so that they can be learned from.

For the next week I'm to concentrate on packing & helping the children adjust to the move. When we get to Bessy's Dome there will be thousands of adjustments to make—new people to meet, new routine, new customs, new duties…& the overwhelming strain of keeping a Family together in such circumstances. Grand Mother says it will be extremely difficult, almost as difficult as if we were going to live outside, because this other Family, to whom their dome already belongs, will be stronger & we will sometimes find ourselves torn between absorption & resistance to it—despite all the goodwill between us, all the desire to see this Family survive. It is already known how difficult this will be, for it was discussed in the meeting at Saturna. Grand Mother says it will be important to keep this problem in the open lest it destroy us.

I'm so anxious, so worried. But I keep working almost without stopping & don't think much about anything except when I'm writing in this journal. It's best that way because I don't think I could bear to think much about everything that's happened in the last month.

24.VII.493

Though we're leaving the Dome, hope is resurging: the effort to hold the government to their longtime agreement with us has some chance—that's what someone in the legislative assembly told the Matriarchs. But we must press the efforts to free them because of what it is doing to those who are prisoners.

The thought of having Daisy back again, holding us together in that way we now realize was truly unique (to take one small example: in her absence meetings are a torture, no one knows what to do, & people attack one another out of frustration, a thing Daisy always prevented from happening), gives me the strength to go through with this wrenching move from home.

But there's no time to write anything of substance—we're barely sleeping, so busy are we these last hours here in Paula's Dome. Saturna is a good place—we all know that. But it won't be home. No place but Paula's Dome could ever be that.

Another rumor about Frogmore's time-trippers tends to be repeated only off-planet and after a few vials of something disinhibiting have been shared. I heard it several times when visiting Holliday, Frogmore's largest moon. It made no sense to me, but the whisper in which the tale was told and the nervous giggles accompanying it left me with the impression that the people sharing the rumor actually believed it.

If one merely says the word "time-tripper" or even thinks about the creature, a time-tripper will "hear" this as an invocation and indefinitely haunt one's dreams. Every person who repeated this rumor had a tale to tell about someone an acquaintance of theirs knew who had been driven mad by this invasion of their dream space. So vivid and unpleasant were their dreams that they had become afraid to sleep. Not one person copped, though, to actually having experienced such dreams.

Since I spent a good deal of time investigating (with scant yield) time-trippers myself, I can attest to the falsity of this rumor. I have occasionally dreamed about time-trippers (on Frogmore and off), but these have been dreams only of frustrated pursuit of a fascinating, elusive creature.

—Enoch Fulmer, *A Star-Hopper's View of the Galaxy*

Twenty-two
INEZ GAUTHIER

"All right, Zagorin." Inez sighed loudly as she flopped onto the massage couch. "Let's get this over with." She signaled the couch to administer a vigorous barrage of needle-sharp pulses both electrical and mechanical.

"How long will you be staying, Madam?"

"An indefinite period of time. I've no idea. Two local days, two local weeks, who knows?"

"Then we must prepare for the maximum length of stay," Zagorin said.

"No, no, it's not that kind of situation. I won't even take the design dresser—I'll make do with masks. Solstice hates designs. And I suspect these people, her Family as she calls them—" she wrinkled her nose and twisted her mouth— "do too."

Zagorin cleared her throat in an oddly hesitant-sounding way. Inez considered rolling over so that she could look at her. "Well, Zagorin?" she said when the silence grew prolonged.

"Where exactly is it we're going, Madam?" the attendant asked in a painstakingly level tone of voice.

Now Inez did roll over. She couldn't stand not seeing what might be happening on Zagorin's face. "To a place called Saturna. I've reserved three suites at the only hotel with a mag slab in the place." The attendant's eyes flew wide; a faint blush stained her cheeks. Her face grew stiff, wooden, *careful.* "So you know Saturna, Zagorin."

Inez both saw and heard Zagorin swallow. Uh-hm. She watched Zagorin intently.

"I've never been there, but of course I know *of* Saturna."

Staring hard at Zagorin's face, Inez realized that her attendant no longer wore masks—ever. She had done so on first returning to Frogmore from her stint off-world for the surgery, but somewhere along the way she had stopped. "Apparently you know more *of* Saturna than I do," Inez said. "Perhaps you'd be so good as to share some of that knowledge with me."

Zagorin's excessively long incisors gnawed at her lip. "It's an odd place for a nonnative to be going, Madam."

"How so?"

"You won't find any amenities there. Few people there wear masks, even."

Inez shifted to accommodate the massage while still watching Zagorin. "If you haven't been there, how do you know that?"

Zagorin appeared to be studying the pattern in the carpet. "We of the Families hear a great deal about Saturna. There are *three* Families there."

Families. Nathalie Stillness had spoken of Families. Both Solstice and Zagorin seemed to be afflicted with this same incomprehensible background and mind-set... And then it struck her: Zagorin had requested that her contract be dissolved so that she could go to her family almost at the same time Solstice had announced that *she* was returning to her family. Both had cited crisis as the reason for their need to go. Coincidence? Or some non-obvious connection? "Are you acquainted with Solstice Balalzalar?" she softly inquired.

Zagorin's gaze darted to her employer's face, then away. "Why do you ask, Madam?"

"You're blushing, Zagorin. Which, I think, indicates that you *do* know her. Why try to conceal that fact from me?"

"I had no intention of concealing it. *Acquainted* is the correct word, Madam. I barely know her."

"When did you first meet her? Here, in the Commander's Residence?"

"No, Madam. I first met her when you sent me for the surgery. She was undergoing it at the same time."

"And you've seen her since then?" It seemed incredible to Inez that she hadn't known of this relationship. Had they deliberately hidden it from her? Had they been meeting behind her back? *Solstice?* What could a brilliant artist like *Solstice* possibly see in a lackluster, boring *attendant* like Zagorin?

Zagorin's hands, clasped before her, twisted and writhed in sudden tension. "If you'll recall, Madam, you summoned me once when Solstice Balalzalar was with you and the general."

"That was the first time you saw her since your return to Frogmore?" She had to know, she had to know *everything*. Every detail and meeting, *everything*. The more she thought about it the angrier it made her, their concealing their relationship—however casual and distant it might be—from her.

"Yes, Madam."

"And then?"

"Is there some problem, Madam?" Zagorin's gaze met Inez's.

"Is there some problem, you wonder? Don't you think it a bit strange that neither of you said anything when you recognized one another?"

Zagorin's brow furrowed. "But Madam. You had called me...the general was present..." Her gaze dropped. "You would have been annoyed if I'd put myself forward like that."

And of course Solstice—eternally secretive—never said much of anything. Almost anyone could become a conspirator with Solstice out of sheer inertia. "And then? I suppose you talked with her after that?"

"Yes, Madam. After we recognized one another, she contacted me, and we met on my half-day off. She also spent some time with me in the evenings when she came to parties. In your dressing room."

In my *dressing room.* No, she wouldn't ask what it was they talked about—the thought of Zagorin—perhaps Solstice… No. She would let it pass. Ignore it. Obviously they hadn't launched into a great friendship, that much was clear. And how could they, given Zagorin's dullness?

Inez rolled back onto her stomach. "All right, Zagorin, let's get on with it. Bring me a screen and start scrolling through the inventory you keep for me. With suggestions. Since you, obviously, have a better idea of Saturna than I do."

Zagorin brought the screen attached to a stand and arranged it to Inez's satisfaction. "I do have one suggestion, Madam," Zagorin said.

"Oh?"

"That you leave that thing, that pet of yours, here. People in Saturna will hate that more than anything else."

Inez resisted the temptation to look over her shoulder at Zagorin. "What could they possibly have against a harmless creature like Little One?" she said. Of course she wouldn't leave Little One behind! It would be *miserable* without her unless she put it in a coldcoma-cocoon while she was away, which she didn't want to do. She liked having the Sweet Thing nestled close. Its purr alone was a great comfort and pleasure. "It's so helpless, Madam, and artificially created," Zagorin said in a dogged tone of voice. "It would offend anyone of the Families."

"Including you, Zagorin?"

"My opinion in the matter isn't relevant. I'm your employee."

"Bearing that fact in mind, I suggest we get on with the selection, then," Inez said, her tone cold though she had intended it to be merely dry.

"Yes, Madam." A section of the inventory lit the previously dead screen. "Shall we start with cling-ons?"

"They *do* have a slab in Saturna?"

"Why no, Madam. Not in Saturna. It would be too expensive."

What in the spacing universe am I *doing* going to a place like that? Inez wondered. Am I out of my mind, pursuing this dancer, brilliance notwithstanding? But she turned her attention to cling-ons and small-boots and elbow scarves and tunics. It would feel good to be taking action for a change. First Saturna, then Janniset. For surely by the time she returned the entire UAP situation would have stabilized... After which she could leave the planet and once again taste, however briefly, civilized society. How sweet it would be, how exquisite, especially by way of contrast to the place Saturna sounded to be.

She'd been fuming since take-off. Aware that they'd be landing soon, Inez consciously labored to quell her irritation, both general and specific. Given the delicacy of the situation, the faintest whiff of irritation could poison the atmosphere. *But how can I not be irritated? If it weren't for me, Nathalie wouldn't have had a chance of getting into this region. Yet she chooses to behave arrogantly, as though totally unaware of her dependence on my help. How* dare *she fuss about the security escort! It doesn't seem to matter to her that the planet's fate could be affected if I were taken hostage by insurgents, say. And she's clearly indifferent to the wishes or feelings of anyone she perceives as getting in the way of her "making an acceptable impression on the people of Saturna."* Acceptable! *The implication being that my presence will damage her reputation with these people. I could point out to her that it still isn't too late for her to postpone this fieldwork and that she's welcome to take one of the escort craft back to the Capitol District. But if I did say something like that, it would be the same boring old story of my being cast as the heavy. Well, she simply has to put up with me whether she likes it or not. So what if she doesn't like it? After all I've done for her... But this is what always happens with these kind of people. Look at her, she must have*

been wearing that same outfit her whole adult life! The same culottes, the same tunic, only the bare minimum of effort necessary for decency. Have you ever seen her wear so much as an earring or an elbow scarf? All she's interested in is her fieldwork. She's ambitious. She's got to be. Otherwise why would she have chosen to study a world no other anthropologist has ever even visited? Or chosen to so isolate herself from people who know who she really is? She'll never get back what's she's lost, separating herself from her family and friends. She'll always be a stranger to them. Does she realize that?

Stavros's message interrupted her thoughts. <<We've touched down and are taxiing, Madam.>> After a pause, Stavros added <<The second craft has set down as well, Madam. Captain Glance has given orders that none of us deboard until all three craft have parked and the escort has established that it is safe to do so.>>

<Very well, Stavros.>

"What's holding things up?" Nathalie asked. She had unfastened her safety straps and now sat on the edge of her seat, as though prepared to spring for the hatch the instant it was opened.

"We aren't deboarding until Captain Glance has determined it's safe to do so," the general's daughter stated in a moderately icy tone of voice. She wanted no further argument on the subject of the escort. If a tone of voice fended off such argument at the cost of causing offense, then so be it. These craft and personnel belonged to her, Inez Gauthier. Or rather, they lay at her disposal. Not Nathalie Stillness's.

"I see." Nathalie flopped back against her seat, folded her arms over her chest, and stared out the window.

The fog and tarmac here looked like the fog and tarmac anywhere else on Frogmore. Inez picked out Glance from among the ordinaries and officers moving about below and smiled as she recalled his gratification at being assigned to direct her escort. He had been pleased with his promotion. And since the general's expressed recognition of Captain Glance had given him a boost up a rung on the ladder all those on the general's staff fiercely competed to climb, he felt himself to be marked by special favor. The general, as his daughter had pointed out to him, needed officers like Glance. He had always appreciated Deaver and Handler but had somehow not seen Glance's worth. She had merely drawn his attention to it.

One of the ordinaries trotted up to Captain Glance, snapped to attention, and reported. Now, Inez thought, he's telling Glance everything has checked out. But no, Glance followed the ordinary into the fog, away from the craft.

About a standard minute later Inez received a tendril from Captain Glance. <Yes?> she subvocalized.

<<Were you expecting the Executive Manager of Saturna Region, Madam?>>

<Why?> she messaged back. <Has such a person come to meet us?>

<<Yes, Madam. With a full entourage accompanying him. And he assures me that he's already checked out the area and can guarantee its security.>>

Courtesy, nervousness, or something else? Some of the local managers had become quite officious and ambitious in their meddling with the new Brainnard Project. Could this one be among the troublemakers? <Transmit his ID to me, Captain> she instructed.

He did so, and the ID duly stimulated data, which she ordered supplemented via the Combine's Frogmore Net. *Elton Blakely; biological age in standard years: sixty-six; educated: Bittner College, Mellman University, Pleth; Executive Manager of Saturna since 10.09.489 Frogmore dating; Representative of Robbestanton District, 05.25.481-05.24.489; currently sitting on the boards of the following: Banyon Net, Inc., Fortescue Organic Chemical*—Inez cut into the listing and queried whether Blakely's name had appeared in any of the correspondence dealing with the new Brainnard Project.

<<Madam?>>

<One moment, Captain, I'll be back to you shortly.> Before all else she needed to know if Blakely had to be counted among the obstreperous local managers who had taken to challenging the primacy of the governor's circle.

The information came quickly. While his name did not figure prominently in the correspondence, it frequently appeared on endorsements by local managers of the positions taken by those leading the dissident group. Great. She had hoped to have a peaceful trip devoted solely to seeing Solstice and working things out with her. Between Nathalie and this upstart local, however, it looked as though she would be lucky to get much time with Solstice at all...

<All right, Captain> she subvocalized. <Tell Executive Manager Blakely I will join him as soon as I have your confirmation that all is indeed secure.>

It seemed one could not escape politics and business in the back of the back of beyond—even on Frogmore.

"What are you doing with my baggage?" Nathalie Stillness demanded of the attendant unloading luggage from the back of the transport. "Leave it there. It's all going on with me to Violet's Dome."

Out of the corner of her eye Inez observed that the attendant continued to pile luggage indiscriminately into the cart. Nathalie grabbed her arm. "Inez, will you *please* tell this person not to include my things with yours?" Her eyes blazed with barely suppressed fury, an emotion Inez had never before seen her display.

"What's the rush?" Inez said. "There's something I want to talk to you about before you go running off to your dome."

Nathalie's lips tightened. After a few seconds she said, almost through her teeth, "The only reason I shared the Executive Regional Manager's transport with you is because you said it would take me on to the dome, sparing me the trouble of finding my own way there." She glanced at the entrance to the Executive Regional Manager's Mansion. "I've no intention of staying *here*, if that's what you have in mind, Inez. I never agreed to do that. The whole point of my trip is to *live* for a few weeks with these natives."

"I understand that," Inez said. "And I must say, of all places, this would be the last I'd invite anyone to stay. I'm not staying here myself. But there's something I want to discuss with you before you go off to your dome. It won't take long, but we must have privacy in which to speak confidentially. And then off you'll go." She fixed Nathalie's angry eyes with a meaningful stare. "I promised you I'd see to it, and I will, Nathalie. I'm not a liar."

Nathalie swallowed. "I never said you're a liar, Inez. But why do you want to talk *now*? We could have done that back in the Capitol District. Or during the flight, for that matter."

Inez gestured toward the entrance. "Please, Nathalie. Let's not quarrel. I know you're anxious to get on with your work, but—"

"Anxious! I've been waiting to do this for months, and then when finally the time is right, the spacing military establishment gets in my way!"

"This will hardly take any time at all. I promise."

Nathalie Stillness trudged behind with the attendants, the security escort, and the luggage cart as the executive regional manager led Inez through the halls of the mansion. She wondered, as they walked, why she hadn't insisted on going straight to her hotel, even as she murmured appreciative response to everything the ERM had to say, much as she often murmured at her father's conversation while her mind remained fixed on weightier matters. And indeed, as she half-listened to the ERM, she did concentrate on a weightier matter. Given the attitude Nathalie Stillness had adopted since landing, it had become clear it would be difficult to maneuver her into helping with the logistics of locating and contacting Solstice.

Inez did not want to enlist the ERM's assistance. Not only would such assistance risk putting up Solstice's back, but it would also thrust her deeper into the debt of someone she had no wish to owe. A thinly veiled hostility—toward off-world people? or toward the general and anyone connected with him?—lurked behind his every word and gesture. She supposed that was why she had said she would join him for lunch. It would be galling to reveal to him her pursuit, for whatever reason, of one of those he had called "those dome people" when Nathalie had declared the purpose of her presence in Saturna.

At last they—Inez, Zagorin, and Nathalie Stillness—found themselves alone in the Governor's Suite (as the ERM called it) where Inez was supposed to "freshen up" before lunch. Inez collapsed into the nearest hammock. The time without slab interaction with her cling-ons had exhausted her. "I don't see how you'll stand the gravity out there," she said to the anthropologist. Nathalie of course already knew what it would be like; she had been out "in the field" before. Perhaps I've misjudged her, Inez thought. Nathalie had always seemed to be so, well, fainthearted, so drab, so timid (under the disguise of phlegmatic stolidity Inez had long ago seen through). But then Nathalie hadn't shown the slightest trace of fear of crashing, had she. She had opened the shutters nearest her and stared out into the fog as though fascinated. And she had said something about how seldom she had had an "opportunity" to take above-surface transport since coming to Frogmore.

"I'll stand it," Nathalie said, digging out a number of unidentifiable objects from the piece of baggage she had opened the instant the attendants had lifted it off the cart. "Believe me, I'll stand it."

"What is all that stuff?" Inez burrowed her fingers into Little One's fur. The top of Little One's head felt strange without the jewels she usually had Zagorin clip to its fur. (She hadn't needed Zagorin to tell her that jewels would be out of place in Saturna.)

"These braces help people without exoskeletal adaptations stand the gravity without the slab-cling-ons anti-grav effect," Nathalie said, tossing another of the strange-looking articles onto the pile beside her.

"Since you're going to the domes," Inez began her pitch, watching as Nathalie stripped off all her clothes—cling-ons included—and attached the braces to various parts of her naked body, all quite unselfconsciously (and probably, Inez thought, without realizing she still wore her day-mask), "I wonder if you'd do me a favor."

Nathalie did not look up from what she was doing.

Inez stared hard at her, willing the anthropologist to recall that she owed her this "favor," that without her, Nathalie Stillness, a mere anthropologist, would still be cooling her heels in the Capitol District, able only to fulminate and fume at her inability to get permission to travel to Saturna. "I know that Solstice Balalzalar is living now in one of those domes," Inez said, striving to suppress the anger so close to slipping her self-control.

Nathalie dropped into a crouch and fastened braces around her ankles, binding the soles of her feet with the broad bands of fabric holding the strange little knobs and springs and magnets (at least Inez thought they must be magnets). Each time a brace was clicked into place, a tiny green light on the clasp glinted. Inez cleared her throat, uncertain that Nathalie was even listening. "Perhaps you could ask after her and then message me which dome she's in?"

Nathalie straightened up out of her crouch and stared directly at her. Uncomfortable at the anthropologist's partial nudity (now studded with numerous tiny green lights),

Inez considered mentioning the day-mask she still wore. "So that's why you insisted I come all the way over here? So you could ask me to be your personal detective?"

She sounded angry. Which made no sense. If anyone should be angry, it should be me, Inez thought. "I'm not asking you to do any detecting," Inez said. "I don't see what the big deal about inquiring for a particular person is. And as to why you should mind having come here when obviously you needed a place for changing into all *that* stuff—" she gestured at the anthropologist's body— "is a mystery to me. I don't know what your problem is, Nathalie. But frankly, you're behaving like a real bitch about all this."

The anthropologist's eyes stared at her through the large almond-shaped holes of her gold and cocoa rigid-mold day-mask. Slowly, deliberately, she turned her back on Inez and began putting her clothes—minus the cling-ons—back on. When she had finished dressing, she turned and faced Inez. "I fully appreciate the favor you've done bringing me here, Inez," she said in a quiet, remote voice. "But I'm not going to jeopardize this or any other fieldwork on Frogmore in order to repay that favor. That wouldn't make sense." Nathalie collected her luggage. "If you can't understand how delicate and important my relations with the natives are, I'm sorry." She started her bags rolling. At the threshold, she turned to face Inez. "I wouldn't have accepted your offer to come here if I'd known you were expecting that sort of quid pro quo."

Inez watched her leave, luggage following close behind. Quid pro quo indeed! How had she let herself get involved with someone so crass? She'd find another solution. There had to be an alternative to sending Captain Glance or one of the ERM's people looking for Solstice. She only had to think about the problem, and the solution would occur to her. If there was one thing she prided herself on, it was her resourcefulness. Which was why she didn't *need* people like

Nathalie Stillness, who did, in fact, need *her*—whether she was willing to admit it or not.

Inez browsed through her box of vials, but finally resorted to pacing, moving from one boring room in her hotel suite to another. She again checked time. Zagorin had been gone nearly two hours. Considering the poor state of communications she had to deal with, as well as the fact that Solstice could be living in any of the three domes—or even outside them, Zagorin hadn't precluded that as a possibility—it was really too early to begin getting impatient with her for taking so long. But Zagorin could at least be keeping her informed of her progress. For a moment Inez considered messaging her, but dropped the idea. Zagorin never responded well to chivying. When she thought she was being "harassed," she employed the irritating tactic of slowing way down.

That thought pulled Inez up short. What really did she know about Zagorin these days? She had once known quite a lot, but it had been years since Zagorin's evaluation. And now that she thought about it, Zagorin had changed considerably over the course of her employment. She used to chatter. Now, however, she seldom said anything except to make an occasional acerbic retort about a particular design, or about Little One, or about a fad she especially disliked. Zagorin had a pathological dislike of fads: whether elbow scarves, feathers, furs, capes, jewels—she had had scathing comments for all of them. But she had simply grown more sophisticated, Inez reasoned about her attendant's evolved reserve. Living in the Commander's Residence had taught Zagorin better social skills than many of the elite in the governor's circle could claim for themselves.

Yet the thought of Zagorin talking to Solstice behind her back...

But Zagorin hadn't been eager to go out looking for Solstice, so it couldn't be that they were close. No, that just wasn't a possibility. Not with *those* two. But why had Zagorin been so reluctant? Her excuse that the gravity would be too much for her altered body was not plausible. Inez had actually had to remind Zagorin of the legal penalties attached to refusal to honor the terms of their contract before Zagorin would agree to find Solstice for her. But Zagorin had stood there, arms folded across her chest, obdurate, refusing to budge. *You have an entire security staff at your disposal, Madam, not to mention all the resources of the Executive Regional Manager.* Through that entire exchange, Inez realized, there had been hints in Zagorin's face and voice intimating something going on beneath the surface, something she was keeping to herself.

Inez frowned at the cliché holoscape of the Glitter District in Janniset's Bergen. Like everyone else in the general's household, Zagorin was subject to random security checks. If the woman had ever had anything to hide, Major Cleveland would certainly have sniffed it out and brought it into the open.

No, no. Zagorin had never been secretive. She had changed, yes. But it was merely that she had learned to be discreet. She no longer said everything she thought, which was as it should be with so expensive an attendant. And so if one were looking for something mysterious, her not saying everything she was thinking would feed the impression of secretiveness. Inez turned away from the holoscape. Of course she knew what Zagorin had been holding back—as any reasonably intelligent person in Zagorin's position would unquestionably hold back. Inez laughed wryly at her own momentary creation of high drama out of nothing more than ordinary, lowdown employer-employee relations...

Zagorin chose this moment to return. Watching the attendant cross the room, Inez smiled at the thought of this stolid dull individual engaging in anything illicit or clandestine. "So, did you find Solstice Balalzalar?" she demanded.

"Yes, Madam, I found her." Zagorin's gaze flicked down at Little One before coming to rest on Inez's non-masked face. "She said she would come here to see you."

"Come *here*?" The atmosphere of this place was terrible. Surely Solstice would be more comfortable meeting with her wherever it was she was living.

"Yes, Madam. She said she thought it best that she come here." Zagorin's gaze strayed back to Little One. "And I think she's right. The gravity is terrible without the slab. I had a hard time coping with it, even using the transport Captain Glance arranged for me."

Zagorin did bear the marks of physical exhaustion. Vertical lines Inez couldn't remember seeing before deeply scoured the attendant's face, making her look as though she had aged a century. Inez sighed acquiescence. "All right. Perhaps you're right. Though I'm not crazy about *this* place."

"I've just been messaged that your lunch is ready to be served if you wish it now, Madam."

She tried to think of inducements to offer the waterdancer, inducements that would be irresistible. Nothing, however, came to her off the top of her head—except the idea of asking Zagorin about what *she* thought the waterdancer might want or need. But Zagorin was one of the last persons she'd ever want to address that question to.

Solstice stood just two steps inside the threshold. She was wearing the same sorts of braces Nathalie Stillness had donned earlier (only in her case, the tiny green lights were not lit up)—and no cling-ons at all. Just the braces and a long, heavily embroidered loose tunic. Inez slid out of the hammock and moved toward Solstice, but before she could speak, Solstice pre-empted her in a rasping, angry voice: "What are you doing here in Saturna?"

Inez stopped in her tracks. The waterdancer's dark eyes were blazing with rage. "What is it?" Inez was puzzled. "Is there some reason you don't want me here? I don't understand your question." She glanced over her shoulder at the pair of hammocks she had ordered hung in the space she had decided would be most conducive of good conversation. "Shall we go over there?" she suggested. "You must be tired, I know adjusting to the gravity here is probably not that easy for you after—"

"Then just tell me what it is you want of me so that I can get back to the comfort of the dome."

Inez hadn't expected Solstice to be *this* difficult. "Why are you so angry with me?" she asked.

"You can ask that?" Solstice fairly flung the words her. "You find me here at Saturna, and you know I came here to be with my Family at a time of terrible crisis, which must mean you know who my Family is. And you can with a straight face ask me why I'm angry?" She hugged her crossed arms even more tightly to her body. "Whatever it is you came here to do or say, let's just get it over with."

Inez moved a few steps closer to Solstice. "I think there's been some misunderstanding here," she said in her firmest, calmest voice. "You're so hostile that I can only think you suspect me of something terrible, I can hardly guess what. Let's get that straightened out first, Solstice."

"Oh, I see. I should have realized you would think I didn't know you are as responsible for everything happening as your father is."

Inez's throat closed. What could such an accusation possibly relate to? "What in the spacing void are you *talking* about, Solstice?" she choked out. "Responsible for *what*?"

"For destroying an entire people's way of life, for devastating my Family! Because of you, Sadora will lose her mother and one of her sisters. Forever. After their trials she'll never see them again. And if she did, they wouldn't be the same people, her own mother wouldn't recognize her! Because of you, we'll both lose several cousins. Because of you, entire domes are vanishing, their children orphaned, their lives permanently disrupted. Because of you—"

"I don't understand what you're talking about!" Inez said. "I haven't done anything to your family. Or to these domes or whatever it is you're talking about! Who's been telling you such scurrilous lies about me, Solstice? Because that's what they are—lies!"

"You'd like that, my telling you who exposed the truth, wouldn't you," Solstice said. "The fact is that we know who most of the stockholders in UAP are, even though you made your involvement in it a big secret. It was bad enough, knowing what your father is. But then, to find out that it was you who was behind UAP's plot to destroy the domes—"

"Why should UAP want to destroy any domes?" Inez said. "Believe me, all UAP cares about is *business,* Solstice. If you imagine that UAP's stockholders sit around plotting the downfall of various Frogmore groups, you're wrong. I don't even know what these domes are that you're talking about! None of us do! Naturally we care about the planet, but we don't try to decide whose interests on the planet to advance. We all support democracy and self-determination, Solstice. Believe me, whatever you've heard to the contrary is a lie! UAP would *never* meddle in local politics!"

Solstice laughed. "Oh, that's beautiful. You've never heard of the domes. You wouldn't interfere with local politics. No, of course not. You'd only dislocate most of the population of Frogmore, that's all."

Inez's desire to placate Solstice became tinged with irritation. "Look. I'm sorry if members of your family have been dislocated." Hearing how that sounded, she tried to put more sympathy into her voice. "Really, I am. In fact, I'm perfectly willing to help out. Not by reversing the UAP decision," she added hastily as it occurred to her that Solstice might actually make that outrageous of a demand. "I couldn't, even if I wanted to. It's a matter of progress, Solstice. I can assure you, Frogmore will be far better off with this new—"

"Don't insult me by giving me the official line. I'm sick to death of hearing it every time I talk to people outside the Dome."

Inez stared dumbly at the waterdancer, for a few seconds at a loss for something to say that would mollify her. "It's really unfair of you to hold me responsible for whatever has happened to these people you mentioned. I am a stockholder of UAP, I admit that, but even given a share in the responsibility for the dislocations suffered—and you know, Solstice, it's not as though attractive alternatives aren't being offered to those who are being dislocated—anyway, even so, you can't blame me for everything that happens to people on the basis that what happened to them happened simply because they were in some way reacting to their dislocations. From what I understand, most people are relocating quite happily, with jobs as good as and sometimes better than the ones they'd had before. Why, the last report I read gave numbers suggesting that—"

"You don't understand at all, do you." Solstice's her raspy voice strained to its limits. "You really don't understand that by forcing people to relocate you're forcing Families to accept being broken up and dispersed, to accept the destruction and obliteration of an entire way of life. And when they *don't* accept the destruction of everything they know and care about, when they *don't* accept being dispersed, then they find themselves being literally destroyed by the judicial system. Is that the choice you're talking about, Inez Gauthier? If so, I don't think much of it!"

"Oh, Solstice." Solstice was making *her* the scapegoat. It was so unfair! "I can't be responsible for the way people choose to live their lives, I can't be responsible for people choosing to break the law. It's not fair of you to suggest that I *am* responsible. But you're deeply upset by what's happening to people you care about. I can understand that, believe me I can. What I don't understand, though, is what you're doing *here*. What about your art, Solstice? Don't you any longer care about *it*?"

The blaze in Solstice's eyes—all this time never once wavering from Inez's—blinked out, leaving a pair of dead cold black stones where fiery onyx had an instant before burned with painful brilliance. "Ah, my art." She laughed bitterly. "So that's why you've come." She choked out another mirthless laugh. "When Florrie showed up at the Dome and said you were here in Saturna, looking for me, my first thought was..." Solstice shook her head. "But no, you're here about my art. Isn't that lovely." Her mouth twisted into something she probably thought could pass for a smile. "Dance was a choice I once made, because I thought it was a choice that was mine to make. But that choice has been taken from me. By you and those like you." Solstice's voice was now as quiet and dull as her eyes had become. "And it's been made clear to me that dance is a luxury. Not a choice. A luxury not open to people like us. When I found out what was happening here, in my home, in my Family, the first question that came to me was how could I even think of indulging such a luxury when so many children need those of us who are left?" Solstice shook her head. "The answer was obvious: I couldn't."

Who were these children Solstice was talking about? Did she mean the children of the people who had been arrested? "But that choice *hasn't* been taken from you," she said. "So far am I anxious to support you that I'll do everything I can to get those people you mentioned—Sadora's mother and sister, I think you said, and some cousins?— I'll pull strings in the Ministry of Justice for you, Solstice. I'm sure that if they each agree to sign a pledge to never again get involved in whatever it was that got them detained in the first place, that the ministry can be persuaded to drop charges against them." When Solstice began to speak, Inez rushed on to forestall the likely further objection of expense: "And I'll even pay the expenses they've already incurred with the ministry." Inez moved the rest of the distance to the dancer and touched her arm. "Believe me, Solstice, I'm anxious to do whatever I can to help clear up whatever problems are standing in the way of your art. I don't think you appreciate just how—"

Solstice stepped back—into the threshold, which cleared. "Do you really mean to suggest such *generosity* on your part would solve everything?"

Inez's temper flared. "If you choose to sneer at my generosity, then there's nothing I can do for you."

Solstice performed a bow more exaggerated than any Inez had ever seen—even in the governor's circle. "Have a safe trip back to the Capitol District." She turned to go.

"Solstice!" Inez called, stepping out into the corridor. "I've made you a concrete offer to help people you claim to care for. You must not care much for them if you can just throw it away like that."

Solstice whirled. Her eyes were again blazing. "Do you think they'd really agree to sign anything that was put before them, just to save themselves from brainwipe?"

"If they cared about these children you keep talking about," Inez began, but Solstice cut her off. "You understand *nothing!* Just keep out of our affairs. You've already done enough damage. Just get the void out of Saturna and leave us alone!"

Shocked, Inez stood frozen; speechless, she watched the waterdancer stride off. Only when Solstice had vanished through the threshold at the end of the corridor did Inez slowly gather herself together and move back into the suite. She's crazy, she whispered to Little One. That woman is crazy. Her thinking is twisted and perverse to the point of self-destruction. No wonder no one has been able to talk to her. She's living in her own weirdly twisted world—crazy. Maybe even as crazy as that biologist. This spacing planet. It must be the Scourge. For how else would one come across so much craziness at one time?

Inez sank into the hammock. She had come to this back-water of a backwater for nothing, nothing at all. Except for the painful revelation that so much talent had been squandered on a crazy woman.

What a bitter, tragic waste.

Ministry of the Interior,
Frogmore Central Governing Authority
[Dossier: Inez Gauthier, File #37401]
SECRET
Report from G. Emphala, 20.VII.493

An informant in the Commander's Residence has report-ed [Doc #G401-29-008-0467] that during a session involv-ing physical intimacies, Margaret Abish, a member of the Station 23 bioforming research team, disclosed to IG the existence of a minority report she wished to bring to the Governor's attention, and requested IG's assistance in con-tacting the Governor. (The research team on Station 23 is charged with determining the feasibility and effectiveness of carrying out a plan recently developed by CDS-sponsored scientists for eliminating the Scourge, among other projects.) [Cf Ministry of Science, Dossier: atmospheric sciences, File #84496553] Abish claimed that the plan carries serious risks to Frogmore's ecosystem that the majority report declines to mention. IG refused to help her and issued orders that she be barred from the Commander's Residence thereafter.

I advise that a copy of the minority report be obtained, clas-sified eyes-only, and reviewed. I see two causes for concern: (1) that the minority report could be leaked on Frogmore, re-sulting in political damage to the CGA; and (2) that the CGA be cut out of the loop and possibly blindsided by certain CDS administrators who see Frogmore merely as a depository of resources to be plundered rather than the home world of an established population.

Twenty-three
ARIEL DOLMA

Ariel Dolma to Livvy Kracauer
21.Vll.493

Dearest,

I don't know why I'm bothering writing to you, now that we've been enjoying the privacy that lets us chat freely. I suppose this may be as much for myself as for you, to try to put into words what, when we talk, eludes me in the confusion of delivering updates and sharing emotions. It's not that talking doesn't help me figure things out—it does. But the last few times we've talked, I've done a lot of mulling afterwards. Maybe it's because I've been working in the crèche, which though demanding of my attention, is full of periods of time when my mind has nothing to do but wander, since at those times I can't allow myself to get too absorbed in anything, lest my lapse of attention come to a bad end.

Okay, maybe I do think I know why I'm taking the time to do this. Granted, this whole mess isn't my trauma, but that of every member of Paula's. And yet I've noticed that I do what people trying to cope with trauma usually do after it's over—struggle to put all the painful, highly charged fragments into some kind of order. I have all these fragments of memory (well, you should know—you're probably sick of hearing the same recitals over and over again. Telling you the same things a zillion times isn't voluntary, I promise you, but irresistibly compulsive, something I can't stop myself from doing, often don't even realize I'm doing until I'm well launched into it) that I keep telling myself would make sense if I could just put them into the correct order. The only order that occurs to me is chronological, but somehow that doesn't satisfy me. And which chronological, anyway? An objective chronological order? Or the order in which I learned about them? I worry about this obsessively, sweetie. I'm all messed up. And I'm just a witness! Watching Claire go about her duties in a numb, mechanical state makes me want to cry with an empathy I never before felt for her.

Since my mother and her sister arrived, I've become intensely aware of my outsider status here. There are all sorts of cultural dissonances, but the most glaring is my mother's cap, which outsiders read as signifying full connection, but which the members of Paula's regard with visceral disgust and suspicion. The adults at first hinted tactfully that she should help with the packing, but then Violet Chang came right out and told her, bluntly, that she needed to stay away from the children. Since her whole focus for coming here was her concern for the children, you can imagine how well that went over, especially when they (grudgingly) allowed Lee, her sister, to help with the pre-adults. (I found this incredibly mortifying, which is why, I guess, I didn't mention it during any of our chats.)

Maybe, though, the most telling sign of our being considered de facto irrelevant was the lack of interest of the few members left to attend meetings in what my mother had to say about her colleagues' response when they heard about the mass arrests. (That they heard about them, as you know, was thanks to my holo, which my mother uploaded to her engineering group's network.) I know you see this as important, especially the questions it raises about the ERM's being so blunt about putting UAP's interests above those of the people living in the region. The Grand Mother's suggestion, that what outsiders are thinking about their treatment is of no significance because that opinion has no power to shift either the judicial system's or UAP's policies, essentially kept my mother from adding that a lot of people are angry that full-scale brainwipe (rather than narrowly directed neural correction) is being prescribed on the grounds that the culture itself is irrational. My father apparently remarked to my mother that by that reasoning they could just as easily prescribe brainwipe for weavers without day jobs (meaning him). The remaining members of Paula's have so withdrawn into themselves that they'd probably not see this response as an identification of common interest but simply as a frivolous, self-centered diversion from their tragedy.

And so, over the last week I've come to see my own presence here as a witness rather than a participant, who is tolerated (still graciously, as it happens) rather than taken for granted. Weirdly, the Grand Mother's report on the meeting of the Matriarchs in Saturna, though it made a point of stressing how all the Families are standing together, insisting that the charter signed by the first elected governor of Frogmore be upheld, only reinforced my sense of not being one of them. All that is left to do, the Grand Mother made plain, is to pack up what can be taken to Bessy's Dome, where the remaining members of Paula's will be accommodated. I, of course, will be leaving for Birth-Home then, to continue my instruction with the First Midwife. The presumption is that the Grand Mother will be too busy handling the survival of her Family to give me special instruction—for now, at least. I'm uneasy about my lack of preparation. Oh, not as a midwife, of course; my internships at those clinics on Holliday assure me of that. But there's much more involved than practical skills in assisting women of the Families through pregnancy, labor, and delivery.

Did I say tragedy? Well yeah. It does feel like watching a tragedy unfold up close and personal—only without the catharsis.

A.

Humans with an idealistic bent have talked about "cultural relativism" for millennia. This term is, and always has been, purely notional; "cultural relativism" has never existed, and may be as possible as trisecting the angle. The most any society has ever achieved in this direction is cultural tolerance—and the word *tolerance* says everything you ever need to know about the fate of people who share a set of cultural practices and values different from the cultural practices and values of those who govern them.

Here on Frogmore, those who govern share a set of cultural practices and values entirely alien to the various cultural groups that together make up a super-majority population. Each member of that super-majority is in *theory* "allowed" to live in accordance with their cultural traditions and customs. In practice, however, they are in every respect treated as isolated monads assumed to share the cultural values and practices of the rulers. This assumption effectively strips them of their culture in every important context, rendering their cultural context invisible, allowing the rulers' cultural values to be projected onto them as though they were blank slates.

Thus, their voices are inaudible and unintelligible when the policies that affect them are being framed. And thus justice, in the rulers' courts of law, is an utter impossibility. *Tolerance* allows for expressions of difference from the hegemonic culture only to the extent that they are cosmetic, and their voices can be heard only to the extent that their words fit with the rulers' perceptions and expectations.

—Imogen Alençon, *The Trouble with Frogmore*

Twenty-four
MADELEINE TAO

When the district supervisor announced that the Minister of Justice himself would be addressing them, Madeleine glanced sidelong at Solange. In all the terms she had served as a judge, she could not recall a single occasion on which the Minister of Justice—or even one of his deputies—had personally addressed the quarterly District Colloquy. In general, the quarterly colloquies served to impart a sense of unity of purpose, in addition to providing an opportunity for discussing common problems and an occasional insight into those problems. At the opening of each colloquy, the district supervisor routinely delivered a standard pep talk—except that this time the pep talk had been pre-empted by the Minister of Justice, who stood now on the dais before them, startlingly appareled in the full regalia of Justice: wearing not only the black, green, and inlaid gilt day-mask all judges wore while holding court, but the austere cap and robes as well.

"Esteemed colleagues," the minister said. Solange groaned—faintly—and nudged Madeleine's arm with her elbow. "I'm pleased to take the opportunity your district supervisor has so graciously offered me for addressing you at this time on an immensely grave matter whose outcome each of you will have some small share in influencing."

When the minister paused to clear his throat, Solange leaned into Madeleine and whispered. "Do you think he ever gets lost in such circumlocutious sentences? Or do you think he's got it all pat in a memory block?"

Madeleine tightened her lips and jabbed her elbow into Solange's arm. Granted he was pompous, but the minister would not have bothered coming to address them on a trivial matter. Sometimes Solange's desire to be amused at the world played her false. Solange just shrugged at Madeleine's glare and turned her head to stare at the minister.

"There isn't a district judge on Frogmore who will not find in the next quarter's assignment cases arising from the planet-wide protests over UAP's relocations. These cases mark a highly disturbing development in known patterns of disruption. In the first place, they are, as I just noted, world-wide. Which is to say, they are globally organized." The minister paused to let that significant phrase sink in. "Indeed, the degree of organization of these disruptions has been made crystal clear by the fact that the people supporting them— and far more people are involved than simply the ones who have been apprehended in the act of committing disruptions—these people supporting them, who are apparently all members of the same anachronistic cult, have launched a lobbying campaign to influence members of the legislative assembly as well as local regional managers to bring pressure to bear on the ministry to drop the disruption charges altogether."

The minister loudly drew in an impressively chest-inflating breath, its capaciousness conspicuous even given the bulk of his judicial robes. "In other words, these people are *organized* agitators as well as fanatical, as indeed are all ACCMs. They represent a threat fully as serious as that posed by the small militant anti-Combine groups that have been blowing up the transport system and deliberately sabotaging industry. Their numbers as well as their high degree of organization—they have an organizational structure and inter-cult authority stretching back to Frogmore's earliest days—demand that we take their efforts very, very seriously." The minister cleared his throat. "I have discussed this with the governor herself," he revealed. "Because of the heavy burden the sheer volume of these cases places on the Ministry of Justice, she and I discussed the possibility of dismissing most of them and pursuing perceived ringleaders only. However, we have both concluded that that tactic would be a mistake. We have every reason to believe that these people will not be deterred by the mere example of the ringleaders' punishment, but will go on following the orders of this ACC's ultimate leadership, women who are known to cult members as 'matriarchs,' as long as they are permitted to do so. It therefore behooves the Ministry of Justice—as embodied by you, the district judges—to see to it that they are *not* permitted to do so."

A nasty feeling settled in the pit of Madeleine's stomach. This situation was going to cause her trouble. The issue adumbrated by the minister reeked of it.

Two months later, caught up in the process of reviewing all the testimony and evaluative documents in the first of the fifteen ACCM cases that had been assigned to her, Madeleine's suspicion was confirmed. Though in the minority, she and several of her colleagues found the political issues raised by the case to be—as they put it when informally meeting among themselves—"of utmost gravity for the future of Frogmore." The problem as they saw it lay not with the question of whether or not citizens had the right to disrupt the lawful business of a corporation like UAP, but whether or not it was justifiable for district judges to sentence to serious therapy the members of a sizable portion of the population of Frogmore who apparently shared a number of opinions and values held by them to be at stake in these cases. Did the district courts have the right to order serious therapy that would in the first instance destroy the peculiar character of that minority's mental and ethical outlook, however non-standard with the rest of the galaxy that outlook happened

to be? "In ordinary circumstances"—one of the members
of the legislative assembly had argued in a letter sent to all
district judges on Frogmore—"a person who has undergone
radical therapy is, at the end of that therapy, most often re-
absorbed into the original social matrix from which she or
he came—unless, of course, that matrix had in fact generated the mind-set that had produced the maladjustment in
the first place." But, the member of the legislative assembly
went on, "in these cases, though this particular ACC has in
fact constituted a long-traditioned subculture sanctioned at
the very origins of Frogmore's settlement, those defendants
sentenced to serious therapy would not be allowed to return
to that matrix and would be forcibly ejected into the culture
at large, which this subculture has regularly designated as
'outside,' for it was the determination to preserve the existence of the ACC that in each case lay behind the incident of
dissent for which the defendants are being prosecuted, and
thus the influence of the ACC that would be held responsible
for the maladjustment." Since every governor and legislative
assembly of Frogmore had from the beginning sanctioned
the existence of this subculture and had implicitly endorsed
the subculture's right to exist, the member reasoned, "the
question then arises as to whether it is just to mete out serious therapy as punishment of such individuals when in fact
such punishment would deprive said individuals of their entire cultural tradition to an extent to which other defendants
never are." The legislative assembly member in sum urged
all district judges to consider handling these particular cases
differently from all others, saying she did not advocate excus-
ing the incidents of dissent—for subcultural imperatives obviously could not be allowed to *excuse* violations of the law,
especially those that endangered public tranquility—but
that she hoped that judges would take under serious consideration the way in which the violators were to be punished.

In addition, a handful of legislative assembly members were promulgating more radical arguments—including the dismissal of all charges against the ACC's defendants on the grounds that because of the perceived threat to the ACC's most cherished values, the defendants had an extraordinary right to dissent and disrupt the peace. Madeleine naturally could not accept such reasoning, but she was troubled by the implications of a sentence of serious therapy for such a large number of individuals, as well as for the sizable minority of citizens this particular ACC represented. One of the legislators advocating the dismissal of all charges argued that this ACC had historically been a significantly positive force for Frogmore's survival and that its demographic contribution had been especially praiseworthy, following as it did the urgings of various governors to greater fertility. Madeleine, reading the report attached to this legislator's brief, had to acknowledge the truth of the statement, however distasteful she found the subject. But the demographic report reminded her of an aspect she had preferred to ignore, which the far more comprehensive report the Deputy Minister of Justice had sent all district judges had clearly spelled out: namely, the unusual child-bearing and -rearing arrangements practiced by the ACC.

What would be a just solution for these cases? When sentencing one always tried to take the circumstances of the crime and the personal history of the defendant into account. But in this case those very factors had created the problem. How could one possibly assess the personal history of the defendants with any degree of fairness when almost all the persons the defendants had any persistent relationships with partook of the same nonstandard values and living arrangements? Taken in isolation, any of them would seem—whether they had committed a crime or not—to be so far off the scale of standard as to be in recognizable need of therapy. Yet one could *not* in this instance take them in isolation (not least because certain advocates spoke for them in the legislative assembly).

The Minister of Justice had all but ordered the ordinary sentencing protocols to be applied to each of these ACC cases, and the deputy minister's as well as the district supervisor's follow-up memos and reports sealed the matter. To go against such pressure would in itself require that one's reasons be carefully and strongly stated. Madeleine knew that ninety-nine percent of her colleagues would without hesitation follow the minister's urging; if she failed to sentence these cases to serious therapy, thereby running counter to the recommendations of her superiors, she would find herself called upon to make detailed explanations for such a decision to the district supervisor—if not to the deputy minister or even the minister himself.

Did she really want to expose herself to that kind of trouble simply because she felt uneasy about the social and political ramifications of these cases?

Remembering their evening discussing *Antigone*, she imagined what Imogen Alençon would likely say about her dilemma. Though in discussion that night Madeleine had thought she knew her own beliefs and instincts on the subject, now, in real life, she wasn't so certain.

Three days before the scheduled sentencing for the first of her ACC disruption cases, a young unaltered Frogmore woman accosted Madeleine as she was leaving her chambers. The way the girl's hands clutched at a slip of paper and her eyes stared at her, so wide and alarmed, reminded Madeleine of the terror she had often observed in relatives of defendants who, out of desperation, waylaid her after discovering she would not schedule appointments with them. "Excuse me," the woman said in thickly accented Standard. "You are Judge Tao, aren't you? Please, it's very very important that I talk to you!"

Despite the heavy accent, something in the girl's appearance reminded Madeleine of Holland that last year before she'd gone to Pleth. The pattern of the facial spalls, perhaps? Or the wide eyes that despite their pleading conveyed some attractive quality of character? "I'm sorry," Madeleine said, "but if it concerns a specific case, procedure requires that you submit a holoview or written deposition." No ID broadcast came from the girl, Madeleine realized without surprise.

"Please." Her voice quavered. "I know it's dangerous to come like this to see a judge, but I have to talk to you."

Had she not understood? Was it possible her Standard wasn't up to it? One never could tell with these people. "I can't simply see people about cases outside the established procedure." Madeleine spoke slowly and distinctly. "There is a proper way to do things, and the defendant's counsel can tell you what it is. That is who you should be talking to." Madeleine moved to step around her, but the girl threw herself onto her knees right in front of Madeleine.

"Please, you don't understand how important this is!" Her eyes, intense and compelling, stared straight up into Madeleine's. "You don't understand! It's a mistake, a terrible mistake! She is the best person I've ever known, the very best, she is *good*—you can't do those terrible things to her!"

"You must not importune me like this." Careful to enunciate her words slowly and distinctly, Madeleine spoke in her sternest voice. "It is against the law to do so, and if you persist you will find yourself in bad trouble. I might agree to see you about this person, but only if you go through the required procedures." She felt a physical pang strike near her heart as the face staring up at her convulsed. "I advise you to go to the defendant's counsel and arrange it through her or him. But it must be done properly, not in this compromising clandestine manner." Madeleine stepped backwards and then around the still-kneeling woman. She felt sick to her stomach—and angry that she had been subjected to such a scene.

As she moved down the hall she tried not to hear the groping, halting words with which the woman pursued her. She would be correct to call a bailiff and have her arrested: the procedure existed precisely to spare judges this sort of painful emotional scene. But though she felt angry, she would not lash out at this young woman and have her arrested. Not in this case, anyway. People in extreme pain often went to uncharacteristic and even irrational lengths in order to feel that they were doing something. This woman was so young. Worse, from the sound of it, the defendant involved was probably her mother.

Madeleine stepped into the lift. Brooding and regretting the inevitable did no one any good. She needed to remain objective, to remember all that a good judge's objectives must be. Empathy with the defendant's relatives must fall far to the bottom of the list—however much their plight wrenched one's heart.

Solange lifted her glass in a half-toasting gesture. "Whatever horrible bit of shop you've got in mind to thrust on me, I'm still pleased you thought of doing this today. It's been a long time since we've had this kind of lunch." She chuckled. "And it sure beats joining the fray downstairs. If you ask me, Jordan is getting out of hand."

Madeleine, watching Solange sip the fruit drink, smiled ruefully. "I've my own fray up here, I'm afraid. I don't promise you peace today, Solange."

"You did warn me. But I still think your conversation is less likely to give me indigestion." She picked up the two-pronged fork and plunged it into the spicy-sauced crab.

Madeleine toyed with her own fork; if it hadn't been for wanting to have Solange here for a shoptalk lunch she wouldn't have bothered with food at all. "I'm down to the wire on a case I've scheduled for sentencing tomorrow," she said.

Solange, chewing, nodded.

"And I'm having difficulties."

Solange prepared another forkful and invited Madeleine to elaborate.

"It's the first of my ACCM cases," Madeleine said.

Solange's fork, only inches from the hole in her anthropomorphized swan's head day-mask-and-cap-ensemble, paused. For a moment her teeth worried at her lower lip. Sighing, she returned the fork to the dish. "What is it, Madeleine? I've already gotten through two of my ACCM load. Is there something in this individual case that's giving you trouble?"

"No, it's not the individual case," Madeleine said. "Rather, it's the general disposition of all these cases."

Solange frowned, but she ate another bite before speaking. "As to that, I suppose we are both working from the same documents?"

"Oh, I'm certain you've been deluged with the same arguments I have." Madeleine forced herself to take a bite of the crab. The image of that distraught girl pleading for her mother kept intruding into her head. She strove to banish it. She *must* not allow such personal considerations to cloud her objectivity. After all, as a district judge she saw family tragedies unfolding before her almost constantly.

"Which points in particular have put you in doubt?"

"It's the cultural factor and the discrimination that sentencing without reference to it implies."

Solange put down her fork. "You mean you buy the argument that because they felt their life-style was being threatened they had the right to disrupt UAP's lawfully conducted business?"

"Oh come, Solange, you know me better than that. Of course I'm not suggesting any such thing. Law is law and must be obeyed. What I'm talking about are the effects resulting from the application of certain sentences. The effects on one of these ACCMs of serious therapy are more far-reaching than the effects on an ordinary run-of-the-mill mainstream Frogmore citizen. It's *that* I'm concerned about."

Solange shook her head and reached for her glass. "As far as I'm concerned, the effects are *so* far-reaching that the cultural factor doesn't really matter." She sipped from her glass before continuing. "Even with a wash, the defendant's most intimate relations are seriously disrupted. All but the most deeply embedded personal memories go. And with a wipe nothing of one's personal background remains at all." She picked up her fork and prepared a new bite.

"I've been thinking a great deal about this. And I have to say that on the cultural level your analysis doesn't hold."

Solange's eyes lifted from her crab to stare at Madeleine. "Is there something I'm missing?"

"Take the simple matter of language," Madeleine said. "It's well-documented that even persons who were raised in nothing but a vernacular Frogmore dialect speak perfect Standard by the time they are finished with therapy—and remember none of the tongue they had previously spent their life thinking and speaking in. The same principle applies to other things than language; but destruction of one's language is surely the most serious sign of cultural tampering."

Solange raised her eyebrows. "Perhaps it's for the best, then. Persons who have been through therapy are far better adjusted than even the most stable of those who haven't been through it. They become exemplars of the standard. Which is to say they become very good citizens indeed." Solange popped a forkful of crab into her mouth. "I don't see the problem, Madeleine."

Madeleine could not manage to eat another bite. Perhaps it was the mother and daughter factor that had gotten to her and was clouding her judgment. Surely Solange was correct? Madeleine picked up her glass to drink; she paused before touching the rim to her lips as the answer to Lawrence's offer came to her. It seemed obvious, now, that she move out of the area of executing and interpreting the law into the potentially more gratifying one of formulating it. With Aureole, the regents would be starting from scratch. There would be none of these dilemmas with Aureole law, at least not to begin with. Even better, her concern would be wholly abstract, without reference to these wrenching personal tragedies she was forced to participate in every day she served the Frogmore legal system.

The weight squeezing her heart eased. Madeleine nodded at Solange. "Thanks for your input, Solange. You've been enormously helpful. And now maybe you could tell me anything new you may have heard about Henrietta West's daughter?"

Solange plunged zestfully into the ongoing scandal of behind-the-scenes maneuverings to secure special treatment for Maida West. Madeleine paid only cursory attention as she silently vowed to notify Lawrence immediately after lunch. Once she had done so and Lawrence had confirmed the offer, it would be assumed settled—unless, of course, she rocked the boat with her ACCM cases.

"Will the defendant please rise and approach the bench," Madeleine intoned in her most neutral and formal tone of voice.

Daisy Scherr rose, moved around the defense table, and walked—her head held high on her thickly boned and chitinous neck—with slow, deliberate steps toward the bench. With the defendant's chair vacated, Madeleine could not help seeing the young woman who had importuned her outside her chambers seated directly behind. The girl's eyes glittered; she held her facial muscles stiff enough to suggest she wore a rigid day-mask deliberately fashioned to look like a young native-born Frogmorian. The defendant's daughter, Madeleine thought. With the strength so painfully visible in that face, she could be Antigone. She glanced at the defense counsel and considered messaging her to get the girl out of there. But no, the tight control in that young woman's face determined her not to do so. The girl would hold up. And clearly it mattered to her to be here, present, for what were essentially the last moments of her recognizable mother's life.

The defense counsel looked into Madeleine's eyes, and Madeleine knew she knew what the sentence would be. Madeleine's gaze strayed back to the daughter, and her throat tightened as the girl's eyes suddenly looked straight into her own. Quickly she looked down at the screen set into the bench and clenched her trembling hands in her lap.

The defendant stood calmly, waiting seemingly without emotion, as though this were a routine ritual she had performed thousands of times before. Madeleine willed her voice to hold steady under the intense wave of emotion that that shocking meeting of eyes had precipitated. Slowly she read out the charges in a voice just barely even. As she read she looked again and again into the defendant's nearly blank eyes—until she realized the strangeness of that blankness. Had they drugged her? Madeleine wondered as her voice automatically droned on.

She paused to draw breath before reading the sentence. She felt the girl's eyes pulling at her but resisted their demand, dividing her gaze between the defendant's eyes (however blank they might be) and the screen containing the words of the sentence. "Daisy Scherr," Madeleine began, "you are hereby sentenced to a fine of five hundred SCUs. In addition, this court requires that you undergo Total Rehabilitative Therapy to be admin—"

"NO! NO! You can't *do* that!" shrieked the daughter in a dialect Madeleine barely understood. By the time Madeleine broke off because the shrieking voice was drowning out her own voice, the girl was already on her feet rushing toward the bench. "You must not, you *cannot* do this to her, it is a crime that anyone would—"

The bailiff, reaching her, clamped a hand over the girl's mouth and dragged her out of the courtroom.

<You spacing, inconsiderate bitch!> Madeleine messaged the defense counsel. <By letting her come here when she was obviously distraught you've let that girl ruin her life over this! You *know* the courtroom is no place for defendants' relatives under emotional strain!> Madeleine put her shaking hand to her throat and made herself stop the stream of invective she wanted to pour into the defense counsel's brain. It was inexcusable, she thought, absolutely inexcusable. *I should have known. I should have let her know the girl's condition.*

Madeleine pressed her lips together and stared down at the defendant—who stood quite still, apparently unmoved. Madeleine swallowed and blinked back the tears sliding down her cheeks under cover of her judicial day-mask. She drew a long, ragged breath. In a forced monotone she began the sentence from the top. "Daisy Scherr, you are hereby sentenced to a fine of five hundred SCUs," she repeated, unheeding of the audible tremor in her voice. "In addition, this court requires…"

The only stories that cease to live and breathe after they've been told are those that end in perfect, unchanging bliss— "happily ever after"—or with the definitive death of their focal character(s). Most other stories, though, remain unfinished, hanging on into the present, projecting their own spectral future, intangible, problematic, messy. They can never be perfect objects, complete and, in the viewer's mind, hypostasized. Unceasing bliss or definitive, perfect death are called the classical modes of drama for a reason. They leave the viewer free of the story itself, which after its telling is finished has become a memory (often pleasurable) set firmly in the past, available for revisiting at will, but contained. In order to emphasize this past-ness of classical dramas, some ancients insisted that the drama be set entirely in one place within one local day. Dramas that remain open and unresolved necessarily employ different conventions, techniques, and narrative structures than do those of classical drama as it has developed over the millennia.

—Alexandra Jador of Pleth, *The Art of Holodrama*

Twenty-five
INEZ GAUTHIER

Inez was submerged in oil so viscid and dark that her eyes could see only a few centimeters before her. Aimlessly she swam through the oil. Somehow she had come to be in the waterdancer's tank. She searched all around but saw nothing but thick oil. If Solstice were in here with her she would not know it—for not only could she not see anything, but she also knew Solstice was not connected and could therefore not be messaged, nor her ID broadcast picked up.

Still she laboriously propelled herself without any sense of where she was going—up, down, or in circles...without any apparent need to take breaths... She wanted to call out to Solstice but knew that if she opened her mouth oil would rush in. Instinct told her to let herself rise to the surface, but she knew that if she *were* in Solstice's tank then up would only bring her into contact with the ceiling of the tank. To get out of the tank ~ and now she wondered if she really were in the tank at all, or whether she might not be in one of Frogmore's horrible, dangerous bodies of water ~ one had to push one's way down, for the door to the tank was through a set of locks built into the floor, extending downwards to the real floor of whatever room now contained it.

Though she struggled against it, panic, inexorable, took her, a panic she knew would strangle her if she failed to master it. *Keep calm, Inez, keep calm, there is a way out of here, it's only a matter of calmly discovering it. And besides, Solstice will come, of course she's in here with me, she wouldn't have let me come in here by myself when I know nothing of what I'm doing.* But why, it suddenly occurred to her to wonder, didn't she know for certain where she was or how she had gotten there?

She forced herself to keep moving through the murk. Her eyes never ceased to strain for signs of any living thing in the oil besides herself. For Solstice, yes, but for inimical things—Scourge plants, hostile sea life—as well—just in case she were not in the tank but had inadvertently fallen into a Frogmore sea or lake.

After an interminable length of time ~ her limbs had begun to tremble from fatigue ~ she thought she could make out an area of murk slightly lighter than the rest. Eagerly she made for it, wondering if Solstice had triggered the program that provided the visual effects she interacted with in her dances.

The closer she got to the light patch, the brighter it grew. Her heart accelerated. At last, at last she would figure out how to get out of this place, the horror of which kept shortening her breath to the point of nearly choking her. On and on she swam—until she connected with a barrier she hadn't seen. Glass, she realized. It must be a glass panel. Puzzled, she peered past the glass—for the source of the light lay outside—and saw Solstice swimming about on the other side of the glass. Frantically she pounded on the glass with her hands and feet. *Solstice* she silently screamed in her throat, desperate to get the other's attention. *Solstice!*

The dancer apparently did not see or hear her. She realized that from Solstice's point of view there was nothing on this side of the glass. For there was nothing here that she had been able to find other than the murky oil untouched by light except that which came from the other side of the glass.

When she tired of pounding on the glass she pressed herself nearly flat against it, to take from it whatever support it might give her tremoring muscles. She stared and stared into the oil on the other side of the glass and watched Solstice, ever graceful, moving freely, easily, through the brilliantly lit fluid. And then she saw, coming up behind Solstice, a glittering silvery iridescent creature, enormous, deadly, swift. Involuntarily she cried out—and oil flowed into her mouth, nearly choking her with its soft, gelid, foul-tasting pressure. She spluttered to expel it, struggling against taking more and more of the horrible stuff into her mouth. When finally the fit of choking had subsided, she looked again to where Solstice had been—and found nothing. Nothing but Scourge plants and the time-tripper.

Her gaze darted about, searching the extent of the lighted area, but instead of finding Solstice she seemed only to notice more and more of the Scourge so far filling the fluid as to darken the light that had been so warm and brilliant when Solstice had been there. Eventually, she lost all hope of seeing Solstice again.

She was pressed listlessly up against the glass, the side of her head flat against its cool smooth surface, when Solstice popped back into sight. Scourge flowers covered the dancer's body and hair, filled her mouth, obscured her eyes. Newly alarmed, Inez pounded on the glass, frantic to get Solstice's attention, to warn her of the danger. But Solstice popped out as instantaneously as she had popped in.

Solstice is a time-tripper, she realized. She doesn't wear the pelt, but she is one of them. Solstice is a time-tripper.

Her dream interrupted, Inez stirred and nearly awakened. But the sleep-cocoon gently rocked and soothed her, protecting her from surfacing into full consciousness. And so the general's daughter slept on and did not wake until morning.

Seattle
January-June, 1987
Revised, Port Townsend
October 2015 and March 2016

Acknowledgments

As one of those writers who regards the initial draft as merely material to be shaped, I owe a debt of deep gratitude to the many people who, over the course of the evolution of "The Waterdancer's World," offered me critical comments as well as insight into the novel I wished it to become. The earliest draft, which I wrote during the first half of 1987, I called "The General's Daughter." Several people read that incarnation of the novel. I gathered that although most of them enjoyed it immensely, a few people noted that it might not be quite right; most of these thought it might be due to the lack of a proper plot. I at first put this down to the novel's refusal to follow the usual narrative arc readers expect to find in a science fiction novel, but, without giving it much thought, slowly came to consider the novel flawed.

Eighteen years later, in October 2015, I allowed myself two months away from my work for Aqueduct Press and, as I considered what to work on, realized that not only would two months devoted entirely to my own work allow me to finish the draft of a new novel long in progress and near completion, it would also give me the space I'd need for looking at and possibly rewriting one of my several unpublished novel mss. Since I'd been away from "The General's Daughter" for so many years, I read it as if it were someone else's ms in need of serious critique or editing (but because it was my own could treat with the utmost ruthlessness, without respect for ideas about style that I seem to have held in 1987). My distanced reading allowed me to conceive a more coherent, unified whole that I soon understood wasn't really about "the general's daughter" at all, but rather about the world known as Frogmore—and not the general's daughter's Frogmore, either.

The novel underwent one final revision thanks to Nisi Shawl's astute comments on "The Waterdancer's World" and my conversation with her about it. This one involved an additional month away from Aqueduct (for which I especially thank Kath Wilham and Tom Duchamp, who generously took up the slack for me during both absences).

Without further ado, I'd like to thank the following people for reading one or more iterations of the novel in ms and speaking frankly about it: Kath Wilham, Tom Duchamp, Dr. Ellen Kittell, Dr. Ann Hibner Koblitz, Dr. Neal Koblitz, Therese Spaude, Elizabeth Walters, Dr. Robert Philmus, Dr. Helen Merrick, and Nisi Shawl. (If I've forgotten anyone, I plead the inadequacy of a sexagenarian memory.) My greatest debt is to Kath Wilham, who diligently edited the novel and encouraged me to take its world-building another step further; I suspect that without her interest and support, it would have forever remained in the drawer

L. Timmel Duchamp
August 21, 2016

Author Biography

L. Timmel Duchamp is the author of the five-volume Marq'ssan Cycle, which won a special Tiptree Award honor in 2009, and the founder and publisher of Aqueduct Press. She has published two collections of short fiction: *Love's Body, Dancing in Time* (Aqueduct, 2004), which was shortlisted for the Tiptree and includes the Sturgeon-finalist story "Dance at the Edge," the Sidewise Award-nominated "The Heloise Archive," and the Titpree-shortlisted "The Apprenticeship of Isabetta di Pietro Cavazzi"; and *Never at Home* (Aqueduct, 2011), which includes a 2011 Tiptree-Honor List story, and co-author, with Maureen McHugh, of a mini-collection, *Plugged In* (Aqueduct, 2008, published in conjunction with the authors' being GoHs at Wis-Con). Her Marq'ssan Cycle consists of *Alanya to Alanya* (Aqueduct, 2005), *Renegade* (Aqueduct, 2006), and *Tsunami* (Aqueduct, 2007), *Blood in the Fruit* (Aqueduct, 2007), and *Stretto* (Aqueduct, 2008). She has also published the short novel, *The Red Rose Rages (Bleeding)* (Aqueduct, 2005), the novella *De Secretis Mulierum* (Aqueduct, 2008); dozens more short stories, including "Motherhood, Etc" (short-listed for the Tiptree) and "Living Trust" (Nebula and Homer Award finalist). She has also published a good deal of nonfiction. Since 2011 she has been the Features Editor of *The Cascadia Subduction Zone.* She is also the editor of *Talking Back: Epistolary Fantasies* (Aqueduct, 2006), *The WisCon Chronicles, Vol. 1* (Aqueduct, 2007), *Narrative Power: Encounters, Celebrations, Struggles* (Aqueduct Press, 2010), *Missing Links and Secret Histories: A Selection of Wikipedia Entries from across the Known Multiverse* (Aqueduct Press, 2013), and co-editor, with Eileen Gunn, of *The WisCon Chronicles, Vol. 2: Provocative essays on feminism, race, revolution, and the future* (Aqueduct, 2008).

In 2008 she appeared as a Guest of Honor at WisCon. In 2009-2010 she was awarded the Neil Clark Special Achievement Award ("recognizing individuals who are proactive behind the scenes but whose efforts often don't receive the measure of public recognition they deserve"). In 2015 she was the Editor Guest at Armadillocon. She has taught at the Clarion West Writers Workshop and has taught one-day Clarion West workshops. She lives in Seattle.